DARKNESS
in Green & Gold

***

Green & Gold, Book Three

Jo Holloway

***

CHAPTER 1

SMALL RUSTLINGS STOPPED as the forest stilled and fell silent. Birdcalls cut off mid-chirp. Cara rolled over with a grunt and sat up on the wet earth. Her nose wrinkled at the smell of rotten leaves and damp earth. Running was supposed to be her happy time. But one moment of lost focus and here she was, flat out in the dirt after scaring the woods into silence. Fantastic.

Grimacing, she rubbed her aching kneecap, smearing mud from her burning palms across her pantlegs. A fern frond brushed the back of her neck, and she swatted it away, ignoring the stinging scrapes on her arms. The forest she loved had turned against her.

Above the trail, evergreen branches blurred together across the dreary winter sky, and she furiously blinked back the tears prickling in her eyes.

Stop it. You are not crying about a stupid fall, Cara Ransome.

Not now. Not with everything else.

The tightness in her chest climbed her throat to her clenched teeth.

"Thanks for the warning," she snapped. "Both of you."

Jenner was already beside her, nudging at her wrist with his wet nose. Usually it was hard to stay mad at her dog when he gazed at her with those liquid brown eyes, black ears flicking back and forth above his furry face, but today, the burning on her hands matched the fire in her belly.

Dampness began to soak through the seat of her pants, and she switched her glare to Wes.

Her friend had stopped as soon as she'd fallen and turned back for her. He'd already extended a hand, but dropped it and raised his eyebrows instead after her little outburst.

"We're . . . sorry?" Wes glanced at Cara's dog. "We didn't realize you needed a warning *not* to trip over your own feet."

Between Jenner's tilted head and the way Wes's eyebrows had vanished into his shiny black hair, she couldn't help another groan. Sarcasm coming from Wes was all wrong. From her, maybe. But not from her logical, direct best friend. That wasn't him at all.

"Crap. I'm doing it again, aren't I?" Cara took a deep breath and forced her tight jaw to relax. This time when Wes reached out, she accepted the hand offered to her and climbed to her feet with a soft thanks.

Jenner circled them, sniffing the air. The familiar green gleam passed across his eyes when the Pyx who lived in her dog spoke from his mind to theirs.

"There is another one of us nearby, though I cannot tell precisely how close," Jenyx said, his voice clear in her head.

"Well, that's helpful," she muttered.

Cara brushed her hands across the back of her pants, feeling the wet spots with a frown. Ever since these others had started coming around, irritation and anger came faster and easier than ever before.

"Cara . . ." Wes prompted again at her grumbling.

"Ugh, I know. I can't turn it off." She shook out her arms like the motion could rid her of the unnatural aggression. "It's so annoying."

"It's not you. It's them. Are you okay, though?"

Tough question. Lately, she never felt okay. Learning she was an empath on top of everything else had been hard enough to accept, even before these newcomers started setting her on edge all the time. She tested a little weight on her knee and then checked her hands. The red rash across the bottoms of her palms caused another flash of anger, but she bit it back. "I think so."

Wes gave her a half-hearted smile. "Good."

"Sorry."

"Stop apologizing. It's not your fault. You know it's just your Pyxsee empathy picking up on one of them."

Jenner had moved off the path, scenting the woods around them, making sure they didn't have unwanted company too close by. Cara closed her eyes. She breathed in slowly and then exhaled. The fresher air above the undergrowth helped clear her mind.

There had to be a way to stop the churning emotions that didn't feel like they belonged to her. At least, she hoped they didn't. Her friends thought her awful moods lately were a product of her ability to sense the Pyx nearby. Maybe they were.

Of course, it was little comfort to think there were such hostile-feeling Pyx in the area. Everything she'd learned from Jenyx in the past two years made her think this wasn't normal for them. The Pyx who lived in her dog had always made it sound like his kind were peaceful observers in the long history of the world, rarely interfering in the lives or events of the times. More than anything, she wanted to feel like herself again, not like she had no control over her own life or feelings.

Her eyelids lifted, and she found Wes still studying her with concern across his dark features. Hundreds of tiny gold flecks in his brown eyes meant he was a Pyxsee too, but they didn't come close to matching the intensity of her solid-gold eyes.

Wes didn't have to deal with the extra ability she had found herself saddled with. He saw and heard the Pyx like she did, like all normal Pyxsees did—if being a Pyxsee could ever be called normal—but he didn't have to feel them. As far as she knew, no one else did. The eye color she'd hated most of her life for how different it made her was coming back to bite her again. She had no idea what normal even was anymore.

"I hope you're right, but we don't know for sure."

He looked at her sideways without a word. She knew that look, but his silent reassurance wasn't what she needed. She needed answers.

"No," she insisted. "We don't know. We don't know anything. That's the point."

Flames of frustration clawed at her ribs again. This time, she was pretty sure the emotions were her own. She shot a dark look at Jenner—not that it had anything to do with her beautiful brown-and-black dog.

"Cara, child, I know you feel left out, but we will share what information we can when the time is right," Jenyx said. His usual soft and gentle voice rang with a sharp edge in her mind.

Wes's jaw twitched as he heard it too.

"The council meeting was three months ago already. How much longer do you need to figure stuff out before you tell us what's going on?" She couldn't keep the acid from her tone.

"It is complicated. The situation is not what we expected, and we have yet to discover the meaning of these new Pyx in the area. They have avoided all the usual communications with others. Your reactions to them, current mood included, are worrisome, to say the least."

"Yeah, or maybe I'm just an angry teenager," she grumbled. "Or I'm going crazy. Again."

"Enough." Wes's low, quiet voice was gentle, but his words were firm. "I might not know what you're going through, but we all know the real you. And angry isn't you. This attitude is coming from them, and you know it."

She started to shake her head. "Maybe I'm like all the people we hear about in the news these days, not acting like themselves. Don't look at me like that. I'm serious. Something's going on. How do you know it's not affecting me too, whatever it is?"

Her gut twisted with a wave of regret she couldn't place, and she glanced at Jenner. She would never get used to being struck by random feelings out of the blue.

"Fine." Wes turned and started down the path.

"Wait up. Where are you going?"

"If you won't listen to reason, maybe a more permanently cheerful friend can make you see things in a different light."

Cara rolled her eyes but fell into step beside him.

"Even if you're right, it's Pyx whose feelings I absorb, not people."

"Not even exceptionally sunny people?" Wes shot her one of his rare smiles.

The corner of her mouth ticked up. She scoffed. "Worth a shot, I guess."

"Besides, getting away from this area can't hurt. If you're feeling this mad, they could be close. They could even be watching us."

She glanced over her shoulder. Shafts of pale winter light split the woods, filtering through the gaps above and illuminating some of the shadows. Nothing jumped out at them, but a tingle worked its way up her spine as she hurried forward.

BY THE TIME THEY STEPPED out of the trees into the open clearing of the school campus, the tingle had receded, and her dark mood began to lighten. She rolled her head from side to side, loosening the tense muscles of her neck while they strolled past wooden fences.

A figure sat on the fence ahead. His familiar crown of golden-blond hair glowed in the late afternoon sun.

Jory turned his head at the sound of their approach and took in Cara's appearance with his trademark enormous grin. "Wow, Cares. Did you leave any mud on the trail?"

"Ha ha, Sunshine. Very funny." She climbed onto the bottom railing of the fence to punch him in the shoulder.

Puddles dotted the sand arena in front of them. A big bay horse trotted along the far side, extending his stride down the long edge before the girl on his back sank into the saddle and gently coaxed him to compress before he splashed through the wet corner.

Wes climbed the fence on her other side and swung his legs over to sit on top like Jory. "Better?"

"Yeah, better." Wes had been right as usual.

Cara allowed herself a moment to appreciate the support of the two guys sitting on either side of her. In spite of their differences from each other—a bright, cheerful grin on one side and a dark, thoughtful expression on the other—they shared a fierce loyalty, both to each other and, now, to her. They were the best friends a girl could ever ask for, and all she'd done lately was snap at them. If she couldn't control herself, they'd probably ditch her soon. Somehow, she had to shut these feelings out and get her life back.

"Seriously. You know running doesn't usually involve rolling in the dirt, right? You're doing it wrong." Jory chuckled when she sneered at him.

"You try running when every muscle fiber in your body gets tight for no reason, and your thoughts spiral off to—" She cut herself off with a small head shake. She didn't feel like discussing where her thoughts had been when she'd fallen, and she forced herself to focus on the horse and rider now coming toward them, instead of spinning back down that particular dark spiral.

She turned to Jory, whose grin had slipped from his face.

"It happened again?" Jory looked across to his childhood best friend. He and Wes barely had to speak to understand each other, and he grimaced at the look on Wes's face. "Damn. We gotta figure out what's going on."

The girl on the horse stopped the animal in front of them and loosened the reins. "Figure out what's going on with what?"

"With Cara and the random fits of rage." Jory gave Cara a wink, and then faced the girl in front of them. A sweeter smile crept across his face as he turned to the newest member of their tight group.

"Again?" Liv stood in her stirrups and swung her right leg over the horse's rear end, dropping to the ground in one fluid motion. Holding the reins in one hand, she slid her helmet off with the other and shook out her shoulder-length auburn hair.

Cara nodded, still clinging to the top rail of the fence. The horse took a step forward and raised his head. She leaned over the fence and held out a hand. His velvety lip nuzzled her stinging palm, searching for treats, and her mood lightened a bit more.

"Sorry, Charlie, I don't have anything for you."

He snorted into her hand. She jerked it back but not before he'd coated her with slime.

"Yuuuck."

Wiping her hand across her thigh added a green-tinged stain to the mud smeared below.

Lovely. Really adds to the look.

Three snickers from all around her brought a flash of amusement. She shot dirty looks at each of them. "Control your beast, Liv."

Liv smirked. "Sorry, Charlie's a real snot-breathing dragon sometimes."

More laughter circled her, but she held back the silencing glares and chuckled along with them.

"So the Pyx still aren't telling you anything?" Jory asked, bringing the serious tone back.

"No." Wes shifted on his perch atop the fence. "But we did say we'd trust them a while longer."

"I want to know what they did with that evil . . ."

She missed Jory's words when a swoop of guilt hit her, causing her to lean out from the railings and wrap one arm across her middle. Out of the corner of her eye, she caught Jenner slinking away into the undergrowth. Was this feeling coming from Jenyx? What was he feeling this awful about?

"Cara?"

A smooth, clear voice from behind them jerked her upright again. She resisted the urge to clap both hands across the wet spots on the seat of her pants. Good thing, since it would have meant letting go of the fence and toppling over backward.

She stepped down from the railing and spun around to put her back to the fence, facing the person approaching.

"Hey, big bro," Liv called out to him.

Rhys waved in his sister's direction without taking his eyes off Cara. "You okay?"

She dropped the arm still wrapped across her and nodded. "Cramps."

Holy crap, Cara. What did you just say?

Heat surged across her cheeks. The gorgeous eyes in front of her twinkled—a perfect thunderstorm of swirling grey with a gold limbal ring that flashed like lightning when he was mad . . . or amused, as he clearly was now.

Say something! Fix it.

"Running . . . running cramps. Stitch in my side," she blurted.

Wow, Cara. Next level humiliating.

The thoughts that had consumed her while she was running with Wes, the ones that had distracted her to the point where she tripped over her own feet, came flooding back. Rhys.

His eyebrows raised as he scanned her filthy clothes. There was no hiding the streaks of mud or the green horse-slobber stain on her pants, no matter how much she wished she could disappear. Thankfully, Wes drew Rhys's attention away.

"She tried to beat me in a sprint at the end."

"And you can't beat her so you tackled her instead?"

Wes shrugged one shoulder. "It's the only way."

The rich notes of Rhys's laugh rang inside her chest.

"So glad I can amuse you all with my misery," she said.

Rhys adopted a serious expression. His lips glistened in the sun when he moistened them, forcing down his smile. "Sorry, Cara. It's a good look, really. But there has to be an easier way to commune with nature. At least a less painful one."

Fighting her own smile as her friends snickered again, she muttered a quiet, "*Et tu*?"

Rhys folded his long, lean frame between the middle railings of the fence and swung his legs through to stand up smoothly on the other side. Her fingertips twitched as he ran a hand through his dark-blond locks. Wes gave a tiny snort from the top of the fence, and she quickly stopped staring. As usual, he was too observant for his own good—the downside of being friends with another Pyxsee who shared her heightened observation skills. Her lips pursed together as she glared him into silence, but at least he'd warned her before Rhys could catch her staring too.

Rhys stopped to pat Charlie's neck before stepping over to drape an arm around Liv, towering over his sister and squeezing her in a sideways hug. Cara couldn't help a small smile. After all they'd been through, it was no surprise they were as close as any siblings she'd ever known.

The rest of the thoughts clouding her focus during the run came back. Rhys with a happy smile while he talked to Liv at breakfast with them, or when he talked to Wes. Rhys with the same easy smile when he sat with Emma at meals, or walked across campus with Emma, or waved to Emma between classes.

No. Stop it. She fled from images of beautiful, perfect Emma.

"So what's new?" Rhys asked, glancing around.

She never got that smile.

When he talked to her, she got quiet Rhys—reserved Rhys. She wished she got this happier, more playful version, but the rare times they found themselves alone for a moment, he usually grew quiet. Maybe she reminded him too much of a bad time in his life. It couldn't be easy being around someone who'd helped plot and carry out his sister's murder, even if it had been necessary to save her. She shuddered to think how easily it could all have gone wrong. Then neither he nor Liv would be here.

Residual guilt trickled through her at the thoughts she'd been having before she'd tripped. She should be glad Rhys had Emma. She should be grateful he had someone who could let him relax without thinking of dark times. He deserved that much after everything he'd been through.

Cara gritted her teeth. It didn't matter how much mud was on her pants or what kind of embarrassing things she said. It wasn't like Rhys would care. She was his little sister's friend now, however they'd first met. All that mattered in this moment was the five of them were together, conveniently away from anyone who could overhear them.

Wes had brought Jory in on the secret of the hidden Pyx from the moment he'd begun to discover his abilities. Liv . . . well, Liv had firsthand knowledge. And as for Rhys, the gold ring in his eyes meant he was the third Pyxsee in their midst. Here at Scovell Academy, the five of them were the only ones who knew.

She stepped up to the fence again.

"What's new is Jenyx thinks there was another unfamiliar Pyx near us today." She managed not to wince when Rhys's smile vanished at her words.

"Seriously?"

Wes nodded. "Not a friendly one, if Cara's emotional radar is any indication."

"It is true," Jenyx said. Jenner had reappeared from the forest. "They are turning up with increasing frequency."

"Do we know what they want?" Jory asked.

"We do not. It is most unusual for any Pyx to avoid communication with the others in the area, but this one, or more than one, does not appear keen to make themselves known."

"They aren't talking." Cara recapped for Jory and Liv who, not being Pyxsees, couldn't hear Jenyx's response.

"Do you have a guess? Does the council?" Rhys straightened and took a step toward the fence. "Do we know if it's safe for her—for anyone, I mean—to be out on the forest trails?" His eyes darted to Cara, sending her heart skittering for a second.

"We aren't certain of much; however, we do have some ideas," Jenyx replied.

"And?"

"Now is not the time."

Cara huffed. "Figures. When is your precious council going to tell us what's up?"

"Soon, child, very soon."

"Why did I know you were going to say that?"

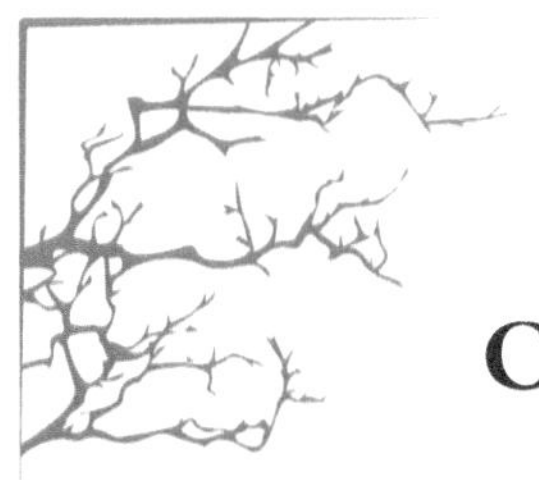

CHAPTER 2

"WHAT COL-OR D-DID SHE say?" Cassidy forced the words out between ragged breaths and swiped at the tears on her cheeks, dislodging Cara's hand from her shoulder with her jerky motions.

Tish paled, staring open-mouthed at the hair color tube on the bathroom counter.

"Smoky silver," Tish breathed.

"Tish!"

"I'm so sorry, Cass. I never—I can't—"

Cara had rushed into the bathroom after Cassidy's scream tore through the halls. There had been a moment of confusion over the appearance of what looked like an old lady crying in the middle of the dorms while Cassidy's two best friends stood over her, wearing matching looks of horror. Then she'd realized the old woman actually *was* Cassidy.

Cara picked up the blonde hair dye box. "The tubes must have gotten swapped."

Cassidy's face reddened in the silence that followed.

Cara gave up trying to console her one-time roommate, whose usual blonde curls were now a tangled mess of grey. Before anyone could throw accusations around, Ms. Lewis charged into the room.

"Who screamed?" The French teacher, and one of their two dorm parents, must have heard Cassidy's shriek through the vents. Ms. Lewis glanced around the crowded bathroom and clutched her chest at the sight of Cassidy's damp grey curls. "*Oh mon Dieu*. That is a bold choice."

Cassidy stomped her foot. "Someone did this to me. On purpose. Look at my hair. I can't be seen like this. You have to punish them."

Cara took one more look and then turned away. Cassidy's complaints and accusations faded as Cara slipped out the door past the other watching girls and headed down the hall. She passed the door to her dorm room where she and her roommate, Delaney, had been studying with Liv and Kaylee moments before the scream, and went to the room on the other side of the hall that she'd shared with Cassidy for the first few months of freshman year.

Turquoise hair bounced on Meygyn's bare shoulders as the girl turned toward the knock at the open door. Cassidy's roommate held, of all things, a glue gun in one hand and the shirt she'd just been wearing in the other. Cara didn't have the energy to ask what she was doing standing in her bra with a superheated weapon in her hand and the door standing wide open.

"Um, did you . . . You didn't swap Cassidy's hair dye, did you?" She couldn't imagine why she would, but Meygyn changed her own hair color at least once a month, so she was the obvious choice. "Because she's really upset."

"She's upset? Why?"

"I guess because she looks like an old lady?"

"So?"

"So most people don't want to go grey before sixteen, I guess."

"I don't know. I think she looks pretty hot as a crone. But I've got plenty of other colors if she wants to change it."

Okay, then. Not Meygyn. Who else . . .?

Cara turned and left Meygyn to do whatever it was Meygyn did with her spare time. She checked her and Delaney's room with a sinking feeling, and found it empty except for Jenner and Marcus, Delaney's cat. The girls hadn't come back to their study session after the excitement. She headed to the lounge in the center of the dorm with Jenner padding after her.

The couch sagged when she sank beside Liv. Liv worked hard to keep watching the television, but her cheeks twitched under the force of Cara's stare. After another moment, she turned her head.

"Yes? Can I help you?"

"Liv?"

"What?"

Cara waited her out.

Liv rolled her eyes. "What? It's a harmless prank. She can dye it back right away. I even have another box of her blonde dye to give her . . . tomorrow." She gave a wicked grin. "After class."

"Why?"

"Someone had to take Queen Bee down a peg."

"Cassidy's nice. A little salty sometimes, a tad superficial, but she's sweet deep down. Why won't you give her a chance?"

"I'm sick of her flirting with Jory all the time."

There it was. Those two needed to sort themselves out.

"Are you serious? Cassidy's a flirt, sure, and Jory too. At least, he was . . . before. But you and him are together all the time now. You must know he likes you."

The Pyx who'd been trapped in her mind had left Liv near death, with ashen skin, sunken eyes, and lifeless hair, unable to speak or react, wasting away to nothing, and Jory had still looked at her like she was the only thing that mattered in the world from the first time he'd seen her.

"I thought so, but it's not like he's asked me out yet."

Cara had no idea what he was waiting for. He certainly wasn't shy. And he was clearly smitten. It was obvious in the way he looked at Liv, the way they reflected each other's expressions without trying, and the special smile he only had for her. Obvious to everyone except Liv, apparently.

One of the girls in the lounge changed the channel, and the background music of the TV show cut out, replaced by a droning voice.

Cara rolled her eyes at Liv and dropped her voice to a hushed tone. "You do know you could ask him out, right? You don't have to wait. Twenty-first century and everything. We have exams next week and a few days off, but then it'll be a new semester, and the Valentine's dance is coming up." When Liv shot her a look that said that wasn't going to happen, she tried another approach. "Fine, but you must see how he looks at you. I've never seen him look at any girl that way. Even when he supposedly had a crush on me for a while, he never—hey!"

Liv had shoved her over sideways on the couch. "When he *what*?"

Cara sat back up, laughing. She raised one finger to hold off Liv's outstretched hands. "Okay, I definitely thought you knew that. And it definitely was not my point. That was before he ever laid eyes on you. My point was he's not the same flirty guy since he met you."

Jenner bumped Cara's knee. "Cara, are you seeing this?" Jenyx's voice sounded deathly serious in her mind.

The babble of voices in the room had vanished into tense silence. She held up a hand to stop Liv from responding and switched her attention to the television.

"You guys are watching the news?" Cara asked the girls around her.

The couch dipped again as Kaylee sat beside her and nodded. "It's awful."

On the screen, the news showed twisted cars scattered across a street. Wreckage lay strewn in haphazard patterns. The newscast switched to an overhead view and panned out. Cara gasped. The crash scene must have stretched for a mile.

"This is in Portland?" She'd run that road often enough with Jenner to recognize it.

She scanned the faces around the arc of couches. Every girl, and a couple visiting boyfriends, stared at the TV or their phones with blank looks of shock. People passing through stopped behind the couches to watch.

The screen changed again to show a reporter standing in front of a bus that was lying on its side looking crumpled and battered.

"As you can see, the bus came to a stop here after crashing into cars on both sides of the road for nearly a mile. Witnesses say the bus engine was revving, and the lack of skid marks is leading many to speculate this was a deliberate act by the driver, who is not known to police and does not appear to have been a part of any extremist groups. The sole survivor from the bus gave a statement to police from the hospital."

The reporter lifted a paper. "This report alleges that the driver was screaming and hitting his head. When passengers attempted to intervene, the driver apparently began a high-speed journey of destruction, ramming cars while shouting about polluting monsters."

Cara's pulse pounded in her throat at the images in front of her. The reporter's next words made it far worse.

"At least two dozen are confirmed dead, including the driver and all but one bus passenger, as well as several other drivers and bystanders. The survivor from the bus remains in the hospital in a serious but stable condition. Another thirty-one people have been taken to the hospital with a variety of injuries, several in critical condition. Jackie has more."

The footage switched to a female reporter standing at a different part of the wreck. Cara's breath caught. In the background of the frame, between crushed cars, police officers worked around a yellow tarp on the ground. Her breathing grew tight and her eyes welled. All those people, all those families. It hit too close to home.

"Need to text my mom," she whispered, standing. Her feet carried her down the hall to her room, where she scooped her phone off the desk and found she already had a message from her mother.

Nowhere near the crash.
In case you were worried.

The road wasn't on her mom's commute, so she hadn't been worried, but she still breathed easier reading the text. She sent a reply.

Glad you're ok.
Try not to watch.
Love you.

She hoped her mom wouldn't watch the coverage. Cara had never gotten over the day she'd found her mom sobbing in their living room with a similar scene playing on the news—a much smaller accident, but a fatality where the same type of tarp showed in the background. It was the day her mom had told her the story of her dad's accident and how she'd been called to identify his body. Police had shown her photos of the scene to see if she could shed some light on what he'd been doing at the time of his death.

The memory of the conversation haunted Cara, so the memory of that awful day would be a million times worse for her mom after seeing a similar crash on TV. She wiped the tears from her eyes.

The phone chimed again.

Love you too, sweetie. Not watching. I'm heading out to the police station to talk to the detective again. It's been another month and still no word on Lydia. Figured another face to face might help light a fire since my phone calls do nothing.

There wasn't much Cara could say, so she replied with a heart emoji to offer a little support, although she didn't expect the visit would do any good. Her mom's friend Lydia had disappeared about three months after the day she'd run out of their law office and right into traffic, luckily only breaking her leg.

Cara's heart gave another squeeze recalling how her mom had done everything she could to help Lydia recover, taking her to all her psychiatrist appointments, feeling terrible about not realizing what had been going on with her. Cara didn't pretend to understand the myriad of ways people could be affected by mental illness, but she wished her mom would stop feeling guilty. No one could have foreseen the woman up and leaving her life behind the way she had. And no one could have done anything more to find her.

Jenner rested his head on Cara's knee, looking as miserable as she felt. She stroked his silky ears and sniffed. A flash of green crossed his eyes as he turned his baleful gaze up to her.

She fought fresh tears. "Stop making my dog sad. And me."

"Apologies, child. It is difficult to see you struggle, although I do admit I am uncertain as to why I am affected so. I do, however, have concerns about what we heard."

"Concerns?"

"Indeed. Is there time yet to head over to speak with Tomyx?"

There was still an hour before curfew. Besides, a visit with Wes and Jory was exactly what she needed right now, so she nodded.

THE LOUNGE IN THE LODGEPOLE Pine dorm, or the Lodge, where the boys lived held the same scene as her lounge over at the Cedars, as they called the Red Cedar dorm. The only differences were the faint musky scent and the people watching the television were a bunch of guys instead of girls.

Wes and Jory sat to one side, spotting her as soon as she and Jenner entered through the main doors. They rose and climbed over the back of the couch to join her.

"Tomyx said you'd be over soon. We were watching for you." Jory attempted a smile, falling short of his usual grin.

She glanced at their TV where the image had returned to the anchors at the news desk.

"In other news, the suicide rate continues to climb. This week saw three more deaths and another six people admitted on suicide watch. That's more than triple the average for Portland, and we're learning this heartbreaking trend is more widespread than was previously thought. Pete, what can you tell us about what the state of Oregon is doing to handle this increasing demand on our mental health facilities?"

The news was full of cheer today. Cara sighed. Noise grew in the lounge and drowned out the television's coverage of a psychiatrist discussing how to make it easier for people to seek and accept help. The guys sitting around the couches all started talking at once, discussing the accident now that the broadcast had moved on from their top story.

"Think he was a terrorist?"

"Weren't you listening? They said the police don't suspect terrorism. Just a guy who snapped."

"Who would do that?"

"Someone insane, obviously."

"The guy's not wrong about polluting monsters, though. I'm getting an electric."

"Sure you are, Mike."

"It didn't look like he cared what type of cars they were."

"He's the monster."

The din of comments started to annoy her, and Cara turned away, leading their group down the hall to the boys' room.

"Hi, Tomyx." Cara greeted the Pyx who lived in Jory's big orange cat. The only answer was another wave of sorrow she didn't need. "Jenyx said we need to talk."

The boys each sat on their beds, and she took a seat beside Wes.

"So what's wrong, aside from the obvious?" she asked.

"A lot." Tomyx usually spoke in a joking, sometimes sarcastic tone, but today, he was mastering a grumpy cat voice to match his pyxis.

"A lot?"

"Indeed," Jenyx replied. "Sadly the events of today are not isolated. A pattern is forming, one which is of terrible concern in light of what the council learned from Livyx."

"The information you refuse to share with us, you mean."

"I do, though that will not be true much longer, unfortunately."

"What? You're finally going to tell us?"

Jory perked up across the room. "They're talking about Livyx? What'd they do to her? She better have paid for what she did to Liv."

"You may reassure young Jory that the Pyx in question is serving out her sentence," Jenyx said.

"She's serving out her sentence? That's it? That's all you have to say about an evil Pyx who almost killed someone?" Cara fumed.

"Easy, child. I know everyone in this room feels strongly about Olivia, and I assure you, the council did not take the decision lightly. The circumstances are not what we expected, and adjustments had to be made."

"We're not the only ones who feel strongly about Liv." Cara's mind flashed to an image of Rhys smiling over his sister at breakfast that morning. There was also her dad, Dr. Randall Whalton, probably busy at the hospital in Portland with crash victims as they spoke. Presumably Liv's mother cared too, though neither Whalton sibling had ever shared anything about her except enough for them to gather she was alive . . . somewhere.

"Of course not," Tomyx said, "but we had to make a call. Letting the Pyx live to ensure her help was the best decision given the situation."

"Her help with what?" Wes narrowed his eyes at the two animals.

Jory fidgeted like he wanted to ask a question, but he held it and trusted them to fill him in as soon as they could. They waited.

Cara's hand rubbed across her middle, and she bent forward. "I can feel that you're uncomfortable telling us, but please." The constant stomachaches lately were really getting old.

Jenner circled the room before sitting. "Allow me to provide some background. You know our three absolute laws: never revealing how we can be killed, never killing another Pyx, and never taking a human pyxis. What you do not know is that for centuries of early human civilization, nothing explicitly forbade the use of human vessels, even though humans' neural complexity had evolved to the point that sharing consciousness became risky. Most of us simply stopped doing it when we saw the increasingly dire consequences for our hosts."

He paused to allow Wes to update Jory, and then continued. "I once mentioned an event that took place in what you would call ancient Greece. It is perhaps time I told you the story of the pyres of Vamis."

Jory had to wait a long time while Jenyx spoke to Cara and Wes, telling the awful tale of a city whose population was cut in half in one terrible night of mass hysteria started by a few humans going insane when Pyx entered their minds. The pyres to burn the bodies had sent towers of smoke to the skies for three solid days after the violence ended.

"The genetic variant that causes the gold color in your eyes and allows you to see and communicate with us dates back to the origins of your species. The trait was once more common. Whole families shared it. Pyxsees like you were instrumental in helping control the mayhem that night and other times since. After Vamis, a consensus was reached that the risk to your species from ours had become too great, and the law was passed. Humans were off limits. As your population has exploded, your genetics have diversified, and the number of you with enough Pyxsee-gold to recognize us has dwindled. We still cooperate with our Pyxsee allies; however, humans in general have forgotten us, making it easier for us to take advantage of human tendencies to overlook the unexplained and allowing us to remain hidden."

Again, he paused, but Cara and Wes were both too stunned by the horrific story to recount it to Jory yet. Jenyx's voice turned grave, laced with the guilt Cara had been feeling from him. "While the majority of Pyx would never intentionally break one of our laws, there *have* been other incidents since then. The Pyx who inhabited Olivia—her actions were clearly inexcusable—but she also did not act on her own."

Cara reeled. Wes's eyes widened, and Jory looked ready to jump out of his skin, waiting to find out what had caused their reactions. Wes gave him a quick recap.

"There are others? More people were attacked like Liv was?" Jory was turning purple.

"What does this have to do with the crash on TV?" Cara asked quickly.

"It likely has everything to do with it, though the following story may have been even more significant in that regard."

"The suicides?"

"Yes, and the growing level of mental illness manifesting in this area."

Her thoughts tumbled back over all the times she'd had out-of-control feelings lately. The unexplained aggression she'd been displaying had her doubting her sanity, not for the first time. A flash of panic coursed through her. What if she was another statistic in the mounting crisis? Would she know if a Pyx had attacked her? Surely she would.

"Are you saying more people are *still* being attacked by Pyx? Why would they all be breaking your sacred laws now?"

"Your questions are better answered by a firsthand account, which is why we need to take you to see the council," Jenyx replied.

"We're going to talk to the council?"

"Wait . . . What are we doing?" Jory interrupted.

"Not we," Tomyx said, "we…" This time, Thomas sat back on his haunches and raised a paw to indicate everyone except Jory, who frowned at the confusing and comical gesture.

"Please explain to Jory that only the Pyxsees will be able to come. Quite aside from his inability to hear the proceedings, there are Pyx among us who will not take kindly to revealing themselves to a normal human."

Cara stared at Jenner, appalled at having to exclude her friend.

Wes saved her from having to say it out loud. "Sorry, man. Looks like it has to be just me and Cara."

"And Rhys," Tomyx added.

Her insides lurched. Wes's eyes flicked from the cat to her and back.

"And Rhys," he repeated for Jory.

"When?" Cara asked.

"We must arrange to assemble as many council members as we can, and summon the guardians, so I expect we should plan for the end of the week."

She swallowed. Setting aside the awful story and the nagging threat, she would be meeting with a bunch of immortal beings deep in the forest the weekend before exams. What could go wrong? Oh, and for good measure, bring along the guy who made her trip over her own feet. Perfect.

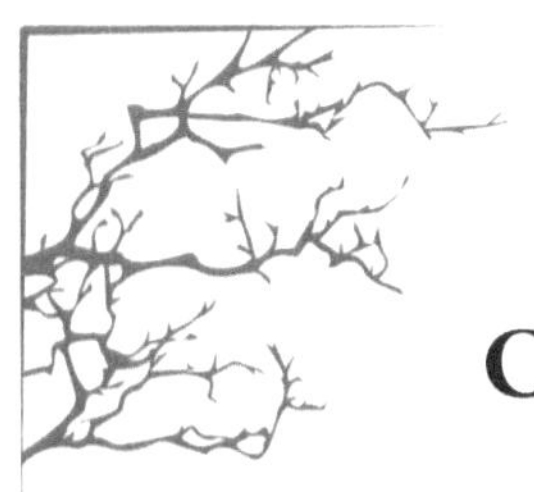

CHAPTER 3

CASSIDY STARTED THE next day in surprising fashion. She waltzed past the glass walls of the dining hall with a posse of friends, before bursting through the doors with her grey head held high. The bottom half of her silver mane had been transformed into a gradient of pinks, ending in a shockingly bright tone to rival the fuchsia bedding in her dorm room.

She paraded past the tables, shaking out her silver and pink curls, touching friends' shoulders and waving to others as she went. When she passed them, she flashed Jory a brilliant smile before giving Liv a terse nod and continuing on her way to grab breakfast.

When Cara turned back, it was to find Jory watching Liv with an amused grin. She kicked his foot and leaned across him to Liv.

"I thought you apologized and gave her the blonde dye last night after I talked to you."

Liv blinked, still staring after Cassidy and her friends. "I did."

A familiar tall figure came into Cara's peripheral vision. There was no need to look. She was way too aware of Rhys to mistake that form. He sat down across the table from her, beside his sister. "What was that about?"

"Nothing. She'll get over it." Liv scowled.

"Liv, what did you do now?" Her brother gave her a sympathetic look. "I know you're still making up for lost time, but why does it always involve getting yourself in trouble?"

Cara ignored Liv's response and grabbed Jory's sleeve. She yanked, pulling him over.

"This is your fault," she hissed in his ear.

He pointed to his chest, dropping his chin.

"Yes, you." She released his shirt and glared at him as he sat up again with that omnipresent grin plastered across his face.

Wes chuckled on Cara's other side.

Rhys glanced up from his conversation with Liv, and his eyes traveled to someone behind them. He smiled and lifted a hand.

"Hey, guys," Emma greeted as she walked by with a group of other senior girls.

A fresh wave of guilt over her angry feelings from the weekend swept through Cara. It wasn't Emma's fault she was totally perfect, and probably perfect for Rhys. Cara had been avoiding Rhys as much as she could ever since he and Emma had grown close again. The last thing she wanted was for him to see her scowl at Emma's presence, especially since the kind older girl had never been anything but gracious to her.

After all, Rhys was supposed to be in the senior class too. He'd only ended up in junior year now after missing a year of school when Liv was in the hospital. He'd dated Emma as a sophomore before he left, and it looked like they'd picked up where they left off.

Avoiding him was supposed to make things easier. *Sure.* She stabbed at her hash browns until a waft of strawberry scent made her close her eyes and suppress a groan.

You should have known it wasn't over.

Cassidy stepped up to their table, sliding in between Cara and Jory. She took one hand off her tray to rest on Jory's shoulder, blocking Cara's view of Liv on his other side.

"Good luck at your baseball game tomorrow, Jory." Her voice dripped with sweetness.

"Thanks, Cass. New hair looks great."

Cara kicked him again under the table, hard enough to make him grunt, as she visualized Liv's hurt face hidden behind him. Cassidy swept away, swinging her hips and her pink-and-grey hair. Cara's exaggerated eye-roll ended in time to catch Rhys watching her. His lips twitched before he could bring the spoonful of cereal to his mouth. Blushing, she gave the foil top on her peach yogurt her full attention as she avoided looking in his direction again.

Wes cleared his throat and leaned over his empty tray. "Should we talk about last night?"

"You haven't told him yet?" Cara gave Wes a sideways look. He had Rhys's number, and she'd assumed he would have messaged him and filled him in by now.

"No. I figured you could tell him."

She kept glaring at Wes. She didn't dare turn an accusing look at Jory, who was probably in on this setup, in case he did something absurd—like wink at her. The fact that her two best friends knew about her crush was beyond annoying sometimes. Jory got a little credit for managing not to spill it to Liv . . . so far, at least.

"Tell me what?"

She resisted the urge to kick Wes, too, and did the only thing she could. Swallowing, she met Rhys's gaze across the table. Wes could join Jory in the doghouse. She'd have words with both of them later.

"Our *other* friends," she said in a quiet voice, glancing to each side to make sure no one was eavesdropping, "said they want to take us—you, me, and Wes—to meet with the council finally, to get the whole story about . . . you know." She nodded her head toward Liv.

His eyebrows rose, and the rings of gold flashed in his steely eyes. "When?"

"They said it would take a few days to assemble the members, and something called a guardian—no idea. Probably this weekend."

"Okay. Let me know." He stood to leave. She couldn't help noticing the tightness in his shoulders and jaw.

They put away their trays and joined the other students heading to class. Rhys walked ahead with some other juniors. Cara trudged between Jory and Wes, chewing her lip and trying not to focus on Kaylee and Ethan holding hands and giggling close together in front of them. At least Rhys and Emma never did that in public. She'd never even seen them holding hands, let alone making out, thankfully.

When they split off to go to their separate classes, she had Jory to herself as they headed for biology.

"Will you ask her out already?" She elbowed him in the ribs.

"Ow. What?"

"Liv. When are you finally going to ask her out? It's obvious you two like each other."

"I don't know. It's not that easy."

"What do you mean? You've never had trouble asking girls out before."

"Exactly. This is different."

She slowed, inspecting his face. "Different how?" There was no reason not to give her friend's love life a little nudge, even if she couldn't do anything about hers.

Jory shrugged. "It just is. She's special. I can't just ask her out like any other girl."

She bumped his shoulder. "Don't tell me you're turning shy on me, Jor."

"No, but . . . Meeting you . . . The whole 'nothing that never was' between us—" He gave her a ridiculous grin, and she smacked his shoulder.

"Thank goodness. Dodged a bullet there."

"Ha ha. Anyway, it made me realize that getting to know her first will make it better. I want it to be perfect. You know, waiting for the right time."

Aw. What a romantic.

When Jory finally got his act together, he and Liv were going to be great. "Well, don't wait too long. She and Cassidy might do something drastic."

For the rest of the week, Cara left him alone about it but watched him closely whenever Liv was with them. When the time came for her and Wes to leave after dinner on Saturday, she pulled him aside again.

"I'm guessing we'll be gone a few hours. Maybe a good time for you and Liv to be alone?" she whispered.

He gave her a grin but no promises. She shook her head with a smile.

"Ready?" Wes asked.

She set her shoulders. "I hope so."

Jenner trotted beside them as they circled behind the dorms close to the forest. Rhys stood waiting at the start of the trail leading into the woods. He relaxed a little when he saw them, his hands unclenching as she approached. Thomas ambled down the path toward them, and a green gleam passed over his eyes.

"They're waiting for us," Tomyx said.

Their somber party hiked single file down the trail deep into the forest, well beyond the school boundary marked by gold-banded trees. She barely gave a thought to breaking that particular rule. It wasn't the first time. The path grew less used, and the undergrowth pressed in on them as the shadows intensified. Cara shivered in the cool evening air. After what felt like half an hour of tense silence, they reached a small clearing. The low angle of the remaining sunlight left it dimly lit, and the surrounding trees were barely lighter than the darkness beyond them.

Wes, who had taken the lead, stopped in front of her before she could move into the open space. Peeking over his shoulder, she took in their surroundings, starting with the boulder in the center. Her eyes darted to the far side, and she understood Wes's hesitation. Several animals watched their approach—the largest among them, a black bear.

She tensed at the sight but took comfort from Wes's quick assessment and acceptance when he stepped forward. Of course. These animals were all pyxides and were here to meet them under complete control of the Pyx within their minds. Predator and prey stood side by side without issue. They were safe. Probably.

Cara joined Wes and pressed a hand to her sternum in an effort to suppress the varied surge of feelings from the Pyx all around them. Her heart stuttered, partly her own nerves, but it seemed many of the Pyx were anxious too. How unusual was it for them to meet with a bunch of Pyxsees?

Aside from the bear, there were two deer, a fox, a squirrel, and a hare ranged around the tree line. In the branches above them, she spotted the owl who'd given them instructions on what to do with the clay pyxis containing the captured Pyx last fall. The owl was perched on a large branch beside an unwelcome sight.

The large black raven fixed her with his beady eyes, but the serious moment meant Ryx didn't taunt her with his usual mocking: "Caw, caw, Cara."

Rhys had come to stand on her other side, and his head lifted toward the birds as well.

The bear shifted across the clearing, and Cara flinched, bumping Rhys's arm beside her.

He glanced down at her. "I've never seen a bear this close before, either. Shouldn't it be hibernating?"

At least she wasn't the only one in awe, although Rhys was doing a better job of keeping his head. Wes had almost certainly seen bears while out bowhunting with his dad and siblings growing up, and he didn't appear intimidated. Jenner moved in front of the humans and glanced back over his shoulder at them.

"Relax. There is nothing to worry about here," Jenyx said.

Cara dropped her hand from her throat and gestured around the circle. "Do they know that? Because I'm picking up plenty of worry. I can't control everyone's feelings. I can't even control my own."

The bear sank back to its haunches and bowed its head. "He's well-fed and perfectly calm, I promise you." The voice of the

Pyx speaking from the bear's mind came out gruff yet friendly enough. Cara tried to relax.

Thomas strutted around the edge of the clearing before leaping onto the boulder.

"Thanks for coming, everyone," Tomyx started. "We couldn't put this off any longer. I know we're not used to sharing these proceedings with humans, but Cara is a special case, and her friends are involved too."

"Thank you for your trust in us," added Jenyx.

"We've all noticed some new Pyx in the area who've managed to stay hidden. After the testimony we heard this past autumn, there's been a lot of discussion about what this means. On top of that, those of us in contact with Pyx in the city, and with more humans in these parts, have noticed some disturbing trends." It was the most serious Tomyx had ever sounded.

A deeper voice picked up where Tomyx had left off. "Attacks on humans in the area by our kind have definitely increased since we first learned about it. It confirms everything the law-breaker told us at the council of eleven when we interrogated her."

Cara knew the voice. The squirrel pyxis hosted one of the elders who usually lived in the small park near her house in Portland. The deep voice booming in her mind from the small squirrel usually made her stifle a laugh, but the somber mood at the moment dampened her amusement.

Jenyx spoke again. "Indeed, the testimony from that time has been borne out by everything we have learned since. Tomyx and I, and several of you here today, have watched Cara for half her life. We long suspected she may have increased abilities due to the intensity of Pyxsee-gold in her eyes. It is exceedingly rare to find a Pyxsee with her solid-gold hue. Last summer, it became clear we were correct when she sensed Livyx trapped and struggling inside young Olivia. Her empathic ability has grown since then, and we can deduce from her reactions to the unknown Pyx in the area that they do not come with friendly intentions." Jenner turned to face the three of them. "The Pyx who attacked Olivia testified to our council that she did not act alone. Since then, we have confirmed numerous other attacks, meaning there is a group of Pyx choosing to break our laws. They appear to be somewhat, er, organized."

Rhys tensed beside her, but Cara kept her eyes on the assembly in front. "Have you found out why?"

"We asked you here not only to fill you in on what the council has learned, but also so you could hear from the Pyx you knew as Livyx yourself. She is known as Linnaeryx now and will be here soon to speak with you. She will tell you what she has told us."

Was that why she'd begun to feel sick? How close was Livyx, or Linnaeryx, to them? Cara rubbed a hand across her middle as she searched the assembled animals. Which of the others had been watching her grow up struggling all those years before she knew about Pyx and what it was that made her so different from everyone else? She didn't know how she felt about it, and wasn't sure she'd be able to tell at the moment anyway. The emotions from the creatures around her were overwhelming her own, and deep regret ate at her.

Wes glanced over. When she nodded that she was okay, he turned to focus on Jenner. "You said last week this had something to do with the bus crash and the mental health crisis Portland's seen lately."

"I did," Jenyx replied. "We believe it has everything to do with that. The city's population did not collectively begin to go insane on its own. You recall my explanation of why we have a law against using a human as a pyxis, and the three possible outcomes?"

Wes nodded. "Our minds reject the Pyx's presence and fight it, causing insanity."

"Unless the human is too strong and shuts their mind down to protect themselves," Cara said, "like Liv."

"Too stubborn, you mean," Rhys muttered.

The tiny smile and shake of his head was out of love for his sister, but the tremor in his voice betrayed his lasting feelings. Liv had done exactly that and trapped Livyx inside her mind, which is how they'd all wound up here together in the first place.

"Which leaves one other option," Jenyx continued, "the few humans who do not fight back against the presence in their minds and instead lose themselves entirely. We believe that is what these Pyx are aiming for."

"Jenyx is right. And humans are far from perfect, but no one deserves to be treated like a skin suit for someone else's purpose, no matter what it is," Tomyx grumbled from the boulder.

Cara fought back the bile in her throat as the disgust of the Pyx around the circle multiplied her own.

"Zombies," she whispered, recalling how she'd thought of it the first time she'd heard of this. Rhys made a noise beside her, also cringing at the notion.

"If that's what they're going for, then how does it explain how all the rest of the people are affected?" Wes asked.

"This faction of law-breakers does not seem to care how many people they go through before finding one compliant enough to allow them to take over," Jenyx answered. "In the process, they may inhabit a dozen humans who fight back for every one they eventually find who does not. They move past those first ones quickly, and those people may fully recover once the Pyx leave them, but not always before they've acted irrationally or outside of their normal behavior. If they are unlucky, they may have lasting damage, or have been injured by their actions, or have hurt others, or—"

"Or have committed suicide." Rhys finished for him.

Waves of sorrow washed over Cara, flooding her own. Her knees threatened to buckle with the torrent of emotion. Wes put a hand on her shoulder, and Rhys leaned closer. Both their faces were downcast too. She reached up to wipe away the tear rolling down her cheek.

Silence extended across the space until Cara managed to swallow and speak again. "So what reason did Livyx—I mean Linnaeryx—give for this string of attacks? And why is it still going on?"

"She can tell you," said the gruff voice from the bear. "She's here."

CHAPTER 4

ONE OF THE SHADOWS deep in the darkness of the surrounding trees moved. The whole shadow. A shape larger and darker than the black bear shifted in the gloom.

Wes rocked onto the balls of his feet. Her mind hadn't processed her fear yet before Rhys put himself between her and the shape, shielding her. His arm extended around her, grasping her wrist to hold her in place behind him.

The spot in the middle of her chest did a weird little flip. It had been a while since that had happened around him, and she almost didn't notice in the sudden motion. The flutter had as much to do with being in shock at what she'd seen as it did with noticing how he'd protected her.

The rest of the Pyx might have moved past their remorse for the poor humans affected by the law-breakers, but this newcomer brought enough sadness with her to keep Cara's feet rooted firmly in place in spite of her flash of fear at the sheer size of whatever it was.

She couldn't see over Rhys's shoulder. But his closeness gave her confidence, and she balanced with her other hand against his back to lean into the safety of his arm and look around him.

All three of them held their breath until the huge shadow shifted again. She was too big to be human. Too tall for an animal. Her arms were too long, and her outline was . . . shaggy?

She stood upright on two legs in the darkness. Cara squinted. Muscles rippled under her hand as a shiver ran up Rhys's back, and they both let out shallow breaths.

Behind the giant form, another shadow shifted, even bigger than the first.

There were two of them.

"What are they?" she breathed.

No one answered.

Jenner turned his back to the beasts in the shadows, and Wes relaxed his stance slightly. Cara took a breath. Jenyx wouldn't put them in danger, and he certainly wouldn't endanger Jenner.

"These Pyx, Linnaeryx now included, are guardians," Jenyx told them. "You know we have watchers, Pyx who stay in one area for long periods and observe the evolution of the region, and wanderers, Pyx who travel the globe bringing news and developments to others. This is how we have operated for millions of years, through many eras and cycles of life since the very beginning, adapting as the earth has changed and species have come and gone."

They'd heard as much before, but Jenyx had their undivided attention for what came next. He was revealing secrets not many people, maybe no one before them, had ever heard. She could tell from the way the clearing crackled with tension as they all anticipated his words.

"Very rarely, we encounter a species that, for various reasons, we cannot allow to be driven to extinction. This has been more frequent in the last millennium than ever before, and humans have been the greatest threat. Several of our kind are now dedicated guardians. They guard the species, inhabiting all remaining members to protect them from human eyes and to help them survive. These species then help us in a variety of ways. In this case, by guarding other Pyx serving sentences for their crimes, and protecting us all. Linnaeryx has voluntarily gone into service with the guardians as her sentence."

Their heads all jerked up to the dark shadows when Jenyx finished speaking.

"I'm happy to serve out my five centuries, and maybe more. I know I deserve it. I might choose to stay and do some good long after this. I know it won't make up for what I did."

The remorseful tone in the new voice hit Cara like a punch in the gut despite the filter of Rhys's warmth. The sharp angle of his shoulder blade dug into her hand as he tensed.

For the first time since the creatures had appeared in the darkness, she realized Liv's would-be killer stood in front of them. She stepped out from behind Rhys but kept her hand on his shoulder, offering what little support she could.

"You're right. It doesn't make up for it. But we're here to learn what you can tell us about the others," she said to the deep shadows.

"I understand. But you must know, I had no idea that would happen. Please allow me to offer my sincerest apologies, though I don't expect you to accept them."

Rhys lurched forward, and Cara's grip tightened on his shoulder. She turned and held him back from throwing himself across the clearing at the enormous figures in the dark. He trembled under her hands.

"I'm so sorry, Rhys. I can't imagine what you're feeling," she whispered up at him. His gaze flickered between her face and the trees behind her. "But I don't have to imagine what she's feeling."

He stopped glancing back and forth and focused on her. If only she could appreciate the lines of his face in the dusk, but the nauseated feeling from Linnaeryx was too overwhelming. Looking into his darkened eyes, she tried to focus on what he needed—what she could say to help—instead of on the awful sensation filling her.

"I need you to trust me on this. She really does regret it. I don't know what I'd have to do in my life to feel this terrible about myself."

"You shouldn't be the one feeling like that." His gaze softened.

"Can't help it. No control." She had to choke down her breaths past the churning sensation that kept building. "You don't have to accept her apologies, but she is sincere, and I think she's here to help now. Please . . . just . . . oh, crap . . . don't move."

She dropped her hands and raced to the tree line, where she vomited into the bushes.

Perfect. Glad you didn't manage to go a day without doing something humiliating, Cara.

Footfalls behind her gave him away, and somehow, she knew it was Rhys who had followed her.

"No, seriously, don't come over here."

She gagged again and spat on the ground.

Ladylike, nice.

He ignored her, because a hand warmed her lower back a moment later. The chill evening air eased her throat when she inhaled and stood upright.

"Sorry," she whispered.

"No, I'm sorry. This is hard enough without me making it worse. I just . . . I can't stop picturing it."

She knew he was imagining the moment he'd once described to her, when Liv had fallen to the ground screaming right in front of him. It was on her mind too, and it must be fresh and raw for him with the culprit standing so close to them now. His hand trailed away as she turned, leaving a warm tingle in its place.

"No one expects you to forgive her, no matter how bad she feels now. We're here for answers, that's all."

"You're right. I know. And for what it's worth, I do trust you. You good to go back?"

Wes waited for them to rejoin him after she took another breath and nodded. The guys stayed close enough together for her to lean into them both for support, and the nausea-inducing remorse from Linnaeryx receded behind their wall until she could think again.

"Where were we?" Tomyx asked, with a hint of his joking tone returning.

"I understand one of you is the girl's family," Linnaeryx said.

"We're all her family now," Cara replied, "but we're not here to talk about what you did to Liv."

Rhys's fingers brushed against the back of her hand. Good. He should know he wasn't alone in protecting Liv anymore. She could think about him saying he trusted her later.

"Tell us who else was involved. What made you do it?"

"Let me start from the beginning."

"Are you coming out where we can see you?" Cara asked.

Remorse, regrets, and her own bitterness aside, she desperately wanted to know what enormous creatures the guardians protected.

"No. I'm a guardian now, and even though I'm new to this, I won't make the mistakes I made before."

The bigger shape behind the first shifted in the dark. Cara got the sense Linnaeryx had a guardian of her own for now.

Linnaeryx continued. "She's shy, as are the rest of her species, for good reason. I won't do anything to make her uncomfortable. I won't do that again."

"Start from the beginning, then." Rhys addressed his sister's attacker for the first time.

"All right. It was two years ago. I had been wandering for ages, but each place had begun to feel more depressing than the last. I heard news from all over of increasingly difficult conditions for so many species on this planet, humans included. The Pyx who convinced me to join the movement promised me we would help. We watch and we wait for so long, until it's too late to save them. I was tired of it. The way she explained using humans didn't sound as bad as I'd always been told. We would enter one mind, and if the human fought back, we would move quickly to the next, not harming anyone. When we found one who didn't fight, we would stay. That person would then be protected by our presence, not harmed, and we could use them to stop other humans who were doing much more damage than we ever could. It really didn't sound so bad. I couldn't see the downside."

"Looks like the rest of them moved on from the idea of not harming anyone." Cara's jaw tightened.

"How many others did you try?" Wes asked.

"Other humans? None. The girl was the first."

"Unlucky," Cara said. Harsh but true. "So who was the leader who convinced you? And how do we stop her?"

"She was not the leader. I never met him. I'm sorry I can't help more."

"Not as sorry as we are," she muttered. She struggled to remember why she'd stopped Rhys from going after this thing, or why she hadn't joined him in lunging across the clearing to exact revenge.

"We should be heading back to the school," Jenyx said. "Darkness is falling."

Wes turned toward Cara and checked her expression. She ran a hand through her hair and rubbed at the base of her neck.

He scanned the woods around them and stepped away from her side. "Thank you all for telling us what you know. We'll be careful."

She snorted. Wes was one to talk about being careful. He was the reason they'd ended up on Rhys's doorstep last year with no plan but to confront him about kidnapping Pyx. That encounter had ended with Jory punching Rhys in the face and her having to smooth things over. Okay, maybe that was a bad example since it had worked out in the end. Still, Wes wasn't exactly the authority on careful.

Wes turned away from all the animals and gave Rhys a pointed look. She grimaced. What was that about?

"Jenyx is right. We should go." Rhys stepped away from her other side, turning for the path back to the school.

Her weight shifted as she rebalanced. Why was everyone keen to leave all of a sudden? She crossed her arms. "We're here. Shouldn't we talk more and ask more questions?"

Thomas landed on the ground with a soft thump. His leap from the boulder took him halfway across the clearing, and he stalked the rest of the way without stopping.

"Jenyx and I can answer anything else now. The council has witnessed what they needed, and you heard from Linnaeryx. Time to go," Tomyx said.

She shook her head.

Rhys rested a hand on her arm. "Cara, come on. I'd like to get back to Liv."

Her eyes narrowed.

Probably a date with Emma is more like it.

Wes started down the path after Thomas. She shrugged her arm out from under Rhys's hand and stormed after Wes, leaving Rhys and Jenner to follow. They trudged along the trail, and her irritation grew steadily into full-blown anger.

They'd been right there with the council they'd been asking about for months. How could Wes and Rhys be satisfied with the little they'd learned? And why had it taken so long for them to be told that much, anyway? Jenyx and Tomyx had been keeping all that from them for far too long. It made her furious. Now they were headed back to the dorms so Rhys and Emma could be together. Trying to say it was so he could see his sister . . . Did he honestly think—Oh.

Uh oh.

A shiver wormed up her spine.

This isn't you, Cara. He probably does want to see Liv after that. And you did learn a lot. And Jenyx and Wes are always protecting you, even from yourself.

They'd started talking about leaving as soon as she'd responded to Linnaeryx with irritation. That feeling was mild compared to the hostility now. She halted in the middle of the path, and Rhys had to put a hand out to stop from bumping into her. She peered into the deep black on either side of them. It really had grown dark.

"They're here. At least one. Close, I think," she whispered. Her insides hardened with bitter hatred that wasn't hers. "I think we should—"

Jenner barked—a deep aggressive bark she'd never heard before. "Run!" Jenyx's voice thundered in their heads. The dog crashed into the bushes, vanishing into the dark. Flames clawed up her ribs, and she lurched to run after him. No one was going to hurt Jenner.

Rhys caught her, holding her back the way she'd done for him. "He'll keep Jenner safe and give us time. Now go." He turned her shoulders and urged her forward on the path.

Reluctantly, she broke into a run that quickly turned to a sprint. She wasn't the only one out there. If someone was after them, then she wasn't the only one in danger. They could hurt Wes, or Rhys. They all raced along the trail, with branches whipping at their arms until they spilled out onto the lawn behind the dorms. They slowed in the open space. A moment later, Jenner burst out of the undergrowth a few yards away.

"Gone. I believe she was alone."

"She?" Cara asked, panting.

"Yes. Jenner drew close enough to make out the outline of a woman, but she retreated, and I steered him away to safety to return to you."

Confirmation of another human pyxis so soon after meeting Liv's attacker and hearing what she had to say was sobering. The forest behind them seemed to teem with hidden dangers as night pressed in.

"Thank you, Jenyx." She knelt beside her dog. "And thank you for the protection, Jenner." Her anger had dissolved along the run, and she rubbed his head. His tongue lolled out the side of his mouth. "Let's get you some water."

THE DOOR TO WES AND Jory's room stood open. Liv jumped up from her perch on Jory's desk and threw her arms around her brother when they walked in.

"You okay? How was it?"

"It was . . . something. Come on. I'll tell you everything," Rhys said, and steered her from the room.

He would want some time alone with his sister to tell her about her attacker, and relay the apology from Linnaeryx if he wanted. If Liv would accept it. The rest of them could talk to her later.

Jenner lapped up water from Thomas's dish in the corner, and Cara flopped down on Wes's bed, completely drained.

"So what happened?" Jory sat on the edge of his bed. "And why do you look like you just sprinted?"

"We did." Wes took a seat beside Cara and told Jory everything, starting with the race from the intruder in the forest, and then circling back to the events of the meeting, including Cara's humiliating vomiting episode.

"Wow. It was really that bad?"

Cara nodded and smoothed her hair. "I've never felt so terrible about anything in my life. Still, half of me wanted to let Rhys attack her. Maybe if she hadn't been so huge."

"Okay, wait. What did they look like?"

Wes rubbed his hands on his knees. "Big, tall, hairy, long arms–"

"No freaking way. No way." Jory jumped up from the bed. His cheeks turned red, and his hands flew in the air. "You're telling me you saw Bigfoot. I can't believe I didn't get to come! I can't believe you saw Bigfoot and I wasn't there."

"We don't know *what* we saw. It was dark, and they stayed in the shadows."

"It was totally Bigfoot. Wasn't it, Jenyx? Ask Jenyx. Ask him. He'll tell you."

Cara looked to Jenner. "Well?"

"You humans do have many strange names for unfamiliar things," Jenyx replied.

She laughed. "Sorry, Jor. That wasn't really an answer."

"I don't care. It was definitely Bigfoot." He sat down with a satisfied smirk and crossed his arms.

"More importantly, did you and Liv get a chance to talk?"

That wiped the smirk off his face.

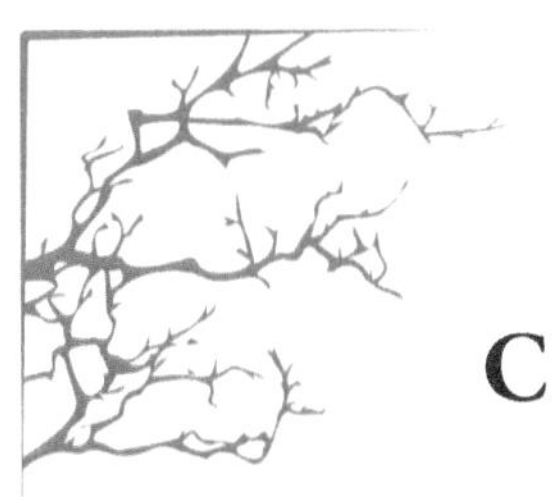

CHAPTER 5

AS IT OFTEN DID WHEN her thoughts were swirling, her brain refused to sleep. Cara rose early while the rest of the dorms slept, and crept out the door with Jenner. She'd added leggings under her sweatpants and layered a long-sleeved shirt beneath her hoodie. It was cold enough for a winter jacket, but she'd be sweating soon.

"If I sense any others nearby, I will let you know," Jenyx said as she broke into a jog along the packed gravel path. "Do the same if you feel anything out of the ordinary."

"I will." All she felt was the hesitancy from Jenyx at having her out here alone and vulnerable if one of the hostile strangers turned up. But she needed her morning runs. When there was this much to think about, it was the only way to clear her head, and she still loved the thrill of this bit of stolen alone time. They stuck to the path around campus, staying out of the trees, circling the stables, and crossing the wide meadow near the huge stone administration building that always reminded her of a castle. Her muscles warmed, and she relished the burn while sweat rose around her in a misty shroud.

Finally, she slowed to a walk past the dining hall. Her steps faltered when she caught sight of a familiar figure sitting on top of one of the picnic tables outside the Dougie, as the students called the Douglas Fir dorm. Rhys had already noticed her and was watching her approach. He lifted a gloved hand in greeting. A cloud of breath surrounded his head, shimmering in the pink air of dawn.

"You look like you're smoking," she said. *More like smoking hot.* She fought a little smirk from betraying her ridiculous rogue thoughts. At least the red in her cheeks from running in the cold would hide any blush.

"Ew. No, I was watching the sunrise. Couldn't sleep after yesterday. I didn't know you were a morning person."

"Ew," she parroted. "I'm not. I'm just a morning runner."

Chuckling softly, his head bowed forward and soft blond hair fell across his eyes. She hadn't been alone with him in months. Usually there were other friends around as buffers. But this was practically a conversation, and her pulse was skipping. Jenner jumped onto the table beside him, and Rhys's arm wrapped around her dog, scratching his ruff so Jenner's chin stretched toward the brightening sky.

Traitor. She gave her dog a look that was probably part jealousy. Why did Rhys have to be a dog person too? It wasn't helpful.

"You sure you're not a morning person?" He pointed over her shoulder to the east.

She turned to find rays of orange bolting from a dark-pink cloud as the first sliver of sun slid over the treetops. It was all she could do not to stare straight into it as the top of the bright circle framed jagged pines beyond the stables and the sky faded to pale blue above the low cloud. This forest, this place, the fresh air, she could almost be convinced to love mornings after all. Her content sigh brought another chuckle from behind her, and she pulled herself together. The company didn't hurt.

"Nah. Not impressed," she said straight-faced. "Plus, morning people are crazy."

Rhys released Jenner and stood. "Oh, really? Well, I'd say I should join you for a morning run sometime—our basketball coach would probably be happy—but that would involve . . . you know . . . running. And runners are the real crazy people." His mouth did that sweet smile it did sometimes, the one that made the world stand still in a brief second of perfection, a lot like that sunrise. It reminded her of the look he had when she saw him at Whalton manor, a place he clearly loved, or for Liv when she did something generous and kind instead of mischievous.

She had to tell her heart to beat again.

"Should you be out here alone?" He turned serious.

"I'm not alone. I have Jenner, and Jenyx."

"It appears safe for now," Jenyx chimed in. There was a hint of another comment in his voice, and Cara tried not to think what things he might say later about this exchange and her teenage hormones. The astute observations of an immortal companion sometimes hit an awkward note.

"I'll walk back with you anyway," Rhys offered.

Cara shrugged her acceptance while warmth bubbled inside her.

Calm yourself. He's just being nice.

"My dad's the real morning person in our family."

"Yeah?" She stole a sideways glance at him as they made their way toward the Cedars.

"Liv and my mom are both night owls. They hate mornings, but I never minded them. Dad's kind of a workaholic, so he usually heads to his office or goes to the hospital early when we're in town. But when we used to all stay out at the manor together, he would come wake me in the mornings. We'd go to the balcony off the upstairs study to watch the sun rise over the trees."

"That sounds beautiful."

"It is. It was."

The tender look he'd had for a moment disappeared as they reached the door to her building. Words abandoned her, and she resisted an unexpected urge to comfort him. Whatever that was about, it wasn't her place. Instead, she thanked him for walking her back.

"Of course," he said, kneeling to rub Jenner's head. "Anything to spend more time with this guy. I should really get a dog."

The sudden image of him cuddling a puppy was too much. Her face was out of control, and she was going to say something stupid any second now. "You can always come walk Jenner," she blurted.

Why, Cara? Go inside. Now.

"But I'm sure you have better things to do. Like, um, head to breakfast." She shook her wrist and glanced at her watch, the only heirloom she had from her dad. As if on cue, Meygyn burst out the doors, indigo hair blowing past them on her way to the dining hall. Cara darted through the opening before she could do anything else she'd regret.

Her thoughts swirled away to her own father and the memories they might have shared if he had lived. Instead, she was left with a hollow longing and an image of Rhys's face when he'd told her about watching sunrises with his dad. She did her best to drown the thoughts in a long, hot shower.

The rest of Sunday was spent in the library with Liv and the guys, studying for their exams. Since Liv had missed the end of her freshman year and then had picked up as a sophomore in November, falling back a year after her ordeal, they'd spent all semester helping her catch up. Cara and Liv continued studying in the lounge at the Cedars long after curfew, where Kaylee and Delaney joined them.

"You've got this, Liv. No problem," Cara said the next morning as they took their seats for their chemistry exam—Liv's worst subject. Cara avoided eye contact with Mrs. Johansen when she handed out the exams, remembering all the stuff they'd stolen from her lab in the fall to make the poison that saved the girl sitting beside her. Liv gave a shaky thumbs-up, and they set to work.

Three days, six exams, and one final project later, they spilled out of their history final to end the first semester of sophomore year.

"We should find a party or something," Liv said.

Cara chuckled. "Wes and I are leaving right away anyway. Try the Treehouse if you have time."

"Maybe. I'm heading over to the manor in a few hours with Rhys, and our dad'll be up here tonight. I'm looking forward to a crackling fire in the study."

"I bet." She could picture curling up with a book in front of that fireplace in Whalton manor. It was sometimes hard to resist running down the familiar forest path to the stone mansion down the road. She missed its stark beauty. But she had no business going there, and it wouldn't be safe at the moment, even if she didn't care about breaking school rules by leaving the grounds.

As if her thoughts had summoned him, Rhys emerged from the science building. Maybe he could read minds, because he immediately caught her looking and held her eyes across the courtyard. She quickly turned back around and found Wes and Jory had joined them.

"Be careful around here the next few days, Liv. You too, Jor," she said. They headed for the dorms and separated from the crowd. "We know they're out here, at least one, so don't go off into the woods. We don't know what they want here, unless it's more victims."

"Tomyx is keeping an eye out, and Ryx said he'd help too. They'll find ways to warn them if any unfamiliar Pyx are nearby." Wes turned to his friend. "But, yeah, be careful this weekend."

The bright-blond head bobbed. "We won't take any risks."

"Don't worry, guys. Rhys and I will visit the school to see friends, and we invited Jory for dinner on Friday." Liv skipped to Cara's side, with her cheeks pink in the wind. "Rhys will drive us back and forth in that hideous van of his so no one's walking through the forest."

"Thanks, Liv. And, um, tell your brother to be careful too." She turned her face to let the wind sting her cheeks, which were already turning pink on their own.

"Of course." Liv spun around, skipping backward. "You're not the only Pyxsees in town."

"Shh," Cara hissed. "Loud enough, Liv?"

"Loud enough for what? Who's a pixie?"

Cara spun around to the figure coming toward them. Speaking of brothers . . . "Hey, Mak. I thought we were meeting you at the parking lot."

"Oh, there you are, shorty." Wes's brother loomed over her and patted the top of her head until she swatted his hand. "Didn't see you down there. I'd have gone with sprite, not pixie, but whatever. Anyway, I came to check what was taking you guys so long."

"I am not short. And we're not late. Be right back." She dashed into the Cedars to grab her bag. When she returned, Jory and Liv had disappeared and the two Vanneau brothers stood waiting for her. Wes wasn't going to catch his basketball-team-captain brother for height, but they were looking more and more alike lately. "I'm ready. We have to grab Jenner from the kennels."

Her mom was waiting for them by the time they arrived at the parking lot. "Do you want to drive, Cara?" Sandra asked her.

"Nope. No thanks."

Driving made her jittery at the best of times, but with Mak in the car—a senior and a friend of Rhys—she'd be a bundle of nerves. Instead, she allowed Mak and his long legs to take the front seat, while she piled in the back with Wes and Jenner.

Mak leaned between the front seats to grin at them as they pulled off the private road onto the highway. "So did Jory ask out Rhys's little sister yet?"

"Not yet."

"Speaking of Rhys—"

Cara's stomach gave a jolt.

"What were you two doing with him last weekend?" Mak asked. "I saw you guys head into the forest together."

Cara met her mom's eyes in the rearview mirror when they flicked up. She looked away quickly.

"Nothing," Wes replied.

"I don't know how I feel about my friend hanging out with my kid brother and his girlfriend."

This time, her mom's whole head jerked up. Cara's mouth opened and closed silently as she shook her head at her mom's reflection. It should be obvious Mak was teasing, although he did keep believing she and Wes were dating, no matter what they said.

"Why are you such a tool, Mak?" Wes leaned forward to punch his brother's arm, but Cara stopped him by smacking the top of Mak's head from behind instead.

"Hey, no fighting in the car."

"Sorry, Mom. He deserved it."

Mak shrugged. "Yeah, I probably did. So why are you ditching the family on Friday?"

"I'm not ditching. It's only a few hours. It's also none of your business, and I'm taking your car," Wes answered.

"No you're not."

"Okay."

Mak's look of triumph was only a flash before it slipped. "You're taking it anyway, aren't you?"

"Yep."

"I'm hiding my keys."

"Fine." Wes watched the trees flashing past the window while Cara's eyes darted between the brothers.

Mak sighed. "How long have you had a copy of my car key?"

"Since I turned sixteen."

Cara nearly choked on her laugh.

"Mom's going to give you so much sh—oops, sorry, Mrs. R."

Sandra was too busy trying not to laugh to respond.

"Three words," Wes said. "Jory's birthday present."

With that, the argument was won. Mak hung his head in defeat and turned around. "Yeah, you're right. Mom'll let you take it to pick up his present. Ugh, fine. But you better not scratch my car." He looked over his shoulder again. "I'm still trying to convince Mom to let me drive it back to school after this weekend."

"Why? You can't take it anywhere."

"Not yet, but I'll be eighteen soon enough, and then I can leave the school on weekends and go into Tillamook or whatever."

"In another two months? Why not wait until then?"

"I have my reasons."

Cara took her chance. *Payback time.* "Do those reasons include a girl, Mak? Trying to impress someone?"

"Shut it, sprite."

She sat back, laughing at the guilty sideways look Mak gave her mom. Wes held out a fist for her to bump. "So who is this mystery girl?" She'd never seen Mak with a girlfriend, though he was plenty popular and always out socializing. She had no idea who he might be dating, though.

"None of your business. And no one. Yet." He fell silent in the front seat.

They'd had their fun and left him alone for the rest of the ride, chatting quietly in the backseat, leaning across Jenner to whisper with Jenyx about the Pyx and the council and what it could all mean. Cara gave Wes a couple meaningful looks behind Jenner's back. They had plans for more than birthday shopping on Friday.

TWO DAYS LATER, CARA walked to the little park she used to cross on her way to and from her old school each day. Wes sat waiting for her in Mak's old beater of a car. She'd told her mom she was taking the bus to meet him at the mall, but she and Wes had made different arrangements.

She climbed into the passenger seat beside him to warm up momentarily.

"Check these out." She held up the custom socks. She'd already sent him a photo as soon as she'd walked in the door of her house and seen them, but the repeating image of Thomas's furry orange face plastered all over them was way better in person, so she'd brought them along.

Wes laughed. "Jory will think those are hilarious. You do know he's actually going to wear them and we have to be seen with him, right?"

"Don't care. They're awesome. Tomyx will choke when he sees them."

"I don't think a being with no body can actually choke."

"Whatever. You know what I mean."

"I stopped by the mall and picked up the other thing already." He reached into the backseat and pulled out a small bag to hand to her.

She unwrapped the silver keychain and turned it over. The photo she'd taken of Jory at his baseball game was etched on the gleaming silver rectangle, looking like a metallic baseball card. The nearly invisible catch on the bottom released under the pressure of her thumb, and the metal slid apart to reveal a color image inside. The three of them had been sitting on the couch in the lounge of the Cedars when she'd asked Delaney to take the picture, and Liv dove across their laps to join in. Liv's face beamed next to Jory's, where he'd caught her and held her for the photo.

"He's gonna love it. Probably more than the car his parents will end up buying him." She carefully slid the pieces back together until they latched and no one could tell the extra picture was there unless they knew to look for it. "Do you know if they're going to show up to see him?"

Wes shook his head. She had yet to meet Jory's parents, and was pretty sure she never wanted to. She had nothing to say to people who would rather have more yacht time than come visit their son for his birthday, no matter what expensive presents they sent him. As far as she was concerned, his grandma and Wes's mom had raised Jory much more than his own parents.

"What'd you do yesterday?" Wes asked.

She leaned back in the passenger seat. "Not much. Walked Jenner. Read a book. My mom and I video chatted with my uncle."

"Where is Josh right now? Any new stories?"

Since her uncle was the only adult Pyxsee they knew, his stories of Pyx around the world were always fascinating. "Indonesia. They were helping relocate a couple villages from some of the low-lying islands that keep flooding. And yeah, he texted me after we hung up to say he worked with some Pyx in the area to save a couple local species too." Her hands clenched in her lap. "It actually made me think about the guardians."

They sat in silence for a moment.

"Jenyx still doesn't know we're doing this?" Wes asked.

"No. He thinks we're going to the mall like we planned."

"Are you sure you want to go behind his back? You've always trusted him before. This could make things awkward when he finds out."

Her stomach tightened. "I know. But he and Tomyx kept so much from us for so long. I can't control all these feelings I keep having, which can't be a good thing. I want to talk to the elders without him around and see if they'll tell me more than what anyone said at the council. If Jenyx were here, he'd only interrupt when he thought we'd heard enough. I don't want enough. I want everything."

"Okay. Just checking."

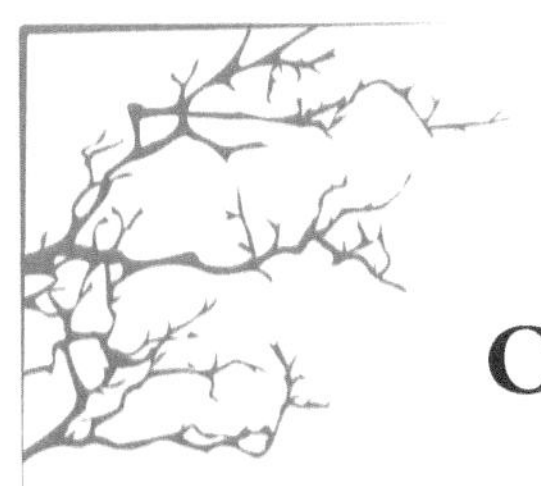

CHAPTER 6

WES CLIMBED OUT OF the car and shrugged on a sweatshirt he'd pulled from the back seat. Cara zipped up her jacket in the biting wind. Together, they hustled into the park where the trees offered some shelter, and stopped in front of the large pine.

Wes rubbed his hands for warmth. "Anything?"

"No strong feelings. All I feel is cold." She peered up the trunk into the thick branches. "Hello?"

After a moment, a large shape shifted in one of the high boughs. "Cara, isn't it? I wondered if I'd see you here eventually." The porcupine lumbered down to a lower branch.

"You did? Where are the other two elders? What happened to the one in the tree?" She'd become oddly accustomed to talking to the Pyx who used to live in this tree, and was surprised to find her gone.

"Ah, they're off on important business. And she had no reason to stay in the tree once you sorted out that other Pyxsee."

"He was only trying to save his sister."

"What important business?" Wes asked.

"Oh, nothing related to what you came here for. Nothing related to the one watching you."

Wes cast a side-eyed glance at Cara before craning his neck up the tree again. "You know about it. So who's watching us?"

"Not both of you. No, no. What would anyone care about you? No, she's watching the girl. Cara's the interesting one."

Cara glanced over at Wes at the insensitive words, but he didn't seem perturbed to be called uninteresting.

"Interesting how?" he asked.

Ouch. Hurtful. He didn't have to spread it around just because the Pyx said no one would care about him. Was that what he thought about her? Huh. Maybe she'd been rude one too many times lately.

"Those eyes—"

"Yeah, yeah. My stupid crazy-colored eyes. Unusual intensity. Blah, blah, blah," she interrupted. "Get to the part where it matters."

"There have been others with extra abilities like you."

Her insides froze. She knew there had been others with the same intense gold eyes. Her dad, for one. And Jenyx had said Pyxsees like her were rare, not unique. But this was the first she was hearing about enhanced abilities like her empathy. Why hadn't Jenyx ever said anything? How many secrets and lies were still out there?

"How many others? What kinds of abilities?"

"Several. We find a few in every generation of Pyxsees. Come back to see me anytime, and we can discuss it."

"Why? What's wrong with right now?" Her fingernails dug into her palms.

"Cara? You okay?" Wes had his hands pulled into his sleeves for warmth, but still shivered beside her. "Are you picking up something again?"

"What?" The harsh tone registered as it came across her lips. He could be right. She didn't usually sound so snarky. "Sorry.

Maybe. Or maybe this is all me. I have no clue anymore. We can go. You're obviously freezing." This rude defensiveness wasn't going to help keep her friends. She snapped her hood up and stomped back the way they'd come.

Wes caught up and fell into step beside her. A woman walked across the park with her head bowed and her coat drawn around her. Clouds of breath floated in front of all their faces, and Cara's came out in tense puffs. The woman passed them without looking up.

There was something familiar about her.

Cara froze. She whirled around.

"Lydia?"

It hit her.

A wave of hostility nearly took out her legs with its ferocity. Her mind flashed back to the hospital room last year after Lydia had run into traffic. Cara hadn't been able to enter the room in the psychiatric unit, let alone visit her mom's friend, thanks to the feelings overwhelming her that day. Nothing had prepared her for it then, and it was just as unexpected here in the park. Her ribs tightened. A blast of cold wind sucked out her last breath and she choked in a gasp, struggling against her body's response.

In a rush, it all connected, her thoughts tumbling over the hundred times she'd snapped at her friends lately without meaning to. Bitter hatred flooded through her. This was it. This was the one she'd been feeling.

The woman stopped walking.

She didn't turn around.

Cara heard her mom's voice again, shaking as she'd filed the police report for her missing friend. Lydia hadn't been seen since her broken leg had healed. Unable to face whatever she was going through, the woman had vanished. After Sandra had helped nurse her back to health, her only thanks had been the mess of unfinished cases Lydia had left her with at work, and a filthy apartment to deal with. All at once, Cara understood exactly what Lydia had been going through.

She flung herself at the woman, grabbed her shoulder, and spun her around.

"Get out of her, you evil piece of—oh, shit!" She recoiled.

Lydia's face glared back, but it wasn't Lydia looking at her, not anymore.

Her eyes glowed a solid, unyielding green.

Wes rushed to Cara's side, pulling her back. It all happened so fast. One moment, she was staring into the unblinking green glow. The next moment, Lydia lunged. Dull silver flashed in the flat winter light.

Knife.

Her brain registered the movement, and she ducked before the thought finished processing. Wes fell back. Lydia stabbed out again as Cara leaped around her and tried to wrap her arms around Lydia's to pin them to her side. The woman was absurdly strong. She shook Cara off, throwing her to the ground, where Cara scrambled back to her feet to lurch forward again.

Lydia hurled the knife, barely missing Cara's shoulder, and then spun around and ran. Cara took off after her in a blind rage. This Pyx was not getting away with this. Lydia deserved her life back, even if she hadn't fought for it. Tomyx was right. No one deserved to be used like this.

She sprinted past the car and onto the street. Lydia was faster than she had any right to be. The Pyx must be influencing her body, the way she'd seen Thomas leap higher and further than a cat his size should be able to. They raced down the sidewalk. Then Lydia stopped.

She'd wrestled another knife out of a deep pocket and whirled on Cara, slashing at her. The blade cut through Cara's sleeve, barely missing skin. Coppery fear flooded her mouth. She backpedaled and stumbled.

A streak of black-and-brown fur flew over her shoulder, colliding with Lydia. Jenner's jaw clamped down on the woman's forearm. The knife clattered to the sidewalk. She flung her arm, and Jenner tumbled to the ground with a yelp. A crack from Lydia's direction sounded like a bone breaking in her arm from the force. Cara burned with rage at the Pyx who would treat her pyxis with such disrespect, but Jenner's unexpected appearance broke her focus and his safety kept her from giving chase again when Lydia fled.

She scrambled across the frozen grass to her dog. "Jenner."

He rose to his feet and shook himself off.

"Jenyx, is he okay?"

"He is. Are you?"

"Yeah, I'm fine. But what the hell? And where did you come from? Did you know Lydia was one of them? One of the zombie people?"

"Are you sure you are uninjured? Jenner smells blood."

"What? From Lydia, right? Jenner bit her."

"No, it is too much for that."

Jenner sniffed the air and whimpered. He darted across the road. She followed, running back to the park.

No. Not Wes.

The red tinge vanished from the edges of her vision. Cold fear brought the world into crisp focus so the snowflakes that had begun to fall descended in slow motion, held in stark white contrast against the steel sky. Wes leaned against the car.

His right sleeve clung to his arm, plastered in place by the crimson blood soaking through.

"Wes." She stumbled over to him with ice streaking through her veins.

His left hand gripped his right arm around the biceps. His arm. Relief flooded through her that she hadn't discovered him with a knife in his chest, but fresh guilt quickly chased it away. Blood trickled between his fingers. How could she have left him? Why had she chased after Lydia?

"How bad is it?"

"Bad enough. You're driving."

"What?"

"Hospital."

Crap. Of course.

"Right. Hospital." She opened the passenger door for him. "Here."

He lowered himself into the car, not letting pressure off his arm.

"Do you need a tourniquet or something? Should you let me look at it?"

"Drive, Cara," he said through clenched teeth.

She shut his door and raced to the driver's side. She climbed in and reached for the ignition where her hand brushed the key slot, expecting a push button like her mom's car.

Double crap.

"Key?"

"Pocket." He shifted his hip forward so she could fish the key out of his front pocket.

He grimaced when she jostled him.

"Sorry, sorry." She started the car and checked around her. "Oh my—Jenner."

She leaped out of the car again, yanked open the door to the back seat so he could jump in, slammed it behind him, and dropped back into the driver's seat.

Wes gave a confused glance, but his pinched face and clenched jaw made talking difficult.

"I don't know where he came from, but he saved me. Oh, Wes, I never should have chased her and left you. I didn't even know you were hurt." She slammed her hand against the steering wheel. "I was literally seeing red. I didn't think. I shouldn't have let her affect me that way, but the feeling was stronger than any of the other times."

He blinked with a tiny sideways motion of his head, and she swallowed. He wasn't mad. But he was in pain and still bleeding badly. She carefully put on the turn signal at the end of the block and made the left turn toward the hospital.

"Where did you come from, Jenyx? How did you get to us?"

"A friend opened the gate for me."

"I thought Ryx was at Whalton manor, keeping an eye on the area." The raven had let Jenner out of their backyard many times before she'd found out about it.

"Squirrels can be equally adept at unlatching things," Jenyx replied.

Cara gripped the wheel harder, driving along the main road. "I didn't think the elders knew I was coming."

"The elders often know more than we realize. We did think we had more time, however. We did not expect you to go directly to the park, and of course, no one expected for one of the outlaw Pyx to show up."

"Outlaw?"

A car sped by them, passing inches from her side mirror, and Cara swerved. Wes took a sharp breath, and her eyes darted to him. Only three more blocks. Driving wasn't helping calm her shot nerves.

"Indeed. As law-breakers, they will face a council of eleven when they are caught. Our laws are sacred for a reason, and we do not take this lightly."

"So you didn't know about her. You didn't know my mom's friend was one of the people they'd taken over?" A wave of sorrow came from Jenyx when he didn't bother to answer, but there was no guilt with it. He hadn't known. "I should have put it together. Once I started feeling all this hostility, I should have remembered how it felt outside her hospital room last summer. I should have realized."

Wes grunted his disagreement.

"Wesley is correct. You cannot blame yourself. Even if you had made the connection, what could you have done? She was already gone."

The sign for the emergency department flashed by her window as she made the turn into the hospital. She pulled up to the entrance, ignoring the no-parking signs, and switched off the car. Slamming the door behind her, she raced to the other side, past a man in scrubs standing at the entrance.

"You can't park—"

"Help me," she shouted at him, opening Wes's door.

When he saw the blood dripping between Wes's fingers, the man stepped inside and emerged a moment later with a wheelchair.

"I'll be back soon," she whispered to Jenyx as she closed the passenger door and followed them inside.

The man wheeled Wes past the triage desk without stopping and called out a few orders. Other emergency staff crowded around, and they took Wes in right away. He'd gone pale, and held his eyes closed as they helped him onto the bed and began to cut away the blood-soaked sweatshirt.

Cara was left to do the talking for the next while, especially once the policeman showed up. "Yes, it was a knife. That's what I said."

The encounter with the Pyx in Lydia had left a sharp bite to her voice. She understood they had to deal with a police report, but she didn't care about any of it. All she cared about was Wes and how she could have screwed up so badly and left him behind.

"Is he going to be okay?"

A doctor turned to answer her. "We'll have to see about his arm, but he's not in any danger now. The bleeding has mostly stopped."

"Did you know your attacker? Was it a fight?"

She stared at the officer asking her questions while her friend received treatment beside them. Her head turned toward Wes, and she met his eye. With a blink, he gave her permission to lie.

"No, we don't know the guy. He was just some crazy guy in the park. Came out of nowhere. Can I go move my car now?"

The policeman asked her a few more questions, and she provided a vague description, saying she'd been too freaked out to notice much, which was basically true. She hadn't even noticed her friend get stabbed. When he finally said they were done, she moved into the space beside Wes's bed. The activity around him had died down, and his face was looking less pinched.

"Did they already call your parents?"

"Yeah."

"You good for a few minutes?"

He gave a slow nod, painkillers kicking in.

By the time she moved Mak's car, made sure Jenner would be warm enough in the shelter of the backseat, and arrived back at Wes's bedside, his eyes were closed, so she stood to the side and brought out her phone. She stared at the black screen. She couldn't bear telling Jory yet. Maybe when Wes woke up, or after the doctors came back to talk to his family when they arrived and to finish stitching his arm.

Her uncle was the only person she could think of to confide in. They couldn't tell anyone else about Lydia. She'd be arrested if they ever found her, and it wasn't her fault. But Cara obviously couldn't explain to anyone that there was an immortal being in Lydia's mind, using her body for its own purposes. Not unless she wanted another visit to the psychiatric unit for herself this time.

She sent Josh a text asking him to call as soon as he woke up. At fourteen hours ahead, it was barely morning in Indonesia and this didn't feel like a text message conversation.

When she looked up, Wes was watching her.

She jumped. "I thought you were sleeping."

"And you were just going to stand there like a creepy stalker, watching me sleep?"

Tension eased from her chest with a snort. "Good thing you're hurt so I can't punch you." She put away her phone and grabbed his hand—the uninjured one—between hers. "I'm so sorry."

"Why?"

"She was coming after me. I don't know why, but it felt personal. But you're the one lying in a hospital bed all because I couldn't see past her anger and walk away. I had to let it turn into my own psycho rage and go after her."

"Of course you did. You wanted to help her."

"I shouldn't have. What was I going to do if I caught her? I don't know what I'm supposed to do if I can't control how I react to them. I put you in danger." She ignored the look he gave her and let the silence go on until she could speak without a break in her voice. "Your parents should be here soon."

"Mak's gonna pitch about his car."

"Mak should be more concerned about his brother."

"Yeah, well, if you're still standing there, he'll concern himself plenty." He cast a meaningful glance at her hands clutching his.

She could have lost one of her best friends today. It didn't matter what assumptions people made. It wasn't up to them to set Mak straight.

"Your brother's not always the sharpest, is he? I don't care if you don't."

He frowned. "You don't care? What about Rhys?"

"Why would he notice . . . or care?"

Wes watched her with lowered brows.

"What? Does it matter to you? Is there someone—?"

His laugh turned into a wince. "Ow. No."

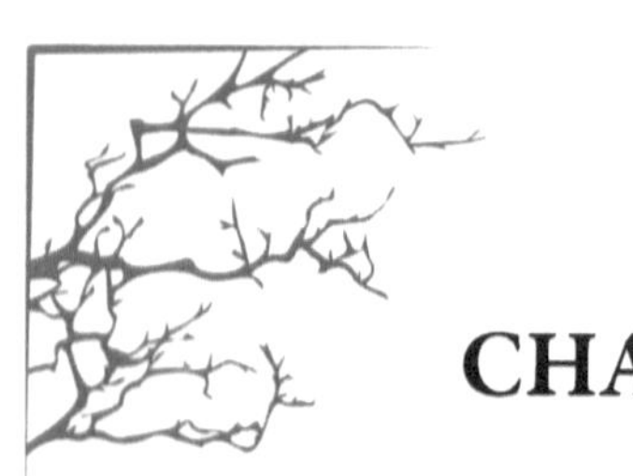

CHAPTER 7

THE PHONE RANG IN HER pocket soon after Wes's family arrived. Mak barely had time to make a face, let alone any comments. She gave Wes's mom a hug and then left the Vanneau family to speak to the doctor, who had reappeared. By the time she hung up and headed back inside, she wasn't sure she should have told Josh anything. He sounded like he might be on the next flight home from Indonesia. She had promised repeatedly to stay safe and stay around people at all times.

Finally, she couldn't put off telling Jory any longer. She typed the message, hit send, and braced herself.

Jory's replies and questions kept coming well after Mak had driven her home from the hospital, leaving his parents to bring Wes home when he was released. Between the annoyed, "You let my brother bleed on my seat?" and the comments about how her dog came to be in the back of the car, she was irritable all night and through to the next day when her mom drove them back to school.

Jory's desire for information had been understandable. Her feelings of guilt and lingering anger were harder to deal with. The whole drive, Wes kept looking over and telling her to stop when he could see her lost in thought again.

When they pulled into the parking lot, Mak stalked away with only a quick thanks to Cara's mom, still upset over not having his own car, and the bloodstains he hadn't been able to completely wash out. Cara's throat tightened when her mom climbed out of the driver's seat to hug her. Sandra had been beside herself when she found out what had happened to them at the park—at least, the version they'd told police. She finally released her daughter, saying, "Take care of yourself."

"It's school, Mom. I'll be fine here." Cara slung her backpack across her shoulder to set out after Jenner and Wes.

"Do you feel any of them near here?" Wes asked as they made their way across campus.

"I honestly don't know. I'm annoyed, but mostly at myself." She cast a guilty look at the brace and sling on his arm.

"You have to stop that. The doctors said I'll be fine with a couple months of physio after this heals. It's only muscle. Lots of blood flow to make it heal well."

"And to make it bleed like crazy."

He shrugged one shoulder. "At least the knife missed the ligaments. The only thing I'm mad about is missing the next couple months of archery, and it's her fault, not yours."

"I'm not sure I can separate the feelings. How am I supposed to know when I'm mad, or when one of them is around me?" The question had been bothering her for weeks, crystallized now by the heightened emotions of the encounter with Lydia.

Jenner slipped between them. "There are only faint impressions nearby, aside from Tomyx and Ryx, of course. None of the others are close enough to recognize."

"So what did Josh say?" Wes asked.

"He was going to talk to some people he knows. Other Pyxsees, I guess. He thinks it's a coincidence this Pyx is using my mom's friend, but I don't know. I told him it seemed like she was coming after me, and he went all quiet. He says there's no reason she would, but it felt . . . off."

"When's the next time he'll be here to visit?"

"Not sure. Easter, maybe, if we're lucky."

"Hm. And you don't have any ideas why a Pyx would hate Cara so much, Jenyx?"

"I do not."

"Then we'll have to figure it out." Wes split off toward the Lodge at the fork in the path.

"Tell Jory I'll be by in a bit so he can yell at me in person," she called to him.

Wes shook his head and walked away. She was being ridiculous, and he didn't need to say it. Jory would never yell at her. His messages had been purely concern for Wes and wanting to know what happened. It didn't stop how she felt.

"Allow me a moment to check the area nearby. I am relatively certain it is safe and your feelings at the moment are your own; however, it does not hurt to be cautious," Jenyx said.

That didn't make it better. Standing alone in the cold air outside the Cedars, she was left with only her thoughts while Jenner sniffed out any scents in the nearby woods. How could Wes expect her to stop feeling terrible? Her actions had put him in danger. Lydia was being used in a horrifying way. And all she could do about any of it was stand around fuming.

She'd have to find a way. She'd have to figure out how to turn off her own feelings enough to pick out the hostility that didn't belong to her. It probably wouldn't work, but she had to try something. If nothing else, she could try to use her emotional radar as an early warning system. She could try to keep her friends safe.

A hand on her shoulder made her jump. She whirled to find Jory's blue eyes looking at her like she was the one who'd been hurt. So much for an early warning system. She hadn't even heard him approach.

He pulled her in close. "Hey, Cares. Are you okay?"

To her horror, tears sprang to her eyes. She nodded against his shoulder.

"That is some freaky stuff." He released her. "I can't believe you saw one of them. You guys scared me. I'm glad you weren't hurt."

"You talked to Wes already?"

"Uh huh. Passed him on the way here. He said you fought like a Viking."

She snorted and sniffed back her tears. "I doubt he said that, but I did go a little berserk."

"My Mathesson ancestors would be proud." Jory's grin split his face, and he draped an arm over her shoulder.

Jenner emerged around the corner of the building, and Jenyx gave her the all clear. They walked in together. They had almost reached the door to her room when she remembered. She ducked from under Jory's arm and turned to smack her friend in the shoulder.

"I forgot. How did dinner go? Do you ask Liv out yet?"

His grin turned sheepish.

"You did. You finally did, didn't you?"

He nodded. She entered her room with a little dance, glad to find it empty. She dropped her backpack and turned to give Jory another hug, a happy one this time.

"I'm so glad," she squealed. "It took you long enough."

"Told you I was waiting for the right time. It was a perfect day." His face flushed. "Sorry, I mean it started out perfect. Once we found out about you and Wes, she was really worried too. We were all freaking out a bit after that. Including Rhys."

"Go back. I want to know about the perfect part." She stamped down the butterflies that had started a familiar dance.

"You mean the part where Rhys asked about you?" He had the nerve to actually wink at her.

"Shut up." The butterflies fought back. She shook her head. Of course Rhys had asked. They'd encountered another one of the Pyx using a human pyxis, like the one who'd attacked his sister. Plus, Wes had been in the hospital at the time, and he would at least have asked about that. "No, Sunshine, go back to the part where you finally asked out the girl of your dreams after almost four months."

He laughed. "No way. Too soon for our first fight. Liv would be pissed if I took away whatever girl talk you two will have later."

"I won't tell her, I swear." She pouted when he shook his head.

"All I can say is dinner with her dad was pretty terrifying, but it went okay. Rhys covered a few times when I wasn't sure what to say. I'm glad he's been so cool. It was intense, but afterward, everything finally felt right. I can't tell you details. That's Liv's territory."

"Fine. Anyway, I'm glad you asked her before I ruined it. Sorry for spoiling your perfect day."

"About that—next time one of my best friends gets stabbed, I expect the other one to tell me right away. Like immediately."

"Next time?"

"You know what I mean. You seem to have some dangerous friends." He shot a look toward Jenner. "Now come see Liv with me. She'll want to see you too."

LIV JUMPED UP WHEN they entered her and Kaylee's crowded room. Ignoring the rest of the people behind her, Liv checked Cara carefully, and totally unnecessarily.

"We were so worried." She pulled Cara into a hug. "I have so much to tell you," she whispered in Cara's ear before she took Jory's hand and they left together.

Cara's heart lifted at the laughter floating down the hall as they walked away. She turned back to the other four people waiting to ask how she was.

"You're okay, right?" Kaylee asked. "You're still good to race on Friday? Liv was telling us some crazy guy attacked you in town. What the heck is going on in Portland?"

"Maybe let her breathe first." Ethan rested a hand on Kaylee's leg, and her intense look softened.

Mike stood up and pulled the other chair out from Liv's desk, placing it beside the one he'd occupied. "Yeah. Here, sit down."

"Thanks, Mike. I'm okay, though." Cara took a seat next to Delaney on Liv's bed. When Mike's face fell, she quickly looked across to Kaylee. "And yes, I'm fine to race."

"Is Wes going to be all right?" Delaney asked.

"Yeah. Wes will be okay. I'm fine. Everyone's all right. A little freaked out, but otherwise fine."

What had Liv told them? The room held a strange vibe.

"What did the guy look like?" Mike asked. "Were you scared?"

She shifted on the bed. "Um, I don't know. He looked like a normal guy, I guess. There wasn't really time to be scared until after."

How was she going to weasel out of this conversation? This was not the group with whom she wanted to discuss specifics. She cast around for anything else.

"So did Liv share her news too? That's great about her and Jory dating now, right?"

"Really great," Mike said.

She wasn't sure she'd ever heard him talk this much. He was around enough since Kaylee had started dating Ethan in the fall, but she'd never given Mike much thought. He and Ethan were basically inseparable. Plus, the four of them were cross country teammates, so she saw him there too, but this chattiness was new. And weird.

Her gold eyes darted between the faces in the room. Kaylee had a strangely hopeful expression, and Ethan stared at the floor with a smirk. Mike met her eyes and then dropped his gaze to his hands. She started to get a sinking feeling.

Jenner whimpered, and the green gleam crossed his eyes.

"You are uncomfortable. Is something wrong?" Jenyx asked in her mind. "If we need to leave, Jenner could provide an excuse." Jenner gave a tiny growl.

"I should probably take Jenner outside . . ."

She did need to work on suppressing her feelings, and everyday awkwardness was probably a good place to start, but the urge to run away right now was strong.

Delaney broke from staring into space and turned to her. "Do you think it'll leave a scar?"

"Huh?"

"Wes. Do you think the cut will leave a scar?"

"Probably. It was really deep." Cara's eyebrows pinched at Delaney's frown.

"Oh, hey, Cara, we were just talking about the Valentine's dance, weren't we, guys?" Kaylee's bright cheer was over the top, even for her.

Yep. Something was up. It looked like she'd have to start practicing now. How did she stop her feelings from bubbling up? She tightened against the squirming sensation.

Breathe, Cara. "Oh yeah? Is everyone going?"

Delaney shrugged, looking lost in thought, but Kaylee and Ethan both nodded.

Mike stopped staring at his hands. "Um, are you? Because I was sort of wondering if you, er, maybe wanted to go . . ."

"Oh." Oh. A slow breath helped her mind push back the discomfort.

Think.

"That's so nice, Mike." It was a good start—polite, kind. Now what? "But I'm already going with someone."

Oops. Where the crap did that come from? Now what?

"Oh. Yeah. Sure. That's cool." He went back to studying his fingers.

The room deflated.

"Is Wes going?"

Cara turned to stare at Delaney after her quiet question. Oh. Before she knew it, she blurted, "Yeah. With me."

Double crap.

What was it about two birds with one stone? That's right—it killed them. But Mike was nice enough. And Delaney was the sweetest person she knew. Feelings or no feelings, she didn't want to kill anything.

"You know . . . because he didn't want to deal with having to dance or anything with his arm all messed up. I said we'd hang out on the fringes together." The lump in her stomach softened when the tension in the room eased. "We can all hang out."

She returned Delaney's smile and stood.

The first attempt at no-feelings Cara was a clear disaster. Now she needed to inform Wes of this whole dance debacle. Inevitably, her mind flashed to an image of Rhys, and a dance a long time ago. Her fingers itched to reach into her pocket and pull out her phone where the only evidence it had ever happened existed in the form of a photo. Ugh, she should really have deleted it by now. It was beyond time to move on. She blinked hard and glanced around. Oh, what the hell . . .

"Save me a dance, Mike?"

His head jerked up. "Sure."

SHE PRACTICALLY RAN along the path to the Lodge. Jory and Liv were still out, but Wes lay on his bed with his splinted arm propped up on a pillow. She crawled across his legs to his other side and lay down beside him with her head on his good arm.

He watched her with raised eyebrows until she settled. "Um, Cara?"

She closed her eyes against his sideways stare. "Don't be mad. I sorta did a thing."

Small sounds told her he was searching for words and coming up with nothing. She opened her eyes and turned her head to meet his gaze.

"So, uh, about the not caring what people think . . . You know, like we said at the hospital?" She took encouragement from his amused nod. "Any chance that would extend to, let's say, maybe, going to the Valentine's dance together?"

He chuckled. "What did you do?"

"Something super awkward. Sorry. If you prefer, I think Delaney would like to go with you, but I wasn't sure you'd want to, and I needed an excuse not to go with Mike. Ugh. Sorry if I messed up."

"Nah, you're fine. All that just happened?"

"Yup."

"Wow." He crossed one foot on top of the other. "Mike, hey?"

"Don't make me hurt you more."

"You know what this makes me think of . . ."

"Shut up, or I won't come watch movies with you anymore. And I have a whole lineup planned while you're healing, vampires and hot werewolves included," she threatened.

Wes made a face. "All the more reason."

"Seriously, I feel bad enough as it is. Poor guy is probably sick and tired of being the third wheel all the time with Kaylee and Ethan."

"Maybe." He made a valiant effort not to laugh.

"But you were right earlier. I really need to stop feeling bad about crap I can't control. There's way more important stuff going on than this. If I can push my own feelings out of the way, I can focus on noticing the Pyx when they come close again."

"How are you going to do that?"

"I don't know. I guess I'll just turn them off. Ignore them."

Jenner lifted his head and flicked his ears when Jenyx spoke. "You cannot dismiss your own feelings. They make you human. Your humanity is what you need, not a lack of emotion."

"Well, I can't do it all at once, clearly. Look at Wes's arm. Something's gotta give. If I stop caring about this unimportant junk, then maybe I can tell when a big wave hits me that it's coming from one of them."

Wes frowned. "I'm not sure that's how it works."

"If either of you have a better idea, let me know." When neither one offered an alternative, she hardened her resolve. It wasn't like she had other options. With a slow breath, she embraced the silence and closed her eyes. Even the knock at the door didn't disturb the peace she was working on.

"Come in," she and Wes both called at the same time, making her smile.

"Hey, Wes. How are—Oh, hi."

The silk-smooth voice melted into her Zen. She opened her eyes to find Rhys standing in the doorway, staring at his feet.

"Hey, man. Come in. What's up?" Wes pulled his arm out from under her head and sat up.

She propped herself up on her elbow and smoothed her hair, glancing at Wes. Weren't they just talking about not caring what people thought?

"I heard you were back. How are you?" Rhys asked.

His eyes scanned the splint on Wes's arm and shifted to Cara. He knew she and Wes were just friends. Not that it mattered. Nope, not caring.

"We're still here, thanks to Cara," Wes answered.

She scoffed. "I think you mean in spite of Cara."

Wes's head shook back and forth in front of her, and she pictured his eye-roll.

"I'm glad you weren't hurt." Rhys blinked and his gaze shifted back to Wes. "Er, hurt worse, I mean."

"Thanks," Wes replied with a hint of amusement in his voice.

Cara grunted and sat up, tired of staring at the back of his head and missing half of what Wes said by not seeing his face.

Rhys angled toward the door. "Oh, I also have a message for you. Dr. Flanagan wants to see you after class tomorrow."

"The headmaster wants to see him?" Cara blurted. "Why?" It came out a little brusque.

He raised a shoulder. "I saw her when Liv and I drove up. She knew about your injury. I'm guessing she wants to check up on you."

"Oh. Okay. Thanks." Wes stood to see him out. When the door closed, he turned back to Cara with an exasperated sigh. "Seriously?"

"What?"

"I get that you're doing this not-caring thing, however dumb I think it is. But none of this was his fault."

"I thought you didn't care what people thought."

"I don't. But you do." He gave her a stern look when she shook her head. "You care about him. Don't make him think you don't."

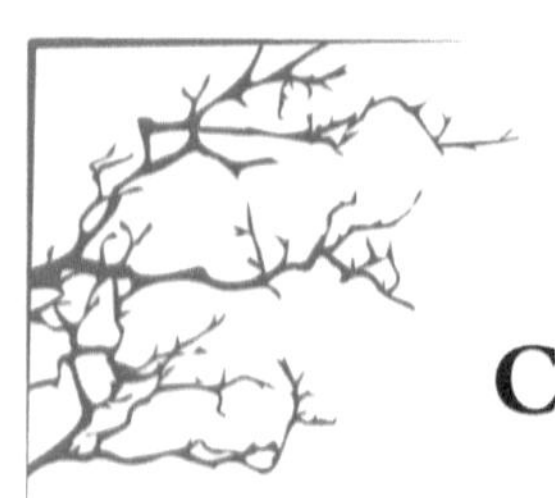

CHAPTER 8

WES CAUGHT UP TO THEM on the way into the dining hall the next evening. The tightness around his jaw said he wasn't exactly pleased.

"So? What did the headmaster want?" Jory asked.

"A tour guide."

"What do you mean?" Cara gave Wes a curious glance.

Liv skipped up beside her. "Is this about the new guy? He was in bio with me and Wes today," she told Cara and Jory.

Wes nodded. "Apparently he chose archery for his active elective. Since I'm hurt, Dr. Flanagan asked if I'd help him catch up to the team and get settled. So now I'm stuck showing around some entitled British prep school transfer."

"He didn't seem so bad," Liv said. "He did have the girls whispering all through class, though. Nothing like a British accent to stoke the gossip fires."

Jory immediately threw his arm around her shoulders, eliciting a giggle and a backhand to his chest.

With a grin, Cara held the glass door open to the dining hall. "I can't wait to meet him, then."

Wes shot her a glare that took her back to the days she'd thought of him as a dark cloud. Man, that felt like forever ago. She reminisced on the bad old days of loneliness and secrets, practicing her new emotional distance from the memories while they grabbed dinner and their usual table.

It would have been impossible not to notice the babble of voices and cluster of people around the table near the spiral staircase in the center of the hall. Their classmates came and went from the surrounding knot of people. No one expected a new kid in the middle of sophomore year, and curiosity drew a crowd.

"Anyone know why he transferred?" Cara asked.

"Something about his dad's job," Wes muttered.

A mischievous look spread across Liv's face. "I don't know. If he was at a boarding school in England, why couldn't he have stayed until the end of the school year? I bet he did something to get kicked out."

Kaylee and Ethan left the new guy's table and sauntered past theirs. Cara's hand darted out to grab Mike's wrist as he passed their table behind his friends. If he was so keen to talk to her all of a sudden, she might as well take advantage. Feelings off and everything.

"Did you meet the new guy? What's he like?"

Mike stepped a little too close to her. He managed to look both pleased and suspicious at the same time. She dropped his wrist and scooted her chair back so her neck didn't have to crane up so far.

"Harrison? Yeah. Not sure what the big deal is."

"Harrison?"

"Uh huh. Preppy name, don't you think?"

"I don't know." She gazed across the room at the guy still surrounded by people. "It's sort of cool."

Wes gave a small headshake and stabbed into his baked potato, clearly still bitter about his relegation to tour guide. Mike wandered away. She caught a glimpse of unfamiliar dark-brown hair in the middle of the attention. Not surprisingly, Cassidy's curls—back to her trademark blonde now—bounced beside the new student as she tossed her head back in a well-practiced flirty laugh. Tish leaned away from the other side of the table, and Cara finally had a view of Harrison.

He was slim and didn't look very tall, although it was hard to tell while he was sitting. Even from a distance, his eyes were a piercing emerald. He caught her watching him and flashed a smile across the space. Maybe she'd found the off switch for her feelings for real, because her insides didn't lurch with any embarrassment at being caught staring. The blush she expected never came. Wes coughed beside her.

She ducked her head toward him. "What?"

Liv and Jory bent their heads together in deep conversation as they cast glances over at the other table and ate slowly. Cara took a few more bites of her pasta before nudging Wes under the table.

"Should you go over and introduce yourself? You know, since you're supposed to show him around and stuff?"

"Nope."

To be fair, from the way Harrison was commanding the table, turning between conversations and flashing that toothy smile at everyone around him, he didn't look like he needed a tour guide. That guy would be fine on his own. A thought struck her out of the blue. They bore no resemblance to one another, but the grin, the self-assuredness, the easy way with people . . .

"He reminds me of Jory," she whispered to Wes.

"You have to be kidding."

"What's got you in a mood? Is your arm bugging you? Do you need another painkiller?"

Jory's voice cut in to their conversation before Wes could do more than scowl. "Hey, guys, Liv realized something."

She and Wes looked up.

"His roommate," Jory started.

Cara was trying to work out what that meant, when Wes gave a little moan and swore softly.

"Theo," he said. "Damn. Poor guy." He stopped scowling and glanced over at the crowded table.

"Oh. Theo's the only one without a roommate, right?" she asked.

Jory nodded and wrinkled his nose. "He's had a room to himself the whole first semester since Nate never came back. Entire place smells like gym socks. It's rank."

Wes's gaze stayed on the far table until Harrison was visible again. He sighed and stood up with his tray. Cara rose to go with him.

"Are we going to say hi?"

"No. I'll see him soon enough at practice tomorrow."

"Why the sigh, then?"

"Look at him. He probably shoots a compound bow."

Cara suppressed a smirk at how serious Wes looked when he talked about bows. "Is that bad?"

He gave a dismissive shrug. "I prefer my recurve bow, that's all."

"Judgy much?"

"Not really." He faced her as they put their trays away. "Compounds are fine. But look at his scrawny arms. I doubt he can handle much draw weight. I'll have to adjust one."

She hadn't noticed Harrison's arms, but she looked over again to check him out. "They look pretty normal to me. Besides, you said archery was more about back muscles."

Wes grunted and headed for the door, leaving Cara to follow.

"Fine. But at least be nice to him tomorrow."

"I thought you were doing the whole *no-feelings* thing. I thought you didn't care," he said.

"*I* don't have to feel any way about it. But he is new. And that's always hard."

"She says . . . not caring." The side of his mouth curved up as Liv and Jory caught up to them. They headed to Cara's room to collect Jenner for an evening of hanging out safely indoors, away from any strangers—new students or otherwise.

CARA DIDN'T HAVE TO wait to learn more from Wes after archery the next day. Harrison was in her math class right after lunch. He walked in smiling and chatting with Mr. Meyers and took an open seat a few rows in front of her. She'd been right about him. He oozed charisma.

She spent the class wondering how Wes was going to handle having to teach him, and how they'd get along. By the end of the long hour, her musings left her considering what would happen if they got along great and started to hang out. He was so similar to Jory, she could picture them becoming friends. And Jory and Liv would be spending all their time together now. Would she be the odd one out like Mike?

The tension mounted when she left the building to head to French. She stuck close behind a group from her class, glancing over her shoulder in the direction of the forest.

Are these your feelings or something else?

She worked to suppress them. Had Lydia or another one of the hostile Pyx returned to the area? Or was this her? If she could shake the sensation, then it was just her. She gritted her teeth. There was nothing to worry about. Her friends wouldn't ditch her. They would still do things as a group. Besides, she'd have Jenyx. She could spend more time with Delaney and Kaylee, even if that meant Ethan, which meant Mike. She swallowed. She would be okay.

As her inner pep talk took hold, the feelings started to recede. They must have been hers.

She packed the emotion away, filled her lungs with crisp air, and tried to clear her head. No sudden anger replaced the thoughts, so she figured she was safe. The babble of voices ahead washed over her, until a crisp accent in the middle reached out and sucked her in like a receding wave.

"I expect I'll be bored. We covered this all last year at my old school," Harrison stated.

The girls around him nodded at how far ahead and sophisticated he must be.

Cara's only thought was: *Wanker.*

Oops. Her insults had turned British at the sound of his voice. Her reading taste had veered away from fantasy lately, and she was clearly reading too many MI6 spy thrillers these days. She snickered.

Harrison glanced over his shoulder at the sound, and his emerald eyes twinkled when she shook her head at him. He fell back a few steps and held out a hand.

"Harrison Winter. A pleasure."

We'll see about that.

"Cara Ransome." She gripped his warm hand, trying not to smirk at the formal gesture.

He leaned in. "I enjoy it when people call me out on my bullshit," he whispered.

"Then you're walking with the wrong crowd," she whispered back.

She dropped his hand and strode into the building with an entertained smile. Wes was going to have an interesting archery practice this afternoon. His bullshit threshold was pretty low.

THAT NIGHT, SHE WAS still trying to weasel details out of Wes as they walked from the dining hall to the gym for the big rivalry basketball game.

"So is he any good at archery?"

"Not as good as he thinks he is," Wes replied.

"Meaning what?"

He shrugged.

"You know, a few more words wouldn't hurt. Is this as much as you talked to him? No wonder you don't have anything to share."

Jory stepped closer, his hand still intertwined with Liv's and swinging between them with each step. "It's not like you just met Wes. Nothing's changed, right, bud?"

"Nope, nothing."

"Fine. I'll have to talk to him myself, I guess," Cara huffed.

Wes shook his head in the semi-dark and then took pity on her. "To be fair to him, he could draw more weight than I expected."

"Well, that's . . . a thing . . . I guess?"

He chuckled at her complete ignorance when it came to archery. They filed into the gym and grabbed seats in the bleachers. Jory and Liv stopped to chat with friends several times and ended up sitting in the row below Cara and Wes as the seats filled up. Soon, the teams emerged for the start of the game, and butterflies jolted through her at the sight of Rhys in his uniform. By the time she stamped those back down, the sounds of squeaking shoes and cheering students echoed through the gym.

A bustle of activity in their row made her look over. Harrison shuffled past people until he reached them. He stopped with a cheeky grin.

"You two are friends? Brill." He rubbed his hands together and inserted himself in between them, forcing Wes to slide over. "I should've guessed."

"Why's that?" Cara asked.

"Similarities, I suppose."

She glanced across him to Wes in time to catch his eye-roll. He stared ahead, watching the game. Harrison glanced at him, too, and followed his gaze to the court.

"So is basketball a big deal here, then?"

Cara scanned the bleachers full of school colors. "Depends. Valley Green is sort of a rival school."

"Ah. I see."

They watched the action in silence for a few minutes.

"That one sure is tall. Good job he's on our team," Harrison said.

Wes scoffed.

Cara muttered an answer for him. "That's Wes's brother, Mak." Her attention had been focused on a different tall figure. It didn't help that Rhys was playing on the far side, facing them, and kept glancing up. Even from a distance, she swore she could make out the ring of gold flashing in his eyes.

"So you've an older brother . . . who also attends this school. I daresay that's a topic we could've discussed." Harrison turned toward Wes, who gave a noncommittal grunt in response.

On the court, Mak passed to Rhys, whose eyes had flicked up to the bleachers again. He managed to catch the ball and snapped his attention back to the game, spinning gracefully away from the Valley Green player. He'd been looking right at her. At least, that was what it felt like, until she remembered his sister was sitting directly in front of her, and then she caught sight of the back of Emma's head another row down and a few seats further over.

"Does this one always prattle on so much?" Harrison rolled his head dramatically back to Cara with a sigh.

"Oh yeah. Wes is a real chatterbox. Watch your secrets around him."

That finally got Wes's attention, and he gave her a scathing look. "That other tall guy . . ."

He leaned over and pointed out Rhys. Cara's mouth narrowed to a thin line as she shot a hard look back at him. He wouldn't dare.

He held her eyes but finally finished with, "That's Liv's brother."

Liv turned around at the sound of her name and nudged Jory. His brow furrowed at Harrison sitting between them.

"Um, have you guys met yet?" Cara asked.

"We haven't had the pleasure." Harrison leaned forward with a hand out.

Liv took it first and introduced herself and Jory.

The grin on Jory's face didn't match his eyes, which darted back and forth between his two best friends before stopping on Harrison. "Do people call you Harry?" he asked.

"Never more than once." Harrison smiled broadly as he answered, but a note in his voice made it clear he was serious.

Liv and Harrison exchanged small talk for a bit, while Jory and Wes held a silent conversation over their bent heads. Cara didn't follow most of what the two old friends could read off each other, but she didn't need to. It would be in line with what she was thinking. Harrison seemed to have decided to insert himself into their group, whether they liked it or not. And with secrets like theirs, that could only be one thing. Complicated.

Her pulse sped up, and for some reason, she wanted to snap at him. He had no right to take over her friends. She pushed back the sleeves of her sweater and rubbed her sweating palms on her knees. She tried to focus on the game, but seeing Rhys look up again, probably to catch Emma's eye, made her seethe even more.

Noticing her feelings taking over, she took a deep breath and tried to push the anger down. Mingling odors of sweat and perfume in the gym air only intensified the burning sensation. She couldn't stop it.

It wasn't her.

When the sharp whistle finally blew and cheers erupted for their team's win, she reached behind Harrison to grab Wes's good arm as they stood. He took one look at her pale face and began to scan the crowd. She'd been searching for the past twenty minutes, but nothing was out of the ordinary inside.

Worry had added to the baseless anger, and she couldn't separate the two.

They drew Jory and Liv close as the surge of students headed for the door.

"Should we wait for Rhys?" Cara spoke quietly, letting kids stream around their tight knot of four. Harrison was swept along in the crowd and away from them.

Liv gave her a funny look. "Why would we wait for my brother?"

"There's someone—something—here," Wes answered for her.

"Oh." Liv's head swiveled. She swallowed. "I'll text him to warn him, but he'll walk back with the team. He'll be in a crowd."

"We should be too. Let's go." Jory took Liv's hand and dragged her forward, with Wes and Cara following close behind.

They caught the huge mass of people going through the outer door. A surge of laughter drifted to them, and Cara caught Jory's name being called. They angled toward the commotion.

"Jory, your cat escaped again."

"How does that cat always know where he is?"

"Jory, your cat needs a leash or something."

Jory hurried forward to collect Thomas, only to stop when he saw the cat in Harrison's arms.

"He's yours?"

"Yeah, thanks." Jory reached out to take Thomas from him.

"I love cats."

"Who is this entitled human?" Tomyx asked.

Cara and Wes shared a glance at the sound of his voice in their minds. She wanted to ask Tomyx what he was doing here, but with all the people around, that wasn't possible.

"He's a little too friendly for his own good sometimes," Jory said.

Harrison handed Thomas over.

A green gleam crossed the cat's eyes. Tomyx got to the point of why he was there, speaking to Cara and Wes. "One of them is close. We're sensing a few strangers in the area, but one who is very near. Are you getting anything, Cara?"

She gave a tiny nod.

"I came to warn you, which I could have done without the manhandling," he grumbled.

Wes smirked at the tone Tomyx often put on. Harrison straightened with a grin and wished them all a good night before wandering away with the crowd. The four of them followed, sticking close to people.

As they approached the safety of the dorms, Liv broke the tense silence. "So what do we think about Harrison?"

Jory grunted. "He might be okay. But does he always have to have that cheesy grin on his face?"

Cara would have joined Liv and Wes, who both burst out laughing at the irony of Sunshine's complaint, but her ribcage still felt too tight. Stuffing her own emotions down meant the tension was all she felt. That had been the plan. It didn't feel great now that it was working.

She stared at Thomas sitting on Jory's shoulder. Icy worry wormed through the lingering burn as his eyes flashed green. The boys walked to the door of the Cedars with them.

"Wes, text us when your brother gets back to the Lodge so we know the team's back safely, or if you hear from Rhys directly." She couldn't help needing to know he was safe.

Liv gave her a funny look but stepped closer to Jory. She stood on her tiptoes to plant a kiss on Jory's lips. Cara and Wes looked away while their friends said a tender goodnight before they each headed to their separate dorms.

"You're pretty worried about my brother all of a sudden," Liv said, holding open the door to the Cedars.

"I'm worried about everyone. And he was with us when we went to the council, so Lydia, or whoever came after us that night, probably saw him too. I figured you'd want to know he was safe," she said.

"Thoughtful of you. Thanks."

Liv gave her a last glance before they each headed down their hallways from the lounge. Cara tried to relax. She couldn't let Liv know about her feelings. It would be too much for her to keep secret. Besides, friends' brothers were supposed to be off-limits, even if, technically, he was the one she'd met first. Somehow she didn't think Liv would see it that way.

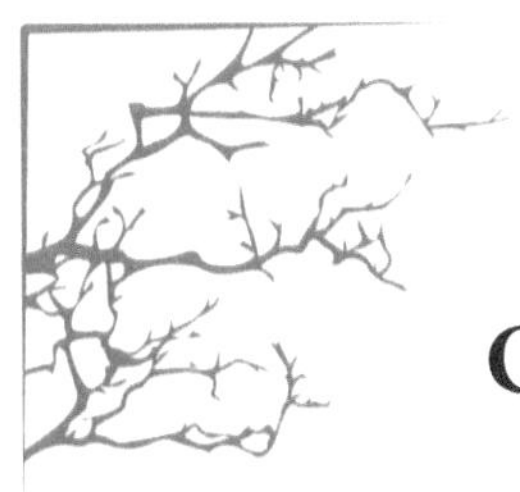

CHAPTER 9

GOLD FABRIC CROSSED her shoulders, meeting a sweeping black skirt at her waist. Gazing at the image on her phone, she studied the arm covering the seam between fabrics and traced the line of the black tuxedo up to Rhys's dark-blond hair and then across to his eyes. In the picture, he stared into the face she barely recognized as her own. After all the times she'd looked at this photo, she'd stopped seeing the angry glares of that night at the gala last summer, and let herself imagine the passionate gaze the camera had captured had been real.

A knock at the door cut off her sigh. She locked the screen and threw the phone onto her bed, where it fell on her coat.

"Yeah?"

Wes opened the door and looked her over. She did a quick twirl, as much to hide her guilty blush as to show off her borrowed dress. "Well?"

"What's up, Buttercup?" Wes joked.

"Shut up. It's Cassidy's. Liv picked it out and made me wear it. Something about the yellow setting off my eyes. I'm sure it looks better on Cassidy."

"No. You look nice."

"Gee, thanks. You're not so bad yourself, for someone I forced into taking me to a dance." She gave him a warm smile, taking in the crisp black pants and black shirt that brought out the russet tones of his skin. He was working a serious tall, dark, and handsome angle tonight.

In the two weeks since the basketball game, the harsh feelings from the hostile Pyx nearby had settled to a steady burn, never gone but never too intense either. She even managed a laugh when he shook his head at her compliment.

"So, if I'm Buttercup, guess that makes you my man in black. Which means"—she picked up her coat and then held out her arm—"my dear, sweet Westley . . . Would you accompany me to this ridiculous dance?"

He somehow managed not to roll his eyes at her. Tucking her arm through his good one, he turned so she could close the door behind them. The brace on his injured arm kept his other elbow at a steady angle until the biceps had time to fully heal, but he didn't need the sling all the time anymore. He had put it on for tonight, though. Too much movement still hurt him.

"What? No 'as you wish' in response? Come on." She grinned. Yep, there was the eye-roll this time. "Seriously, though. Thank you. I'm glad to have someone to go with." It would take some of the sting out of watching Rhys dance with Emma. At least she wouldn't be alone sitting out.

Not that she'd been alone at all lately. She hadn't been allowed to go anywhere unaccompanied for the past few weeks. No morning runs alone. No walking down to the stables on her own to collect Jenner. She had chaperones everywhere.

Jory or Wes came on runs with her when she wanted, but they always stuck to the path around campus and never entered the forest. Coach Francis had been keeping the team to the track, so she hadn't needed an excuse to skip any practices yet. Harrison had shown up once and joined her when she walked down to the stables with Liv and Jory, and they'd stayed to watch Liv ride Charlie.

Wes had stopped complaining about having to help Harrison, but he didn't have much else to say about the newcomer. He was being quiet lately, even for him. Between the constant low level of anger Cara now had to live with, and everyone being on high alert, they were a somber group to hang around. For some reason, Harrison still sought them out. He wasn't pushy, but he was persistent.

Mostly, she stayed indoors and tried not to let her bad mood spill out to the people around her. She struggled to keep it separate from herself and hoped she would notice if it grew stronger, signaling one of the outlaws was close. Jenyx checked the woods daily, so Jenner got plenty of exercise without her. He'd found new scents in the area a few times, but hadn't encountered anyone. The strangers were keeping their distance.

Cara and Wes met up with Liv and Jory in the lounge.

"Wow, Liv. You look amazing," Cara gushed.

"This old thing?" Liv ran a hand over her sleek bright-red dress before giving her a dazzling smile with matching red lips.

Jory beamed with a fierce pride at his date. He draped her coat over her shoulders and wrapped his arm around her waist as they left the Cedars. Cara pulled her own coat together and crossed her arms to keep warm.

A sky the color of a ripe peach set their faces aglow as they hurried along the gravel path. Watching Jory and Liv walking together—all dressed up and smiling at each other in the sunset—was enough to make Cara want to believe in soulmates. She sighed into the collar of her coat, allowing a bit of warmth for her friends to rise past the nagging burn in her chest.

By the time they reached the gym, she wished she could stay outside to enjoy the colorful sky and a few more minutes of tranquility. But the biting cold on her bare legs and the ongoing danger nearby drove her indoors again.

"Oh no. It's worse than I thought," she whispered to Wes, grimacing at the sea of silver and pink decorations.

Wes wrinkled his nose in commiseration, and they quickly found one of the bar-height tables along the walls to claim as their own. She and Wes held it down while Jory and Liv went off for their first dance.

"Aw, look at Sunshine. I never would have thought he could look happier than he always did before."

Wes had a distant look. "I did."

Harrison sauntered up, looking perfectly preppy in his plaid bowtie and purple shirt. Cara could have sworn Wes actually growled under his breath, but she raised a hand in greeting. It wasn't like they could keep him away. Delaney wandered in behind him and settled herself beside Cara.

"Excellent," Harrison said. "Is this our home base for the evening? How does this work? Do people simply stand around, waiting to be asked to dance?"

"I guess," Cara answered. "I mean, a lot of people came with dates, so they'll dance together. Wes can't dance thanks to his arm, obviously, so we'll just hang out."

"He may not be about to spin a gal around, but surely he can still dance?"

"*He* is right here. And what Cara meant to say is I don't dance." Wes leaned on the table.

She snickered and turned to Delaney. "Did you walk over with Kaylee?"

"Uh huh. And Ethan and Mike. He's looking for you, by the way."

Cara's stomach sank. Why had she promised him a dance? A shadow of guilt passed through her, but she quickly let it go, leaving only the steady annoyed feeling she'd almost grown used to.

When Mike came into view at the next slow song, she had a moment's thought of throwing herself at Harrison and begging him to dance with her. Instead, she sucked it up and put on a pleasant expression. Might as well get it over with. How bad could it be? Maybe Mike would surprise her.

Three and a half minutes of awkward swaying later, Cara slipped away from Mike's sweaty palms and rushed back to the sanctuary of Wes's side. What had she possibly been thinking?

Liv and Jory had rejoined the table, and Delaney had wandered away again.

Liv sidled up to her. "So . . . that looked miserable."

Cara winced. "It was, but he's so nice. I wish I liked him more."

"Don't feel bad. We'll find someone better for you," Liv proclaimed. She began to search the crowd, like she could find someone for Cara in the gym somewhere.

There was only one person she wanted to dance with . . .

"Hey, big bro." Liv raised a hand. Cara held her breath, inner freak out in full force, but Liv turned to them and continued. "Excuse me, guys. I need to go show these pathetic swaying bumpkins how it's done."

She poked Jory in the shoulder with a wink, gave her auburn hair a flip, and then flitted across the space to her brother. Rhys listened to Liv before leaning back with a reluctant tilt to his head and a sigh, but Cara could tell he'd give in. After an indulgent look at his sister, he took her arm and they moved to the dance floor.

Twirling, gliding, and spinning around the gym, Liv and Rhys put on a show that stopped all but the bravest pairs from joining them. Most people just stood around gaping at them. All Cara could think of was the way he'd looked when he'd first told her the story of what happened to Liv, while she was still in the hospital—how he'd been willing to do anything to save her, even if it meant condemning himself. She'd never forgotten that guy she'd first met, so broken and yet so fierce in his love for his family. Even if the magical moment when he'd caught her during the Skai run had never happened, Cara still would have fallen for him that day at his house.

When the song ended, the two of them gave a little bow to a round of applause like it had been a professional competition, and Cara found herself clapping along. A memory of a photo she'd seen in Liv's bedroom last summer floated to the surface. Oh. They *had* competed. That was why he was such a good dancer. And Liv had been his partner, not a series of other girls like she had assumed at the gala.

She turned to Jory with a lightness she hadn't felt in a long time. "You might need to take some classes, Sunshine."

He picked up his slack jaw and tore his gaze from Liv. "Um, yeah. I'm in trouble."

Peeking back over at Rhys, she knew the feeling. It was one she had to swallow when he headed toward Emma and her friends. Cara turned to the table with her back to the dance floor. Fortunately, the rhythm changed and a fast song came on. She could be spared a little longer from watching him dance with

Emma. Liv returned, bouncing to the beat. Harrison joined in and held out a hand to each of the two girls.

"Ladies?" He dragged Cara and Liv out to dance, leaving Jory and Wes watching after them from the table.

By the time the slow songs came back, they were out of breath and sweating from trying to keep up with Harrison. They walked back over to the table, laughing. Harrison could be pretty fun sometimes. Cara's eyes twinkled at Wes's darkened face as she tried not to laugh at her friend's exasperation with the new guy. Harrison eventually sighed at all the standing around and asked the closest girl, a junior, to dance. The girl looked surprised, but shrugged and went with him.

Liv stood on Cara's other side, facing the gym and leaning against the table. She grabbed Cara's hand. "Uh oh," she hissed, "Mike is headed this way again."

Cara's eyes widened. She searched for an escape.

"Quick. Find someone to dance with. Jory—nope. Where'd he go?" Liv said, turning to find Jory had stepped away. "Oh, here—"

Her other hand darted past Cara, latching onto someone approaching behind her. The knot in Cara's stomach flipped over when she saw who it was.

"Rhys, do me a favor. Cara needs a savior." Liv pressed their hands together and shooed them away before Mike could arrive.

The warmth from dancing with Liv and Harrison had started to fade, but heat rushed back up her neck. This wasn't at all like she'd imagined.

"Sorry this keeps happening to you," she said over the music.

Rhys looked down at her. "What do you mean?"

"People keep forcing you to dance with me."

"Oh." He stopped in the crowd of people and turned to face her. "I guess that's true. But I didn't think of it like that. Not this time, anyway."

He held out a hand, and a gold flash of amusement in his eyes met her gaze. She stepped into his waiting arm with a fierce rush of nerves and her pulse thudding in her neck. The music faded behind the rushing in her ears.

Once again, as they had at the gala, her steps fell easily into a rhythm with his. Her body responded all on its own to the light pressure of his hand on her back, and they moved effortlessly together. With Rhys confidently guiding her, the rest of the gym faded into the background and the music broke through once again. What had she ever been anxious about? What was that lingering angry feeling she'd been having? She had no idea anymore. None of it mattered while she was floating in his arms.

"Nice dress," he offered.

She glanced down and then craned her neck up to see his face again. "Thanks. Your sister has good taste. Much better than mine, as she likes to remind me."

He laughed. "That sounds like her." A quick step led to a faster twirl, and her head spun. His eyes swept her neckline, and she hoped her hammering pulse wasn't too obvious. "I'm glad you and Wes are, you know . . ."

"Yeah. We're both fine. I mean, he's still recovering, obviously, but it could have been worse."

"Right. Yeah. No more morning runs, though, hey?"

She looked up, surprised he would have thought of it. "No sunrises, no."

"Sorry. You must miss it."

"I do."

He drew her a little closer to sidestep between two other couples and turn in a sweeping arc. She took a sharp breath. A wave of cedar wood washed over her, and her eyes fluttered closed for a moment in the wake of his heady scent. Whether it was his soap or cologne, wow, it was worth every penny. Even though he hadn't been the one to ask her, she started to let herself enjoy the moment. Until she spotted the girl.

A senior girl stood at the far side of the dance floor, staring with wide eyes. Rhys spun Cara to face her, and the girl's mouth fell open. Cara looked away quickly, hoping it meant nothing, but an echo of Cassidy's voice on the first day back at school last fall came to her.

"I heard some of the girls from upstairs talking about him. I guess one of them swears she saw a picture of him at a big fancy party this summer looking all steamy with some brunette. No one can find it now, so who knows if it's true," Cassidy had gossiped.

One of the seniors claimed to have seen the gala photo before it had mysteriously disappeared from the internet, but hadn't recognized the girl—her. When no one could find the picture, people stopped believing it existed. The internet was supposed to be forever. Now the girl was streaking toward Emma at the bleachers with recognition all over her face. Cara's head swiveled to follow her progress.

"You okay?" Rhys asked.

She swallowed and nodded. The next time she peeked over, Emma was staring at her while the girl talked feverishly in her ear.

The song ended, and Cara took a quick step back. "Thanks again for saving me."

She rushed away, barely hearing his, "Anytime." Why had she pinned her hair up the way she'd worn it to the gala? Why had she let herself obsess over some dumb picture or agreed to dance with Rhys? And, oh crap, what was Emma saying to him right now?

He must have gone straight to her. Or Emma had called him over. Cara's head whipped away when Emma caught her eye. She practically ran for the safety of the table and her friends, but she arrived to find it abandoned. She searched the gym for Wes or Liv or Jory, or even Harrison. All she saw was Emma.

The graceful girl had her long fingers wrapped around Rhys's arm, and leaned in to talk beside his ear. Emma was so perfect, she even had a sweet smile when she was angry. How was that fair? And why did Cara feel bad? It wasn't like she'd done anything wrong. Rhys had only danced with her at the gala because he'd been forced to, and the same thing had happened tonight—minus the ending where he'd yelled at her to stay away from him and his sister, and then clearly used his family's resources to have the picture removed from the charity's website and socials. He was obviously embarrassed by it, and she hadn't asked for any of this.

Rhys's tiny flinch of surprise was so subtle, she would have missed it if she weren't a super-observant Pyxsee. He shook his head, trying to pretend he had no idea what Emma was talking about. They both glanced at her. The gnawing irritation that had faded away came clawing back with a sickening burn. She had to get out of there.

She grabbed her coat and swept the room again for one of her friends. Wes would go back with her, if only she could find him. Emma's girlfriends had surrounded her when Rhys walked away, and they kept shooting looks across the gym even when Emma steered them away with a glance back over her shoulder as she went. Their eyes met, and Cara's teeth clenched. She clutched her coat to her middle and decided to risk it. She could run back to the dorms in no time, and Jenner was waiting there for her. She'd only be alone for a few minutes.

CHAPTER 10

CHARGING THROUGH THE door, Cara tried to clear her mind in the blast of cold air. A delicate frosting of white coated the ground. The burning anger inside her refused to be suppressed by the frozen night. She zipped her coat and tried to jog.

Why did that idiot girl have to be there? Without her, she could have had a nice couple minutes in fantasyland, and Emma wouldn't have known or cared that her boyfriend had shared one dance with his little sister's friend. What did it matter? But no. That gossiping cow—Her foot slipped in the frost-tipped grass, and her arms flailed for balance.

Why had she let Liv talk her into these useless ballet flats? At least she'd said no to the heels, but every rock on the gravel path now ground into her feet through the flimsy soles. She slowed to a walk. There was no winning between the painful gravel and the slippery grass.

By now, the girl back at the gym had probably told ten more people, who would have told a bunch more people. Cassidy was probably looking to pounce on her for details at this very moment. If only she had skipped the dumb dance altogether. Her friends would have been able to enjoy it more without having to look out for her all the time. Harrison could convince Wes to talk to him, and they could bond over archery and whatever other stuff guys talked about. Jory and Liv could ride off into the sunset together. Rhys could be enjoying a romantic Valentine's Day with Emma.

Instead, her and her weird eyes and bizarre empathy were standing in everyone's way. She glanced between the buildings to the forest. Maybe she should leave school. If these hate-filled Pyx were after her, then her friends would be safer without her. They'd be better off.

She huffed into the collar of her coat. What was she thinking? If she didn't shake these thoughts off, she'd never feel if there were outlaws nearby. She needed to be able to pick up on their hostility if they were close.

Then it hit her.

These feelings were hatred . . . directed at her . . . turning her own thoughts against her.

Oh no.

Motion registered in her peripheral vision. *Too late.*

A body slammed into her side.

The breath rushed from her chest when she hit the ground. Lydia's face came into view against the dark sky. Cara struggled to free herself, but Lydia pinned her down. Her lungs screamed as she fought to refill them.

"No bodyguards?" Lydia's mouth stretched into a leering grin while her eyes glared with a harsh green glow. "That was accommodating of you."

She shifted off Cara's legs. Cara started to kick and buck, driven by fiery hatred as much as panic. A buzz flowed through her body, urging her to fight harder. But Lydia was too fast. Her body was too strong with the Pyx in control of her nerves and muscles.

The woman slid behind Cara's shoulders and dragged her upright. With terrifying ease, she hauled Cara between two buildings, heading for the forest.

"Let's go, Pyxsee," she spat.

"You don't have to use her voice," Cara hissed between shallow breaths. "You know I can hear you with your own voice."

"You don't deserve that."

Cara thrust with her heels as hard as she could and succeeded in driving Lydia back against the brick wall of the science building. She flinched at the thud. Acid rose in her throat at having to hurt the poor woman who had surrendered control of her body to this usurper. But it made no difference to the vice grip pinning her arms to her sides. Pain radiated from her ribs.

Jagged planks of wood surrounded Lydia's forearm, wrapped into a crude splint with duct tape. Their brutal edges squeezed against her. The horrifying sight of Lydia's untreated broken arm brought a new surge of strength.

A roar burst through her lips. "Get out of her, you sick, twisted monster! What did Lydia ever do to you? What did I do to you?"

She jerked and twisted, throwing herself against the arms holding her tight. That broken arm had to hurt, but it appeared the Pyx had total control over the woman's body, including her pain response, and the grip didn't loosen. Breathing became harder, and she was forced to still. Panic surged.

Lydia started to drag her again. Soon, they'd be on the other side of the building, and no one who might be passing by would be able to see them. Her eyes darted down to the wood-covered arm.

Sorry, Lydia.

She let herself fall.

Her knees buckled, and all her weight sagged onto Lydia's broken arm. With a screech, Lydia dropped her. Apparently, some pain could make it through the Pyx's influence over her. Cara swallowed her guilt and scrambled backward across the ground. Lydia drew herself upright. Fresh anger surged through Cara's mind as Lydia advanced once more. The Pyx was done playing games.

"Cara!"

The sweet sound of his voice blanketed her panic with a glimmer of hope.

Rhys's shout distracted the Pyx long enough for Cara to pull her feet under her. She ducked to the side when Lydia's arm swung through the air. The wooden planks whistled above her head.

A hand grasped her arm, and Rhys pulled her out of range of Lydia's next swing. Together, they stepped back toward the forest, facing Lydia as she turned and charged at them. Rhys threw his arm across Cara. He only made it a half-step forward before she shoved him out of the way. Hard.

He stumbled from her side, and she braced herself. She couldn't allow him to protect her the way he had at the clearing, or risk anyone getting hurt in her place again. Not like Wes had, or worse. Not Rhys.

Tucking her head, she drove her shoulder into Lydia's ribs as they collided. Even with the breath knocked out of her, Lydia stayed upright and grabbed her again. Cara's feet came off the ground as Lydia's good arm squeezed around her ribcage with superhuman strength.

She couldn't breathe.

Oblivious to Cara's heels kicking against her shins, Lydia carried her forward.

Cara's lungs burned for air.

"Stop," Lydia's voice called out. "Unless you want to see her die, I suggest you step aside."

Cara stopped struggling. A dark haze closed in on the sides of her vision. Rhys stood right in front of them.

He froze in place with his chest heaving. His eyes locked on hers, and gold lightning ignited the grey storm. Their intensity shocked her. Those burning eyes were all she could see. Just as she'd thought the first time she'd seen them, losing herself in them was like a warm blanket wrapping around her in a thunderstorm. Raw emotion surged against the hatred she'd been sensing, and its comfort almost made the vise grip around her ribs feel like it loosened for a moment.

If that was the last thing she saw before she died, that wouldn't be so bad.

But his eyes flicked to the side. He lunged forward and crashed into her. Now she was sandwiched between them with no chance of taking another breath ever again. Not a great plan as far as saviors went. What was he doing? Killing her faster? Lungs screaming, the tunnel in her vision closed in. If only she could see his eyes again before she went.

Lydia crumpled behind her.

Now only Rhys held her up, and she sagged in his arms while a breath tore into her throat. Sweet, precious oxygen filled her in huge gasps until her vision cleared.

She turned to see what had happened. Wes stood behind Lydia's collapsed form with a rock raised in his left hand.

"I hope I didn't hit her too hard," he said.

"Cara." Rhys steadied her. "Are you . . .?"

Greedy, gulping breaths prevented her from speaking, but she raised a hand to indicate she was all right. Sore ribs were a small price to pay compared to what could have happened.

Wes dropped the rock. "Is she—Is the Pyx still here?"

Lydia's collapse had not only released the death grip around her ribs, it had also loosened the tightness inside. With her lungs refilled, Cara stood and took the first full breath she could remember in months.

"She's . . . gone? At least, that's what it feels like. But she can't be gone."

"No. Her eyes stayed green right up until they rolled back in her head," Rhys said.

"That's weird. Jenyx doesn't go away when Jenner falls asleep."

"No, Tomyx either," Wes confirmed. "We have whole conversations after Jory and the cat fall asleep."

"She has to still be there. Maybe Pyx can be knocked out too," Rhys said.

Cara unzipped her coat and shrugged out of it. "Then this is our chance. We have to give Lydia her life back. And I need to find out what this Pyx wants with me." She draped her coat over Lydia's face and lifted her head gently off the ground to wrap it all the way around.

When she stood, she found both guys staring at her.

"It's goose down. Organic but not living. Remember?" Cara reminded them of the conditions for keeping a Pyx in its current pyxis. This solution wasn't as good as the proper organic-laced clay pyxis they'd used when they'd saved Liv, but they also didn't have anything big enough for a human, so this was the best she could think of. "If she's really still in there, she'll wake up when Lydia does. We have to get her somewhere we can control before then. It'll be stuffy, but Lydia won't suffocate, and the extra layer should make it harder for the Pyx to escape."

"Good thinking. The other part of the equation . . . the remnants. Is there anything we can use?" Rhys asked.

The conversation last fall with Jenyx and Tomyx outside the hospital came back to her. Since only one Pyx could inhabit a pyxis at a time, the presence of one Pyx prevented use of the same pyxis by another. The protection infused all parts of the host, extending even to pieces that were no longer connected. Those pieces of an active pyxis—known as remnants—could act as a ward of sorts, preventing a Pyx from passing through a barrier laced with them. The protection only stopped if the Pyx moved on and left that pyxis available as a host once more.

"Jenner's hair is bound to be on my coat. It gets everywhere. So there should be a bit of extra protection from that."

"I'm sure there's some Thomas hair on here." Wes peeled off his wool coat and added a layer around Cara's. He sat Lydia up and tied the sleeves behind her back to pin her arms.

"Gentle," Cara warned when Wes set Lydia down again.

Rhys gave her an incredulous look. "How can you be so forgiving? She just tried to kill you."

"No, she didn't. The Pyx did. It's not Lydia's fault. And now that she's unconscious and the bitterness disappeared, I feel . . . sort of fantastic, actually." She looked up into his eyes and nearly lost herself for a moment. She overcame the sudden urge to throw herself back into his arms and kiss him until she couldn't breathe again. Where was her head? She must still be delusional from the lack of oxygen. "Thank you. You saved me."

"Actually, Wes did the saving. I'm sorry I had to crush you to hold her in place."

"Don't be. I would have been gone already if it weren't for you. How did you find me?"

Rhys looked away. "I was outside. Getting some air after . . . doesn't matter. I heard you shout."

"And you?" She turned to Wes.

"Your coat was gone. I figured I should check in case you did something epically stupid like leave on your own."

She blinked. With the new lightness and the flood of relief at being alive, she couldn't bring herself to feel bad. Besides, all three of them had gone out on their own, so they were all guilty of the same thing.

"What now?" she asked.

"My van," Rhys suggested. "We keep the coats on her and hope it's enough to get her over to the manor."

He removed his jacket too. Instead of adding to the layers around Lydia, he draped it over Cara's shoulders.

She hadn't realized she was shivering in her flimsy dress until his warmth enveloped her. "Oh. Thanks." The mix of cedar wood and oranges made her practically giddy as she inhaled his scent. Her ribs ached with the movement as she drew in a deep breath, but her insides fizzed with pleasure.

Pull it together, Cara.

"So, how are we going to carry her? I'm not sure how much I can hold right now, and Wes can only use one arm."

"I could run to get Jory," Wes offered.

Rhys shook his head. "No. I don't want Liv to come. I don't even want my sister to know about this right now. I can take her shoulders. Wes, can you take her legs?"

"If someone helps me get ahold of them with my good arm."

"We have to make sure the jackets don't move from her head, too. Just in case," Cara added.

"You do that, and Wes and I will carry her."

How was she supposed to take Lydia's head if Rhys was taking her shoulders? This wasn't going to work.

"We need another set of hands unless I'm supposed to fit between you and Lydia while you're carrying her." Picturing herself walking between his arms, pressed up against him, was not helping her think straight. At least it was too dark for him to see her blush.

Approaching footsteps made them all whirl around and close together to shield Lydia from view.

"If it's spare hands you need, I've a set." Harrison sauntered toward them. He stopped and peeked around Wes. "Bloody hell, what've you got there?"

"Nothing," Cara answered. "We're fine. Thanks, though."

Harrison ignored her and pressed forward between her and Wes.

She raised her palms at Wes when he stepped aside to let Harrison by. "What are you doing?" she hissed at her friend.

Wes shrugged. "He already saw."

Harrison stared for a moment at the covered body on the ground. "Student? Teacher?" He checked each of their faces. "No answers? I don't generally help move bodies without some sort of explanation."

Cara's jaw dropped. "That's not—She's not dead."

A twinkle in his eye gave away his amusement. So he'd seen Lydia's chest rising and falling. He was messing with her.

"Maybe not, but your evening's certainly gone pear-shaped, hasn't it? Who is she?"

"My aunt," Rhys lied. "She's staying at our place. Must have wandered up here and passed out."

"Your place?"

Cara nodded. "Rhys and Liv's family own this land. Whalton manor is just down the road."

"Ooh. Sounds posh. How do we get there?" Harrison replied, looking suitably impressed.

"No." Wes stepped in. "We'd appreciate your help carrying her to the parking lot, but you're not coming. And you can't tell anyone."

His tone was flat. Not threatening, but completely serious. Harrison stared at him, meeting his even gaze in kind, and contemplating. Finally, he broke away from Wes and shot Cara a grin.

"Right. The aunt with a secret drinking problem. Classic sad tale." With a curious look at the coats wrapped around her, he moved to Lydia's shoulder to take one side. "Shall we?"

CHAPTER 11

CARA AND WES FLATTENED themselves on the floor of the van. Cara landed on top of Lydia with a jarring pain in her ribs. The door slammed closed behind them, extinguishing the overhead light and plunging them into darkness.

"Evening, Professor. Or, Mr. Meyers, that is. Still adjusting. Sorry, sir." Harrison circled the van, distracting the teacher, who had appeared with the worst possible timing.

Cara risked peeking up to see how close he was. Their math teacher had come within a few steps of the van and leaned toward the back windows. For a second, she swore he looked right at her. Then Harrison stepped between them, and she reminded herself of the tinting on the windows.

"What are you doing here, Mr. Winter?" Mr. Meyers asked.

Inside the van, Wes reached across and slowly pressed her head down with a whispered, "Keep your pale face down." Her heart thumped its relief, and she fought a nervous giggle by burying her face in the coats around Lydia's head. Nothing could be less funny, but the adrenaline had made her lightheaded.

Outside, Harrison covered smoothly for them. "Enjoying some night air, sir. I left the dance and bumped into Rhys, so I thought I would stroll up here with him. I love these cold evenings, don't you? Oh, since I've got you, I had a question about that formula you showed us."

Their voices faded as Harrison steered the teacher away from the parking lot. Rhys hopped into the front seat and started the engine without a word.

Cara finally took a deep breath and shifted off Lydia's body. Her nose wrinkled in disgust. The woman reeked. How long had she been wandering the woods and stalking the school in the same clothes? What had she had to eat or drink, and where had she been able to sleep? Or had she? Her sallow skin and bony limbs said she had only had the bare minimum to survive. Enough to stay useful, no more.

"It's safe," Rhys informed them.

Cara's oddly light mood began to settle as the reality of Lydia's situation sank in. She and Wes sat up in the back as they left the clearing of the school and the trees closed in on the sides of the road. No one said a word until they climbed out at the mansion.

Her eyes drank in the darkened stone walls casting shadows in the moonlight across the wintery meadow. It was the first time she'd been back since they had come to meet Liv. Officially, that was the only time she'd ever been here. Of course, unofficially, she'd been here plenty of times before that ever happened, but not since. She snuck a sideways glance at Rhys. Heart skipping, she watched his face lighten the way she remembered. Even during the hardest times when Liv had still been in the hospital, he'd always seemed to love it here.

She headed toward the end of the long garage where they'd spent so much time. Wes stayed to watch Lydia, but Rhys followed and stepped in front of her to open the door. When she entered the closed space they had used as a makeshift lab in the fall, she didn't recognize it.

She turned to ask Rhys what had been going on in here and found him silhouetted in the moonlit doorway. The windows had been boarded over, and the only light came from the space around him. Her breath caught in her throat at his perfect outline. It almost sounded like his breathing hitched, too, when she turned, but the pale glow of the moon reflecting off her face meant his was in shadow, and she couldn't tell. The question she'd been about to ask died on her lips as the rest of the world fell away until there was only the two of them.

Slowly, his silhouetted arm reached around the door to flick on the light, and the single naked bulb illuminated the space. She blinked in the harsh glare as the illusion of something between them faded into the night.

"Um, what—?" She swept an arm across the space.

Bags of peat moss had been stacked like building blocks forming walls for a bizarre structure. A plywood roof covered with more peat moss and a doorway of layered blankets completed it.

"We thought we might need it at some point."

She bent to peer inside, finding more blankets covering an uneven floor. "You built a cell? Out of dirt?"

"Not dirt. Organics—peat moss, wood, cotton—and it's liberally sprinkled with ash remnants."

Her eyes rounded. Ash of a deceased pyxis was the strongest ward against other Pyx that existed. If a pyxis had shared its body with a Pyx until the moment of death, then the protection infused in their cells stayed with them. No other Pyx would ever be able to use them as a host again, so their remnants formed a powerful barrier. Jenyx and Tomyx had reluctantly shared this closely guarded secret in order to explain how to safely capture the Pyx they removed from Liv.

"Wes gave me instructions and more of the ashes Tomyx had supplied him with for the clay last fall. We hope this will work like a human-sized outer pyxis. With all the hostile Pyx in the area, and the way they affect you, it seemed like we might eventually need to hold one. I wanted to be ready. We both did."

"You and Wes did all this?"

He nodded.

"Why didn't you tell me about it?"

"Cara, in case you haven't noticed, you've sort of been dealing with a lot lately. We didn't want to add to it. But if this could help keep you safe . . . I guess we just felt like we had to do something." His smooth voice pierced her heart like a dagger. He had to reach out to steady her as her legs turned to jelly. "Are you hurt? Do you need to lie down?"

"No. No, I'm okay. I just didn't realize how much I was missing while I focused on . . . other stuff."

Other stuff like turning off your feelings. Remember that?

It felt impossible. Not these feelings.

She gulped. Her hand ran down the blankets. "Cotton. Smart."

He nodded with a small smile. "Organic but not living. Right?"

"Who supplies the ash?"

"I haven't asked, but after seeing them, I assume the guardians do the cremations."

It made sense. "Your dad still doesn't come in here?"

"No. I changed the outside lock, but he wouldn't. This was my mom's space."

The dagger in her heart twisted. "Rhys . . . Your mom . . . Is she—"

"Not now. Sometime, okay? But we have more important stuff to deal with right now." The sweet curve of his lips told her he didn't mind that she'd asked, but he wasn't going to talk about it.

She dropped her gaze and gave the side of the dirt cell a little kick. He probably talked to Emma about it enough. He didn't need her butting into his business.

"I guess we better get her in here."

"Are you feeling her? Is she waking up?"

Is that why bitter thoughts prickled through her mind? "Yeah, maybe." She stepped around him to return to the van where Wes waited with Lydia.

"Ready?" Wes asked. "How does it look?"

"You haven't seen it yet?"

"No. I couldn't leave the school through the woods, so Rhys had to take care of it."

Great. So Rhys had done it all himself. He'd been out here alone, working outside with no one to protect him, just to keep her safe. But all it had done so far was put him in danger. Who was to say these Pyx wouldn't go after him?

"You shouldn't have let him do that," she snapped.

"He had Ryx and some of the other friendly Pyx watching the area. It was safe."

"Then it was safe enough for you and me to come help."

"There was no need. It was a good plan, Cara."

"It wasn't a plan. Did you stop to think that I wouldn't want anyone risking themselves for me?" The voice in the back of her mind told her she wasn't being fair, but her control was slipping.

"As usual with you, it was easier to do whatever you wanted without talking to anyone else."

Wes flinched like she'd slapped him. Then he turned to the van. "She's coming around, isn't she?"

"Yep," Rhys said as he approached carrying a lawn chair. "We'd better hurry."

Cara shook out her hands. "Sorry, Wes. I'm sorry. I didn't mean—"

"I know you didn't. Now grab her legs for me."

They tugged Lydia out of the van, and Rhys picked her up to place her in the chair. Using the chair made it much easier to carry her into the garage, and Rhys managed it on his own.

The opening between the peat moss walls would be barely large enough to slide the chair through and allow maybe one more person to fit inside with her.

"Pass me those ropes," Rhys said.

He worked to tie her to the chair.

"I'm not going anywhere." Lydia's muffled voice spoke through the coats still wrapped around her head.

A shiver ran up Cara's spine. At the same time, a cold voice had spoken the words in her mind. From the way Rhys and Wes both froze, they'd heard it too. The voice made her want to shed her own skin to escape the goosebumps crawling across it. The fact that they could hear it through the barrier of coats meant there wasn't enough protection. The Pyx could escape anytime.

Cara waved her hand frantically to indicate they should get the chair into the cell immediately. It wasn't fast enough to stop the bile from rising in her throat and the tension from squeezing her lungs. Rhys picked up the chair and thrust it inside, prisoner and all. He stepped in with her to finish tying her up, ducking under the makeshift roof and dropping the blankets over the space behind him. The effect was instant. Breathing came easier, and Cara's pulse slowed. The world stopped hating her from the inside out.

"Damn, that thing works." She gave Wes a smile and was relieved to see him return it.

At least her logical best friend knew enough not to take her outburst personally. He'd immediately guessed the real problem and moved on. Her hand rubbed across her sore ribs, and she tried not to feel guilty for lashing out. This had to stop. Finding out what these Pyx wanted and why they were making her feel this way was her top priority. There had to be some explanation.

Rhys backed out past the blankets. He was careful to make sure there was always a layer between Lydia and the opening.

"She—it—wants to talk to you," he told her. "But I don't think you should go in there."

She shuddered. "Then what do we do now?"

"We could get Jenyx and Tomyx," Wes replied.

"What are they going to do? They can't assemble a council of eleven fast enough to deal with this. We don't know how well this thing will work, although it's doing a pretty good job right now." She nodded toward the makeshift outer pyxis holding Lydia. "I don't feel her out here, but she wasn't alone in the woods these past few months. We know there's more than one of them. Not to mention their leader, whoever he is. Others could come after her."

Rhys's lips pressed together, but Wes nodded his agreement.

"That's true. And we can't move her. No matter how strong the pyxis—like that black bear or whatever the guardians are—it only takes a second for her to jump to a new pyxis nearby and escape."

"Yeah. This isn't like the ones I took," Rhys added. "She doesn't care about Lydia. She won't stay to try to protect her."

"Ha." Lydia's human voice called out. "This body is fun to torture, but you're right. You can't hold me forever. And the guardians are a joke. We can't protect species from you, and you can't protect yourselves from us. Not if we choose to fight back."

"We're not at war with you," Cara shouted back. "Who are you fighting? What did we do?"

Lydia fell silent.

Cara understood. She'd have to go in if she wanted her answers.

She sighed. "If these walls don't hold, she's gone. All it takes is a bird flying too close, or a mouse running by, or a bug underground. Not to mention all the trees surrounding us. We don't have time. I need to talk to her, and for some reason, I think I'm the only one she'll talk to. It's me she wants."

"Clever little Pyxsee," Lydia's voice taunted from behind the blankets.

The cold voice had stopped accompanying her human voice, blocked by the barrier of organic walls and remnants, but Cara's skin crawled nonetheless.

After overruling all the objections from Rhys and Wes, Cara entered the small dark space with Lydia. She switched on the flashlight on her phone and set it on the floor beside her. Standing upright in the low space was impossible, so she knelt on the barely padded floor. Rhys had taken the coats off Lydia's head, and glowing green eyes stared her down. The up lighting from her phone was straight out of a bad horror movie, the kind she never watched for exactly this reason.

Creepiness factor: Eleven.

As soon as she'd moved past the organic barrier, all her symptoms had flooded back. Her chest tightened, and her eyes narrowed. The tiny space was ripe with Lydia's stench, and she was forced to breathe through her mouth. She struggled to push down the hatred foisted upon her and focus on what she needed. Answers.

"Why are you doing this?" She forced the words past clenched teeth and willed her jaw to relax.

"Wrong question."

The cold voice in her mind was back. She flinched. The Pyx wasn't using Lydia's voice anymore, so Rhys and Wes would only hear one side of the conversation from outside the barrier. Fine. She'd play by these rules. For now.

"What's the right question, then?"

"The right question? Probably what can you do to stop me. To stop us. Pointless thing to ask, though, since the answer is nothing."

"Then *what* is it you're trying to do?"

"Nothing more than correct a terrible mistake and eliminate the worst threat this planet has ever seen."

"Threat? You mean humans."

"Name something worse."

Her mind raced. The hostility radiating to her from the Pyx grew the longer she hesitated. "If that's how you feel, why not work with us instead? I thought Pyx were observers. You don't get involved unless the consequences are too dire, which maybe they are, but then you're supposed to intervene to help. That's how Jenyx has always explained it to me."

The voice came back colder than ever, steely and sharp. "Idealism has no place in this world. Not anymore. Some of us have yet to accept the truth in front of us. There is only one solution remaining. Your precious Jenyx and the others who believe as he does can perish along with the scourge of humanity. The world will be better off. *This is* how we help."

Even without a straight answer, she was starting to get a pretty clear picture of why they were taking over humans. It sank in like a stone through her soul.

"But how does taking over a handful of humans do anything? All you're doing is ruining lives. Not enough to have a global effect."

"It may look that way, but you have no idea. The past few decades have seen our number of supporters explode. We started small, and we may have suffered setbacks, but we're at a turning point now. You'll see. Or maybe you won't be around long enough to see."

At the mention of setbacks, Cara's back stiffened and the anger she'd suppressed pushed to the surface.

"It's personal, isn't it? What happened? What does it have to do with me?"

A seething wave washed over her. She doubled over at the nauseating swirl of emotions. Gasping for air brought Lydia's rank odor together with the sharp tang of the peat moss walls. She gagged. Her eyes stung and streamed in the foul air.

Don't you dare throw up now. She couldn't leave without answers.

"Did you think you were special, little Pyxsee? Did you think there had never been others with your unnatural eyes and fancy abilities?"

"What?" She'd known her eyes weren't unique, but she knew almost nothing about her empathy or what other abilities golden Pyxsees like her possessed. Ever since the elder in the porcupine had mentioned others, it had been on her mind a lot. "No. But why is that relevant? What did I do?"

"Maybe if daddy dearest had stuck around, you'd have more of a clue."

The silence that followed died beneath the rushing in Cara's ears.

"What did you say?" she thundered. The blankets twitched, and she shouted again. "No. Don't come in here." This was between her and this Pyx, and whatever it had to do with her dad. She chose her next words carefully. "What do you know about . . . that?"

Ice replaced the fire in her veins, and she found the cold distance she'd been striving for. Her own loathing had a completely different feel to it than the one she got from the Pyx.

"Tell me. Now." She glared into the glowing green of Lydia's eyes.

"Hit a nerve, did I? I think this conversation is over. You won't kill this unfortunate woman, and you can't move me any other way. So I'll simply wait for my supporters to come for me. No point telling you my plan when I'm about to escape to enact it, is there? That would be the height of foolishness."

"What do you know? What did you do?" she hissed.

Silence slammed through her mind.

"Answer me. How is this related? How am I related to this?"

In response, Lydia closed her eyes and let her chin drop. Cara's shoulders rose and fell with rapid breaths. She shook Lydia's knee. "Hey." There was no response. She nudged the woman's broken arm, grimacing at the pain it would cause. Still nothing.

Her mind spun, going over her options until a plan formed. With her choice made, she backed out of the small space, careful to move through the blankets one layer at a time. Outside, the light did nothing to brighten her mood. Icy venom stuck with her, and her limbs trembled.

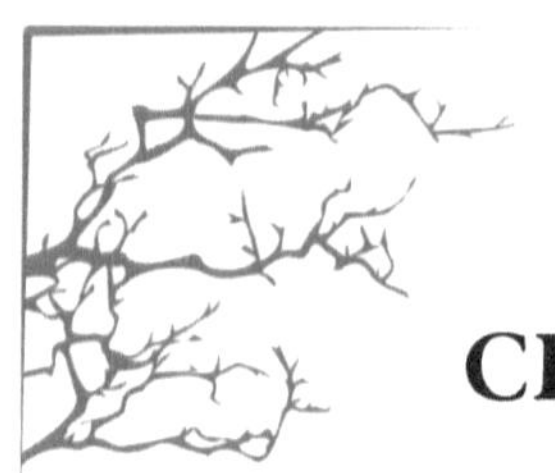

CHAPTER 12

"WHAT HAPPENED?" RHYS asked as she emerged from the cell.

Cara couldn't look at him. She couldn't bear to see those eyes while she felt like her world was caving in.

"I need a pyxis," she said.

"Cara, we need to do this carefully." Wes placed a hand on her arm.

She shrugged him off and moved around the room, ignoring their whispers behind her. Her sharp gold eyes took inventory. She picked up a clay pyxis. Wes must have made more, because there were several stocked along the tall bench. At one end, the glass terrarium that had once held a few frogs sat idle. The fresh greenery inside registered as odd.

"What's this?" She glanced over her shoulder.

Rhys stepped over and lifted the lid. "I've been keeping a couple beetles. Just in case."

"Perfect."

"No, it isn't," Wes objected. "You can't risk . . . whatever you're planning."

She didn't bother responding. Instead, she found the other items she was looking for in one of the drawers. More leftovers from their bold plan to save Liv.

"Beetle, please." She held out a hand toward Rhys.

"Cara. Let us help." His tone almost made her look up, but those eyes would undo her resolve, and that wasn't about to happen. He sighed and placed a wriggling black beetle in her palm. His hand closed around hers. "Please don't do this."

She nearly broke. The blind trust Rhys was showing her meant more than she could say, in spite of his clear objections. But Lydia was her mom's friend. And this was somehow related to her dad. If she knew what the story was with Rhys's mom, then maybe she could have explained it in a way he would understand. But she couldn't. She only knew she had to do this.

This was personal. Her fight. That thing was leaving Lydia, and that was it. Then she'd figure out how to get answers.

Returning to the dark cell, the hostility in the small space fueled the cold detachment she'd found in her choice, and she approached Lydia with determination.

"You don't think I'll hurt Lydia?" she asked.

Lydia's eyelids flicked open. Cara stared into the glowing green as her hand grasped the splinted and broken arm. She pulled.

Lydia didn't react, but the cold voice spoke. "Nice try. You caught me off guard last time, but that won't work again."

Cara's face stayed stony, but inside, she smiled. It was the response she'd been hoping for. Lydia was feeling nothing. She pulled the other two items from her pocket. When the needle had been fitted to the syringe, she unsheathed it. Drawing back the plunger to fill it with air, she pulled Lydia's broken arm out to the side.

"You know what a huge air bubble injected into her bloodstream will do, don't you?" she whispered so the boys wouldn't hear. No matter how much trust they put in her, mention of cold-blooded murder would bring them through the walls to stop her.

"You wouldn't dare. I know you think you're a good person. Not a killer. You don't have what it takes."

"No?" She leaned over Lydia's twisted arm, exposing tender skin and protruding veins. When she finished, she held up the syringe with its plunger fully depressed. She twisted Lydia's arm to show her the drop of blood blooming from a fresh puncture mark in the crook of her elbow.

Her mouth went dry at what she'd done. The wave of fear sweeping through her made her gulp. It lasted only a moment before it was replaced by fresh bitterness.

"Stupid child. I liked using this wretched creature."

Cara held out the beetle between trembling hands. "Time for a new one."

All the emotions from the past months coursed through her again. Isolation piled onto anger. Fear undermined hostility. And worry gnawed at her. She felt it all with a new intensity.

But mostly, the rage.

Cara's world exploded in a blinding flash of pain and light. The clay vessel and the beetle fell from her hands, and she was vaguely aware of tumbling to the ground. Millions of images rampaged through her mind.

She swam. She ran. She flew.

She skipped through meadows of long grass. She swayed in a stiff wind. She was ravaged by a bitter snowstorm. Floodwaters rose all around her. Fire chased her through a smoky forest of enormous trees and prehistoric plants.

Her body was covered in fur, scales, slippery skin, and everything in between, each one chasing away the last. She felt pleasure and pride, and then sorrow and loss. She experienced hunger and sickness. She stood atop a mountain, soared high above a glistening ocean, and crawled in a dark cave below monolithic cliffs.

She fought. She cowered in fear. She loved. And she screamed in despair.

The anguished howl rang in her ears. Pain tore through her knees. When she sucked in a breath, the screaming stopped. With air in her lungs, it started again.

She struggled to regain control.

Stop.

Stop the screams. Stop the blinding images and savage sensations. Stop everything.

When the light began to fade and the sounds deadened inside her mind, she thought she was winning. Until she realized she was choking—drowning. She sank through murky, watery depths until all she knew was darkness.

"CARA. CARA." HER NAME drifted to her from far away. "Cara." Why was she so cold? "Cara." Closer that time. Softer.

A hard surface under her right side spread a chill through her body until she drifted away from that too. Then cushioned warmth met her skin. She hadn't drifted; she'd been carried. Her eyes fought their way open.

Two stricken faces stared back at her.

Dark-brown eyes full of golden flecks. Wes.

Swirling grey irises with a ring of gold. Rhys.

What had happened to make them look that way?

"Cara?" Rhys's voice had none of its usual smooth, clear tone.

The throaty rasp reminded her of how he'd sounded in the hospital, when they weren't sure Liv would survive. She started to reach for him, for an anchor to her jumbled thoughts, but stopped when she remembered herself. Blinking, she looked around.

Low roof, windows, a smooth dash—it was the front seat of his van. Wes held her up with one hand where she sagged toward him and Rhys standing in the open door. The brace on Wes's other arm meant Rhys must have been the one to carry her to the seat. But from where? She frowned.

Pulling herself upright, she gasped at the pain shooting up her legs. Blood and dirt covered her knees.

"What happened?" she asked, leaning forward to rub them.

The guys exchanged a glance.

"I can't," Rhys said.

Wes nodded his head toward the garage, and Rhys stepped away. He stuffed his hands in his pockets and vanished through the door.

Memories surged back to her. "What—Lydia—is she . . .?"

"He'll check on her," Wes replied. "How do you feel?"

"Beat up. I remember most of it, but not what happened to my knees, or how I got here." Something close to pity spread across his face, and her heart fell. "Wes. What is it?"

He didn't answer.

Her mind raced, trying to piece together the events. Lydia had attacked her at the school. They'd brought her here, to Whalton manor. She'd talked to the Pyx inside the warded cell.

There'd been something about fighting back against humans, but that wasn't all. Oh, crap. The Pyx had said something about her dad and Pyxsees with eyes like hers having extra abilities.

If daddy dearest had stuck around . . .

The words came back, and with them, the rest of the pieces. *Double crap.*

"I got so mad. All I knew was I had to get that thing out of Lydia so we could deal with him. Where is he?"

"The Pyx? She's gone." Wes studied her carefully, his eyes narrowing from shock into worry.

"Gone? What? How?"

"She used you."

"No." Her shoulder pressed into the seat cushion, and her head shook back and forth. "No."

But the memory of blinding light and searing pain in her head was enough to know he was right. The tumbling string of images and the swirling vortex of emotions and experiences—there was no other explanation. Her stomach pitched at the truth in his words. The Pyx had used her. And escaped.

Tears spilled down her cheeks. She pressed her forehead into Wes's chest, and he rested a hand on the back of her head until she stopped shaking.

"I'm sorry, Cara. We should never have let you go in there alone."

She shook her head against him before looking up. "It's my fault. It's all my fault. I let him affect me, like before. All I could think of was the anger. Some of the things he said . . . And now he's gone."

"He?"

"What?"

"You keep saying he. But the Pyx was in Lydia and then you. Female hosts, female identifiers."

"Oh. Yeah." Why had she switched how she referred to the Pyx? She couldn't explain it, but it seemed right. "I don't know."

Rhys returned and replaced Wes at the door, handing her a damp towel. "Are you okay? I mean, I know you're hurt, but are you . . . okay?"

She nodded and stared at her knees while she pressed the towel to them so he wouldn't see her red-rimmed eyes. "What happened to Lydia?"

"She's unconscious," he answered. "What did you do to make the Pyx leave? Should we be worried about her?"

"I didn't actually do anything. I only made it look like I did. I showed her a syringe full of air, but I pushed the air out where she couldn't see and then pricked her with the needle and showed her the blood. But we should probably still be worried about her. She's half starved. That broken arm . . . Who knows what else?"

"I'll call an ambulance, but I needed to make sure you're okay to go back to the school first. With Wes, of course. You shouldn't be alone, and you can't be here."

"No. We can't leave you here. How are you going to explain finding someone who's been missing for months? Plus, what if he comes back?"

He reached out and brushed her hair back over her shoulder so he could see her face. "I'll be fine. What do you feel?"

He waited for her to answer, but all she felt was humiliated. How could she have messed things up so badly? If only the ground would open up and swallow her so he'd stop looking at her that way—like she wasn't the reason everything had gone to crap.

"Nothing," she muttered.

"Meaning no anger? No hostility?"

She shook her head.

"Good. It must have left the area. They'll need time to regroup after this."

"Did you guys see where the Pyx went after . . . you know?"

They both shook their heads.

"You were screaming and thrashing"—Wes rubbed a red mark beside his eye where she must have struck him—"until you fell. When the screaming stopped, you collapsed. We saw the green gleam leave your eyes, but we were both too busy running to you to see where she went when she left."

She stared at him and then at Rhys. "That sounds . . ."

"Like nothing I ever want to see again," Rhys finished for her.

His words punched her in the chest. *Of course.* That was why he'd been so shaken and had to walk away. He'd seen it before. He'd seen Liv screaming and thrashing when a Pyx attacked her.

His face showed the effort it cost him to shake it off again. "I'm safe for now. And I won't be alone for long. You two take the van. Liv and Jory are meeting you in the parking lot. I messaged her already. Jory and Wes will help you back to the dorms, and Liv will go for the school nurse to come back here with her. We're going to say Liv was with me and raced back to the school for help. Ambulances take forever to reach here, and I'm worried what'll happen if Lydia wakes up."

Cara couldn't see any holes in his plan. "What's the story for how she got here?"

He shrugged. "We'll say we found her on the doorstep when we arrived or something. She's been missing, right? So no one knows where she's been or how she might have ended up here."

"Okay." She winced as she shifted forward in the seat.

"Easy. What are you doing?"

"Moving to the driver's seat."

"I can drive that far with one hand. Stay where you are," Wes said.

Rhys started the van for him and then let Wes into the driver's seat.

"Please text, or get Liv to, when it's over." Cara mustered the courage to look Rhys in the eye one last time before they pulled away. The pain she saw there made her cringe.

Their headlights swept the dark ditches on either side of the narrow road, and Cara sat silently biting her lip so Wes could focus on driving one-handed. She smoothed the buttery-soft fabric of the dress across her legs. It had gone grey in the ghostly light, but stains spread across it to give it a mottled look. A tear in the skirt exposed some of the skin at her hip, whether from the first attack at the school or from falling on the cobblestones, she had no idea. She definitely owed Cassidy a new dress.

Wes's eyes darted over to her. "You still okay?"

She couldn't answer, so she changed the subject.

"When you said I was thrashing around . . . um, how much exactly?"

A little humor tinted his words. "You didn't flash anyone, if that's what you're asking."

It was.

"That's good." She struggled to sound like she was smiling too. If Jory so much as hugged her when they arrived, she'd probably burst into tears again.

"Honestly, Cara, it was so scary, it wouldn't have mattered."

"Maybe not to you." But she was embarrassed enough without adding the extra layer of humiliating herself for the hundredth time.

The silence that fell between them as Wes made the turn toward the school felt strained, like he was working out what to say. Or maybe whether he should say anything.

"Look, when Rhys walked away, it wasn't because he doesn't care. I think—"

"It's okay, Wes," she interrupted. "I know how he feels."

"You do?"

"It would be hard to miss." She managed to sound normal. "Pyxsee, remember? Super observant and all of that."

She'd known it all along with the way Rhys lost his easy smile around her and the way he often fell silent when she was around. Maybe there'd been a few times when she thought she felt something more from him, but whatever she'd deluded herself into believing wouldn't matter anymore. If she hadn't been a terrible reminder of Liv's ordeal before, she certainly would be now. Just when it had started to feel like a wall was coming down between them . . . He'd probably never be able to look at her again.

"Oh. Well, good, then."

Maybe it was. It was well past time she moved on.

The van cleared the last of the trees, and Cara ducked to hide. Wes parked facing away from the castle-like building, and they scooted out in the dark, closing the doors quietly behind them. Jory and Liv stepped forward from the wall where they'd been hiding in a pool of shadows. They'd brought Jenner and Thomas with them.

"Key's still in it," Wes told Liv. "Go grab Amy."

Liv cast an uncharacteristically silent look across them, and then darted into the building to fetch the nurse. Jory took one look at Cara's face and stood quietly beside her. Somehow he knew she couldn't handle his concern right now. She buried her hands in Jenner's fur for comfort.

"Cara, child, what went on tonight? We sensed the Pyx come close again, but then it simply vanished. Clearly something terrible happened for your friends to have shown up in your place."

"Long story," she whispered. She couldn't deal. Not yet.

They hid around the corner of the building out of view until Amy dashed by behind Liv. Once the van had carried them down the road, their little group stepped out of hiding to sneak back to the dorms.

As she turned the corner, a blast of icy wind cut across Cara's face and exposed legs. Before she knew what was happening, she was lost in a snowstorm. Icy darts blasted her skin, and her eyes closed against the blinding white. The cold took her breath away with a gasp and filled her with emptiness.

The shocking blizzard ended as quickly as it started, and her eyes opened to the same dark, chilly night of a moment ago. Cold, but nothing like what she'd just experienced.

What the hell was that?

"Cara, what's wrong?" Jory held her arm.

Good question.

"Nothing." She shook her head but allowed him to keep holding her up.

"Are you sure we should take you to the dorms? Maybe—" Jory looked up to the building full of teacher's apartments and the nurse's station, but froze as the door opened.

Dr. Flanagan stepped outside and folded her long coat around her petite frame. "What are you three doing out here?"

They glanced at each other but found nothing to say.

The headmaster's eyes stopped on Cara. "Oh, dear. What happened to you?"

"I slipped. Walking back from the dance."

"Your knees look pretty torn up."

"Yeah. I slipped on the wet grass, but, um, I fell onto the gravel."

"Sounds like some fall. You'd better come in. Amy's been called away to an emergency, but we can get you cleaned up while we wait."

Cara wanted to shake her head and say she'd rather return to her room, but then they'd lose the excuse of why they were there.

Dr. Flanagan held the boys back when they started to follow her inside. "Thank you, Wes and Jory. You were right to bring her here instead of her room. But it is after curfew, so you'd better head back. I'll call ahead so Mr. Meyers is expecting you and understands the circumstances causing you to miss curfew."

"But we don't want to leave her alone," Jory protested.

"Spoken like a true friend. Rest assured, Jory, she won't be alone. I promise I'll stay with her until Amy returns. Deal?"

Without much choice, Jory looked to Cara.

She bobbed her head once. "It's fine, guys. I'll see you in the morning."

"Jory," Dr. Flanagan called after them, "aren't you forgetting something?" She gave a pointed look at Thomas.

"Oh. Uh. It's just . . . he might want to stay with Cara."

"Don't be silly. Jenner's staying. Your cat should go with you."

Cara could have sworn she looked at Wes when she spoke. But their headmaster turned too quickly for her to be sure and closed the door behind them. It didn't matter. Tomyx could hear his update from Wes, and she'd have a little longer before she had to fill in Jenyx since she couldn't talk to him in front of Dr. Flanagan.

They walked slowly for the sake of Cara's aching knees.

Dr. Flanagan tapped her phone a few times and held it to her ear. "Hi, Owen, it's Eve. I've sent Jory and Wes back your way. They were escorting a friend to the nurse's station." She paused to listen. "Yes. Thanks."

Her math teacher's first name was Owen? File that bit of info under interesting but useless. Cara's hand curled in Jenner's scruff as she trudged down the hall, glad for anything to take her out of her own head.

She eased herself onto one of the beds and fought the urge to immediately collapse.

"You should let your roommate know you'll be spending the night here, Cara. I'm sure Delaney's worried."

Crap. Delaney.

She must be wondering where Cara was. Lots of students would have returned from the dance right at curfew, though, so she might not have started worrying yet. After all, she could simply be in someone else's room, reliving who had danced with whom or other gossip.

Double crap.

She'd completely forgotten about the gossip. Rhys had disappeared from the dance, too. What must Emma be thinking? It paled in significance after everything that had transpired in the last couple hours, but it still managed to make her skin tighten. The constant layer of anger recently had come to feel like a cushion for any other feelings, but now it was gone, and the rest prickled with new intensity.

Swallowing, she found her phone in the jacket pocket—Rhys's jacket, she realized with a jolt—and messaged Delaney to tell her where she was.

"This is going to sting." Dr. Flanagan brought gauze and antiseptic and began cleaning the wounds on Cara's knees.

Jenner nudged Cara's hand as she gritted her teeth.

"The Pyx who was here, was it the one we encountered in the city? The one using your mother's friend as a pyxis?" Jenyx asked.

"Mmm." Her grunt could be taken as confirmation or as pain.

"She attacked you? Is that how you received these injuries?"

She gave her dog a long, slow blink as confirmation. Jenyx knew her well enough to figure out her code.

"I can no longer sense her nearby. Is she still around?"

Cara's eyelashes fluttered, along with an imperceptible sideways movement of her head. It could have been a flinch from the stinging in her knees.

"There," Dr. Flanagan said, "that's as much as I can do. Now let me find you some clothes to change into, and we'll call your mom."

"My mom?"

"Sorry. Protocol. You did get hurt on school property, right?"

"Oh. Right. Yep."

"I'll tell her what happened, and then I'm sure she'll want to speak with you herself."

The past couple years had involved hiding a lot from her mom, and it never stopped feeling awful. She took the sweatpants and the school T-shirt Dr. Flanagan handed her and trudged into the bathroom.

With mounting dread, her eyes landed on the mirror. Dirt streaked across her forehead and one side of her chin. Her eyelashes were still clumped together from the tears that had flowed through them earlier. She gingerly peeled off Rhys's jacket and dropped it to the floor. The top of the dress had been protected from the worst of the grime, but the skirt was now a completely different color. Not that it mattered. It was tattered and blood-stained beyond repair.

She picked debris from her hair, letting it down and running her fingers through the tangled brown waves, and then turned on the water. When she finished scrubbing her face, fresh scrapes and red skin emerged where the dirt had been. She stripped off the dress and examined her hip. Washing the long scrape carefully, she prodded the tender flesh. That would make for an impressive bruise by tomorrow.

Finally, she turned off the water and patted herself dry with a soft towel from the shelf. Things were still bad, but cleaned up and dressed in fresh clothes, she regained enough strength to face them again.

"Here she is." Dr. Flanagan handed her the phone.

After a lot of, "Yes, Mom," "No, Mom," and, "Really, I'm fine. Just some scrapes," she hung up and climbed back into the tall bed.

"I know it's not the most comfortable arrangement, but I'd rather have Amy check you out before we let you go. Get some rest. I'll be right over there in Amy's office until she returns, and then she'll stay with you tonight. Plus, you've got Jenner there." Dr. Flanagan left the room, turning off the overhead lights so only the glow from the office window lit the space.

"Jenyx, I know you have questions. Tomorrow, okay?" Her eyelids sagged.

"Of course. It is enough that you are safe. I am sorry I was not with you, but I will be here when you awaken."

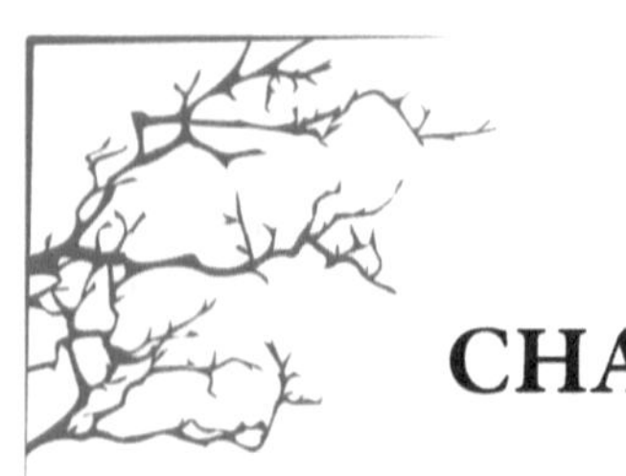

CHAPTER 13

RUMBLING TREMORS INTERRUPTED the stillness of the night. She jerked awake. The sound grew to a deafening roar, and she jumped up. On four legs, she dashed for the mouth of the cave, faster than she'd ever run before. Faster than she should be capable of running. Fresh air ruffled the fur on her face before a cloud of dust exploded from the cave and blocked out the twinkling stars above. She choked and turned toward the opening, toward the avalanche of rock where the back half had collapsed. Her anguished roar split the dark. Her mate had been in there . . . and her cub.

"I'm sorry." The voice in her mind ached with her.

Cara fell out of bed with a *crash*, and the cry from her lips fell silent. Swearing, she scrambled to her feet.

"Sorry, Delaney."

Her roommate reeled back at the sudden motion. Delaney had been leaning over her, probably trying to shake her awake. Again.

Cara stumbled to the window and sagged against the windowsill, pushing the glass open wider. The start of April had brought nice weather, but for some stupid reason, the heaters in the dorms kept pushing out hot air. If only she could blame the heat for the sheen of sweat on her skin.

146

"Do you want me to get Liv?" Delaney whispered with a note of panic. "Talking to her always makes you feel better after one of your . . ."

Don't say episodes.

"Nightmares," Cara filled in. She checked the dial of her dad's watch by the moonlight and wished for the thousandth time he was around to talk to about this. Three o'clock in the morning. "No. I'll be fine. Don't wake her. I'm sorry I woke you up, D."

"Don't be. Do you want to tell me about it?" Delaney sat on the edge of her bed.

She shook her head at her friend's offer. How could she explain a nightmare where she hadn't been herself? Hadn't even been human? Especially when it felt so real.

Especially when they kept happening when she was awake too.

That first night after the disastrous encounter with the Pyx at Whalton manor, and after the first waking nightmare of the blizzard, she'd woken to the sound of Amy returning well past midnight. While the quiet murmurs of Amy talking to Dr. Flanagan had trickled out of the office, Cara had checked her phone.

The message from Rhys said the ambulance had taken Lydia away and the police had arrived. At the time, they had been waiting for their dad to drive up from the city so he could be there while Rhys and Liv were interviewed, and then they would all stay at the manor that night. Her surprise that he'd been the one to message her instead of Liv had been quickly overwhelmed by concern for them both being forced to lie to the police about how they'd found Lydia. Liv hadn't even been there. Fortunately, they had so few details to offer that their story didn't really matter.

Naturally, like any secret around here, the whole school had buzzed with rumors about it within the day. The upside of this was that rumors about the photo from the gala, or whatever the girl had told Emma at the dance, never really materialized. Cara had hidden out with Wes and Jory, and Wes had recounted the full story so Jenyx, Tomyx, and Jory were all caught up. Cara's mom had also phoned to share the "news" about Lydia. Apparently she was still listed as the woman's emergency contact and had been called to the hospital where Lydia was being treated.

When Liv had returned late that afternoon and marched into the boys' room, she'd ignored Jory entirely for once and pulled Cara into her arms. Then she'd kicked the boys out of their own room and made them take the animals with them, leaving her and Cara completely alone.

"Rhys told me everything. I've never seen him so freaked out," she'd said.

"I know. I hate that he's reliving what he went through with you, and it's all my fault."

"No, listen. What I'm trying to say is, he's freaked, but he doesn't really know what it's like. I mean, I know what happened to me was different, but I'm the only other person you know who's had one of them in her head, unless you go talk to Lydia. But I think she'll be out of commission for a while."

"No, Liv. You're right. It's totally different. It was a year and a half for you, and you almost died. Actually, you did die. That's a million times worse. No comparison. Don't feel bad for me."

"Cara. Of course I do. I wouldn't want this for anyone, least of all my best friend." Liv had held her while she fought off tears. "Promise me you'll talk to me. Having you guys around helped me so much when I first came back. Don't shut down, okay?"

It was fine for Liv to say. And Cara had tried. She'd really tried at first.

The next vision, or whatever they were, had hit her while she and Liv walked through the lounge of the Cedars on their way back to their rooms. When she had come back to herself, slumped over the back of one of the couches, Liv had explained to the girls in the room that Cara's injured knees had caused her to cry out and gasp. That didn't stop them all from looking at her as if she'd grown three heads and it might be contagious.

So she'd tried. She'd explained it to Liv in the privacy of her room.

"It's like I went somewhere else. And I was someone else. Actually, I'm pretty sure I was an animal. It happened so fast. I saw the hunter's orange vest. Then I was dying and thinking how beautiful the sun was in the sky above me. I didn't feel anything. Not physically. But now, inside, I feel like I actually died. Does that make any sense at all? Did you get these weird vision things after you came back? How long did it take for them to stop?"

"I—no. I sort of have some vague memories I know aren't mine. They're like stories I heard or something. Sometimes I think I can picture places I've never seen before. But nothing like actually being in the memory. And not feeling like it was happening to me."

"Oh."

After the first few, she had learned to control her physical response. She stopped gasping or shrieking or crying. These things weren't actually happening to her. But she had to live with the emotions afterward. Those were one hundred percent real, even if they weren't hers.

She almost wished for the days when all she'd felt was angry and bitter all the time when the Pyx had been stalking her. But those feelings hadn't come back since that night. The Pyx had left the area for now.

After six weeks of this, the worst that happened during the day now was she tripped or spaced out for a while. Her classmates noticed occasionally, and most of them were giving her a wide berth these days. It was an unwelcome reminder of her old life, when it had been a choice between mockery or isolation, and she'd done her best to be invisible. Now here she was again. Even Mike stopped finding reasons to talk to her. She avoided being around people whenever she could.

The difference now was she had real friends, and somehow that was making the loneliness worse. Her friends kept a close eye on her, but that only made her feel like a live grenade. Like they were all holding their breath, waiting for her to explode.

She stopped telling them about all the visions. Only Jenyx knew the full breadth of what she saw.

But hiding her reactions during the day was one thing. Nights were another.

She stepped away from the window, skin prickling with drying sweat.

"Go back to bed, D. I'm gonna go take a shower."

"At 3 a.m.?" Delaney asked.

"Yeah. And tomorrow I'm going to complain about this ridiculous heat situation again. Honestly, if people are cold, they can put on a sweater." She gathered her things and stumbled out the door, with Jenner following.

"Which one was it this time?" Jenyx asked once they were alone.

"New one. Some sort of bear, I think. It felt like a long time ago. Maybe a cave bear from prehistoric times or something." She turned on the faucet and splashed some water on her face.

"Not prehistoric to us. The lives of all our past pyxides live on in us. That *is* our history."

"I know. Believe me. How do you live with all these memories? And why are they all focused on death and loss?"

"They are not normally so centered on negative events the way these memories are for you. My guess is this Pyx has been focusing on death and destruction, and likely whatever has driven him to the mindset he finds himself in now."

"I've got you using 'him' now too. He saved us in this memory. He got me out of the cave even though I didn't want to leave them. Or she did. Oh, I don't even know anymore. It's so confusing. In the memories, he still identifies with his hosts, but that night at the manor—when he was in my mind—I got the sense he's taken his own identity now, not honoring his pyxis anymore. Which I guess makes sense if he's using humans and he hates us so much. Why would he honor a pyxis he hates?"

"I am terribly sorry these are the only memories being presented to you. Most of mine are full of joy and love from the pyxides who have shared their minds with me. I wish I could share those with you instead."

"Well, I don't. Sorry, Jenyx. Those do sound nicer than what I've got going on up here"—she tapped her temple—"but there's already too much swirling around. It's hard enough to figure out how to suppress the emotions I'm left with after these visions, and I'm getting sort of used to all the misery."

An ache in her heart told her Jenyx was feeling bad for her.

"Not helping," she said. "Turn that off by the time I'm done."

She stepped into one of the shower stalls and closed the door on Jenner's brown eyes and sweet furry face. Setting down her towel and clothes, she stripped off her sweaty pajamas and turned on the water. Closing her eyes, she worked to clear her head and push away the last of the grief from the vision. Learning to turn off her emotions was a slow process. Now she had a little ritual that was half meditation and half pure stubborn will. She'd even let Cassidy teach her a bit of yoga one day, and she focused on breathing from her core while she stood in the hot water.

The shower was fast. She was really quick lately, as if the Pyx was shaming her from inside her own mind not to waste water, but she stayed in the lingering steam after she turned off the taps. Droplets fell from her body, and she tried to release as much of her tension with them as she could. The refreshing citrus smell from her shampoo carried to her on the steam, and she inhaled deeply.

Dry and dressed, she emerged to find Jenyx exuding a much happier vibe for her to pick up on.

"I see you found a happy memory to draw on?"

"Yes. One of Jenner's, in fact. It's from the day he met you on that park bench."

"Aw. Thanks, buddy." She ruffled the top of her dog's head. "I needed that." Maybe she had a tiny chance of falling back asleep for a few hours.

SHE WOKE UP BY ALMOST rolling out of bed again. Instead of falling, her hip ran into something solid.

"Morning."

Cara opened her eyes to find Liv sitting on her bed. The dip in the mattress had made her roll into Liv's back.

"Is it?"

"I just said morning. Not good."

"Oh. Right."

"Here." Liv held out a blueberry muffin.

Cara sat up and rubbed her sleepy face instead of taking the muffin. "What time is it?"

"You have half an hour until your biology midterm. Jory's waiting for you in our lounge."

"Crap. Where's my phone? Why didn't my alarm go off?"

Liv handed her the phone with a smug smile before she turned serious. "Delaney came in this morning and said you were up half the night. You needed as much sleep as you could get, and when I came to check on you, you were snoring away. So I snagged your phone and then brought breakfast back with me. I figured you might not want to face the dining hall."

The irritation with her friend faded. "Thanks." She pulled her pillow out from behind her and used it to thump Liv across the back. "And I was not snoring."

"Oh, but how would you know?" Liv jumped up with a laugh. "Now get dressed. You do still have to pass these last few exams before the break."

Cara threw off her covers and went to her closet. Good thing they were about to have a break, because she desperately needed to do some laundry. At least she could take her clothes home with her instead of dealing with the laundry room here.

"So, do you want to talk about it?" Liv prompted.

Cara found a clean T-shirt to pull on and crossed the room for her jeans, which she'd left hanging over her desk chair. "Not much to tell. It was like all the rest. I didn't die in this one, but my family did."

Liv sucked in a breath, and Cara turned away to grab her backpack. Ignoring the look of pity on Liv's face, she reached for the muffin. Liv handed it over, and Cara started to pick at it as they left the room.

"And Jenyx still doesn't know why you're seeing these things?" Liv glanced down at the dog following at their heels.

"No. It's not like we have any other empath Pyxsees who've had their minds taken over by a Pyx to ask. We don't even know any others alive right now with eyes like mine, let alone with the same ability. I hope the visions stay away through these exams. I can't afford to lose even a few minutes."

Her studying had been far below her usual standard this time. Partly she'd been avoiding people, so she hadn't spent as much time with Wes in the library, or in study parties with the girls in Liv and Kaylee's room. Also, she simply couldn't focus. Six weeks should have been enough time for the shock to wear off and for her to stop seeing things that had nothing to do with her, but it was only getting worse. The biggest part, though, was it felt like nothing mattered anymore. Not when everything in life was death and loss, over and over, day and night. Who cared about school? Her head still told her she had to care. But her heart? Not so much.

Jory greeted them in the lounge. Even though they'd obviously just been to breakfast together, his eyes lit up when they landed on Liv coming back toward him. Cara's heavy heart lightened for a few beats. Every once in a while, there was more than the doom and gloom in her mind. What would it be like to have someone look at her that way? The moment passed, and her heart hardened again. It didn't matter. At this rate, she'd never find out.

Liv stood on her tiptoes to kiss Jory and then skipped out the door with a wave to head to her own exams.

"Hey, Cares. Rough night?" Jory turned to her.

"Apparently. We'd better hurry. I can't believe you guys let me sleep in so late."

"You needed it. Should we jog?" Jory had a twinkle in his eye that said it would turn into a race.

They settled for a brisk walk down to the stables to leave Jenner at the kennels for the day, and then raced up the hill. The burn in her thighs felt good enough to take her mind off the dream and put it back on their biology exam where it belonged. Jory's infectious grin didn't hurt either.

After their two morning exams, which she made it through without interruption from her malfunctioning brain, her stomach growled when they entered the dining hall. She'd have to remember to tell Liv, for future reference, that a single muffin wasn't exactly enough food for a whole morning. She loaded up a tray and headed for their usual table. The sight of a familiar figure sitting with Wes and Liv stopped her in her tracks. Even sitting down, and with his back to her, Rhys's long, lean shape was unmistakable.

She'd been right about him not being able to look her in the eye after that night. In the first few days, they'd had a couple short conversations. He'd asked her how she was feeling, staring at his feet the whole time, and she'd kept it to a few simple words about her sore knees and bruised ribs. Those injuries had long since healed, but the awkward exchanges with him were worse than not talking to him at all, so she'd avoided him along with everyone else. Well, maybe she'd avoided him a little more than everyone else.

She turned away from the table, scooped her sandwich and drink from her tray, and dropped it off. The desire for time alone rose from a place deep in her past and drove her outside. The grey sky matched her feelings—flat, heavy, featureless. After all the time she'd spent pushing down her emotions so she could sense the Pyx, it was like those had left the area too. She'd gone numb.

That old life she'd thought she'd left behind, all that time spent hiding what made her different, was still closer than she'd like. With her emotions dulled now, this new life felt like a ghost of those dark memories.

Only the emotions after the visions were vivid. The pain, the grief, the misery—those were real.

Her eyes scanned the area outside for somewhere to eat alone. A few other students had ventured out to enjoy the scattered picnic tables, so she quickly dismissed those. Maybe she should head toward the science building where her math exam would be taking place after lunch. Her feet moved without direction until she found herself at the path leading into the forest. It had been so long since she'd run those trails alone, or sat by herself in the shady silence. If the Pyx had left the area, then why shouldn't she? She'd had enough of the constant chaperones and avoiding any possibility of danger. Besides, it was safe if they were gone.

The first steps into the woods made her close her eyes and breathe in the forest smell. Spring growth gave the whole place a fresh scent, overpowering the winter decomposition as last year's dead things brought forward new life. The grey sky vanished behind a canopy of green, and the only sounds were the chirping birds and a faint breeze rustling the new leaves on the branches. And footsteps.

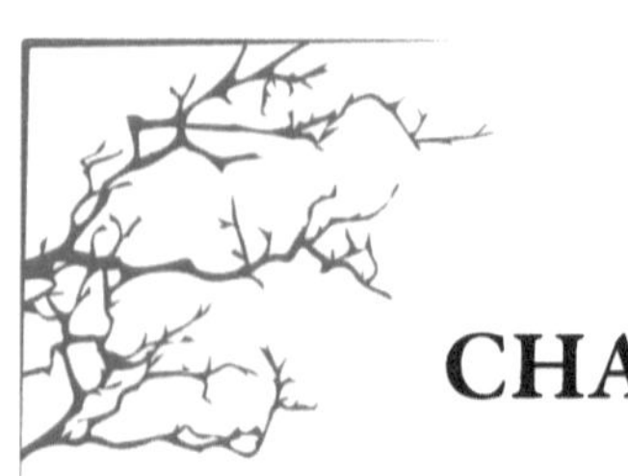

CHAPTER 14

HER EYES SPRANG OPEN as Cara whipped around on the trail. A slice of tomato flew out of the sandwich flopping open in her hand and torpedoed through the trees.

Harrison held up his hands. "Easy, love. I didn't mean to startle you."

Her pulse skipped a few beats before leveling out. "You scared the crap out of me. And I'm not your love."

"Right." Harrison forced his voice into an American accent. "Sorry . . . Cara . . . Didn't mean to scare the crap out of you."

She squinted at him and then snorted. She kicked at a pinecone on the path, sending it skittering into the bushes. "It's not your fault. I didn't know I was so jumpy. Sorry. I was just trying to be alone for a bit."

"Fancy that. Me too. We can be alone together." He took a few steps closer and gestured for her to go ahead down the path.

Again, her feet found a direction before her brain kicked in. They walked in single file. Alone. Together. She smirked.

"So you're not in danger?"

Her head whipped up at the gruff voice.

Bear. Bear!

Her brain short-circuited. A large black bear stood to one side of the path, a low growl rumbling from its throat. Shock rippled through her body, electrifying her nerves as adrenaline

158

dumped into her system. Her heart restarted when the familiar green gleam crossed its eyes. The voice had been inside her head. This must be the same bear from the council meeting.

"Did you just growl?" Harrison asked behind her.

She blinked at the bear standing right in front of them.

"Um, my stomach. Guess I'm hungry."

Good one. Maybe adrenaline makes you smarter.

The gruff voice spoke in her mind again. "You seemed scared. But if you're all right, I'll leave you."

She gave a tiny nod and turned back to Harrison, who was looking way too amused for her liking. The Pyx was clearly manipulating Harrison's human perception so he saw nothing unexpected.

"Anyone ever tell you your stomach growls like a bear?"

"Anyone ever tell *you* you pronounce 'grawlls' like you have rocks in your mouth?" she challenged, mocking his accent.

"Oho, so it's like that, is it?"

The bear disappeared through the forest.

"Yeah, it's like that," she returned. "Grawlls. Honestly." Well, if the bear was going to be hanging around, at least she had something to call it now. Harrison's head snapped over at the loud crack of a branch from the bear's direction.

"Did you hear that?"

"Now who's jumpy? Dead branches fall in the forest, you know."

Her legs began to shake as the double rushes of fear wore off. Spotting a familiar mossy boulder, she made her way to it. First Harrison, then the bear. Her heart could barely take it. She sat and steadied her breathing. Harrison sat beside her, apparently not about to leave her alone.

Somehow, she'd held on to her sandwich the whole time, and she took a bite so she wouldn't have to talk. Harrison let her eat in comfortable silence until she finished.

He gazed up at the branches and sighed. "Rather peaceful here, isn't it?"

Fine. She might as well talk to him. "Mm hmm. I used to come in here alone all the time. I miss it."

"Why'd you stop?"

She raised a shoulder. Not for any reasons she could tell him about, that was for sure.

"So are you and Wes—"

"Not dating. But people always assume, and we got sick of correcting everyone all the time."

Harrison chuckled. "I was going to say fighting, actually. You've not been around much lately. I think he's worried for you."

"Oh. No, we're not fighting. Wes is great. I'm just dealing with some . . . stuff."

"Ah, yes . . . stuff."

She shot him a look. "So how is archery going? Is Wes still helping you now that his arm is better?"

"It's fantastic. And yes, Wes is still helping. He's not half bad at teaching, really."

"Yeah. I had a feeling he'd be good at it."

"If you like it here in the woods, you should come hang with us at the range sometime."

"Thanks. Maybe I will."

"Did you know you're shaking?" Harrison pointed at her hand holding her drink.

She set it down against her leg and tried to force it to be still. It wasn't like she could explain an adrenaline rush from seeing a bear he hadn't been able to see.

He looked from her hand up to her face. "The, ah . . . stuff . . . Anything you care to discuss?"

She glanced at him. He didn't know about any of it. Well, that wasn't quite true. He sort of knew about Lydia. But the story of Rhys's drunken aunt was nowhere close to the truth. He knew nothing about Pyx or Pyxsees. He certainly knew nothing about her visions or nightmares, beyond whatever he might have heard through the rumor mill. The idea of talking to someone who couldn't possibly understand, and therefore couldn't read too much into anything, seemed oddly freeing.

She shifted on the rock, turning to face him. "Have you ever learned something about someone that made you see them completely differently? Like, even if you hated them at first?"

For some reason, Harrison let out a huge, "Ha." He started to laugh. "If you only knew."

"Will you tell me? Please? I could use the distraction."

"Worried about your last exams?"

"Something like that."

"The short version, then. There was a guy at my last school. Privileged. Entitled. And I mean more so than the rest of us. Total arse. You know the type."

She laughed, reveling in the lightness it brought her after so long. Talking to Harrison was allowing her to let go.

"I do, yeah. You're sleeping in his old bed," she answered, thinking of Nate from her freshman year. He'd been expelled, and now poor, unfortunate Harrison had the joy of living with his old roommate, who was nearly as bad.

"Right. Well, I learned something about this bloke, something private. He thought I'd tell the school, but I would never expose something like that. It was his secret to tell, you know?"

She nodded.

"Besides, it made me see he wasn't really such a prick. His arrogance was a show. It was how he protected himself. I mean, his way was stupid, but I can still understand it."

"So what happened after you changed your mind about him? Did you become friends?"

"Hardly. He sort of got me tossed out. And here I am."

"What? That's terrible."

"Perhaps." Harrison shrugged. "Perhaps not."

They shared a long look.

His brilliant green eyes could have reminded her of the glowing green Lydia had stared back with, but they didn't. They did have an inner glow of their own, but it wasn't the cold control of the Pyx. Maybe the biggest difference stemmed from not having the veil of hatred between them that she'd had with the Pyx. Whatever it was, the lightness stayed for more than a few heartbeats.

"I think you might have the greenest eyes I've ever seen," she blurted.

His eyebrows shot up. "Do you really think you're a person who gets to comment about crazy eye color?" He stood up from the boulder and held out a hand. "Now come along, or we'll be late for this maths test."

"Math," she corrected with a laugh as she took his hand to stand up. "It's just one math here."

At the end of the path where they spilled out onto the lawn around the buildings, Harrison stopped to point. "Isn't that Jory's cat?"

Sure enough, Thomas stalked along the forest's edge. "I'm going to have to trade guard duty if you're going to romance this awful adolescent."

"What? That's not—" She started to answer Tomyx before she caught herself.

"It's not?" Harrison replied. "I could have sworn . . ."

"Oh. That cat. Yep, that's Jory's cat."

"Please. Thomas belongs to no man." Tomyx's voice lingered in her mind after the cat swished his tail and turned to go the other way.

She suppressed another laugh. He always had to have the last word, didn't he? But he'd been there. Even when she'd thought she was going off to be alone, she wasn't.

HARRISON CAUGHT UP to her on the way out of their exam. "That went well. I'm quite sure I got all the maths right." He winked and nudged her with his elbow.

A little scoff came easily again. They stepped out of the building to a sky that had cleared since lunch, and both screened their eyes.

"So, one more, then." Harrison spotted Liv emerging from the building behind them, having completed her biology exam. He hooked his arm through Cara's and held the other one out for Liv. "*Français. Avec la belle* Liv."

He grinned at her and puffed out his chest to stride off to their French exam with Liv on one arm and Cara on the other. Liv gave her a *"What the heck is going on?"* look behind his head, but Cara only responded by raising her eyebrows while a smile spread across her face. That earned another surprised look from Liv.

At the end of the hour, Cara heaved a sigh of relief. She'd made it through the long day without any unwelcome interruptions since the one in the middle of the night. She barely reached the hallway before Liv caught up to her with Jory a few steps behind.

"Glad that's over," Jory said. "What did you put for the translation on question four?"

Cara started to answer, but Liv's elbow in her ribs cut her short. She nodded toward Harrison, who waved a friendly goodbye as they went their separate ways outside.

Liv grabbed her arm and glued herself to Cara's side. "Since when are you two thick as thieves?"

"Uh, since lunch, I guess?"

"Are you switching Robin Hoods on me?"

"What are you talking about, Liv?"

"You know . . . If you're not gonna date Wes anytime soon, you could still date a dreamy archer." Liv's eyes traveled to Harrison, who passed a group of juniors down the hill, which Cara couldn't help noticing included Rhys.

"Excuse me?" Jory cut in on the conversation.

"Don't worry. No one's dreamier than you, babe. But you're taken." Liv kissed the air in his direction.

Cara looked away from Rhys, whose face had turned up the hill at them after he'd watched Harrison breeze by. She focused on Jory and laughed. "Are you actually blushing, Sunshine?"

Wow. She'd forgotten how good it felt to joke around with her friends. And anything to escape having to answer Liv about dating anyone, when her brother . . .

Nope. Not going there.

Maybe she should consider Liv's suggestion. Hadn't she been thinking she should move on? How long could a girl keep crushing on the same guy, anyway? Being around Harrison did feel easy. There was no pressure there, no history. She didn't get the sideways looks her friends kept giving her, or the tension she kept avoiding around Rhys. Sure, there were no butterflies and blushes around Harrison, and the scary giddy feeling was missing, but maybe that was how it was supposed to be. Easy. Simple. Just nice.

"Well, if you do want to play Maid Marion, you better get your hooks in him soon. You should see the girls lining up to flirt with him at the Treehouse every night. Which you would, if you ever came with us anymore."

"Oh. Does he flirt back?"

"Shamelessly. But not with anyone in particular that I've seen. It's more like he's amused. He reminds me of Rhys in a way." She laughed at the incredulous look on Cara's face. "I know what you're thinking. My brother's so boring and serious now, but I swear he used to be way more fun. He was like Harrison, joking around but not really letting anyone in. Downside of coming from a family like ours—not knowing who actually likes you and who just likes your name and money. Until Emma, he never let anyone get too close. It's hard for him to trust people but he used to hide it better—more of a good times vibe, you know?" Liv hid her feelings in a little shrug, and then dropped Cara's arm and grabbed Jory's hand instead.

Cara let her feet drag and fell behind, the hollowness threatening to creep back in. She stuffed back the thoughts of Rhys and the awful things that had made him withdraw from most people, with only a few exceptions. If she wanted to hang out with Harrison more, then the last thing she needed was another Emma situation. She'd avoided the graceful senior as much as she could. But team practices were an exercise in positioning so she always had someone between them. So far, Emma hadn't said anything about the dance or the gala photo, or about where Rhys had vanished to that night. But she kept trying to catch Cara's eye—always with a look Cara couldn't interpret.

Once, she had been sure Emma was eyeing the seat next to her on the team bus. She'd had to make a big show of calling out to Kaylee, who was still a long way down the aisle, to give Emma the hint that the seat was spoken for. Ever since then, she'd been careful to board the bus last when they traveled to a race.

But if she dated someone else, all those suspicions would go away. She could breathe easier around Emma again, and maybe eventually act normal around Rhys too. Her cheek twitched as a little guilt gnawed at her. Would that be fair to Harrison? He was definitely attractive, and she enjoyed his company. Could she make herself like him enough to get past the way she felt about Rhys?

Stepping into the cool stables, she inhaled the sweet smell of hay. She had the whole break to think it over. She didn't need to decide anything now. That way, she could hold on to this light feeling for a little longer. There was no need to fall right back into the numb darkness.

Liv and Jory's voices floated down the aisle past the horse stalls, talking and laughing together in the tack room while Liv gathered her gear to saddle Charlie. Cara stopped in before continuing down to the kennels.

"I never asked. Are you staying out at the manor, Liv, or going into the city for the break?"

"We're going to the house in town. Dad has to work next week, and he didn't want me and Rhys staying on our own. Especially when he thought Jory was staying at school." Liv gave him a look and giggled.

"I thought you were going home for the break, Jor."

"I am," he replied, returning Liv's look.

"Jeez, guys, get a room. Oh. Ack. Never mind. Forget I said that." She'd forgotten Jory basically had a house to himself with only his grandmother around. She turned to go.

"No, wait." Liv turned serious and came toward her. "I wanted to ask you something before you leave. If I pick you up, would you go somewhere with me next week?"

"Where?"

"I'll, uh—I'll tell you when we get there." Liv's pale-blue eyes pleaded with her.

"Yeah. Of course, Liv. Whatever you need."

"Good." Liv clapped her hands, and the serious mood lifted. "I'll text you the deets."

A quick look to Jory found no answers. He only raised a shoulder to say he had no idea either, and Cara left, mystified.

At the kennels, Jenner's tail wagged in greeting, and he jumped on her when she opened the door.

"Hi, buddy. Miss me?" She rubbed the fur on his shoulders.

"You seem to be feeling better than in quite some time," Jenyx said. "Jenner senses it too. Did something happen?"

"Not really." She picked up his dish and carried it to the sink to wash it out. "I had a nice conversation with someone. That's all."

"Wonderful. I am pleased to hear you found someone else with whom you feel comfortable."

"Tomyx came down here and talked to you, didn't he?"

"He did mention you'd been in the woods. But if it helped to talk, then perhaps you would consider a few more people. Or at least one while you are at home."

She was sure Tomyx mentioned more than the mere fact she'd been in the woods. But Jenyx was right. "Assuming you don't suddenly want me to tell my mom all about you, I'm guessing you mean my uncle."

"Indeed. He is planning to visit, is he not?"

"Yep. And yeah, you're probably right. I should talk to him."

She set the clean dish back in the kennel and closed the door behind them. She'd already been thinking about this. The idea of telling her uncle everything that had been going on was daunting. But if anyone would be able to help her, it was probably him.

Her dad was the only other Pyxsee she knew of with eyes the same intensity as hers, and since she couldn't talk to him, talking to his brother seemed like a good place to start. If the Pyx in the porcupine was right, then her dad must have had some sort of enhanced ability too. Plus, Josh knew lots of other Pyxsees from his travels around the world. Maybe he'd learned more since she'd confided in him about her empathic ability last summer. He hadn't said any more about it at Christmas when he'd visited, but he could have found out something since then. It probably wasn't the type of thing he'd text her about, and they hadn't spoken on the phone in a while.

The only thing she wouldn't tell him was the thing she hadn't told anyone. Not even Jenyx. She wouldn't say anything about the Pyx bringing up her dad. Although she didn't know what he'd meant by, "Maybe if daddy dearest had stuck around, you'd have more of a clue," the words still echoed through her mind daily. What had he been referring to? Or had he only said it to torture her? Until she knew more, she wouldn't hurt her uncle with those words the way they were hurting her.

CHAPTER 15

JOSH SCOOPED HER INTO his arms for a crushing hug the way he'd always done ever since she was a little kid. "How are you, Care Bear?"

When he set her down, instead of answering, she stuck out her tongue like that little kid would have done. He was still the only one who got away with that particular nickname, among a never-ending string of others.

"Uh huh. That's what I thought." He looked her over and winced at the new scars on her knees. He'd heard about her so-called fall at school and probably figured there was more to the story. There always was lately.

"I'm glad you're here, Uncle Josh."

His eyes darted to Jenner, then back to her face. Yeah, the observant Pyxsee thing could be handy. It didn't take more than a note in her voice or a flick of her eyes toward Jenner for him to know there was something more she wanted to say but couldn't in front of her mom.

"Me too, Carageen. I've been pining for a forest hike with you. Get it? Pine-ing?"

She groaned. "Please, stop. If you promise no puns, I'll go hiking with you."

"No promises." He winked at her.

The following day, they drove out to their favorite trail in the Tillamook State Forest, about two-thirds of the way between Portland and Scovell Academy. Jenner jumped from the backseat and began to sniff all around the area. Cara tried to sense anything from nearby Pyx, but she couldn't. So far, the outlaws hadn't been back, and there was no reason to think they would find her here.

She'd been chewing the inside of her lip for most of the drive while her uncle caught her up on some of what he'd been doing lately. None of this conversation was going to be fun or easy. Her uncle was going to be so mad and disappointed when he heard what she'd done. The idea of it was enough to make her throat constrict. What would he say when she told him she'd confronted the Pyx in Lydia again after he'd pleaded with her to be careful following the attack in Portland? It was bad enough Wes had gotten hurt that time. And look at the end result when she hadn't listened. The Pyx was gone. He was out there, free to attack any number of other innocent people now.

The car doors slammed closed, and the smell of pine filled her nostrils.

"How's Wes doing?" Josh asked as if he'd been reading her mind. "Is his arm better?"

Enough self-pity. She'd tell him and take the consequences. "Yeah. Wes is good. It's basically healed. He's still doing physio and working on regaining his strength, but it looks like he won't have any lasting effects. Just a scar."

"A couple manly scars never hurt anyone, right?"

She scoffed. "I guess."

"And Jory?"

"Jory's fine. He and Liv are all official now." She smiled down at her shoes. "They're kind of adorable together, actually."

"Oh? And you're . . ."

"Also fine, yes."

No way was he getting away with throwing in a question about her love life all casually like that. Besides, it was non-existent. He took the hint and moved on when she started up the trail.

"You'll have to invite them over for dinner one night this week so I can see them while I'm here."

"Definitely." She needed to apologize to Wes for being so distant lately, as Harrison had reminded her. But she didn't need to give it any more thought right now. She breathed the fresh air and tried to prepare herself.

"Your mom was telling me about Lydia last night. You didn't exactly do justice to the details in your messages about it. I know she was found at Whalton manor—uncomfortably close to you at Scovell. And I know you're friends with Olivia Whalton, not to mention the stuff about the rest of that family you kids were asking me last year. I'm still not sure how you got yourself all tangled up with them. But I'm guessing it's not as much of a coincidence that Lydia was found there as I want it to be, is it?" He paused when she shook her head. "I had no idea of the terrible condition Lydia had been found in. It sounds awful. Is that what this is about?"

She nodded. He waited for her to elaborate, but she took a moment to look around at the forest. Clear blue sky opened above the trail and lit all the spaces between the trees. No anger pressed in on her, and she took heart from the airy feel all around. Talking to Harrison had felt freeing. Joking with Jory and Liv again had felt normal. She'd always been able to trust her uncle. Since learning she was a Pyxsee, and discovering he was too, he was the only adult she *could* talk to about this stuff. She took a deep breath.

"She wasn't found at Whalton manor. I mean, officially she was. But a bunch of stuff happened before that."

How far back should she go? Was *she* even sure when everything had started? She'd definitely been feeling the hostile Pyx around the school since the beginning of January, but did it go back further? It was so hard to separate her feelings from theirs.

"Last summer, I told you about the empath stuff I was starting to have with Pyx, remember?"

"Of course I do. I've been asking around but haven't found any other empaths among any Pyxsees I know, or any they know of."

"And do any of them have eyes like me and my dad?"

Josh stopped walking. "Is that what causes it?"

Jenner turned back to look at them from ahead on the trail, and the green gleam crossed his eyes. "It does appear that those Pyxsees with pure-gold eyes are the ones who have additional abilities. Since we have begun asking around, we have learned of others in the past; however, the trait is rare enough that this was not well known. It is consistent with what Cara learned."

"What Cara learned? What did Cara learn?" Josh turned to stare at her.

"Let me start at the beginning." They carried on along the path, and she told him about the hostile feelings and the council and how she'd gone to talk to the elders afterward. "I was tired of the secrets and not being in control. I kept snapping at my friends for no reason. I wanted answers."

"And she felt we were letting her down," Jenyx added.

She considered denying it, but there was no point. Instead, she continued and told Josh what the Pyx in the porcupine had said about golden Pyxsees with extra abilities, and how Lydia had attacked as they left. She explained how they had played it safe after that first encounter with Lydia. "I was never alone and never went near the woods, but they were always around. I basically got used to feeling angry all the time. Then I screwed up."

She stared at her feet. Her uncle waited. The only sounds came from their boots crunching on little rocks along the path, and small rustlings in the undergrowth.

"I left a school dance by myself—doesn't matter why. I thought I could run back to the dorms fast enough that nothing would happen, but Lydia found me."

She glossed over the fight without going into detail on how close she'd come to dying, and only said they'd managed to knock her out and take her over to the mansion. Josh made sounds as if to interrupt several times, but in the end, he only placed a hand on her shoulder and let her keep talking.

"We had the Pyx trapped. But all I could think about was how mad I felt all the time and how evil this Pyx was and how much Lydia had already been through. It's my fault he escaped. If I had listened to Wes and Rhys . . ." Her voice cracked as the regret boiled up and broke over her.

"Hey," Josh murmured. He stopped her and turned her toward him. "Hey, it's okay. You didn't do anything wrong, Cara. All that matters is you're all right. Your friends are all fine, and

Lydia is back too. Even if the Pyx escaped, you saved her. You're basically a hero."

She burst into tears, and he pulled her close. It was all wrong. Shaking her head, she pulled back from the hug.

"No. You don't understand. The way he escaped—I thought I could catch him . . . But, I . . ." She was wrong. She couldn't tell him.

Jenyx took over. "He used Cara's mind to escape."

Josh's whole body jerked. No words came out of his open mouth. He stared, dumbfounded, until she nodded her confirmation.

"Obviously, I didn't fall at school. I'm sure you guessed that already. Most of the injuries I had were from those few minutes when I wasn't myself. I woke up after it was over, and the guys had to tell me what happened." She sniffed. Now he knew.

"You went in to talk to her alone? You forced her to leave Lydia?"

See? What did you expect, Cara? Of course he's mad.

She nodded miserably and waited for him to yell at her, or at least give her a stern lecture about not being so rash and irresponsible.

When he spoke, his voice was so tight, she couldn't look at him. She studied the ground.

"I'm so—"

Angry? Disappointed?

"Proud of you."

Her head snapped up.

His eyes wavered behind bright moisture. "Oh, Cara, I'm sorry this happened to you, but you were so brave. You couldn't let injustice like that stand, and you did something about it and saved Lydia. I'm terrified at how much danger it put you in, but, kiddo . . . Your dad would have been proud of you too. Jordan always was big on standing up for others."

Tears streaked down her cheeks, and she missed the soft words he muttered to himself. She buried her face in her hands, and he wrapped his arms around her again. They stood in silence for several minutes. Eventually, she straightened and took a long breath.

"I'm glad you're not mad, but there's more."

Josh put a hand to his heart. "I don't think I can take any more." His eyes twinkled, and she could tell he was trying to make her feel better. The trouble was, as guilty as she felt about the night at the mansion, the way things had gone since then were worse.

"I don't know if it's a Pyxsee thing or an empath thing or a me thing . . . but ever since that night, I get these visions of the Pyx's past. I get glimpses of the lives of every pyxis he's ever had. Usually the moments of their deaths or some big trauma." She started to walk so she didn't have to look at the horror dawning on her uncle's face. "I'm dealing with it. I wish it would stop, but it won't. I just have to learn how to shut off the emotions it leaves me with all the time." And ignore the constant worry that the Pyx had done something to her brain to make this happen, and the fear that she was permanently damaged now.

"You're dealing with it? Are you serious? How could you not have told me this before today?"

"It didn't really feel like a phone call type of thing. And I—I don't know how to explain how it makes me feel."

"Dying over and over again? Yeah, I imagine that's a little hard to describe."

"Not that. I mean, yes, that part sucks. But as much as I hated the Pyx before, and still do—poor Lydia, and all those other people . . . " She swallowed. She hadn't voiced this part yet to anyone. "I feel bad for him too," she whispered. "He's lost so much, and I'm starting to understand why he'd hate humans for parts of it. In some ways, I get why he wants to wipe us out. Sometimes, after a vision, I feel that way too." What if she *was* damaged? Would she turn out like him, twisted and bitter, full of plans for retribution?

"But all Pyx have lost like that. Jenyx can tell you. They're not all running around hellbent on destroying us."

"Your uncle is right, child. We accept this as a part of our lives. Immortality comes with terrible burdens, but it is our choice how to respond. It is not our way to seek revenge or justice. Not for most of us."

"Exactly," Josh agreed.

"I know. I know. It's stupid. I can't sympathize with him. He's evil." The remains of her breakfast soured. Sympathizing with the creature who'd left her with these thoughts, and whose cold voice still haunted her—it was disgusting. She was repulsive.

"It's not stupid at all." Josh took her by the shoulders and looked her in the eye. "It's a mark of your strength that you're able to see why this Pyx might be making these choices. That empathy, natural or enhanced or whatever, that's what you need to fight back. Most wars worth fighting are won by influence, not by confrontation. Fear mongering and violence, those are for the weak. You? You're strong. Always have been. Just look at what you've dealt with already."

She shrugged.

"No, Cara. I need you to hear me. Understanding an enemy's motivations does not make you the same as them. You get to make your own choices too. You're more powerful than you give yourself credit for." He studied her. "Got it?"

She tried for a small smile. "Got it."

If only it were that easy.

He let go of her shoulders and turned to continue along their hike. Before he could make it more than a few steps, he froze. "Quick, grab the bear spray, side pocket of my pack."

Cara whirled around and almost laughed. "It's okay. Hi, Grawllyx. How did you know where I was?"

"Let's say a little birdie told me you'd be here." The black bear lumbered out from the trees. "Sorry, I tried to stay out of sight so I didn't scare anyone this time."

"This time?" Josh asked. "Grawllyx?"

Jenner looked at her too.

"What? I named a bear. It happens." She walked right past Grawlls, down the path, leaving Josh and Jenner to sort it out for themselves.

SHE AND JOSH TALKED more in the car on the way back, and Cara began to feel a little better. It wasn't much, but she did have some choices. She would start by choosing to let her friends back in and trying to enjoy herself sometimes. That was her mindset when her phone chimed.

The message was from Liv, and whatever Liv wanted her to do, she was in. She replied immediately.

We'll pick you up on Monday. 1 p.m.

Sounds good.

Then she messaged Wes and Jory to extend an invitation to dinner one night to see her uncle. She'd invite Liv, too, when she saw her.

The fact that Liv had said "we" escaped her until the maroon van pulled up to her curb on Monday, and she whipped out her phone to check again.

Crap. How did you miss that?

She'd made the choice to stop avoiding her friends, even if they still looked at her like a ticking time bomb, but she hadn't considered who else she might stop avoiding yet. Wes, Jory, and Liv were enough of a start, weren't they? Did she have to be thrown in the deep end with Rhys right away too?

Liv's auburn hair bounced as she waved from the front seat. Cara opened the back door, trying to decide how much of a traitor Liv really was. Jory beamed at her from the far side. Okay. Better. At least this was some sort of group excursion.

"Cara, tell my brother he needs a new car. I've been trying to tell him forever, and he won't listen," Liv said as they left Cara's block.

"Why?"

"Look at this thing. It's an embarrassment. It's so . . . old."

Cara looked around the interior. The first time she'd been inside, she'd sat in the front seat while they drove all the way from the city to the mansion to research a cure for Liv. She held weirdly fond memories of that sweltering day in spite of the task they'd been working on. The carpet at her feet was where Lydia's unconscious body had lain more recently. But as her uncle had said, that night had ended with them saving Lydia too, even if it was tainted by other events. She could choose to focus on the positive.

"See? Cara thinks it's hideous too." Liv interpreted her silence.

"I didn't say that. I don't know why we need new things all the time. This van"—she searched for the right words—"runs."

Liv looked scandalized until Rhys burst out laughing.

Hiding a little grin, Cara asked, "Why don't you buy a car, Liv? Wouldn't that be easier?"

Rhys spoke for the first time. "That's what I said. Cara gets it."

Liv made a face at her brother. "I prefer being chauffeured. Besides, I'll look great riding in my boyfriend's new Jaguar."

Cara turned to Jory. "Does that mean you finally decided what your parents are getting you for your birthday, Sunshine? It was two months ago after all."

"Not yet. I'm not in a rush. I'm narrowing down the list," Jory replied with a grin.

She glanced around and wanted to ask where they were going. Something about the vibe in the front seats made her bite her tongue. Liv had said she'd tell her when they got there, after all.

They pulled into a parking lot ten minutes later.

ROSE RIVER CARE CENTER

Cara stared at the sign in confusion.

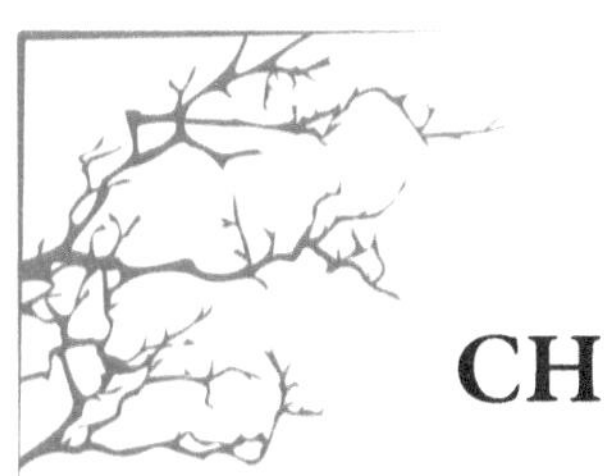

CHAPTER 16

RHYS TURNED OFF THE engine and handed the key over to Liv, who made no move to get out. Without a word, he pulled on a baseball cap and climbed out of the driver's seat. His shoulders hunched forward as he hustled to the main entrance and disappeared.

Liv turned around in the front seat to face them with a pained expression on her face. Jory was looking as serious as the first time he'd laid eyes on Liv in her hospital bed. Instead of freezing this time, he leaned forward to take Liv's hand. The tender look they shared carved a hole in Cara's heart, and the pieces clicked into place. Jory had figured it out first, but now she knew why they were here.

Her mouth wouldn't form the words, so she waited for Liv to speak.

"You guys know our family is private. We try to keep our personal lives out of the media so the focus stays on the Whalton foundation and the charities, so we don't tell anyone this. We try not to be seen or recognized outside of here. But I wanted you guys to meet my mom, and Rhys agreed."

Cara forced out a breath past her sluggish heart.

"I'm sorry I didn't tell you this was what we were doing. It's just . . . hard to talk about." Liv stared at her hand still clasped in

Jory's. "She's not herself anymore. But she's still our mom, even if she doesn't remember us."

One hand covered Cara's mouth, but she reached out to Liv's shoulder with the other. Tears welled in the corners of her eyes. After a few more moments of silence, she lowered her hand.

"Liv, that's awful. She doesn't remember you?"

"No. She got worse while I was in the hospital. Before, she used to have some good days when she could remember things. But not anymore. That's why Rhys went in first. He's gone to make sure she's okay today and to tell her who we are again. She usually remembers what we tell her for a while. But it's brand new again the next time we visit. She's more confused in the mornings and evenings, which is why we're here now."

Cara couldn't think of anything to say that wouldn't sound like pity. And Liv didn't need her pity.

Jory took a big breath. "Well, I'm excited to meet her. I can't believe you're introducing me to your mom and you didn't tell me. Do I look okay?"

The girls stared at him until they both started to laugh. This was Jory, after all. He always looked good.

"You're perfect," Liv answered. "Plus, she won't remember you after this, anyway, so there's no pressure. Luckiest boyfriend ever, right?"

They climbed out of the van after Liv, who tucked her hair into a scarf and added big sunglasses to her movie star look. Cara walked beside her.

"Thank you for bringing me here. It means a lot."

"Of course."

"Why, though? I get why you'd want Jory to meet your mom, but why me?"

"You're my best friend, silly. I wanted to tell you guys before, but couldn't really figure out how to bring it up. Honestly, I thought Rhys might object, but he agreed way easier than I expected."

A flutter hit Cara's chest, but as hard as it was not to read anything into that, she made herself move on. "I'm sorry I've been a crappy friend lately. You keep coming to listen to me, but I haven't been there for you."

"Forget it. You're here now." Liv bumped her hip into Cara's and shot her a genuine smile as they reached the entrance.

A blast of warm air hit her as they entered the double doors, and she was transported. Flames raged all around her as the timber-dry forest of her vision crackled and burned. Terrified doe eyes searched for an escape while her hooves pounded the earth. She bounded through the trees until a blaze cut off the only opening.

Cara froze, determined not to let the Pyx's memory coursing through her mind affect her in the real world. It would pass. She just had to breathe. In the forest fire, smoke choked her lungs, and she fell to the ground. The only thing Cara truly felt was the terrible realization that her life was over even though the physical pain never came when the flames took the poor deer. Suddenly looking down from above, she mourned its loss as she flapped her brand-new wings and fled the heat waves of the fire in a new pyxis.

She took a sharp breath, and the lobby of the care center reappeared around her, along with Jory and Liv. They'd recognized her momentary freeze, and Jory covered by stopping to tie his shoe as her friends had done so many times over the last couple months. At the change in her breathing, he stood up.

"You good?" he whispered.

She nodded. She didn't need to take on the emotions lingering from the vision. It was about choices, like her uncle had said. Right now, she was choosing to be strong and support Liv. She squared her shoulders. Some sadness lingered, but it made sense given everything Liv had shared and the reason they were here. She would let herself feel some of it, but this was about her own life, not millions of other creatures' past lives she couldn't do anything about.

"I'm sorry, Liv," she said. "I'm here. I promise."

"No apologies today. We can be here for each other."

Liv squeezed her hand and then let go to greet the staff at the front desk. After stopping to wait for the door to be buzzed open, she led Jory and Cara down a corridor. Plush carpet padded their footsteps, and sleek lighting showed off expensive-looking wallpaper in modern geometric forms. Wooden doors were numbered like fancy apartments. This place screamed attention to detail and exclusivity. No wonder the Whaltons had chosen it when privacy was so important.

The door to number twelve stood open, and Rhys's voice floated out to the hall, causing another pang in Cara's chest. She couldn't make out the words, but his tone was patient and warm. This might be harder than she'd thought. She swallowed as Liv entered first.

The woman on the couch next to Rhys looked up at the group coming in. Her dark-blonde hair matched her son's, but her oval face was an older version of Liv's. Cara had seen a picture of her in Liv's room last year, but Elizabeth Whalton had aged more than the dozen or so years that had passed since that photo had been taken. Grey hair streaked her temples, merging into deep wrinkles extending from the corners of her eyes. Their pale blue-grey examined the people entering her room.

"Olivia?" she asked.

She searched back and forth between Cara and Liv, and Cara hung back so Liv could make it clear to her mother who she was.

"Hi, Mom." Liv moved to the couch, and Rhys stood. He squeezed his sister's shoulder and let her slide past him. Liv took his place beside their mom.

"I'll be outside." He cast a glance at Jory and gave him a nod. Then his eyes found Cara's, and she did her best to tell whether he was happy she was here. She still hadn't figured it out when he dropped his gaze and moved past them out the door.

Her focus returned to the people inside the room as Liv introduced her and Jory.

"Cara's my best friend. You'll like her way better than some of my old friends you used to know. And Jory is my boyfriend." Liv held her mom's hand while she talked. "You won't remember, but I've told you a lot about him before."

"You have?" Jory beamed.

Liv gave his leg a playful tap. "Of course, dummy."

He sank down onto the ottoman in front of them. Cara moved to the armchair on the other side and perched on the edge.

"I've told her all about how you two saved my life. And how generally awesome you are."

"Why did your life need saving?" Elizabeth turned to her daughter. She sounded mildly curious, but she could have been asking about a neighbor or a distant relative.

"Long story," Liv answered, then turned to Cara and Jory. "I've told her about Pyx before. I figured it didn't matter since she won't remember. It's not like anyone else would believe it."

"Believe what?" Elizabeth asked.

"It doesn't matter, Mom. Basically I had a sort of infection in my brain and they cured me."

Cara frowned. "That's not exactly—" She stopped when Liv shook her head. She was right. It wasn't worth going into the details. "Technically, Rhys saved you. We helped, along with our other friend Wes."

"So you and your brother look after each other?" A few of her words slurred together, but Liv answered without hesitation.

"Oh, yeah. I lucked out in the family department. Dad too. He'll be here to have dinner with you later, I'm sure." Liv squeezed her mom's hand. Turning to them, she added, "He comes here for dinner almost every night."

Cara's heart ached for their family and all they'd been through. No matter how wealthy they were or how many charities they supported, money couldn't fix plain bad luck. Liv still thought she was lucky in spite of the situation. In spite of everything that had happened to her personally, and with her mother sitting with a bland expression like someone hearing about a stranger's life story, Liv still found a way to look on the bright side. She was choosing it. Looking at Elizabeth Whalton's face, barely affected by her daughter's story, was another stark reminder to Cara that she had to stop shutting people out. She was lucky to have that choice.

While Liv and Jory told stories from school, Cara's mind wandered over the people in her life and how she could let them in again.

Her gaze settled on Jory. Friendship with him had always been easy, no matter what awkward patches they'd gone through. Besides, he'd had Liv these last few months, so it wasn't like he'd needed her. She'd be able to patch up that friendship without much trouble, and Liv already seemed fine.

Which led her to Wes. How could she have shut him out after he'd been there for her at the mansion and so many times before? Of course, he'd been quiet lately too, even for him. But that was how he was. She knew that.

You have to fix it, Cara.

She pursed her lips with a fiery resolve. Wes was like family. No way she was losing him over a bunch of random memories and crazy emotional roller coaster rides. Not happening.

And what about Harrison? Talking to him had been really nice and might be exactly what she needed. This guy who didn't know about Pyx at all had been the person to make her remember she could feel things for herself too. Not everything had to be doom and gloom all the time. But as much as she could admire his emerald eyes and listen to his accent tell her . . . well, pretty much anything, she wasn't ready to give up on the fantasy of butterflies and blushes. She wasn't ready to settle for nice and easy.

Another one for the friend zone.

Her lips twisted with a sarcastic little scoff. She sure was getting to be good at being friends with guys. Maybe that was all she was good at. Crap. Maybe that was what she needed to be with Rhys—friends. The idea sat heavy, but if she was supposed to let people back in, she'd have to stop avoiding him.

"So if this is your boyfriend"—Elizabeth turned away from Liv to Cara—"then does that mean you're dating my son?"

The heat in her cheeks was instant. "Oh, no. No. I'm friends with Liv."

"Remember, Mom? I told you Cara was my best friend."

"Too bad. You're very pretty, and you seem nice."

Cara stared at the cluster of feet on the plush carpet while Elizabeth Whalton watched her. "Um, thank you?" She looked up to Liv to save her, but Elizabeth continued instead, and Cara met her eyes.

"He deserves a nice girl."

"Yes, he does." She answered sincerely because she meant it. A flush of pleasure ran through her that his mom, no matter how misguided, thought she could be that girl. It was a beautiful idea for a second. Then Emma came to mind, and she snapped back to reality. He already had a nice girl.

Jory cleared his throat. "I'm so happy to meet you, Mrs. Whalton. You have an amazing daughter. I'm sure she takes after you."

Liv laughed. "You don't have to suck up, babe."

"What? I'm not. It's true."

Cara shot Jory a grateful look. Count on Sunshine to charm his way through any situation. "I'll give you guys a minute," she whispered. She rose and left the room.

Rhys sat on the floor in the hallway with his back against the wall, staring at his phone with a little curve to his lips. Liv and Jory's voices floated out to them. Oh no. Had he heard his mom's awkward suggestion?

"Hey."

He looked up from the screen. "Hey."

The quiet word was all it took for her to want to be closer. She moved to the wall and slid down beside him. Knowing about his mom now, and how few others knew, meant she was one of the only people he'd be able to talk to about it, and that wasn't something she wanted to take away from him. For him, she'd find a way to be a friend, no matter how difficult.

"Thanks for letting me come today. It means a lot."

His face softened, and he turned his head to look at her. "I did say I'd tell you. I've wanted to for a while now, but there was never a good time."

"That's what Liv said too." She'd been too out of it lately. Too focused on what was going on with her. "Is it okay for me to ask what—?"

"She had a stroke. Almost three years ago now. Actually, she had a whole series of mini strokes, but we didn't know until after the big one. Dad hates himself for not recognizing the signs soon enough to get her treatment before." He drew his knees in closer, staring at his hands. "Now she has dementia from the damage."

Cara's brow wrinkled, and her lips pressed into her teeth. There was nothing she could say.

"She was outside, gardening. They think it was a few hours before our gardener found her and called the ambulance. We're lucky she survived at all, but it was too late to prevent the damage to her brain. She's regained a bunch of mobility and speech since then, although she used to talk up a storm. If you'd met her before, she'd have talked your ear off and learned your whole life story before she let you go." He paused, staring through his knees, and a lump rose in her throat. "She has okay short-term memory for now, but the cells that died affected her long-term memory. It hit the perfect spot in her brain to erase most of her life. Just really shitty luck."

"Rhys, I'm so sorry."

Without thinking, she reached out a hand and placed it on his arm for comfort. His forearm gave a slight jump under her touch, but he didn't pull away. Instead, he turned to look at her.

"It could be worse. At least I still get to talk to her."

Cara's head dropped, and she let her hand slide back to her lap, ignoring the beautiful curve of his mouth and the urge to hold him. She wasn't sure this was better. Would she rather go talk to her dad's gravestone, or have to remind him who she was every time they spoke? There were no winners here. She lifted her sleeve to dry her eyes before she could look at him again.

"I know it's a secret, but is it okay for Wes to know? You know he wouldn't tell anyone."

"He already knows."

"He does?"

"Uh huh. He actually figured it out. Most of it, anyway, and guessed at the rest. Something about finding a bunch of tiny clues in all sorts of articles last year and finally putting all the pieces together. Smart guy."

"You two talk a lot, don't you? I don't think I realized how much."

"Aside from Emma, he's probably the person I talk to most. My old friends are all graduating soon and moving on. After I missed a year and fell back a grade, most of them couldn't figure out what to say to me anymore, anyway. Emma helped keep me sane when I first got back to school in the fall, when Liv was still in the hospital and I didn't really know my new classmates yet. But Wes is the only one I can talk to about the Pyxsee stuff."

Somehow, she'd never been more jealous of Emma, or more grateful to her. She could have kicked herself. He should have been able to talk to her too, not just Wes. He clearly needed more friends, and she could have been that to him even if it wasn't anything more. Why had she let her feelings get in the way?

"Especially the last few months with everything that happened after the dance." His forearms rested on his knees in front of him with his phone dangling in his hands.

It lit up with an incoming message, but he clicked it off quickly, and she almost smiled. It was something she'd noticed about him. He never checked his phone when other people were around. Quirky, maybe, but she admired it.

"Don't you want to check that?"

"Nah. It's not important." He set the phone down on the carpet.

"I'm sorry I've been a bit . . . whatever. I should have been more like Wes. I mean, you went through this with your mom"—her arm swept an arc across the open door in front of them—"and then everything with Liv not long after. I can't even imagine what you thought when that happened. I feel terrible that I didn't know the whole story, and then I made everything worse when you had to relive it. If only I'd listened to you and Wes that night."

"Are you kidding?" His head snapped over to her, soft blond hair bouncing on his forehead above stormy eyes. "I've been trying to find a way to apologize to you since that night. I should never have handed you that beetle or let you go back in there. Seeing everything you've been going through since then . . . I hate myself for letting you get hurt."

"You've been feeling guilty?" It was so unexpected, it took Cara a moment to process his words. "I was happy you trusted me that night. But after, I thought I reminded you too much of what happened with Liv when she was attacked. I was avoiding you because you couldn't stand to be around me."

"Why I couldn't—What? No. Cara, you . . . you don't remind me of my sister. Not in any way." He almost laughed.

His eyes held hers with a warmth she had forgotten. It soothed the ache in her soul after hearing his story. When his gaze felt like the sun warming her skin, being his friend was going to be even harder than she'd thought.

CHAPTER 17

"CARAVANSARY," JOSH called up the stairs. "Got a minute?"

Cara poked her head out her bedroom door to look down the staircase at her uncle. "You're running out of nicknames."

"Never. I might have to get more creative, that's all."

She moved into the hall and placed her hands on her hips. "That's a scary thought."

"Come downstairs."

"Fine, just a sec."

Returning to her room, she checked her phone again for a new message. She'd been chatting with Wes over the last few days and was finally feeling better about things. Not that he'd been mad.

No new message. Oh well. She'd see him soon anyway when they all got together for dinner tonight. Then she could finish her apology in person.

Rich smells poured from the kitchen where her mom was using practically every special olive oil and herb, and all the gourmet cheeses she'd received from Lydia. The gift basket had arrived the day before, a week after Lydia was finally released from the hospital. Her long road to recovery had included surgery to rebreak and place pins in her arm, an extensive nutrition program to bring her weight back up, and a long course of antibiotics for the varied infections in her other injuries. Oh, and there'd been that nasty parasite. Cara shuddered. It hadn't been easy on the poor woman, and the lavish gift basket was a thank-you to Sandra for all her support throughout.

Sandra seemed happy—when she wasn't looking stunned—that Lydia was acting like her old self again. Cara struggled to keep her face neutral whenever her mom commented about how it was as if the past year and a half had never happened. For Lydia, it basically hadn't. Blissfully, she had almost no memories of it. Cara had visited her once in the hospital, when she'd been home for a track meet in the city one weekend. It was hard to say whether the odd look Lydia gave her was because the last time she remembered seeing Cara had been at her eighth-grade graduation and she'd grown up a lot since then, or whether she had some other faint memories stirring beneath the surface.

"Come on, Jenner." She pulled on a pair of socks and headed downstairs with her dog in tow to see what Josh wanted.

She found him in the kitchen.

"That sounds like a disaster," Josh was saying to Sandra.

"It really is. The environmental impact of the Brookfire Dam has been far worse than any predictions. It's a mess. The only upside—which is selfish of me to even think, let alone say—is that I might be appointed lead counsel on the class action. It's a career case."

"Don't feel bad about it, Sandy. You'll be on the right side of things." Josh picked up a bowl to move it out of the way.

"Too bad that doesn't undo the damage. Here—" Sandra held out a hand for the bowl, which she promptly put right back where it had started.

Uncle Josh's version of helping looked a lot like getting in the way. Her mom shot her a grateful look when she asked what he wanted to see her about.

"You okay here, Sandy? Anything else I can do?"

"No. I'm fine. Go. Please go." Sandra laughed and shooed them out of her space.

"I think she's excited to have people to cook for," Josh whispered as they entered the living room. "I'm glad your friends are coming over."

"Me too. It was a good idea."

"That's what I'm here for, Cara-guay."

She shook her head. "Nope. Fail. New low."

He shrugged and gestured to the couch where he picked up his laptop and opened it. She sank down beside him.

"This is what I wanted to show you."

She peered at the screen. "The local news?"

"This story specifically." He pointed to a headline beneath an article about graffiti tags of bizarre symbols popping up around the city. It was Portland, there was weird art all over, and that article looked more fun than the one he was indicating.

"Shocking turn in Oregon's mental health crisis," Cara read aloud.

"Uh huh."

"Ugh. I've been avoiding the news. I hate knowing there's another Pyx out there taking over more people again. Since he left Lydia, who knows how many innocent lives he's affected? If he's out there searching for someone to turn into a new zombie slave, he could have gone through dozens of people by now before finding one who didn't fight back. If I see specific stories on the news, I'll always wonder if it's him." She swallowed. "I know I should be glad Lydia is safe, but I can't help thinking that somewhere out there, someone else is going through the same thing now. And it's my fault."

"It's absolutely not your fault. Not at all."

Jenyx didn't need to verbalize his objections to her statements. She felt his rejection of her words deep in her throat.

"The worst part is it's not like he's the only one. As horrible as it is to say, what's one more when there are so many of them doing this right now? But we already know all this. We know the surge in suicides and mental health issues is from the outlaws jumping between humans until they find cooperative ones. So why show me?"

"That's not what this is. Watch." Josh clicked the play button on the video.

A familiar-looking blonde reporter stood outside an impressive building.

"We're here outside Locckart Center, where two more long-term patients were released from care today with what doctors are calling miraculous recoveries. Both patients had been diagnosed with undisclosed mental illnesses and had not responded to treatments so far. Both were expected to remain here"—the woman on the screen gestured over her shoulder, and the camera panned in—"under close observation and in the care of physicians. They were deemed unstable and potential threats to themselves, so their incredible recoveries and subsequent discharges are very much unexpected. These two patients bring the total long-term patients released to five for this week alone, a stunning record, according to the spokeswoman for the center."

The view switched to a woman in a power suit who stood with her shoulders square to the camera. "Locckart Center is incredibly proud of the work done by our medical and support staff every day. But days like today truly stand apart from the rest. It's a wonderful feeling to see patients recovering and able to return to their families with appropriate treatment and follow-ups. We absolutely credit our wonderful doctors and nurses for this success."

The story returned to the female reporter. "While this is one of the largest mental health facilities in the state, five so-called miraculous recoveries in the span of a week—with several more in the weeks leading up to this—have some experts questioning what Oregon is doing so right. This trend appears to extend across the city of Portland and even around the nearby counties and throughout the state. The same groups who, until recently, could be found criticizing politicians for their lack of action following the dramatic rise in mental health admissions over the past year are now left unsure of how to respond. Some skeptics are even suggesting these recoveries are part of an elaborate cover-up. Pete has that story at eleven."

The video ended, and Cara found her uncle gazing expectantly at her. She glanced toward the kitchen door, but her mom was still occupied by her dinner preparations. Even so, she kept her voice down.

"I don't get it. What does it mean?"

"Well, I don't know anything for sure, obviously. It's guesswork right now. But suicide rates have normalized too. This isn't the only story like this, either. There have been a few of them in the last several weeks now that I started looking."

"You think the Pyx aren't hopping around people's heads anymore?"

"I think it's more than that. Skeptics aside, I don't know how to explain mental health facilities emptying out. Unless . . ."

"Unless they were people who had Pyx in their minds and now don't? Is that what you're thinking?"

"It had occurred to me." Josh closed the laptop and set it on the coffee table. "After our conversation the other day—"

"About choices," Cara said.

"Yes, about choices. It got me thinking. Ever since that Pyx"—he stopped with a little shudder and put a hand on her shoulder—"ever since it used you, you've been affected by its emotions. You're still seeing these visions and then experiencing the feelings that went along with them even though the Pyx is long gone. When I came across these news stories, I wondered. What if using your mind also affected the Pyx after it left you? You're influenced by them. Why couldn't it have been influenced by you?"

She blinked and leaned back. "What? That's crazy. Right, Jenyx?"

Jenner's ears flicked back and forth. "I honestly don't know. Though we have had cases of Pyx occupying human minds before, your situation appears to be something new. Perhaps it is the nature of being a Pyxsee, but more likely it is your additional empath ability. Regardless, I could not say what is or is not possible at this point."

"You really think the few minutes in my mind was enough to make this Pyx change his whole plan? Maybe I should take both of you to that facility on the news because that's insane. I'm telling you, I got a good sense of him. He's not about to change his mind. Besides, we'd have to be talking about a bunch of them leaving the people they'd taken over if that many patients are recovering."

Josh squeezed her shoulder for reassurance before he took his hand away. "Well, I can't explain why people are suddenly flooding out of mental health hospitals. Like I said before, I think you're more powerful than you know."

She scoffed. "Sheesh. Have you been reading my old fantasy books? Because they're called fantasy for a reason. I'll get you some of the crime thrillers I'm into right now. That'll help you find your way back to the real world. News flash: It's broken."

Josh gave a sad sigh and looked like he might say something about her view of the "real world," but Sandra emerged from the kitchen. "What are you two whispering about out here?" She put a hand on her hip. "Never mind. Cara, can you set the table, please? Your friends will be here soon. Use the nice silverware."

Cara gave her uncle and Jenner one more disbelieving glance and rose. As funny as her mom's desire to impress Liv with the fancy silverware was, it was nothing compared to the ludicrous suggestion that she could have stopped the Pyx with her mind.

You're no Jedi. Honestly. What do they think this is? The Matrix?

She gave a little laugh. Clearly too many old movies with Wes on weekends. Actually, they should go back to that tradition. One more thing to add to her apology plan.

LIV TURNED HER CHARM up to a level even Jory couldn't meet and had Sandra blushing from compliments all evening.

While Cara filled Jenner's food and water dishes after dinner, she watched Liv and Jory clear the dishes from the table.

When her mom leaned against the counter to chat with Liv like old friends, Jory made his way to the couch where Cara had already found a seat. Wes and Josh stood in the corner. They'd had their heads bent together in serious discussion for the past few minutes.

"I don't know what I did to deserve Liv. She's amazing." Jory settled beside her, looking as content as she'd ever seen him.

"Of course you deserve her. You're lucky I think she's good enough to deserve you, or I'd have to rethink all that stuff I said last year about just wanting to be friends." She nudged him with her elbow.

Jory chuckled. Seeing how adorable they were together made her feel a glowing kind of happy. She could have been jealous of what they had, but somehow it never felt like that with them. They belonged together in a way that didn't make anyone else feel left out. Even when she'd been mired in the last six weeks of darkness, they'd been a little spot of warm light when she let herself appreciate it. Which hadn't been enough.

"I'm really glad Liv's with us now, and that you had her around to talk to, Jor. I'm sorry I've been so distant lately. Thanks for sticking around."

His expression turned serious when he faced her. "You know we're here for you. Whatever you need, Cares. But it's easier if you ask so we don't have to guess."

"I know. I knew you'd be okay. I did feel bad about Wes, though. He says he's not mad at me, thank goodness. Have you talked to him about the stuff that happened that night?"

"He was never mad at you. And yeah, we've talked some. But he's seemed distant lately, too. And I don't think it's just because of that night. I've been thinking about it since it started bugging me, and now I can't help feeling it's been for a lot longer than that."

"Well, you're not kids anymore. It's natural for your friendship to change a bit over time."

"I guess."

"You've also been busy with Liv. Your dynamic with Wes already shifted when I started hanging out with you two, then she came along. Now you have this serious girlfriend. That's bound to change things."

"Still. It's more like there's something he's not saying. Remember when he decided to get in better shape and took up running without telling us?"

"How could I forget? For months, I wondered what he was hiding. But it was super obvious that time. Have I really missed that much these past six weeks?" Her shoulders tightened. She tried to replay the limited conversations she'd had with Wes before this week. It wasn't like she hadn't seen him. She'd been closed off but not gone entirely. Surely she couldn't have missed something major.

"No, you haven't missed it. It's way subtler than that. Maybe it's my imagination. It just feels like he's holding his breath or something. I don't know. It sounds stupid when I say it out loud." Jory picked at a spot on his jeans.

"Jor, with everything that's been going on, the only thing I'm surprised about is that we're not all falling apart. I basically was, but the rest of you are holding it together. I'm glad Harrison came along when he did. At least Wes has had him to talk to when they're training."

Jory's lip curled back at Harrison's name. "Yeah, I guess he's not *that* bad. I'm still not sure who he thinks he's fooling with his over-the-top grin all the time. I mean, come on."

She laughed and punched him in the shoulder. "Missed you, Sunshine."

"You too, Cares." He leaned close to whisper to her. "Now, speaking of people being good enough to deserve us, what are we doing about you and the Rutabaga?"

She choked in surprise at his old root-vegetable nickname for Rhys. The first time they'd been in the same room, Rhys had knocked Jory unconscious and left him with a concussion. The next time they met, Jory had punched him in the face and nearly broken Rhys's nose. All around, it had been a rocky start until Liv came into the picture.

"I'm really *so* glad to hear you approve of Rhys now, because I was *totally* going to ask for your blessing. Seriously, though, we're not doing anything about it. I'm going to try actually being a normal person and being his friend."

"That's dumb. You guys obviously belong together. Liv's going to notice soon, too. You should probably tell her before she figures it out."

Cara scoffed. "What kind of herbs did you have in your salad, Sunshine? Are you high?"

"I don't think so." He grinned at her. "Come on. You like each other. And yes, he does happen to have my approval now that I apparently earned his. I was worried at first, with how protective he is over Liv, but he came around. He had some pretty big walls built up, but it seems like they're coming down slowly. Plus, Wes likes him, which is pretty much all I ever need to know about a person. So what's the hold up? It's like with me and Liv, and you kept pushing me to do something about it. Why aren't you doing the same thing?"

"It's not the same thing at all. And he doesn't like me. I mean, maybe he likes me fine . . . as a person. As his sister's friend or whatever. But not like that. You and Liv were totally different. Everyone could see how you looked at each other. It was obvious to the whole world how you both felt. This isn't the same. I don't know where you got that crazy idea, but I promise, no one else sees it that way, least of all him."

"Well, maybe the whole world doesn't see it, but you don't need them to. Maybe only super-observant people notice it."

"Did Wes say something? Because he told me he knew how things were." She glanced over at her friend. He caught her eye from across the room with a questioning look.

That night in the van, after they'd left Rhys at Whalton manor, hadn't Wes said Rhys walked away, not because he didn't care, but because the similarity to the attack on Liv was too difficult? Or maybe she'd filled in the blank for him. But surely that was what Wes had been about to say.

Jory's grin slipped, and his face took on a more serious expression. "Look. Wes has been quiet, but it's not like we haven't talked at all. We've talked about you and the Pyx stuff. You told him you knew how Rhys felt."

"I thought I did. Turns out I was wrong about reminding him of all the bad stuff that happened to Liv. But it doesn't mean I'm wrong about the rest." It didn't, right? Wes couldn't actually think Rhys had feelings for her. They were talking about the guy who'd told her to stay away from him—twice. Sure, they'd long since moved past that, but he still grew quiet around her all the time.

Jory shrugged. "If you say so. I wouldn't bet against Wes, though. He's not wrong often."

"Maybe his superpowers don't work when it comes to other Pyxsees. Don't forget he hated me at first."

"Misunderstandings." He waved a hand dismissively.

"Exactly. It doesn't matter, anyway. There's still Emma."

"Emma? What does Emma have to do with—?"

"You know what? Never mind. I'll talk to Wes about it later. Let's enjoy the rest of the night."

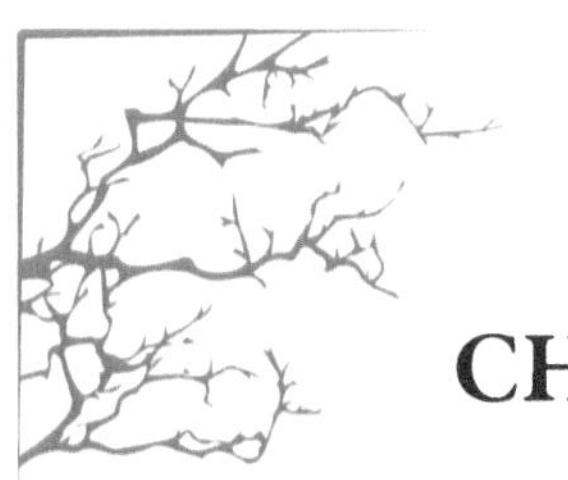

CHAPTER 18

"WATCH YOUR ANCHOR." Wes touched Harrison's hand at his jaw where it drew back the bowstring. "And soften that elbow. Did you forget everything while I was away?"

"Not everything." Harrison breathed the words through barely parted lips so he didn't mess up his position.

Wes stepped back. "Okay, you're good."

The arrow flew to the target, thudding into the backstop above and to the right of the bullseye. Cara smiled from her seat on the bench off to the side. It was better than his last shot, which had almost missed the rings altogether. She was enjoying watching Wes in this coaching role.

He stepped closer to Harrison. "Try again."

Harrison raised the bow. Cara had made the mistake of asking what kind it was when she'd first arrived at the range. How was she supposed to know? Wes's dark look at her question said he was not amused, but Harrison had answered.

"Recurve. Wes convinced me to give it a try. I do like it, but now my release is rubbish. I swear I used to be better at this with a compound bow. Don't judge, love." He'd shot her a grin while she moved to the bench.

She was glad she'd listened to his invitation to join them. After the break, she'd returned to school still firming her resolve to be a better friend to everyone. The conversations of that week were behind her, and this week had been all about reconnecting with old Cara and the people she cared about. Sitting in the woods with friends after dinner on a Friday was perfect. She focused on her connection to those old feelings she'd missed out on recently.

Unfortunately, her brain had a few other ideas. Unlike the visions, she kept revisiting a memory. It was the last thing she'd seen and felt before she hit the cobblestones and blacked out at Whalton manor. The one where she sank through murky waters, drowning. Not a pleasant memory to relive over and over.

Well, it wasn't going to be like flipping a switch. She knew that. It was going to take more work to get back in touch with herself after the negative emotions had taken over for so long. Flashes of the old anger and bitterness swept through, and she closed her eyes.

Deep breath in . . .

Counting to four, she inhaled the earthy air laced with the freshness of spring leaves.

And out.

She was careful to breathe slowly so it didn't make a noise that could distract Harrison. The black ocean's depths faded from her mind's eye, and her throat relaxed so it didn't feel so much like she was choking anymore.

Jenner looked up at her from the ground. The gleam crossed his brown eyes, and Jenyx spoke. "Is there something here? I sense Pyx in the area, but we do have several stationed around to keep an eye out. Are you picking up on something?"

She couldn't answer with Harrison close by, so she simply gave a tiny shake of her head. It was only the uncomfortable images and the memories of how it felt to choke and drown. She shook her head again, this time to dispel the lingering effects.

"I would feel better if I checked," Jenyx said. Jenner stood and trotted off through the ferns along the edge of the trees.

Cara tried to read the textbook she'd brought along to study, but the paragraphs blurred together and surged in front of her tired eyes, reminding her of waves and drowning again. Setting it down, she stared up through the branches for a while instead. Glimpses of windswept clouds lacing the early evening sky peeked between the openings before they crossed the larger clearing above. Down at ground level, there wasn't a hint of a breeze. The forest hung in thick silence around her. A little shiver trickled down her spine, and she shifted her position to put her feet flat on the ground.

"Watch your front foot," Wes told Harrison. "It keeps creeping this way."

He nudged Harrison's toe with his own to push it backward.

Harrison let him adjust it without looking down and with only a small twitch to his mouth to indicate anything had happened.

"Go ahead," Wes said, stepping back again.

This time, the arrow buried home in the center circle.

Cara let out a cheer and jumped to her feet.

"Better," was all Wes allowed before stepping over to the bench where Cara stood celebrating.

Harrison beamed in the middle of the clearing. He held his arms out to the sides in triumph. "Better? That was brilliant. I knew we had Cara along for a reason. Someone has to appreciate my sheer excellence." He moved toward her with a hand raised for a high five.

Their hands never connected.

"Down!" Wes hurtled toward them. He tackled them both to the ground in a crushing heap.

She landed awkwardly on her side with her shoulder in Harrison's chest, and barely kept the back of her head from smashing into his face.

"Ouf." The sound came out of him with a rush of breath, but he recovered quickly beneath her as soon as her weight shifted to her hip on the ground, allowing him to breathe again. "At least buy a fellow dinner first," he chuckled beside her ear.

"Sorry, sorry." She rolled off him and up to her knees where she could turn around.

His sparking gaze was already on Wes, who rose quickly from his other side to a low crouch. Wes scanned the woods, and Harrison's spark faded as he followed Wes's intense stare to the trees. A glint of metal above them came into focus. A knife still quivered, buried deep in the tree behind where she had been standing. Cara's mouth went dry.

With the danger of the situation rapidly becoming clear, her head whipped around to the tree line beyond the archery range clearing. She leaped to her feet, darted to the tree, and threw her entire body weight into yanking the blade from the bark. With difficulty, she quieted the urge to plunge it into the next set of glowing eyes she saw. Rage from the Pyx whose knife had barely missed her now flooded her empathic senses and knocked her breath out again. Intense feelings surged from multiple directions.

They were back.

"More than one, I think," she grunted, backing up toward Wes.

He bent to pick up the bow Harrison had been using and nocked an arrow to the string. Even with his arm still recovering its former strength, he held the bow with confidence and searched the opposite side of the clearing with a hunter's gaze.

Harrison started to rise.

"What's going on? What are you two doing?"

"Stay down," Wes snapped at him. Then, as though realizing how insane they must look standing over him, armed and back to back, staring at the trees, he softened his voice. "Please."

A vicious bark tore through the air ahead of a brown-and-black streak as Jenner burst from the bushes and across the clearing. He skidded to a halt at the far side with his hackles standing straight up. His growls rumbled in their ears.

Hot anger receded into icy fingers of fear. They'd come after her. Here. At school. And with apparently no regard for other people in the way. They hadn't waited to catch her alone this time.

Crashing sounds in the trees off to her left gave her another jolt. She whirled with the knife raised in front of her.

The lumbering black bear rose to his hind legs as he emerged from the trees.

She exhaled. Grawlls was still around. The huge, powerful pyxis was a welcome sight.

His gruff voice sounded in her mind. "It's all clear. The one with the knives took off as soon as he attacked, and another one hightailed it when she caught sight of the guardians."

The guardians were still around too? How many Pyx were out in the woods, looking out for her? As she had the thought, a blur of orange moved in her peripheral vision. Expecting Thomas, she blinked at the fox weaving around a log to enter the clearing. The collection of Pyx around her gave her comfort along with Grawllyx's reassurances, and she lowered the knife.

Harrison finally found his voice again. He raised a trembling arm from the ground and pointed. "Bear."

He shouldn't be able to see it. She and Wes exchanged a curious glance.

Jenner's growls had ceased, and he trotted over. Jenyx explained. "Humans can become more observant at times of heightened emotional intensity, such as fear . . . or arousal."

"Seriously, Jenyx? How can you make a moment like this embarrassing?" Cara rubbed a hand across her forehead.

"Fear, obviously," Wes said. He helped Harrison to his feet by taking hold of the hand still extended and pointing at the black bear.

"Obviously." Cara shook her head and glanced from the bear, to Jenner, to the fox beyond him. "Thanks for the help. And thank the guardians, too. And whoever else you have out there."

More forms moved in the shadows of the trees deep into the forest. How had they all known to come so quickly? Some had begun to turn and melt away again. A few, like the fox, sat quietly, as though standing guard.

"Am I seeing things?" Harrison asked, staring around the clearing. "Is someone going to explain what the bloody hell is happening?"

Cara's lips pursed together. "Hmm. What do we do now?"

Wes met her eye. "You know my vote will always be for the simplest solution."

"You think we should tell him?"

"Easier than trying to think of a lame story."

Her heart thumped at the thought of explaining the situation. Wes had that open, honest look he wore sometimes when he let his guard down. He might be right. How could they possibly explain any of this? The truth might be their only option.

"But then he'll be involved."

"He is involved. After this, they'll assume he's with us, anyway."

"*He* is standing right here, in case you forgot. Now what the devil is going on?" Harrison clasped his hands together, not quite hiding the way they trembled as he looked back and forth between them.

Wes faced him with his shoulders squared. He watched Harrison with a little tilt to his head. After another moment's consideration, he looked across to Cara. Her shoulders raised and her head nodded at the same time. What else could they do? Her situation had put another friend in danger. He needed to understand it so he could be safe. Or safer, anyway.

"Come to my room at eight," Wes said, turning back to Harrison. "Cara, you should come too. Bring Liv along. She and Jory can help explain what it's like from that perspective."

"What what's like?" Harrison's face had fallen slack, but he studied Wes with intensity in his eyes.

"Tonight. We'll explain."

"Good, let us please get out of these woods now," Jenyx said.

Cara turned around again, but Grawlls had vanished. A rustle of leaves signaled his direction, and she breathed easier knowing he was around.

As they followed the path out to the fields near the front of the school campus, several more forms moved away through the trees. Harrison had calmed down enough that he no longer noticed them, but Wes's eyes darted to the sides as often as hers did.

"Jenyx, where did they all come from?"

Harrison turned his head at the sound of her voice, his eyes searching.

Jenyx answered. "We have had friends nearby for some time now in anticipation of this possibility. You must have recognized several from the council. I will admit, more Pyx appeared tonight than I was aware were on our side."

"Really? What do you make of that?"

"I am not certain. All I know is, I thought I had found the stranger until I was suddenly aware you needed help back where I had left you. There were too many signatures in the area for me to identify friend from foe."

"Oh."

Harrison stopped as they stepped out of the woods near the football field. "Who are you talking to?"

The question had been directed at Cara, who must have seemed like she was talking to herself since he couldn't hear Jenyx answering. When he stopped, though, he turned to Wes for answers.

Wes sighed and clapped a hand to Harrison's back. "We tried to keep you away. You kept pushing your way in, and now, here we are. All I can say is . . . keep an open mind."

Harrison studied him. His eyebrows pinched together until, slowly, his shoulders relaxed. "I can do that."

Cara tried to look reassuring when he turned back to her. "Sorry. I think you might be stuck with us and our, um, interesting lives now."

Either Harrison couldn't think of a response or he'd decided to trust them and wait. They made their way across the grass toward the safety of the middle of campus. Cara cast glances to her left each time a small flash of orange appeared along the edge of the woods. The fox was tracking their movement and keeping pace with them.

She wove her hand into the fur at Jenner's neck. "So you saw them, Jenyx?"

"Not the two who escaped, no. There was a third. Another woman."

"One who didn't escape?" Wes asked.

Harrison's curiosity looked like it was causing him physical pain, but he held his tongue.

"Indeed. This woman did not attempt to attack or to escape. She turned herself in to the guardians."

"What?" Cara couldn't believe Jenyx's words. "Why would she turn herself in?"

"She has not yet said. She seems cooperative for some reason, and appears willing to release her human pyxis in exchange for a chance to speak with us. Perhaps she is another who is disillusioned with the purpose set forth by their leader."

"I really doubt it will be that simple. What did she look like? Was she as abused and broken as Lydia?"

"No. She looked to be in good health. Presumably she is a more recent host. Do not worry, child. We will make sure the woman gets the help she needs once the Pyx leaves her. She will not suffer as poor Lydia has."

"Okay. I'm glad you were there to look out for me. I don't know why I didn't sense them sooner."

She peeked over at Harrison walking beside her to see if he would react to her mentioning her extra sense. He looked as bewildered by it as he did by everything else, and it occurred to her that no part of this would be any stranger than another. It would all seem totally crazy.

In a way, she was glad. She'd enjoyed being able to talk to him because he didn't know about any of it. Now he'd learn all about it, but her extra weirdness would probably blend right in with all the rest.

He caught her looking and gave her a dull, crooked grin. "This had really better be good."

"Please do be careful what you share with him," Jenyx pleaded.

"We know." She wouldn't betray their bigger secrets, like the guardians. She wasn't even sure they'd tell Harrison about the Pyx using humans yet. Learning about their existence at all would be a big enough dose of honesty for one evening. "Where's Tomyx? I didn't see him at the clearing."

"No. I'm sure he sensed all the others congregating there, but he won't leave his charges."

"Charges?"

"Yes. He is keeping an eye on Jory and Liv to be safe. We don't expect them to be in danger, but he could still warn them if any unfamiliar Pyx come too close. Jory would pay attention if Thomas were acting strangely."

"Oh. That's good. I'm glad he's taking their safety seriously."

"Of course, child. Tomyx may not show it, but he cares very much for Jory."

Wes scratched his head, hiding a small laugh with his arm. Cara had often sensed that from Tomyx, but Jenyx was right.

He definitely didn't show it. Even if the Pyx didn't expect Jory and Liv to be in any danger, she was happy to know he was there for them. But if the Pyxsees were the ones who might be threatened by the Pyx returning to the area, there were two more who needed protection.

"Who's watching Rhys?"

"Ryx is ensuring his safety."

Cara groaned. Poor Rhys. She spent a few moments contemplating whether she'd rather get stabbed than put up with Ryx hanging around her. She glanced down at her fist where white knuckles clenched the knife from the attack. When she imagined the sharp edge dripping with blood, she shuddered. She wouldn't rather see Rhys injured. A sudden appreciation bloomed for the rude Pyx in the raven. If he kept Rhys safe, he'd seriously climb the ranks in her esteem.

"What about Wes when he's not with me?"

"That would be me." The fox was still weaving between trees along the edge of the forest, close enough to them to hear their conversation with its sensitive hearing.

She turned to see if Wes had known.

"Oh, yeah. She's been around."

Wes commented so casually she almost thought he didn't care. But the tiny crinkle beside his eye gave him away. He liked having her around.

"You didn't tell me that."

Harrison finally couldn't hold it any longer. "Who's been around?"

"The fox you saw at the clearing," Cara answered. "She's been, um . . . nope. That's not going to make any sense until we explain everything else. Sorry."

"A fox?" Harrison looked like he might laugh. "*She* is a fox?"

Was it relief that he hadn't been seeing things? The poor guy had been through a lot in the past ten or fifteen minutes. Laughter wouldn't be the weirdest response. She should know.

"Have you named her, Wes?"

"Have I named a wild animal? No, Cara. I haven't named the fox."

"Why not? I named a bear. Actually, Harrison sort of named the bear by accident."

Wes rolled his eyes and gave Harrison a look as if to say, "*Are you sure you want to be a part of this?*"

The spark had returned to Harrison's bright emerald eyes. His smile evened out and spread across his face. "It sounds as though you've a lot to tell me. After our little roll-about in the dirt, I think I'd like a shower first." He left them at the fork in the path between the dorms and went ahead to the Lodge.

Wes watched him go. "That"—his eyes pivoted from Harrison to Cara—"is going to be complicated."

She raised an eyebrow. "I think it already was." Still smiling to herself, she turned and went into the Cedars.

CHAPTER 19

"THEY HAVE NO BODIES?" Harrison sat on the desk chair. He'd pulled it close to Wes's bed where Cara sat beside Wes while he explained.

"Right. They live in animal hosts, like a shared consciousness type of thing. A host, or a vessel for them, is a pyxis. Normally they're animals or, at least, complex life forms, but not people. The ones who attacked us are part of a group of Pyx who are breaking their laws by taking human pyxides."

They had decided to tell him about the human hosts. It only made sense when that was where the biggest threat was coming from right now. They kept other secrets for the Pyx for now, but this was about his safety.

"And there's one of these creatures in each of your animals."

Cara nodded. "Yep. Jenyx and Tomyx. They take their identifiers from their hosts."

Jenner and Thomas had found positions on the floor as far across the room from Harrison as they could. They both curled into harmless balls of fur on the floor and watched Harrison absorb what he was being told. It was as non-threatening as they could possibly look. Maybe Jenyx and Tomyx thought it would be more reassuring this way.

"And that's why you named the bear. So you'd have something to call this . . . this Pyx who lives inside him." Harrison gave a feeble attempt at a smile.

All things considered, he was taking it like a champ. Certainly better than she'd done, and she'd been able to see and hear them. Come to think of it, that might have made things worse.

"So a Pyx is one of these creatures with no corporeal form, only energy. A pyxis is the vessel they live in, usually an animal. And a Pyxsee is a human with this gene that gives you gold eye color and lets you communicate with them. Have I got that straight?"

"Yep. Nailed it. Oh, and Pyx are immortal." That was still the part she had the hardest time wrapping her head around, although it was being driven home by all the memories now plaguing her with visions. She still found it weird.

Not Harrison. "Well, clearly. That makes sense if they have no bodies. Nothing to age and decay, is there?"

Smarty pants.

"Fine, Mr. Expert on the Thing You Just Learned About. Any other questions?"

"Only about a million. How old are these two? How many are there? How do they reproduce? They may be immortal, but they must have evolved and expanded their population over time. Can they be killed?"

"Whoa. One step at a time. They don't tell us everything either." Jory still didn't look impressed at initiating Harrison into their bizarre and exclusive little club.

Cara leaned forward, thinking. "They can be killed but don't ask us how. We don't know." She ignored the twinge of discomfort from the other side of the room. "They're hundreds of millions of years old, so I doubt the exact number matters much, and there are plenty of them. Again, exact numbers probably aren't important. And, you know, I don't think we've ever asked how new Pyx are born."

"I have," Wes said. "Tomyx wouldn't say."

Harrison steepled his fingers. "Fascinating. And only the two of you can hear them?" He watched Cara and Wes, who nodded.

"And my brother," Liv added from the other bed where she sat beside Jory. "Don't worry, though. These guys are always recapping for us. We don't feel too left out or anything. You'll see."

"We try." Cara gave Liv a bright smile before focusing on Harrison again. "We also see when they're in an animal. When they take over control of the mind, even for a moment, a green gleam passes across their eyes. You won't see it. You'd only see the animal's movement."

In response, Thomas's eyes flashed and the cat nodded his head. Harrison gave a small snort while Jory glared at Thomas as if his cat had personally betrayed him by amusing the new guy.

Cara continued quickly before Jory said something he'd regret later. "The ones who are taking over humans stay in control all the time, and the people's eyes stay green to us. Like a creepy glow, though, not green like yours."

"I should hope not."

HARRISON STUCK WITH them all weekend. The days of keeping him on the fringes were well and truly over now. After all they'd told him, and their warnings about what had been going on lately, he was still there.

"You believed us so easily. Why?" Cara walked beside him along the path around campus after dinner on Sunday.

"Couldn't see why you'd spew a load of rubbish. I am aware I can be a bit pushy, but from what I've seen, your group don't seem the type for cruel jokes. It's part of why I chose your lot to befriend."

"Thanks? I guess?"

"It's a bit too unbelievable not to believe, you know? I did see those animals at the range, after all. And Wes strikes me as being rather direct. I have trouble picturing him lying, particularly for laughs."

Wes had gone to the library after they'd finished eating, and Liv and Jory had climbed the spiral staircase to the Treehouse to hang out for a while. But Harrison had looked like he wanted to talk, so Cara had asked if he wanted to walk Jenner with her. At the far end of campus, away from most of the students out enjoying the warm spring evening, they were free to talk. Jenner crisscrossed the path ahead, sniffing for unfamiliar scents, and Jenyx would be on high alert for other Pyx nearby.

Cara smiled down at the path in front of them. "No. If Wes says something, you can be sure it's the truth, at least his version of it. It's reading all the stuff he doesn't say that's trickier."

Harrison returned her smile when she looked up, and gratitude warmed her like the pleasant breeze ruffling her hair.

"I was worried it wouldn't be as easy to talk to you now that you know all this."

"Why? Shouldn't it be easier?"

She laughed. "You'd think. But I liked talking to you because you didn't know any of the craziness. For years, all I wanted was to fit in. Now I don't need to, because I have this amazing group, like you said. Meeting Wes and Jory changed my life more than learning about Pyx did." She laughed again at his disbelieving look. "No, really. It's a close race. Trust me. But they did. The thing is, I still just want to feel normal sometimes. I love hanging out with Delaney and Kaylee, or even Cassidy and those girls occasionally, but there's always this invisible barrier I can't quite get rid of. Like the veil of secrets between me and them is a physical wall and I'm on the wrong side."

"Not the wrong side, surely. Perhaps . . . well, perhaps just another side."

"Maybe. Anyway, for some reason, it didn't feel like that with you. But I worried I'd lose that now because I don't get to be normal-version Cara anymore." Her feet ground a little harder against the gravel on the path. Clouds of dust swirled ahead of the toes of her shoes. They could use some rain, which was a weird thought for this time of year in Oregon.

"True. You're upgraded-version Cara with super-spidey senses." He nudged her and winked, making her give a little scoff. "Regardless, I am perfectly happy to talk normal topics with either version of Cara anytime you like, love."

"Thanks. I'd like that." She was finding she really did want to spend more time with Harrison.

"I'm also fairly well-versed in secrets myself."

"Oh, really?" She used a joking tone, hoping he'd feel comfortable sharing more. "Maybe that's why it felt natural with you. We're on the same side of the secrets veil. So does that mean you're going to tell me why you really got kicked out of your last school?"

"I didn't lie before."

"But you haven't told the whole story."

"No." He touched a finger to his nose, looking pensive for several steps. He dropped his hand with a shrug. "I don't suppose it matters here."

"You're still keeping that awful guy's secret? Even after he got you kicked out?"

"He wasn't awful at all. Far from it, actually." His gaze sank to his feet. "Sadly, he also wasn't ready for people to know when the headmaster caught us snogging."

Cara's mouth opened. She quickly covered her surprise at his openness when Harrison looked up. "But that's—What decade is this? You can't get kicked out of school for kissing another boy. That's insane."

"Well, apparently you can when the boy in question is the headmaster's son. Especially when he denies being gay. And definitely when you admit to kissing him against his will. Then, it turns out you can be expelled for harassment."

"Was it against his will?"

"Oh no. He definitely wanted me to kiss him." His mouth quirked into a lopsided grin at the memory. "But I could see he didn't want to tell his father, so I told a teensy little lie."

"That lie wasn't so little. And your dad? Does he know? Was his job transfer the real reason you moved here?"

"Yes, my family all know what really happened. And we really did move for my father's work. Only, we had to move up the timeline a bit when I found myself needing a new school. My mum and sisters are still back in England, finishing out the year."

"I'm glad. That's probably selfish to say, because now you're in danger because of me and my friends. But I'm happy you're here. And I'm glad you're one of us now."

"Do you know what? I'm rather pleased about it myself." His emerald eyes sparkled with eagerness at the new adventures he seemed to think he'd found. She hoped neither of them would come to regret it.

They rounded the corner of the science building and started across the open space toward the dorms. Jenner lifted his nose.

"Jenyx."

The voice sounded in her mind as another Pyx called to Jenyx, and Cara glanced around for its source. A large shadow shifted at the tree line. Her sharp intake of breath caught Harrison's attention, and he followed her gaze but kept scanning past the enormous shaggy form.

"Please do not stray far, child. Let me check what Linnaeryx has to tell me, and stay here with your friend," Jenyx said. Jenner bounded to the woods.

"I don't see anything this time. But it's one of them, isn't it?" Harrison asked.

Cara could only nod, still staring open-mouthed at the guardian in the trees. The anxiety worming through her mind contributed to her racing pulse and her own shock. Jory would be so mad he'd missed it again.

You were right, Jor. That's no bear.

She stared at the outline of what had to be the source of the Bigfoot legends of the Pacific Northwest. And if Sasquatch was real, what else was out there? Her mind reeled with sudden possibilities, and images burst one after another through her memory.

Places and things she was sure she'd never seen in her life strung out like a high-speed slideshow. She couldn't focus on any of the Pyx's memories long enough to make sense of them, but there were definitely a few creatures she didn't recognize among them. Species long dead and gone before the time of humans . . . or maybe not. The world around her blinked back into view, and she released Harrison's arm. She must have reached out to him to steady herself without realizing.

He rubbed his arm after she let go. "Why can I see Jenner and Thomas but not these others? At least, not usually?"

Her mouth snapped closed, and she turned to Harrison with a start. Grabbing him had been a reflex, but she'd practically forgotten he was there after the flurry of other lives she'd flown through in a second. The question made her realize Jory would be missing it, anyway, even if he were standing here next to her.

"They can influence people's perception so you don't notice them. People tend to be unobservant and dismiss things that don't fit their preconceptions. The Pyx take advantage of that and sort of enhance it. Unless you know what to look for, or they choose to let you see them, or something like fear overrides their influence, you'll overlook them. The more of them that are together, the more power they have. Jenyx and Tomyx have no reason to hide their pyxides, but a bear in the middle of the path would cause a little more of an issue."

"But now I know there's something there, so why do I still not see it?"

"If I told you it was the bear you saw before, and pointed to where it was standing, you'd see it. But anything less than that, and you're not going to see unless you already know what you would see if you did see it. Sorry. That came out super confusing."

"So it's not a bear."

"It. Is. Not."

"Well . . . What is it?"

"I'm sorry. I can't tell you." Her brows pinched together, but the guardians were one of the things they'd agreed not to share with Harrison yet. She hoped he'd understand.

"Huh. Bit rude. I thought you trusted me."

"I do. But you said it yourself. Some secrets aren't ours to tell."

Disappointment settled on his face, but he accepted her explanation and didn't appear overly hurt by it. She grimaced. It sucked not being able to tell him everything, but he'd have to earn more trust from the Pyx before that happened. In the meantime, she'd have to live up to his trust in her.

"Thanks for telling me what really happened back in England. I won't say anything. Not if you don't want me to."

"About me being gay? Oh, I don't care. It's not a secret. It's only that . . . no one ever asks."

She chuckled. "Fair enough."

"Of course, my poor roommate may be better off left in the dark. For all his bravado and brute size, the fellow doesn't seem to be made of particularly strong stuff. He's barely over my foreignness and what he calls 'nancy boy' accent. Bit old fashioned. This might be more than he can handle. Although given his comments about Brits in general, he may already assume as much about our entire population."

"Ugh. Theo is such a caveman. You deserve a better roommate. Not that anyone else deserves to be stuck with Theo either."

"Agreed. Complete tosser, that one." When she giggled, he threw in a few more for good measure. "Total prat. Gormless twit. Manky muppet."

"Okay, you're teaching me some more of those." She'd barely stopped laughing by the time Jenner rejoined them. "What did she want?"

Jenyx's mood brought her crashing back down from the momentary high of Harrison's good humor.

"To pass along a message," Jenyx replied. "Can we go see Tomyx?"

The door to the boys' room stood open, and they walked right in. Liv sat in her usual spot on Jory's bed, but he had taken a position at his desk chair instead of at her side. They were almost always within distance of a casual touch, or an easy reach to hold hands. The reason for Jory's polite distance became apparent when Cara turned around to find Rhys straightening up from a spot against the wall. He held a drink from the Treehouse in one hand. Liv and Jory must have bumped into him there.

She couldn't stop the electric jolt to her heart at seeing him unexpectedly, but she shoved down the feelings that followed and managed to limit the heat blooming across her cheeks.

You said you'd be his friend, Cara. That's all.

"I heard what happened on Friday. I can't believe I didn't know about it." Rhys's hands gripped the bottle a little too firmly, his forearms flexing.

"Sorry. We should have told you. We had a bit of a situation." She jerked a thumb in Harrison's direction.

"That would be me. I was the situation."

Rhys looked as displeased as Jory at the notion that they'd let Harrison in on their secret. "I heard about that too."

Aside from Wes, who wasn't back from the library yet, everyone who knew what was going on was in this room. They could fill Wes in later, but she wanted to hear what Jenyx had to say. She eased the door closed with a soft click and looked up at Rhys. "Since you're here now, you should know Linnaeryx just passed a message to Jenyx." She moved to perch on the edge of Wes's tidy bed and waited for Jenyx to take over.

"The Pyx who turned herself in rather than join the attack yesterday has requested to speak with Cara. Alone."

"No way. Absolutely not." Rhys didn't wait to fill in anyone else in the room. Only he and Cara knew what Jenyx had said. "Way too dangerous."

"I agree with you," Jenyx said. "Our terms are that the guardians will be there, along with myself, Grawllyx, and a few other Pyx who will stay around the perimeter."

"I'm going too, then," Rhys added.

"No other humans. She was resolute on that point. I am sorry, but you'll have to trust us to keep Cara safe."

"Is someone going to tell us what the huge freak-out is about? Big bro?" Liv had shuffled forward on the bed and reached a hand out to her brother's elbow.

Cara broke her gaze away from the hard look in Rhys's eyes to answer. "The Pyx who surrendered wants to talk to me, but she doesn't want any other humans there. Only other Pyx."

Jory sat up straighter. "What? Well, then I'm with Rhys. That sounds way too dangerous, Cares. Please tell me you aren't considering it."

Liv nodded her agreement. Leaning back with a sigh, Cara bit the inside of her lip. They might not understand, but she had to at least consider it. The outlaw Pyx had attacked her on school grounds with Harrison and Wes right there. Who knew what they'd do next? Someone else was going to get hurt if this kept up. If this Pyx knew what the outlaws wanted with her, didn't she have to go find out? Besides, the Pyx had turned herself in. What if she'd switched sides? Maybe she only wanted to warn Cara and pass along information. It could be a good thing.

After months of fighting off the hostile feelings, not to mention the physical attacks, she needed answers above all else. How could she keep her friends safe if she didn't know what the rogue Pyx wanted with her? There were other students to consider too. How would she feel if anything happened to Delaney or Kaylee? They weren't part of this. Then there was the whole rest of the school. This was all about her. It was her responsibility.

Harrison sat down close beside her. He took her hand, looking worried.

"I think I have to," she finally answered. "The stuff in my head makes no sense. They're coming to the school now. I need to know what she has to say. I have to go."

Rhys stalked out of the room without another word. Harrison fidgeted but stayed silent. Jory asked her to reconsider one more time, but stopped when Liv crossed the room to sit on Cara's other side and pick up her other hand.

"I know you need to go. But promise us you'll be careful. If anything feels off, just leave, okay?" Liv stared at her. "Trust your instincts, or feelings, or whatever. Just trust yourself."

Cara nodded at her. She tried and failed not to let her eyes dart to the open door. Couldn't Rhys have cared a tiny bit more? Some part of her had hoped he would insist on going with her or that he'd beg her not to go. He'd left like nothing mattered. She took some reassurance from Jenyx supporting the plan. He wouldn't put her at risk if he weren't feeling confident they could keep her safe. More importantly, a little danger was worth it if it meant finding answers.

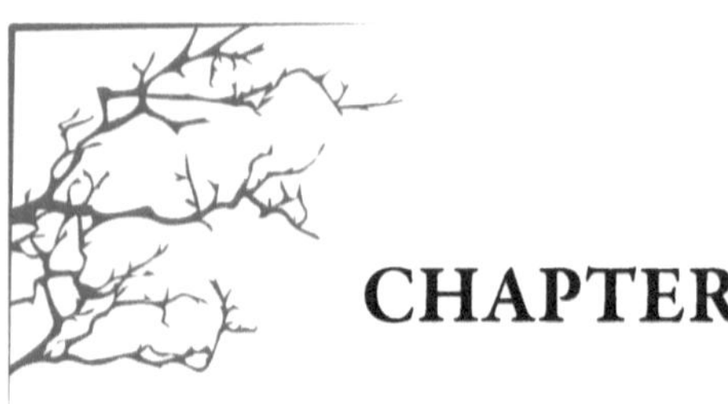

CHAPTER 20

RELIEVED TO FIND HER room empty, aside from Delaney's cat, Marcus, curled up on her pillow, Cara checked her phone. She'd missed a text from her mom.

> **Before you see it on the news . . .**
> **I got it. Lead counsel on the Brookfire Dam lawsuit.**

Cara's heart swelled with pride, and Mr. Jackson, her mom's boss, earned a warm thought for placing his trust in her. Her mom completely deserved it.

> **You'll totally kick their butts.**
> **Go Mom!**

From everything her mom had been talking about at home, the project had been a complete environmental disaster. The news had covered the massive decline in fish populations since the dam's construction, but apparently there were a ton of other issues too. It set her teeth on edge just thinking about it, and before she knew it, her sight began to blur.

When wind began to whip at her face even though she was inside her dorm room, she reached behind her for her bed. She was tired of fighting back against the visions, and no one was around, anyway. She sank to her pillow and let the vision take her.

Wind lashed the driving rain across the top of the ridge and whipped Lydia's hair across her face. The clothes she wore offered no protection from the elements, but her body—Lydia's body—felt nothing. Stretched out below her, a dam cut off the river.

The water swirling away below the obstruction was a trickle compared to the flooded reservoir behind it. She stood and watched for hours, until dark fell on the valley, as the basin filled and overflowed in the torrential rain. The vile humans thought they could control nature itself, and now their monstrosity drowned habitats and killed the innocent creatures who called this valley home. The worst part was it would all dry out again soon, and there wouldn't be enough water after the floods passed. Death and destruction would continue all because this plague on the earth had to try to control everything around them instead of existing with it. Icy resentment filled her already frozen chest.

Around her, the valley dissipated. Flashes of a thousand images flew by—city streets, shopping malls, paved lots, and people—people everywhere. She raged through them, as many as she could. Flying backward through the memories, she flitted through mind after mind with no regard to what the people did while she was there. One fell from a bridge while she jumped to another, who crashed his toxin-spewing truck into a tree. She felt worse about the damage to the tree than the man's broken limbs.

The tree's only offense had been managing to grow in this filthy place. She'd be careful not to do that again. She could find others who felt the same way. There were more like her who had lost so many pyxides lately much closer together than usual. They'd do something to fix this. They'd wage war if they had to. She apologized to the tree, and the vision melted to another scene.

Her legs rooted to the ground in her despair, and her limbs multiplied, stretching skyward, covered in rough bark. Stepping back through time again, she recalled the giant Sequoia fondly. She should have had a couple centuries in the tree to recover from the last aching loss of another pyxis before she had to endure it again. After the string of lives cut short recently, she needed the break. Then the men showed up with their brutality and bulldozers. It was more than she could take. She snapped and entered her first human mind.

The memory that followed was full of hate, not to mention violence and bloodshed as she'd used him to slaughter his shocked friends. Nothing less than they deserved. She flinched from those thoughts and slipped further back in time instead. More trees . . . hundreds of them . . . but all one. Their roots connected them, binding them and offering ongoing life even as the individual aspens died out. This clonal forest had been here for thousands of years, with thousands more in front of it. She could inhabit this rich and vital life for as long as she needed. Then the soil dried and crumbled around her. Her roots shriveled and died in the drought, and the trees failed. Leaves fell, never to be replaced. By the time she left, nothing remained but skeletons clawing at the sky. The irony of this death after the drowning of the last pyxis broke her all over again.

The last pyxis . . . She rewound further to visit that memory. The sea turtle had been one of her favorites of all time, which was saying a lot after so many millions of years. He'd had such a joyful spirit and vibrant personality. She'd loved surfing the currents with him, feeling his bliss at the freedom his world offered. She felt his confusion when the trash rode in on those same currents. Floating junk crowded his ocean and cut at his flippers when he tried to surf and swim. Then the fateful day came. Guilt crushed her lungs. She hadn't been paying attention, and she'd failed to keep him safe. The plastic bag must have looked like a jellyfish. Instead of a meal, it stuck in his throat. She used every bit of influence she had over his body, but couldn't expel it. Together, they sank to a watery grave, and she thought about staying there forever. It might not be worth living anymore.

"Cara. Wake up. Cara."

Her eyes flew open in her dorm room. Jenner had jumped onto the bed, and his wet nose bumped at her face. She gasped, and pain ripped through her lungs as they refilled.

"Cara. Oh, thank goodness. There you are." Jenyx sounded close to panic.

Wiping her face, she found it streaked with tears. Her chest hollowed. After all she'd witnessed in her mind, she wanted to rage at the world too. For a moment, she sided entirely with the Pyx who had experienced those losses, and shared his need to cleanse the earth. At the same time, she was sick at the actions he'd taken already, and sicker for having felt herself do them in the vision. It carved a hole inside her. But something else burned through her to fill the emptiness left behind. Purpose. Understanding.

No single person was responsible for the mess the world was in, and more mass destruction wasn't the answer. She could understand the choice he'd made, but it wouldn't be hers.

Choking down the emotions stuck in her throat like the plastic bag, she sat up.

She gulped air. "How long was I out?"

"It has been at least a half hour. But you stopped breathing nearly a minute ago and would not wake. It was terrifying. I did not realize these visions would be capable of affecting you so."

"Sorry. Neither did I. But after what I saw . . . I know you've been through worse than this. Even if I died."

"Do not say such things. No matter how much death we witness, all life is precious."

"I know it is. I know. But for most of us, death is inevitable and it only happens once. For you, though . . . I wouldn't want to watch it and feel it over and over like this. I don't want to when I keep seeing it from his memories. But I understand him better now. I know why he's doing this." She swung her legs to the floor and stared at her socks. Jenner jumped down from the bed and came over to rest his chin on her knee. She laid a hand on his silky soft head and sighed. "He's broken. We broke him."

"It is no excuse for his actions."

"Maybe not to us. But he thinks it's justified. He thinks he's saving the rest of the world from us."

"This Pyx . . . he is terribly misguided."

"Messoryx. His name is Messoryx." She took her hand away as Jenyx's surprise rippled through her. "At the start of the vision, I was in Lydia, and I knew. That was my name. Lydia tried to fight back for a while when she realized something was wrong. I think I—*he*—used her to kill someone. She didn't want to be used for more violence. That's when she ran into traffic. Afterward, he took stronger control, but he already had his own identity. He'd already been gathering followers. He'd been doing it for years before Lydia."

Jenner stared at her with sad eyes.

"I don't think he meant for me to see all of that. I don't know how I did or why I know all this now, but I do. It's him, Jenyx. He's their leader. He's the one who started all this."

"Are you sure?"

She nodded. By letting herself go into the vision, deeper than she'd ever been into his consciousness before, she'd seen who he was. She'd touched his pain and felt his fall into bitterness. But she'd also seen the men he'd killed when he'd snapped and ripped them apart with their own chainsaws. She swallowed the bile from his memories—from being him while he took his own identity so he'd have stronger control over that first human. Lead weights settled inside her at the way he'd overridden the man's will to fight back and used him to murder his friends. She cringed at the string of faces of the people he'd killed, injured, and ruined since then. He'd never stop.

"I'm still not sure why he's coming after me. But I do know I'm only a tiny part of his plan. I'm just something he has to deal with before he can move forward, for some reason. Then he'll be able to move on to the rest. He's going to keep recruiting. He's already found a lot of other Pyx who feel the same way and are ready to be a part of his war. They're going to use us to destroy ourselves before we can destroy everything."

"Perhaps we should not proceed with speaking to the Pyx who surrendered yesterday."

"No. I have to. Maybe she changed her mind and wants to help us, or maybe he sent her and the others to kill me. Either way, she could have information that will help us figure out what he's planning. He managed to keep that from me. I have his memories, not his plans for the future, but I know it's bad."

"She is only one, and we will be many. Still, we will have to proceed with extreme caution."

The thought she'd had when she'd come back to herself burned through the hollow space inside her. She hated the idea, but he had to be stopped. And there was only one way. It was clear now he was too broken to turn back.

"Jenyx, I need to know how to kill him. I know you'd be breaking your laws by telling me, but it's the only way. I've seen how much hatred he has now. It's all he thinks about."

As she spoke, Jenyx's reluctance and anguish at her words pierced through the fire in her belly. But she couldn't let it stop her. The fire would have to forge those emotions into new, hardened weapons she could yield when the time came. Her mind went to the knife tucked away in her sock drawer.

She had to kill Messoryx. Nothing less would stop him. Even if he was right about the problem, he was wrong about the solution. Whatever his exact plan was, too many people would die if he had his way.

"I cannot tell you that, child. You know this. Even if it were not against our laws, I would never want you to resort to such measures. We will find another solution, Cara. Together."

It would be pointless to try to convince him, she could tell. But that didn't sway her. Maybe the Pyx would tell her something useful tomorrow. She'd figure something out. There was no other way.

"I'M NOT HERE TO HELP you, you sad, sad human. I'm here to give you a message from our leader."

"Messoryx." Cara's gold eyes were locked on the glowing green pair in the middle of the clearing. The heart-shaped face of the sturdy woman in front of her gave nothing away, but she sensed the surprise of the Pyx inside when she used Messoryx's name.

"That's right." The Pyx recovered quickly. "He sees what needs to be done. We've let this go on long enough, and if we don't step in now, it'll be too late for all of us." The woman turned her glowing eyes to the Pyx surrounding the clearing, ignoring the guardians on either side of her. "You should all be joining us. Fight back for every other species on this planet. Do your duty to the world we've inhabited longer than any other."

Grawlls rumbled a warning at Cara's side. She put a hand in the bear's long, coarse fur, and he quieted.

From the moment she had approached the clearing, she'd known this wasn't going to go the way she'd hoped. The outlaw before her radiated condescension and disgust that coursed through Cara's body. Even her shock at seeing the two guardians up close standing in the clearing in all their enormous glory wasn't enough to cut through the feelings. This wasn't someone who had seen the error in her ways and wanted to help defeat Messoryx. This was a loyal soldier, here on his command. She'd willingly turned herself in to whatever consequences awaited her just to deliver his message.

"Nice speech. Really. You'd fit right in with the drama club."

The woman's creepy eyes snapped back to her. "And you. So naïve. You don't think this is about saving people, do you? Because even if we stop, you'll wipe a whole bunch of yourselves out soon enough, the way you're going. The trouble is, you'll take too many others with you."

Cara's teeth clenched. The truth and bitterness in the words climbed her throat. It wasn't like she wasn't aware of the crisis, no matter how much the world tried to ignore it. She choked down the acid and fought to remember which side she was on.

"So what's the message you're supposed to deliver?"

"Don't try to stop us. Your precious school and friends aren't as safe as you think they are. If you don't leave us alone, we'll find ways to convince you. Or eliminate you. Our work is noble. Don't try to convince us otherwise."

Even if they had a point, a few ominous words weren't going to convince her mass murder was the best solution to the problem. Not happening. "Then work with us instead. Stop stealing people's lives and help us. Messoryx and his death campaign have to end, but the rest of you could still turn back and help us set things right."

"Don't you think it's too late for that?" the Pyx seethed.

The bitterness rose again, but this time, there was sorrow too. It felt like it was on the other side of a wall in her mind. Like two sides of a shared space.

Her stomach sank. "I hope not."

It almost felt like the hatred from the Pyx eased up for a moment. Then the lead weight settled back into place in time to match her next words. "Hope died decades ago. You humans failed to notice through your greed. Messoryx sees. He knows the path forward, and he'll lead us there."

All the things Cara had been through thanks to their leader ran through her thoughts. The first time she'd seen Liv in the hospital with one of Messoryx's recruits trapped in her mind.

The times she'd snapped at her friends with hostility she couldn't place. The attack in Portland, and Wes's injury and long recovery. Even Jory's concussion at Rhys's hands had been a result of the path Rhys had taken trying to save Liv. It was all because of Messoryx and his followers. It was all connected. Then there were the visions haunting her days and nights now. In spite of all that, she was one of the lucky ones. When she thought of Lydia and all the other people impacted, she shuddered. It had to stop.

It was a choice between letting him continue with his disregard and disdain for human life, or stopping him and hoping the others would decide to find another way to help. Could she get this Pyx to see that? Josh had said she could be more persuasive than she knew. Maybe it was worth a try.

"Messoryx won't be able to lead you. As soon as I learn how to kill him, I will. Find another way, and tell the others who feel like you do to find ways to help, instead of hurting."

Now who's giving drama club speeches, Cara? You don't expect that to work, do you?

"Ha. You protect this weak human. You let her influence your decisions and yet, you won't trust her with simple secrets. You're pathetic. All of you. You deserve the fates awaiting you." The woman's glowing green eyes stopped prowling across the other Pyx and fixed on Cara like a wild cat staring down its dinner. "You want to know how to kill us? How about I show you?"

She whirled and flung herself at the guardian on her left.

CHAPTER 21

GRAWLLS WAS BETWEEN them before Cara could see anything more than the woman's legs kick through the air as she landed on the guardian's shoulders. Linnaeryx joined the fight with her enormous pyxis, rushing to save her fellow guardian, and Cara craned to see what was happening while the forest erupted into motion around her. Grawlls stood on his hind legs and let out a terrifying roar, turning her legs to trembling mush.

"Cara, we must go. Please," Jenyx urged her, using Jenner to nudge at her legs.

The danger of the situation electrified her skin, zipping warnings up and down her limbs, but her feet stuck to the ground. She was torn. She didn't want to see the Pyx in the guardian get hurt, and she'd promised Liv she'd leave immediately if anything felt off, which meant she should have left before they ever reached the clearing. But the burning resolve since she'd fallen through Messoryx's memories yesterday meant she desperately wanted to know how to kill him.

She lurched forward, trying to step around Grawlls to find a view of the noisy battle raging in the middle of the clearing. The bear's broad, furry side slammed against her and sent her sprawling through the branches off the side of the path.

A hand grabbed at her arm. "Get up. Let's go," Wes's low voice whispered beside her ear as his firm grip looped under her shoulder and helped her scramble to her feet.

The shock of seeing his face right beside her spurred her into motion, and they spilled back onto the path and ran for the school. Jenner barked his encouragement for them to run faster, and darted past to take the lead. Branches crashed behind them. She chanced a peek over her shoulder and found Grawlls following them, protecting the back of their group.

They burst out from the trees into the clear grass behind the Cedars dorm, and Cara put her hands on her knees to catch her breath. Wes was doing the same, with his bow dangling from one hand and a quiver of arrows across his back.

"Where did you come from?" she asked between gasps for air.

"I got there early. Found a spot up a tree, downwind and out of sight. I figured they'd use that clearing again for the meeting."

"You shouldn't have been there. You weren't supposed to be. What if they'd caught you?" He could have ruined everything. He could have gotten hurt again. Protectiveness and anger fought for dominance inside her. She couldn't decide which was worse. "You didn't trust me to take care of it alone." Or betrayal. Maybe that was it.

"Good thing, Cara." Wes raised his eyes and shot her a look that made her flinch when he swore. "You don't need protection from them as much as from yourself. You knew she was still on the other side when you got there. I could tell from your face. Why did you stay after you knew it was dangerous?"

"I had to know."

"How to kill them?"

"Yes. Did you see from where you were? Did you see what she was trying to do?" She dismissed the flashes of fear and disappointment from Jenyx and Grawllyx listening in. It didn't matter what they thought.

"No. I was a little busy making sure you didn't get yourself killed."

"And what were you going to do?" She gestured to the bow in his hand. "You can't kill the woman, and you don't know how to kill the Pyx. What good was that going to do?"

"I don't want to kill anyone, but I'd damn sure slow her down and do whatever I had to to stop her from killing you. I thought you'd be smarter after the archery range. Wasn't it bad enough putting Harrison in danger then? It wasn't your fault that time. We didn't know that would happen. But if you keep putting yourself in these situations, they're going to keep coming after you, and it won't just be you in the way."

Before she could snap off a retort or let the brutal honesty of his words sink in, a keening howl rent the air.

Jenner and Grawlls both lifted their heads to the sky and let out howls and roars of their own. Ice froze every muscle and nerve in Cara's body at the chilling sound.

Deep in the woods, the battle between the Pyx was over. Without needing to ask, she knew. A guardian was dead.

WINDOWS OPENED ON BOTH floors of the dorm behind them. Grawlls slipped into hiding in the woods. The roar he'd made would have overridden any ability he had to hide in plain sight from the rest of the students. There was no way they'd missed the loud howling, and fear would heighten everyone's senses. Some braver girls spilled around the sides of the dorms and came close to where she stood with Wes.

Similarly, guys came through the gap between the Cedars and the Lodge, talking animatedly to one another. A shout came down from one of the windows behind them.

"What was that?"

No one answered.

"Get inside, everyone." Mr. Meyers came running from the direction of the Lodge. He shooed students away from the forest. "Sounded like a wolf, or maybe a few. Let's all get inside for a bit, please. Cara"—he looked at her with a ghost-white face and narrow lips—"take your dog inside. Before anything happens."

Her eyes narrowed.

Dramatic much, Owen?

The teacher's first name rang through her mind because his reaction struck her as odd. For starters, there were barely any wolves in Oregon, so the explanation was weak. Why wasn't he curious like the students? Then again, it was his job to keep them away from danger. He was probably playing it safe or following some sort of school protocol.

She started to move, following the crowd. Maybe she'd go with Wes to the Lodge so they could fill Jory in on the details before he worried about the sound. When Wes continued past the corner of the building where they should have turned, she stopped.

"Where are you going?"

"I said I'd text Rhys when it was over and you were back safely. After that racket, I should probably go tell him we're fine in person."

Rhys. *Of course.*

She should have thought of him first. Not because of the guardian's death, or the weird protection pact he and Wes had going on, but because of his past. He might be the only one who could help her now.

"I'll go. You go tell Jory. And Liv. Oh, and Harrison." She sent him off and turned to whisper to Jenner. "Jenyx, if you need to go deal with that situation, go. I'm safe. I'll follow the crowd, and I'm going further into campus, not near the woods."

And you can't be with me for this, she added to herself.

"Are you sure? I can stay with you."

"I'm sure. Go."

She turned to the forward dorms. How could she have forgotten about Rhys? He'd done more than any of them to learn how to kill a Pyx back when he was trying to save Liv. At the time, Cara had been convinced it was the wrong way to do things. And for that situation, it had been. He hadn't known the difference between the good, innocent Pyx he was abducting and the real evil of Messoryx who thought he could solve problems with genocide.

She knew better now, and something Rhys had learned along the way might be able to help her.

The idea of talking to him alone made her queasy. Her decision to swallow her feelings and be his friend was still fresh, but she'd have to get over it. The situation they were in now was more critical than her pride. After what she'd seen and heard, she needed to talk to him. Just talk. She'd done that much before.

Her feet carried her to the door of the Douglas Fir dorm without any further thought. A tall teacher she didn't know ushered the freshman and junior boys inside, along with anyone else in the immediate area. She followed a scrawny kid through the doors. Like a magnet, her gaze immediately found Rhys trying to convince the other dorm parent to let him out again. His eyes landed on her, and his face changed. Her heart stuttered as he rushed over.

"Cara. You're okay? What was that sound? What happened?"

"Not here."

His eyebrows lifted, and he glanced around the crowded main floor. A few people looked their way as he led her toward the stairs. As soon as they climbed to the second floor, the noise level died, and the place was deserted. Everyone had gathered in the downstairs lounge to discuss whatever was going on. He paused at the top to wait for her, or maybe to see if she wanted to talk right there. With her hands trembling, she moved past him down the hall to his room. She'd been up here with Liv before, but only as far as his doorway.

Just friends. Just talking.

He opened the door to let her in, and she brushed past him, feeling the heat from his body as she passed. Pressing a hand to her middle, she told the dancing butterflies to chill out.

A soft click behind her meant he'd figured out this wasn't a conversation they could risk being overheard. Her eyes swept across the room and followed Rhys as he passed beside her with a shallow breath. He perched on the edge of his desk and waited for her to speak.

Her mouth went dry as she took in the rumpled bedcovers and other details of his space. She'd never been inside any of the single bedrooms on the upper floors. The space closed in around them, small and intimate. Books lined the shelf along his wall, and she held back a smile as she recognized several she owned herself. He favored dark blue, like his room at Whalton manor, which she'd been inside but not with him there.

Doesn't matter. Not why you're here, Cara. Use your words.

"The meeting was a warning message. There was a fight, but we got out fine. Wes is back at the Lodge now, even though he shouldn't have been out there with me in the first place."

Rhys wasn't surprised. And he didn't look the slightest bit sorry. A little annoyance at whatever part he had played in that side plan flared up, and her hands clenched into fists at her sides.

"A guardian is dead. That's what the sound was. Some sort of collective mourning."

His shoulders rolled forward, and his face softened. "Wow. What about the Pyx who surrendered? Did she escape?"

"I don't know." She didn't care, either. Only one of them mattered. "That's not why I'm here. I need to talk to you. I need to know everything you did when you were trying to learn how to kill them."

She forced herself to look him in the eye. This was what she needed to do, and he could help her. He might be the only one who could.

"What? Why?"

Confusion played across his features, along with something else. He almost looked hurt. She squared her shoulders and faced him. She couldn't be distracted by whatever it was.

"I have to know how to kill him. It's the only way to end this. If you tell me everything, including all the questions Jenyx and Tomyx asked you that day at Jory's house, maybe we can figure it out together." Her limbs tingled as his gaze intensified. He stood up from the desk. She felt aware of every inch of her body in his presence. This friends thing was never going to work, but he could still help her. "Unless you already know."

His eyes searched hers with fresh depth. She never would have guessed they could be any more captivating than they already were when the deep grey swirled and the gold sparked with electricity. But it was like the last layer of stone behind them had crumbled.

"No, I don't know." His normally smooth voice roughened with emotion.

She blinked and lowered her eyes from his. Of course, that only meant she found herself staring at the way his shirt hugged his shoulders and chest, rising and falling with each breath. Not helping. She had to break his hold on her and stick to her plan. "Well, then, we'll figure it out. We have to. Otherwise, he's going to come after other people to get to me. The warning said as much. I can't stand the thought of anyone else getting hurt in my place. If anything happened to my friends, or you, any of the people I love—"

His eyes had narrowed with concern as she spoke. Now they widened again.

Crap. What did you say? Dammit, Cara, focus.

She wanted to look away again, but she couldn't bring herself to break the electricity between them. Her words came out breathy, almost desperate. "He'll send his soldiers here. I have to kill him. It's the only way."

"I don't believe that." He stepped closer to her. "It isn't the only way. You showed me that."

She stared up at him, locked in his gaze. The air shifted between them.

His hand reached out to brush a lock of hair from her forehead. "You're the one who told me we'd find a better way when I was sure killing them was the only solution. And we did. We saved my sister. Together."

His fingertips trailed across her skin and wound into her hair as his hand cupped the side of her face. The smell of his skin so close to her made her want to curl into him, but she didn't dare move in case it broke the magic.

"You saw through me when I was lost. That day you showed up at my house, you talked me off the ledge. You saw how I hated myself for what I was doing, and I'd never want that for you." His thumb brushed her cheek. "You're the one who made me see past this dark path. Please don't fall down it now."

He was looking down at her with a tenderness she'd never dared to imagine. The gold rings danced in his heated eyes, and their warmth wrapped around her heart. Their faces were only inches apart. His breath tickled her, and she breathed him in while his gaze dropped to her lips.

"Cara—I—"

She couldn't stand against the glorious storm raging all around her.

Her body swayed, leaning into him of its own accord, responding to his touch the way it had when they'd danced.

This couldn't be happening. What was she doing? Her thoughts detached themselves and swirled away in the tempest. Her hands lifted to his arms, feeling as if they belonged to someone else. When his other hand slid around her waist, her pulse surged. The thunderstorm rushing from his eyes tore through her soul.

Her eyes closed as their lips brushed together with feathery softness. The kiss was tentative at first. Tender. Perfect. She melted into it, and her mouth pressed more firmly against his. While the spot in the middle of her chest somersaulted in a dizzying endless loop, her hand slid across and twisted into the fabric of his soft T-shirt to ground her. His lips on hers were all that tethered her to the world.

CHAPTER 22

A KNOCK AT THE DOOR burst through the bubble of the small space.

They sprang apart.

The heat that had gathered inside her spread with a rush up Cara's cheeks. The doorknob turned, and the door swung open.

"Hey, Rhys, Coach Flynn wanted me to tell you . . . Oh." Mak burst into the room and stopped dead. "Whoa. Am I interrupting something?"

Rhys rubbed a hand across the back of his neck. "Nope. What's up?"

He couldn't hide the wrinkles in his shirt or Cara's furious blush.

Mak stared back and forth between them. "Uh, Coach sent me over . . ."

Ugh. Basketball.

She'd never hated basketball more in her entire life.

"You sure nothing was going on? Because that's my brother's girlfriend."

Cara's head whipped up. "Seriously? Now is when you decide to stick up for Wes? What is wrong with you, Mak? For the last damn time, Wes and I aren't dating." The heat in her face grew with frustration. She glared at him with her jaw set until she couldn't hold it back anymore and swore with a shake of her head. "He's your brother. Open your eyes. Or better yet, try talking to him for a change."

Shoving past his towering frame, she fled down the hall to the stairs. Her tingling lips and the spot on her hip still warm from Rhys's hand were the only betrayals to the rest of her feelings. Her heart tripped down the stairs ahead of her.

The problem was the word "girlfriend." It had brought her rational thoughts lurching back into place when her brain reconnected to her body after that kiss. Her first kiss. If only she could float on a cloud back to her own girlfriends and describe its perfection, but that couldn't happen.

Wes might not have a girlfriend, but Rhys did. So what was he doing kissing her? Unless he and Emma had broken up. Shame followed the flash of happiness that idea brought. She had no idea what had been going on with them since the Valentine's dance, but surely she would have noticed if her teammate had gone through a breakup. If anything, Emma had looked happier lately. It wasn't like she'd had anything to be mad about after the dance. That had been nothing. Totally innocent. It was all nothing—until now.

On top of that, the girl she would want to run to tell was Rhys's sister. What was she thinking? Two of the best girls she knew, and she'd betrayed them both. How could she have let this happen?

The door to the Dougie crashed closed behind her. No teacher tried to stop her, so they must have decided the threat of wolves, or whatever they were calling it, was over. She kicked at a rock on the gravel path, mentally kicking herself for being so awful. She wasn't this person.

But the more she thought about it, the more confused she became, and mad too. She could feel bad about hiding her crush from Liv, lying about her feelings for her friend's brother. But the Emma thing wasn't on her. What the hell was Rhys doing? How could he kiss someone else when he had such an amazing girlfriend? And he had kissed her back, hadn't he? Her lips still burned from the heat, but the fire in her chest died to ashes. She hadn't even learned anything useful from him. What a mess.

She nearly collided with Grawlls as she turned the corner of the building. His brownish-black fur was close enough for her to smell the woods mingled with notes of something sharp, like vinegar. But what made her step back after her hand flew to her mouth in shock wasn't his scent. It was the low rumble in his throat.

"What are you doing here?" she asked, casting quick glances in every direction. Thankfully everyone was still indoors. "Aren't you worried your mind tricks won't work so well out in the open like this?"

"I have reinforcements." Grawllyx practically growled the words as if he really was the bear he inhabited.

Jenner stood beside him, and she spotted a squirrel lurking near one of the picnic tables on the lawn. Her heart still pounded from the surprise and from a growing fury at the position she found herself in. That anger reflected back at her from Grawlls until she couldn't be sure whose emotions were feeding into whose anymore.

"Who do I need to teach a lesson?"

"What?" She licked her lips. They'd stopped tingling and gone dry. What was Grawllyx mad about if it wasn't to do with the fight in the woods? He couldn't be mad at Rhys like she was. He couldn't even know anything had happened.

"You're angry. Who's to blame?" Grawllyx flashed across the bear's eyes like a warning.

Jenner looked up at her, and a similar defensiveness wrapped around her from Jenyx. It was almost sweet. Almost comforting. The tension eased slightly.

"No one, Grawllyx. Nothing happened. Isn't the situation with the guardian enough to be mad about?"

"I suppose so." He didn't sound sure.

"What happened? Did she get away?"

Jenyx's anguish chilled the remainder of her anger. She'd think about Rhys later. She couldn't do it right now. It was too much. Too fresh.

"She will not cause any more harm. And Linnaeryx and her guardian are no longer with us."

"Linnaeryx?" It wasn't the other one who had been killed? She blinked back a surprising tear. It wasn't like she cared about the Pyx who had put Liv through so much. She had wanted her dead from the start, hadn't she? Another tear chased the first one down her cheek. Her heart was too raw for this right now.

"Yes. We knew of two other mysterious Pyx deaths last year. Now we know the truth. It appears Messoryx does not take kindly to anyone having second thoughts. Her first attack was a diversion. Her real target was always Linnaeryx."

"And what about her? And the woman?"

Cara was too riddled with emotion to tell what sensation came from the Pyx, but when bear and dog both hung their heads, the situation became clear.

"She never intended to release the woman. We tried to stop her, but—"

"She sacrificed herself, killing the woman in the process," Grawllyx finished.

Once the tears started, Cara couldn't stop them. Her hands balled into fists at her sides. Couldn't she just deal with one thing at a time? Why did Rhys have to pick today to flip her world on its head? Why did she have to feel this way about him at all? Here, another innocent person been sacrificed for the sake of toxic hatred. Two more Pyx were dead, too, and one of the most interesting and majestic creatures she'd ever laid eyes on had died along with them. But the pain and anger at their loss and Messoryx's role in all of it again had to share space on the other side of the wall in her mind from the intensity of her feelings for Rhys. Or about Rhys. Whatever.

"Are you sure I can't beat someone up?" Grawlls stretched out a massive paw, and she appreciated his long claws properly for the first time. He settled when she gulped, her tears drying up. "Not that I would actually hurt another living creature. But with this brawny beast, I could put the fear of Pyx in someone for you."

"That's really not—" She stopped and wiped her face. "Did you just refer to yourself as a god?"

"Sorry. Running joke. There have been some, er, misinterpretations over the years. Did you know humans used to worship a cat goddess in Egypt? And in India, there are these—"

Cara held up a hand to cut him off. She'd figured those ones out freshman year. Pyx in animals, talking to Pyxsees, making the animals act strangely . . . It didn't take much imagination to put those together and come up with legends and gods. Instead of amusing her, today, it rubbed her the wrong way.

"You all talk a big game about not interfering. Messoryx might be taking things way too far with his human zombie murder plans, but you're not all as innocent as you make yourselves out to be." Her shoulders dropped, and she stepped past the bear. "Go hide somewhere properly. You're tricking people right now. I'm tired of all the manipulating and deceiving people." She flinched at the image of Emma's kind face. She didn't want her own deceit to be the cause of any more pain. It was all too much. "Leave me alone."

Voices carried around the building as people started to emerge. Shoving her hands in her pockets, she left Grawlls and the squirrel to make their way to the woods while she stormed down the path.

"Coming, Jenyx?"

"Sorry, child. You said you wanted to be alone. I was not certain."

"I didn't mean you. I never mean you."

Almost never. Except when you need to go behind his back. Because you're not any better than they are.

Her lips pursed. Everything was a mess. If she'd thought her life was out of control before, it was nothing compared to now. How on earth could she fix any of this? She couldn't rein in her own actions, let alone deal with a battle with another race. The next person who suggested she had any sort of power over anything was going to get an earful.

Before she could spiral into thinking too much about all the things she hid and the lives her actions could impact, Jenyx threw a little calming energy her way.

"I am glad to hear you say so."

SHE SPENT THE EVENING with Delaney, watching her roommate paint in the art room. No one would come looking for her there, and watching Delaney layer colors on a canvas until white clouds slid across blue sky, and orange flowers rose and bloomed from green grass was the most soothing thing she could imagine. With her thoughts quieted and as much control mustered as she could manage, she even slept okay.

When she spotted Rhys at breakfast with Emma, she fully expected the shattering heartbreak. Of course he looked great, his smile glowing above a dark-red Henley that framed the solid shoulders her hands had run across last night. She'd steeled herself for this moment and managed to hold back the tears. But how could he sit there smiling with Emma like nothing had happened? Or worse, like he was happy with her? Obviously, he hadn't told Emma anything, because her smile seemed more excited than usual too. She even shot Cara a grin when she spotted her slinking by on her way to hide behind the loud table of football guys at the far edge of the room.

When Emma reached over to Rhys's arm with a teasing touch, Cara had to look away. She sat down with a thump. "I kissed your boyfriend" might as well have been scrawled across her forehead in black marker, and Emma would see it any second now.

No crying. You promised.

She spread strawberry cream cheese on the giant bagel she'd chosen for breakfast. If she wasn't going to let herself cry, carbs and sugar were the next best thing. Of course there'd been no peach yogurt left. That would be too much to ask for on such a terrible day. Ice cream would be on the agenda for tonight. And more time with Delaney, who never asked too many questions.

"Hey."

Her head snapped up at his voice. What in the holiest crap was Rhys doing?

He slid out the chair beside her and sat down. She couldn't make her jaw close again. It was like he wanted to get busted. Why would he leave Emma to move over here? Maybe it was normal to come sit with them when it was a whole table with his sister and Wes and Jory, but not with just her. She spotted Emma leaving the dining hall with a furtive glance over her shoulder. No chance she hadn't noticed, then.

Cara turned back to Rhys.

He looked a little more uncertain after following her gaze. "Um, about yesterday . . ."

Oh. That's what this is.

She struggled to control her voice. "It was a mistake."

While she'd sat and watched Delaney create beauty from nothing last night, she'd gone over it all in her mind. It had been an emotional moment that went too far. Shared secrets had layered over misplaced gratitude and blossoming friendship to paint a singularly perfect moment. That was all. Acrylics on canvas—nothing more. Whether he'd kissed her back or not, it wasn't real.

Knowing it had been a mistake didn't mean she wanted to hear him say the words. Her heart already hurt enough, so she'd said them first.

"Pretend it never happened, okay?" Somehow, her voice held steady.

Tears prickled in spite of her vow to herself, so she focused on her tray and took a bite of her bagel. While her jaw mashed each bite, she blinked and willed the moisture in her eyes back where it belonged.

"Oh. That's, um . . . sure. If that's what you want."

Her head did an awkward nod-shake thing in dismissal. She wouldn't look at him. He should probably just leave already.

"Okay, then. I'll see you later, Cara." He rose with his mostly full tray. "Oh . . . here. It was the last one, so I thought . . . whatever." He set a peach yogurt on her tray and walked away.

If it wasn't real, why did it hurt so much?

After several moments of clenching her jaw, she won the battle against the urge to cry. But she lost her appetite.

"Where's he going?" Liv looked after her brother, and Cara glanced up in time to see his back as he slumped out the door while her friends joined her. "It didn't look like he even ate anything aside from the apple he took with him. What is up with him? He was acting all strange when I went to see him last night, too."

Wes took the seat beside Cara and studied her expression with a crease between his brows.

Jory sat down on her other side. "Why the change in table?"

She shrugged. "Change of scenery." Only Wes seemed to notice anything was up with her. After her promise not to shut her friends out again, and her thoughts about hiding things since yesterday, everything about this morning felt gross. Awful. Sick.

No wonder Rhys hadn't wanted to finish his breakfast. She knew the feeling.

She pushed her tray away.

"Why is no one hungry today?" Liv reached out and took the yogurt from Cara's tray. "You don't mind, do you? There was no peach left."

Cara shook her head. At least it wouldn't go to waste. She almost snickered, but it would have come out too dark. Her whole world could be going to crap, and she was worried about wasting one yogurt. Messoryx was having the last laugh right now, toying with her thoughts without even being there. At least it had the benefit of reminding her what the real problem was.

Time for some perspective, Cara.

Who needed boy trouble when someone was out to kill you? Not to mention his plans to eliminate as many humans as he could manage. And then there were his pretty valid reasons for wanting to.

Seriously. Someone should tell the aching hole in her chest that they had bigger problems.

CHAPTER 23

AFTER MONDAY HAD LIVED up to its awful reputation, the next few days crawled by the same way. Emma had stopped looking so happy. She wore a frown that alternated between disappointment and exasperation.

In her darkest moments, Cara hoped that meant she and Rhys were breaking up, but they still sat together most meals, Rhys looking equally miserable. Her better side hoped the fact they were still together meant they would work it out. Which meant it hadn't been a big deal. It couldn't have mattered to him that much. There was no way Emma would stay if it had meant something to him. If he'd been affected the way she was, Emma would look more than frustrated. She'd be downright mad. Or, if she felt the way Cara did, she'd look like Cara felt . . .

Crushed. You can say it. Nothing matters, anyway.

She told the voice in her head—the stupid, negative one everyone had—to shut up. The Pyx voices in her head were the ones she should pay attention to. Things still mattered. Big things mattered. The warning from the Pyx in the forest rang through her mind.

"Our cause is noble. Don't try to convince us otherwise."

How did they think she was going to convince them of anything? Why was that a warning they needed to give her? The whole thing made no sense.

She was still chewing on the annoyingly cryptic message when she boarded the team bus on Thursday afternoon. She'd been worried about being close to Emma at Tuesday's track practice, but the older girl had ignored her, casting only a few confused glances her way. Presumably that would continue today for their annual friendly spring cross country meet with Valley Green. The whole team had been looking forward to the fun meet, and it might cheer up Emma. Cara waited to board the bus last as usual, but she was too lost in her musings about the warning to avoid Emma's sneak attack.

"Sit." The tall girl stood in the aisle near the front of the bus, blocking her way.

With a drop in her stomach, Cara glanced over her shoulder for another seat she could take instead, but the first three rows were all empty aside from Coach Francis. Coach held a fixed stare out the front windshield as if she didn't notice her star team member staging a blockade three rows back. With her skin feeling two sizes too small, Cara slumped into the window seat, letting Emma trap her.

They sat in tense silence while the bus rumbled to life and lurched out of the parking lot. The gold band across the shoulders of her school shirt—the band indicating she was part of the top team—might as well have turned to lead. Surely it must look as heavy and tarnished as it felt sitting next to Emma in her matching shirt. The gold band of hers set off shimmering highlights in her amber hair and gleamed with the pride it deserved. Cara's insides squirmed while she held perfectly still as trees blurred by the window.

Emma stirred beside her when they passed the fork in the private road. A flutter rose under Cara's breastbone at the pull of the beautiful mansion lying beyond the trees up the narrow driveway. Right now, at the start of May, the meadows surrounding the grey stone walls would be spun with wildflowers woven through the grasses. The early blossoms of the fruit trees in the small orchard would have dropped to litter the ground with petals and give way to budding fruit.

An image of the cobblestone driveway brought a ghostly ache to her knees where she'd hurt them when she'd fallen. The visual of the long garage and all that had happened there drove a shiver down her spine and landed her firmly back in her present situation. She startled at the sight of Emma watching her face.

"It's gorgeous, isn't it?"

Cara could only blink.

After trapping her here, Emma seemed unsure what to say. "Whalton manor. You've been there. When you went to meet Liv . . . and other times, right?"

Cara's throat had gone dry, and she had difficulty swallowing. She nodded instead of trusting her voice. The cold metal side of the bus pressed into one shoulder as she leaned away from Emma's scrutiny.

"Did I do something?" Emma asked.

"What?"

"I know we're two grades apart, but we used to talk. We are teammates after all. Now you avoid me like a bad disease."

"No, I—No, Emma. You didn't do anything." Her head shook too quickly. She rubbed the strap of her dad's watch around her wrist. What was she going to say to make this right?

"Well, I'm graduating in a month, and I don't want to leave it like this. I've wanted to talk to you since February. I think you saw Fiona run over to me at the dance, and I'm guessing you know what she said. You left before I could talk to you."

Cara gulped. She could see the scene in her head: Fiona darting across the gym to Emma's ear. Rhys standing with Emma and glancing her way after she ducked out at the end of their dance. Emma's face tracking her movements before she ran out.

"Emma, that photo wasn't what it looked like. The gala was—"

"None of my business. Whatever it was is between you and him."

She gave a disgusted snort. "It was nothing." *To him.*

"Doesn't matter. I asked Fiona to keep it to herself. She gossips too much for her own good, anyway. But I never asked you about it after that night. I wanted to, but you became so withdrawn right after, and . . . I don't know what it was. I know something bad happened that night. Rhys was gone too."

It was the first time Emma had said his name. It felt like she'd been avoiding it up until now. Emma's head lowered, studying her response. Her eyebrows rose when Cara flinched at the name and the memory.

"Yeah. I figured. He wasn't the same after that night either. He won't tell me about it, but he was pretty dark for a while there, too. I left it alone for a bit to give him time to open up when he was ready. After Easter break, he seemed lighter. Then I noticed you did too. It's like you two mirror each other."

Her belly clenched around the bubbling emotions rising through her core. If she could forget she was talking to Emma, those words would be filled with a shimmering hope. Maybe she wasn't so invisible to him. Maybe the connection she felt was real. And maybe that kiss hadn't been such a horrible mistake.

But this was Emma searching her face with squinting brown eyes. Her arms sagged heavily to her sides.

"At least, you did," Emma continued, "until Monday morning."

And there it was. She knew.

Beyond any remaining doubt, she knew about the kiss.

All the bubbles turned to stones as guilt weighed her down. What could she say? All she could do was apologize. Say she hadn't meant to. Before she could find the words, Emma's gaze opened. Her voice softened with her next words.

"You really like him. Don't you?"

"What? No."

Emma had sounded uncertain. Hesitant. Cara *had* to reassure her.

"Of course not. Nothing like that. I mean, he's great, but it's not like that. I won't say nothing happened, but it didn't mean anything. I swear." She had to make Emma believe it. If there was a chance she could fix things for them, she owed Rhys that much. He'd saved her life from Messoryx that night when Lydia attacked, and he'd protected her a bunch of other times. The least she could do was back up whatever he'd told Emma about the kiss.

"Are you sure?"

"Totally. Big mistake."

Everything in her body fought against the lie. Saying that kiss had been a meaningless mistake to her was like saying the sun rose in the west or the Earth was flat. It turned her inside out. As much as she'd tried to deny it before, telling Emma made it real. The truth had to be obvious in the heart beating outside her body, completely exposed.

They fell into silence as Emma fidgeted and stared at her hands, but finally decided she had nothing else to say about it. When she spoke again, she changed the subject. By the time they pulled into the parking lot of Valley Green High for the meet, Cara couldn't recall a single topic or any of the bland answers her mouth had provided while her brain brooded in the corner.

"You coming?" Emma stood in the aisle.

Cara willed her heavy legs to carry her off the bus. This race was a write-off before it ever started. She considered telling Coach she was going to be sick. Or actually being sick.

She looked for a handy bush in case she needed it, and found a familiar face in a nearby tree instead. The great horned owl's eyes gleamed green, and she swore its head bobbed for her. It lightened her mood a fraction to know there were still Pyx nearby lending some support. Not that it helped with the Rhys and Emma situation, but that wasn't the only thing in her life. She couldn't thank the owl for the reminder in the midst of her teammates, so she simply trudged along with the group as they checked the course.

Kaylee caught up to her so they could warm up together like they always did.

"Did Emma want to talk strategy with you?"

"Something like that."

"This will be a good test for next season for us. I hope I did enough last season for Coach to consider me for the green team in the fall. There's only you and three juniors from this year, so she'll have to name three more . . . Are you listening?"

"Mm hm."

Her mind had been so far from sports for the last few months, she had no clue what Kaylee was saying. The words washed over her and swept back out into the sea of things that didn't really matter. It had been hard to focus on school stuff or even the team she usually loved while she was obsessing over a genocidal mastermind bent on eliminating untold numbers of people . . . after he eliminated her. And why? There had to be a reason he felt the need to threaten her.

She pulled the wrong shoes from her bag, and Kaylee had to stop her and point out the right spikes with a confused look. Without any conscious thought, she reached for the tape and secured the shoes on her feet, though there was no mud to worry about today. Blindly, she moved to the starting line with the rest of the girls. For once, she had no pre-race jitters. She was slow to start when the crowd surged forward at the signal, and found herself near the back.

"Caw caw, Cara." Ryx's voice cut through her daze.

Annoyed more than startled, she found the raven flying low along the trees beside the grassy track. The grumble in her throat made its way past her lips, and the Valley Green girl running beside her shot her a worried glance and moved to the far side of the wide path. Cara's irritation brought a bit of the blood flowing back through her body, and she pushed her stride out to move past a few more girls into an open space ahead. This stride felt more natural, and she found a rhythm to fall into. Her thoughts quieted as her feet covered the ground, and the minutes flew by.

The raven's shadow swept the grass in front of her. She stretched, feeling the urge to stomp on it. She had no idea how good a raven's hearing was, but she might as well find out.

"What are you doing here?" she mumbled as her feet pounded the dry earth. "Shouldn't you be watching over Rhys?"

Ryx's only redeeming quality was he was keeping Rhys safe. Or he was supposed to be.

"I don't take my orders from humans. Well . . . not many humans."

Why did he always avoid answering her directly? It wasn't humans who had asked him to guard Rhys—it was the other Pyx. What was he talking about?

Even this small separation from the school made her miss Jenyx. He would give her an answer. She wished Grawlls were here, too. The powerful black bear lent her a sense of security. She regretted the way she'd spoken to Grawllyx outside the Dougie on Sunday.

"Maybe no one asked me to come. Maybe I *wanted* to check on you," Ryx added.

A derisive snort came out her nose. *Doubtful.*

She focused and pushed through a tight spot on the track where racers bunched together at a narrowing between the trees. She passed August in her green-and-gold shirt as she burst forward from the bottleneck of people.

"Fine. I'll go. But there are others here," Ryx said. The raven flew off and left her feeling strangely alone.

She might hate that stinking bird, or at least the Pyx who flew with him, but a cold feeling stole through her when he left. He'd said there were others. Other Pyx? How did he know if they were friendly?

She stumbled and caught herself. A crowd of parents and teachers from Valley Green had gathered at the top of the rise where they could see the final hill and the sprints to the finish line. Some instinctive sense pushed her steps away from the crowd to the other side of the open area where only trees lined the edge. The people were loosely clustered in twos and threes, cheering on their kids and students.

That was when she saw him.

Glowing green eyes moved up to the front of the crowd. The man was well ahead of her. He turned his head and fixed her with his creepy eyes in the bright afternoon sun. A chill of dread flooded down her limbs. She threw herself up the hill with every bit of strength she could draw. She had to reach him before he could act.

A knife glinted in the sun in his right hand, and he took a step forward. It was a twin of the one she'd wrenched from the tree and now had stashed in her dorm room. Cara followed the direction of his step and cried out.

"No!"

Emma's amber ponytail swayed across her back in line with the man's front foot as he dropped to one knee and brought his arm up and forward. Cara was too far behind. She wouldn't reach Emma. She couldn't stop him.

The hand with the knife plunged to the ground. Emma ran on.

No one reacted to him. Several people turned at her shriek, and the girls running directly ahead of her glanced over their shoulders. But no one responded to the man, who now appeared to be harmlessly tying his shoe. She was the only one who saw him for what he was.

He stood as she reached him, and her pace slowed. A black streak flashed through the air as Ryx flew between them and rose vertically in front of the group of spectators. He must not have been hiding, because a few people at the sidelines ducked and gasped. They hadn't noticed anything out of the ordinary from the true threat walking among them, but they were scared of the raven.

With a nasty sneer, the man stepped back into the crowd and turned away from her.

She ended up in the chute at the finish line with no idea how she'd made it there. Her feet had carried her along with the surrounding girls while she reeled in disbelief. She barely acknowledged her team or her coach, who offered a "great job" to Emma and a few others before turning to her.

"I don't know what that race was, Cara. That was the worst start I've ever seen from you, but then you found your stride and you were running great. Until you completely fell apart again at the end. I know it's only a friendly competition, but I've never seen you so inconsistent. Are you feeling okay?"

She mumbled a response about feeling sick and stepped away. Ryx was nowhere to be seen, but the owl soared a loose loop above her, and she sensed his wariness as he searched the area for any lingering threat. When their group began walking back toward the parking lot after the boys' race ended, she caught sight of more animals standing around the edges of the grounds. Deer blended in amongst the trees. A flash of white in a shadow turned out to be a skunk. Several more birds joined the owl's view from above, flying in overlapping circles. Green gleams caught her attention deeper in the woods from whatever pyxides stood watch out there.

Where had they all come from? Again, she wondered how they'd known. Had they heard her shout, or had they already been on their way? Whose side were they really on, and how would she know?

All she knew was Messoryx's messenger had made his threat perfectly clear. He could reach her here. He could harm others. Had he targeted Emma specifically? Had he seen them climb off the bus together and believed they were friends? That meant he wouldn't hesitate to go after her actual friends even if he couldn't get to her. It didn't matter how much she avoided the woods or kept Pyx close by as bodyguards. As long as she was around, no one was safe.

CHAPTER 24

THE BUS RIDE BACK WAS mercifully quiet and lonely. Both Kaylee and Emma gave her questioning looks as they boarded the bus and moved past her. But she took out her phone and refused to make eye contact with anyone until, eventually, everyone left her alone.

She texted the two people she could talk to about anything. Starting with her uncle, she told him there were still plenty of the outlaw Pyx around. Whatever he thought was happening, he was wrong.

Then she messaged Wes.

One of the controlled people was at my race.
He threatened Emma right in front of me.
Don't tell Rhys.

I know. And Rhys knows.
Ryx beat you back here.
We had one here too. Everyone's okay.

What?
Where?

At the range again.
I only caught a glimpse of her eyes in the trees.
The fox warned me, and your bear got rid of her.

271

Was Harrison with you?

Yep, but nothing actually happened.
They're scare tactics.

They're working.

She'd thought she wanted to talk to them all about it. But when she walked into the room full of almost everyone she cared most about at school, their worried faces sucked the words right out of her mouth.

Rhys's presence, leaning against the wall across the room from where she sank down onto Wes's bed, didn't help her ability to think straight. It was the first time she'd been this close to him since the breakfast table on Monday morning, and the ache in her chest throbbed with new pain. The distress on his face tugged at her, but there was nothing she could do about it. They were all scared for people they cared about.

Wes stood by the window, staring at the forest beyond the glass. After Liv hugged Cara and then returned to sit beside Jory, Harrison rose from the desk chair and sank down beside Cara on Wes's bed.

The room grew tense. Across from her, Rhys stood a little taller against the wall and brushed his hair off his forehead. She couldn't help noticing he'd left it natural and soft today instead of styling it. Her fingers itched to run through it but she'd missed her only chance.

A twinge of guilt hit her. After her talk with Emma, it wasn't something she should even let herself think about. She focused on the friend beside her instead and leaned against Harrison's shoulder.

"Scary day, love. You're all right, though?"

"Mm hm. I'm all right. Thanks." She gave Harrison a small smile, and he patted her leg in a reassuring way. Covering his hand with hers and giving it a squeeze, she took comfort from his presence beside her and sensed Jenyx and Tomyx ease a little as well.

Rhys shifted again, and her eye went to him before she could stop herself. A little color dotted his cheeks when Harrison spoke softly to her.

"Care to share your thoughts?" Harrison asked.

"If anything had happened here or to Emma . . ." She stared at her knees when she couldn't continue.

Wes turned from the window and drew the curtain. The light in the room shifted from the natural cool blue of the evening outside to the warm yellow of the room lights, making everything feel both more intimate and more serious at the same time. She didn't dare look back to Rhys, but let go of Harrison's hand and felt the coolness on her thigh when he took it away.

"So what do we do to make sure that doesn't happen?" Wes directed his question to the floor where Jenner and Thomas sat at attention.

"Our first priority is your safety until this group of Pyx has been dealt with."

Cara wanted to rage at Jenyx. She wanted to yell and scream and throw things and tell him and Tomyx that it wasn't enough. But the words wouldn't come out past the emptiness from talking to Emma and then nearly seeing her hurt, or worse. The others in the room spoke, but their voices were a wash of sound.

Her mind went through the week again, starting with the warning from the Pyx in the clearing, carefully skipping over the stuff with Rhys, and ending with the glowing green eyes and the sneer from the man warning her he could get to anyone, anytime. The plans they were discussing wouldn't matter. They couldn't keep her safe. They definitely couldn't keep everyone at the school safe. She represented something to Messoryx. Something he hated and needed to eliminate. Maybe it didn't matter why, even though the question still burned.

"I'm walking Liv and Cara home. She's been through enough for today." His clear, smooth voice cut through the noise of the rest, and she realized it was the first time Rhys had spoken.

She'd kept her eyes on a patch of floor in front of Jenner's paws, but the surprising softness in his voice made her glance up without meaning to. The pained look she found on his face jolted her heart. Her mind flashed back to the tenderness in his eyes right before he'd kissed her, and her throat closed. It was too much. Tears welled and ran over to stream down her cheeks.

Liv jumped up and rushed over. "Hey, we've got you. No one's hurting our Cara." She took Cara's hands and pulled her to her feet and into an embrace.

"Not . . . me . . ." was all Cara could whisper.

Her shoulder warmed under Wes's hand when he closed ranks behind her. She let Liv steer her to the door and down the hall. One side of her body tingled with awareness the whole way back to their dorm as Rhys walked close beside her. After the last few hours, she couldn't bear to think about what she needed to do now. Tomorrow, she could talk it over with Jenyx, but tonight called for a hot shower and cold ice cream.

ALL DAY FRIDAY, SHE reconsidered her decision and gave herself one more night before she could bring herself to talk to Jenyx. A few things became clear by the weekend. For one, she couldn't help how she felt about Rhys, but he had no right to look so concerned for her after the mess he'd made. It wasn't fair for him to seem like he cared, and she couldn't be his friend either. That plan had been doomed from the start.

So she'd have to stay away. Which meant trusting Ryx to keep him safe, and leaving him alone to fix things with Emma. She hadn't seen him since lunch on Friday, so that was probably what he was off doing right now. The heartbreak of it all had grown each day as she caught his sideways glances and pained looks. Getting away from that might not be a bad thing, although the idea of being physically separated from where he was felt like it might tear her in two. Even now, when he was presumably somewhere on campus, the distance between them twisted an uncomfortable knot under her ribs.

Then there was Wes. She was still mad at him for turning up at the meeting in the forest.

"They can't keep trying to help me or keep me safe, Jenyx." She was hiding out in her room with Jenner and had finally brought up what had been bugging her since the man showed up at the race. "The people I care about are going to get hurt, and it will be my fault."

"It will be no one's fault but Messoryx. We cannot even blame an army for following the direction of its leader, especially when the alternative is death."

"Those Pyx did have a choice about following him in the first place, though."

Jenner gave a little gruff from his spot on the floor. She wasn't sure whether Jenyx was agreeing with her or not, but it felt like a response to the disgust, making her lip curl. A lot of Pyx seemed more than willing to jump on Messoryx's message and join his forces. Despite what Josh thought might be happening now, it didn't feel like any fewer of them were around. Not from what she'd seen in the memories left in her mind. Not from what she felt when she came into close proximity with any of them.

"They did," Jenyx replied. "We are all capable of making wrong choices."

"I don't feel the hostility as intensely as I used to. Do you think that's because there are more friendly, supportive Pyx around too? Where are they all coming from?" She'd spotted more unfamiliar pyxides watching the school. When she walked to the stables—always with an escort or two—and even outside classroom windows, there was usually a Pyx somewhere in sight. A flash of green would draw her attention, and she'd check to see if the animal looked familiar. Some did, but a lot were new. As long as they weren't people, that was all that mattered.

"I cannot say. There are certainly more. It has become impossible for us to determine if one of the rogue Pyx are near with so many new signatures to sort through. As far as why—all I have to go on is the way I feel drawn to where you are when you need me. That could simply be from spending so much time around you over the years, or even from Jenner's love for you."

She reached down to rub Jenner's belly. "At least I'll still have you, buddy."

"Cara, child, I will say one more time that I wish you would reconsider." He paused while she shook her head, and then continued. "However, I do support you, and I will help you in any way I can. Always."

She swallowed and nodded. "I guess I need to talk to them. Starting with Wes."

In spite of her declaration and her resolve, she lay on her bed a while longer, dreading the next step. Her phone lit up with a message, and she heaved a sigh, barely glancing at the screen. The words registered slowly, and her heart stuttered. It was a message from Rhys. He hadn't texted her since the night after Messoryx had escaped. Sitting up, she flicked a thumb across the screen to check it and found it was a group message sent to her, Wes, Jory, and Liv.

> **We have a big problem.**
> **Coming back early.**
> **Meet me at the manor in 2 hrs.**

She frowned at the screen. They couldn't sneak over to the mansion through the forest. What was he thinking? And where was he? She'd assumed he was nearby with Emma, but it sounded like he'd gone into Portland if it was going to be two hours before he could meet them. She stood up with a groan. They obviously weren't going to go, but she flipped through her closet for a clean shirt anyway.

Liv showed up first, bursting through the door while Cara yanked the fresh shirt over her head.

"Don't you knock?"

"Why? Who are you hiding in here?" Liv gave a dramatic look around. "No, seriously, though. You saw this?" She raised her phone.

"I saw. You don't know what it's about either?"

"Nope."

"Where is he?"

"In town. He goes back most weekends to see our parents." Liv's face fell, and she stooped to pick up Marcus, Delaney's fluffy Himalayan. She stroked his soft fur and held him close. "I should go with him more. It's just so hard to see my mom now. But I'm glad he goes."

Cara's heart clenched for them. She'd had no idea Rhys was going into Portland alone on the weekends instead of spending time at school hanging out with his friends and . . . others.

Don't think about it.

"I'm sorry, Liv. But we can't go over there. It would be insane to go off through the forest after what's been going on."

"He knows that. He wouldn't have asked us if it wasn't important. And if there wasn't a good reason to keep it away from prying eyes and ears at school. Talking in the guys' room the other night was risky. You know the vents have ears."

Wes and Jory showed up at the open door.

"She's right. We have to go," Wes said.

"That's stupid, Wes. It's too dangerous." Cara's jaw tightened at the impassive look on his face. Rude words weren't going to stop him once he got an idea in his head.

"I don't think it's stupid. All they've done is warn us. I doubt they'll try anything if we go in a group, and with you there, we'll know they're coming."

She grumbled at the determination around her. Jory would go along with Liv, and Wes had already decided.

Liv took Jory's hand and glanced between Wes and Cara. "Should we find Harrison? I don't think he got the message."

"No," Wes answered. "He's probably at the Treehouse. Let's leave him out of this."

If they were going to do this, Cara was happy to have fewer people in danger. One extra person in the group wouldn't make the walk any safer and would only endanger Harrison. At least she'd have the rest of them in one place. She might as well tell them her decision all at once when they were together.

"Fine. We'll go. But I still think this is stupid," she said.

"I shall inform some of the Pyx so we have some added protection for you on the way. Will you let Jenner outside, please?" Jenyx asked.

They met up in the lobby an hour later. Cara wore a small bag across one shoulder. Her hand rested across the opening, brushing the edge of her phone on which she'd been messaging for the last half hour. Her thumb ran across the hilt of the knife she'd taken from her drawer. She might not know how to use it properly, but she felt better with something on her. One of the first things she'd do after this was learn to protect herself better.

The walk through the forest was nothing like the times she'd run down the path last year. Then, she'd been drawn to the mansion with a fluttery pull and had enjoyed the beauty of the trees around her while anticipating the peacefulness she'd feel when she arrived. After meeting Rhys and Liv last summer, the trips to the mansion in the fall had been full of hope at being able to do something to save Liv. The pull had turned into anticipation of seeing Rhys again each time.

Now her body and mind fought a silent battle. While she watched the forest and felt for any sense of danger from the Pyx in the trees around them, she also struggled between craving another moment of closeness with Rhys on the one hand, and on the other, not wanting the heartache of seeing him again, knowing they couldn't have what she wanted. Grawlls padded along the trail behind the group, and other Pyx fanned out around them, but the mood was somber. It suited her fine—like the Pyx all knew how she was feeling, so what she picked up from them was only more of what she felt herself.

In spite of her worries, they made it to Whalton manor without incident. Rhys's van sat on the cobblestone driveway, still ticking with heat from the long drive. Cara shuddered at the sight of the door on the edge of the garage leading to the room where they'd held Lydia. Wes squeezed close to her as they crossed the cobblestones where she'd fallen to her knees, drowning in the first visions. She leaned against his shoulder and climbed the stairs with a sigh. Whatever Rhys had to say first, sharing her decision was going to be hard.

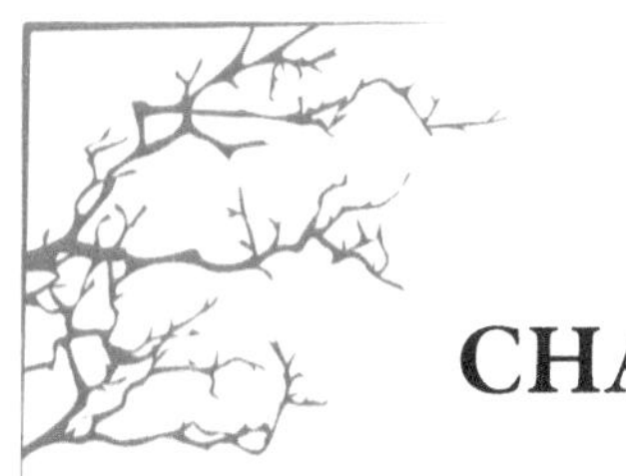

CHAPTER 25

THEY FOLLOWED LIV INSIDE her family's home. Rhys stepped into the hall from the doors to the library and beckoned them in. The wood polish scent and faint echoes of their footsteps off the dark floors brought a flood of memories of the other times she'd been inside the mansion. Now wasn't the time to traipse down memory lane, so she gave her head a shake and entered the library.

"What happened?" Wes got directly to the point.

"You know the news reports about mental health patients having so-called miraculous recoveries?" Rhys asked.

Cara had discussed her uncle's theory with Wes. Apparently Wes had shared it with Rhys.

Wes nodded. "We thought it was possible they were recovering because Pyx who had taken over their minds were now leaving."

Rhys glanced to her and paused. Her nostrils flared. Did they all think she'd miraculously convinced a bunch of Pyx to change their evil ways? It was time to stop living in a fairy tale where one good person could fix the world's problems. Honestly.

"Anyway"—Rhys moved his gaze to his sister and continued—"I was visiting Mom. When I went to leave, the lobby was louder than usual. The staff were all congratulating Hank—you know, the guy from room fourteen? It sounded like he was going home. Cured, or whatever." He shook his head, and his face took on a haunted expression. A chill ran up Cara's spine. "He turned around and saw me. His eyes glow green now. We thought it was Pyx leaving people who only seemed insane. But it's the opposite. These Pyx are taking over sick people and making them act cured so they get released. They're all controlled."

The air sucked out of the room.

The full impact of his words hit her, and she fought the urge to throw up. They were taking advantage of a vulnerable population, and for what? Had they found them to be easier to control? Did something about their illnesses, or maybe their treatments, make them more receptive to giving over control to the Pyx in their minds?

Cara made a choking sound. These people's families thought their loved ones were recovering, when in fact, they'd been stolen away. They were being controlled by another being who could access their memories and take over their lives, but it wasn't them. How many lives had they taken?

"Soldiers," she whispered.

The other four faces, six counting Jenner and Thomas, turned to look at her.

"He's building an army. He stopped randomly taking over all sorts of people and hoping for the best. He might have enjoyed that for a while, toying with humans until they stumbled into ones they could control. But now he's being more calculating. Something about this population makes them better targets, so he's focused his efforts. He's building to something."

Jory let out a low whistle at her analysis. "I know it was serious before, but . . . wow."

The silence around the room said that everyone agreed.

"Then we need a plan," Wes said.

"No. This has to stop." Cara stood from the couch. "All of this has to stop. Messoryx is the leader, and he's threatening me specifically for some reason. If he's gone, then this stops. What he wants right now is me. So I'm leaving."

She held up her hands when everyone in the room protested at once.

"I've already decided. He's sent people to the school. He injured Wes when I was with him. His soldiers attacked when I was at the range with Harrison—who isn't a Pyxsee and didn't know about any of this before then. Then he sent them to threaten anyone close to me at a busy place full of innocent people. I'm not staying here where it constantly puts all of you, let alone the rest of the school, in danger."

"Cares, you can't leave. There's less than a month of school left. We have exams."

"Jory, do you hear yourself?" she practically screeched, and he recoiled when she used his actual name for once. "Who cares about exams? Someone's going to get killed because of me. Fine"—she snapped a look at Jenner when she felt Jenyx's denial—"because of him, but he's only here because of me. Actually, I don't think he's here at all. He's off working on the rest of his plan, but he's sending controlled people after me here. I can't stay."

"So you're going to go off on your own instead? Bad plan, Cara." Irritation dripped from Wes's usually calm voice.

Yeah, he could be mad she hadn't talked it over with him first. He could even be mad that it wasn't his plan. But she had to make him see. She had to make them all see this was the only way.

"My life, my plan," she said. She'd practiced this part in her mind, but forcing the words out took everything she had. The lies tasted rotten and bitter on her tongue, but she pushed forward. "Liv and Jory, you don't need anyone but each other. No one else matters to you, so who cares if I leave?"

Jory's jaw dropped, and Liv looked like she'd been slapped. Cara turned away.

"And you really have nothing to say about my plan, Wes. You're running through the woods with a bow playing hero without a care for what anyone else wants."

His jaw flexed. She couldn't look at Rhys, so she stared at the carpet instead. "And, Rhys, I think you've got enough going on in your own life to figure out. No need to involve me." The quick exhale from his direction was more than she could take. She moved toward the door.

"I'm only taking Jenyx. The rest of you can't help me, and you'll be better off if I'm gone."

Liv dissolved into tears, and Jory stayed to comfort her, but Wes and Rhys followed her to the front entrance. Wes reached out a hand and held the door closed when she tried to jerk it open.

"Nice martyr speech, but if you expect any of us to buy it, you're out of your damn mind. You can't actually think that was going to work on us. Though making your friend cry was a nice touch."

She'd never seen Wes look so mad. His cheeks were redder than ever, and his arm quivered against the door. As if she needed the extra guilt trip. She was already a hollowed-out wreck.

"Take it easy, Wes," Rhys warned him before turning to her. "But we can't let you do this, Cara. He's right about that."

Anger found its way in, and her eyes flashed to his. "You don't get to decide things for me."

He couldn't have it both ways. He didn't get to kiss her, flip her world over, and then go on like they could still be friends. She opened the door when Wes crossed his arms in frustration.

Rhys's eyes bore into hers with all the intensity of the day in his room. Their heat could have melted her, but she let it fuel her frustration instead. They might overlook her speech, but surely they could see this was for the best.

"I know you have no reason to listen to me. But where will you go? How will you get there?" Rhys asked.

"I messaged my uncle. He hasn't agreed yet, but if I travel with him, I can try to find a Pyxsee who knows how they can be killed. Then I can get rid of Messoryx. Eventually."

"At least let me drive you home."

She'd been planning to ask to take his van but was sorely tempted to accept his offer. It was hard enough contemplating leaving the school she thought of as home, and all her friends. A couple more hours with him sounded like both heaven and torture. Biting her lip, she turned to the open doorway and stepped outside. She stopped short before she crashed into the person standing on the steps.

"No one's going anywhere. Now get back inside." Dr. Flanagan stared them down.

The headmaster glanced over her shoulder and shooed them indoors, closing the heavy oak door behind her.

"Rhys, I hope you don't mind me inviting myself in." She stood with her hands crossed in front of her and waited in their stunned silence.

"Uh, no, of course not. Um, please come in," Rhys stuttered.

"Thank you." Dr. Flanagan proceeded down the hall where Jory came out of the library, followed by Liv, who was wiping tears from her wide eyes.

Crap. Now they were all in trouble with the school on top of everything. At least, she and Wes and Jory were. Rhys and Liv were technically allowed to be here since it was their house and they had an arrangement with the school. And really, only Wes and Jory were in trouble. It didn't matter much for her if she was leaving anyway. She had to hope it wouldn't be a problem for Wes's scholarship.

"This is my fault. I invited them all over. I know I should have cleared it with you first." Rhys tried to take the blame.

"I asked him to," Liv added. "I wanted to plan a birthday party for him."

Cara caught his glance when her head snapped over to him. His eighteenth birthday. She'd forgotten it was coming up in a few days.

"I'm not here to dole out detentions, Olivia. However, I would appreciate a word with Cara. Alone, although you may bring Jenner." Dr. Flanagan gave Cara a pointed look.

Cara stared at her headmaster, stunned. How had she known they were here, and why did it sound like she knew something about Jenner?

"Sure. Of course. Ah, you can use the conservatory." Rhys led them through an arch off the front entrance and gestured to a room with large bay windows overlooking the driveway and front gardens.

Cara followed without a word. Jenner padded beside her, and Jenyx radiated the same curious unease she was feeling. Rhys left them after his eyes found hers one last time. Neither of them could figure out what this was about, so the look provided no answers, but he nodded his reassurance to her and then backed out of the room when she dropped her eyes to the marble floor. Once he was gone, she took in her surroundings.

A large piano occupied a third of the room, gleaming with a high gloss finish. On either side, a chaise stretched at an angle beneath pale-green walls so someone sitting there could listen while gazing out the picture window across the room. A low ivory couch spanned the wall beneath the window, tufted with small brass buttons set into its soft leather.

"Please sit, Cara."

People telling her to sit was turning into a bad omen. Her kind headmaster's face was forged into a much stronger and hardened expression than Cara could recall seeing there before. The time she'd been called into her office freshman year after being caught with Jory in the dorm during school hours (a horribly embarrassing misunderstanding) held no comparison to this look. Dr. Flanagan didn't appear curious or disappointed this time. She actually looked pretty fierce.

"I wanted to clear some things up before he arrives," she started. She didn't give Cara time to ask who "he" was. "I understand your desire to leave, and I respect your wish to keep your friends safe. But I promise there is no safer place for you at the moment, or for your friends."

Cara sat with a thud, and the breath rushed out of her to match the whoosh from the leather sofa. What exactly did their headmaster know? Her shock must have shown, because Dr. Flanagan sat down beside her and her face softened.

"Oh yes, I know all about it. And no, before you ask—because I see you trying to search my eyes—I'm not a Pyxsee myself. But I do know what you are. And Wesley and Rhys." She paused to let that sink in. "It's no coincidence you're all at Scovell Academy. Not that we're a school for Pyxsees or anything, but none of you are the first in your families to have these abilities, and we are uniquely positioned to make sure you don't lose your way as you discover what it means to recognize the Pyx among us. There's one in Jenner, isn't there?"

"Remarkable," Jenyx said in Cara's mind. "I truly did not suspect."

"How—?" Cara wasn't sure what to ask.

"I learned of the Pyx from Randall Whalton Senior, Rhys and Olivia's grandfather, when I was hired on to my position fifteen years ago. He passed away a couple years after that, long before Rhys would have begun to show signs of recognizing Pyx. It's a shame. His son, their father, didn't inherit the gene, so he never knew. I would have helped Rhys myself when the time came, but he hadn't shown signs of the ability yet, and then he left abruptly after Olivia fell ill. I blame myself for not recognizing that situation sooner. He's lucky you three found him and were able to help, though I wish you'd trusted someone with that ordeal rather than deal with it yourselves. When I realized what had happened . . ." She clutched at her throat and fell silent.

It was all Cara could do not to fall off the couch. She found one of the brass buttons under her finger and traced the smooth circle while her thoughts raced. All this time . . .

"Wes's family?"

"A great-aunt, I think, and some others further back. The tribal elders who know of Pyxsees suspected his sister Kaiah might develop the ability. She has some gold flecks in her eyes. They arranged for her scholarship first, and it made sense for the rest of the family to follow, especially with Wesley showing so much more Pyxsee-gold even than his sister. Kaiah never demonstrated recognition, though she's a bright and observant young woman. Then, of course, Wesley had fully realized his world before he even arrived. It was interesting that it took you two as long as it did to recognize it in each other, though."

Her mind reeled with how much Dr. Flanagan had known all along. Had she been watching them? "Are there others?"

"Other Pyxsees at Scovell? Not at the moment. Some of the other staff know. Not many."

"Mr. Meyers . . ." She recalled his strange reaction to the noises and howls of anguish from other Pyx after Linnaeryx and the guardian were killed.

"Yes, Owen knows. He's a friend of your uncle's. Did you know?" She carried on after Cara shook her head. "He's kept an eye on Wes. We try to have a dorm parent who understands the situation in each dorm."

"Ms. Lewis?"

"No, but Claire—Mrs. Black—she knows."

Cara didn't have Mrs. Black for any classes, so she'd never interacted much with her other dorm parent. She always went to

Ms. Lewis, whom she knew from French class, when she needed anything, which wasn't often.

"Why keep it a secret? And do Liv and Rhys know their grandfather knew about this? Wait, was he a Pyxsee?"

"Grandpa Whalton?" Liv burst into the room.

"Liv!" Rhys called down the hall and followed her in a moment later. "Sorry. She wouldn't take no for an answer."

Cara could practically hear his voice from last fall joking about how stubborn his sister could be.

"Our grandfather was a Pyxsee? Why didn't he tell us? Why didn't he tell Dad?

Rhys put a hand to his sister's shoulder and tried to steer her away. "Liv, you were, like, three when he died. You don't even remember him."

"I was three when my dad died. I remember a few things." Cara barely recognized her voice as the words came out. The room stilled. "Not much, but some."

"Cara . . . I'm sorry. I didn't think . . ." Rhys dropped his hands from his sister's arm and turned into the room. His face shone in the light from the window as he focused on her. For a moment, it was only the two of them.

Dr. Flanagan cleared her throat. "Rhys, Olivia, you may as well come in. To answer your question, Olivia, yes, your grandfather was a Pyxsee. As was Oliver Whalton, who founded Scovell Academy back in the forties. Your grandfather never told your father because he's not a Pyxsee, but I'm sure he would have told Rhys if he'd lived long enough. Given everything that happened with you, Rhys, I'm inclined to say we may want to consider telling Randall." She gave him a sympathetic look. "I seem to think there's been some unnecessary strain on your relationship while he fails to understand your actions in, er, killing Olivia. I know it was to save her, and your father is happy with the outcome and so has chosen to protect you, but it would probably help him to understand if he knew the reason behind what you did. The decision is yours, but I'll help you explain it to him if you'd like."

Rhys sat down hard on the piano bench. "I don't know."

"Give it some thought."

Cara took in his strained face and yearned to go to him, to comfort him. She'd had no idea his relationship with his dad hadn't recovered when Liv did. Did Wes know? Did Emma?

Stop. Danger. Don't think about that.

She couldn't be the one to help him, even when flashes of the broken guy she'd first met came flooding back as he lowered his elbows to his knees and stared at the floor. She tore her eyes away. "How do you know so much about what's been going on?" she asked the headmaster.

"Partly, I'm naturally observant. Just ask Jory. I told you I see things, didn't I?" Their headmaster looked up.

Cara followed her gaze and found Wes and Jory leaning on either side of the doorway with Thomas between their legs. *Stealthy.* There'd never been a point in keeping this conversation private, anyway. If she stayed, she would have told them all eventually.

"I believe it was one of the things that earned me this job in the first place. I may not be a Pyxsee, but picking up things most people don't notice or see can come in handy in a lot of ways as a headmaster. Like when I spot a bear hanging around my school. It helps to know if he's under a safe and friendly influence, wouldn't you say?" Dr. Flanagan gave them all a knowing look and focused on Jenner. "He is one of yours, isn't he?"

Jenyx's surprise rolled through Cara, and she sat back, letting go of the brass button she'd been twisting. Jenyx rarely controlled Jenner in any way that would be unnatural for him, but the dog dropped his head once in an unmistakable nod.

"I thought so. After the roar accompanying the howls that day, I wasn't about to miss a bear strolling into the middle of campus with a dog I already had a suspicious eye on. And aside from being more observant than most, I also have sources." Dr. Flanagan turned to the window at the sound of an approaching car. "Here's one of them now."

Cara turned on the couch and then stood up to see better. A bright-blue car pulled into the driveway. She couldn't see the driver past the tinted windows, but she didn't recognize the vehicle. When the door opened and the driver climbed out, she gasped.

"Uncle Josh!"

She ran for the front door.

Josh stepped around the car to meet her, and she threw herself into her uncle's waiting arms.

"But, wait a second." She immediately pulled back again. "I was just texting you. Why didn't you say something? Are you here to take me with you? How long have you been spying on me?"

"Whoa, calm down, kiddo."

It was the wrong thing to say. All the anger, fear, and frustration that had faded behind the shock of Dr. Flanagan's revelations surged back to the surface.

"Calm down? Are you serious? You knew all this, and you let me sneak out of school and risk coming through the woods with my friends instead of just coming to get me? Do you have any idea—How are you even here? I thought you were—" Actually, she had no idea where she thought he'd been. She'd forgotten to ask where he was off to next after seeing him over spring break. She was too used to him leaving again all the time.

He held up his hands in surrender. "I know, I know. Sorry. Poor choice of words. And I never left. I'm glad you didn't ask, though. I wouldn't have wanted to lie to you. To answer one of your questions, letting you kids meet over here was a convenient way to set this up secretly so we didn't have to hide it from other people at the school. Now let's go in and I'll answer the rest."

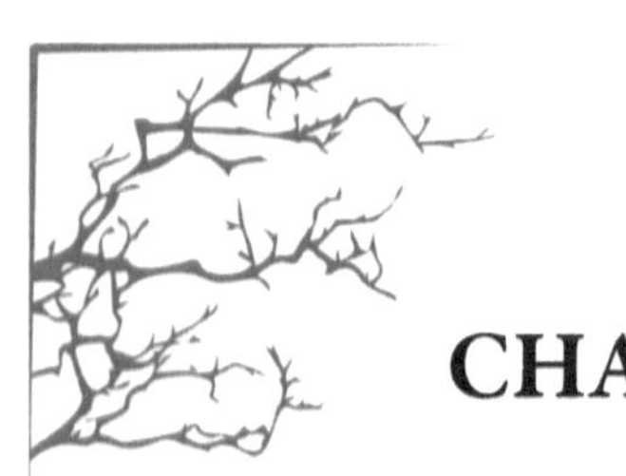

CHAPTER 26

"AGAIN," CARA SAID. She wiped the sweat from her brow and turned back to Josh.

He raised his eyebrows at her and then lunged forward to grab at her arm. She tried not to flinch and quickly balled her hand into a tight fist below his grasp. Fighting the urge to pull away, she stepped into him, grabbed her own fist with her other hand, and started to turn.

"Elbow up." Josh corrected her form.

She raised the elbow and twisted again. This time, she was able to wrench away from his grasp. She stood upright and rubbed at her wrist.

"Don't forget to use your core the whole time so you aren't flailing around. Your jerk will be cleaner and won't hurt so much. Then what?"

"Run, if I can."

"Or?"

"Pivot and don't stop fighting. Eyes, nose, throat, groin."

"Good. Ready for a break? Let's get you a cool cloth for that wrist."

For two weeks of training, it didn't feel like she'd learned much yet, but it was better than nothing. At least she'd finally stopped tripping over backward every time her uncle attacked. Josh and Dr. Flanagan had managed to convince her to stay for only two reasons. Number one, it was true there was only a month of school left. Down to only two more weeks now, and exams would take up the last one. And number two, Josh was staying on campus with the sole purpose of teaching her some self-defense and working with her on separating her emotions from the Pyx. They were focused on keeping her safe, and she was focused on how she could use it to keep the rest of her friends safe.

After the day at Whalton manor, her friends had forgiven her, though she still wasn't sure she deserved it. A twinge of guilt still hit her every time she ended up alone with Liv and Jory. They'd never made her feel awkward before, but by lying and saying they did, she'd made things a little tense. It was improving, and Jory seemed fine, but she could tell she'd hurt Liv more than she could make up for in two short weeks.

"Is Mr. Cook coming back tonight?" she called to her uncle.

Josh stepped out from the kitchen and handed her the wet cloth. He sat down beside her on the couch. "No, he'll be back in time for Monday morning classes."

Her English teacher had one of the staff apartments with a small second bedroom. Since he went home to his wife and kid in Portland on the weekends, he'd graciously offered the room to Josh when Dr. Flanagan asked around. They cleared out the living room for practice space from the time he left on Thursday evenings until he returned on Sunday night or Monday morning. Since Josh's friend who taught at the school turned out to be Owen, and since Mr. Meyers lived in the boys' dorm, Josh couldn't simply crash at his place. Too many legal complications and background checks to be resolved in a short amount of time.

This was the next best solution so he could be on campus but not directly with all the students.

"Where did you learn all this stuff?" she asked. Her uncle's knowledge had been a surprise—one of many that day and in the two weeks since.

"We all take basic training and then refresher courses twice a year for work. Some of us who enjoy it do extra; plus, we get some advanced training depending on where we're going. It's a pretty good idea to know how to avoid being abducted in a lot of places."

She suppressed a chuckle. Someone should have taught all the Pyx Rhys had abducted. The laugh died in her throat when she thought of all the people basically being abducted now as Pyx took them over. "When are you going to teach me attacking stuff? I want to know how to use that knife."

"One step at a time. Master defense before you go attacking anyone."

She liked that her uncle never tried to talk her out of it. Sometimes it seemed like he had just been waiting for the right time to prepare her for this fight. Whatever the reason, she was grateful after the reluctance from both Jenyx and Rhys when she'd tried to convince them to help her learn how to kill Messoryx. This summer would be non-stop training with her uncle sticking around. He'd already found a place to rent in Portland for the next few months, and he'd bought the car since he'd be staying.

"Fine, but I want to learn that move to break a hold from behind next." She couldn't forget the feeling of Lydia's arms squeezing the life from her while she struggled uselessly against her grip.

"We'll get there. That one's all about the hips. Unless you're lifted off the ground, then it's all about the heels." Josh smiled. "Part two?"

She groaned. As much as she enjoyed the self-defense lessons, she barely endured the lectures that always followed.

"Do we have to? Scrappiness for beginners I'm all over, but Politics and Persuasion 101 is not my thing."

Now that they knew the Pyx weren't leaving people in droves, and the opposite was true, she figured everyone would leave her alone about how she might be affecting them. For some reason, Josh hadn't let the idea go, and he insisted on trying to teach her how to use her so-called powers of persuasion.

"Like it or not, the world has a lot of politics in it. My job has it, your school has it, and the Pyx are no different. It's about reading people. You saw the angles I worked for fundraising at the gala last year. That's one side of persuasion in my job, but there are a lot more sensitive areas to navigate when we're working with foreign governments and local people in the areas we try to help. It's not my favorite part of the whole thing, but it's a critical piece to know and understand so you can use it to your advantage. You're naturally trustworthy, Care-a-lot." He gave her shoulder a squeeze and ignored her exasperated look. "I've seen it. People gravitate to you, especially now that you've opened up and let people in. Look at Wes and Jory. They went from your sworn enemies to loyal best friends in, what, under two months?"

"Great. I convinced a couple high school kids to like me. Next step, world domination." Why did people keep thinking she could magically convince others to follow her? "Be serious. I need more than a pep talk. If you want me to learn this, I need specifics."

"Good. I don't want it to be a pep talk. This is too important. How are you doing with separating your emotions from theirs?"

This should really be called part three to this whole training thing. As much as she hated the pointers on manipulating people, which was how she insisted on thinking about it, this was the part she was struggling with the most. Her nose wrinkled.

"The same." She practiced with Jenyx most nights. He'd work on projecting some emotion to her, and she'd try to sense it without feeling it herself. So far, she'd startled Delaney by crying, bursting out laughing, and literally growling from her bed. So yeah . . . it wasn't going great.

"Are you using the visuals we talked about?"

"Trying to. I did a little meditation before Jenyx and I started, like we said. I pictured the room with the wall dividing it like I imagined that one time. I can't make it work, though." For a brief moment, when she'd confronted the vicious Pyx in the clearing before the attack on Linnaeryx, Cara remembered feeling the Pyx's anger as if it were on another side of a wall from her own sorrow. It had been like her mind had opened up two sides of the space where she felt things—one for herself and one for the Pyx. But she hadn't been able to replicate it since.

"Keep trying. That's important too."

That one she believed him on. She'd been wanting to separate her emotions from the Pyx since she'd started feeling the hostility in the area, and especially since Wes's injury after she'd let herself be swept up in it. But by the time Josh walked her back to the dorms before dinner, Cara's eyes had glazed over from all the talk of the power of persuasion. She'd earn her black belt *and* master knife-throwing before she ever learned this leadership crap.

"HOW ARE YOU SO GOOD at this, Wes?" Cara gave the knife in her hand a dirty look.

He looked at her with a serious expression. "Genetics."

"Ha ha. Not falling for that again. I guess it makes sense you'd have a bit of an edge with the aim, being so good with your bow. Your mom did tell me you were a natural when you started that too."

"Aha. So it is an unfair advantage," Harrison said. "I knew it."

"Natural talent or not, any target activity takes practice. A lot of it. This is no different." Josh wrenched the knives from the backstop of the archery range and picked up the ones that had fallen uselessly to the ground. "Don't worry about the rings for now. Work on a consistent throw and figuring out your distance."

Cara and her uncle had decided to use the archery range when she insisted he start training her how to throw knives. He'd been hesitant, saying he was no expert at it, but eventually gave in and said he knew enough to show her the basics. She'd been the one to suggest the range, and checked with Wes when it would be free. They'd decided to go together since Harrison had asked Wes for one last training session before exams and the end of school. He didn't need it. The school teams were all done for the year, but Wes had agreed to one more as a favor, so they joined Cara and Josh and practiced alongside them.

"If you get decent at this, you'll need a proper instructor who knows what they're doing. I still don't think I should be trying to show you this. And your mom will probably kill me, Cara-vel." Josh gave her a conspiratorial grin to go with his never-ending nicknames and handed her two of the knives.

He wouldn't let her use the knife she'd taken from the tree.

"That's a multipurpose knife," he'd said. "It has an edge all the way along it. Too dangerous and difficult for you to start with. These are throwing knives. They have a point but barely any sharp edge to them. We'll start with these, at least until you know what you're doing. Plus, they're made for this, so they're a little easier to learn with."

On the plus side, he also hadn't taken that knife away, and with the sheath he'd found for her, it was tucked carefully inside her shorts, fastened to a thin belt resting against her hip and hidden from view. They'd agreed not to tell anyone she was walking around school with a knife now. Dr. Flanagan might be tempted to allow it if she knew, given the circumstances, but then she'd lose her job if anyone found out. This way, the headmaster could deny knowing anything about it. Cara tugged at the tank top she wore, making sure it was covered. The flared bottom of the shirt was more fashionable than her usual athletic look, but it hid the top of the knife perfectly without a weird bulge she couldn't explain.

Wes and Harrison had abandoned their bows to watch her, and they each took a few turns when Josh offered. So far, Wes was the only one who'd managed to hit one of the targets. Cara had only hit the backstop properly a couple times. All the other times, even if she hit the rings, the knife was the wrong way around and clattered off the wood to fall to the dirt. Harrison was worse than she was.

"Try again. Straight wrist. Like swinging a hammer," Josh encouraged her.

She set her left foot forward and shifted her weight until she felt comfortable. Holding the knife with her fingers in the groove at the end of the handle, she let it settle against her hand between her thumb and forefinger like Josh had shown her. Her eyes focused on the target in front of her, and she took a couple breaths before raising the knife. Her hand moved in a smooth arc in her peripheral vision, and the blade spun across the space to dig in with a satisfying *thunk*.

It was high. Off target. But it was pointy end first, and that was a win for today. Harrison gave her a cheer that far exceeded what she'd accomplished, but she grinned back at him.

"Enough for today?" Josh asked. "You don't want to be too sore for our training tomorrow if you want to work on that hold break you keep asking about."

"Sounds good." She perked up to hear he would finally show her how to break the hold Lydia had used on her. The memory of the woman's preternaturally strong grasp around her ribs still haunted her.

She didn't mind quitting for today with that promise for tomorrow. Besides, the Pyx would be happier once she was out of the woods. Grawlls stood from his position in the trees at the southern edge of the range, ready to accompany them. Jenner shook bits of forest from his coat when he rose from his spot near the bench. Their unease had prickled the back of her mind the whole time they'd been here, but with no other sign of the outlaws, it was background noise among her other thoughts and feelings.

Harrison and Wes gathered their gear to leave too. The little red fox slipped out from the underbrush and trotted over to weave around Wes's ankles once before she led the way down the path toward the football field and the rest of campus. Her tail swished in the air with each step, and Cara had to suppress an urge to skip along the trail after her. With a quiet giggle, she looped her hand through Wes's free arm.

"I think she likes you," she whispered.

He couldn't help a little smirk, and she squeezed his arm. After his anger at her for upsetting Liv and Jory when she'd tried to leave, he'd gone right back to being her stoic best friend. She couldn't express how grateful she was that he hadn't believed her rants for even a second. She'd always thought Jory was the fiercely loyal type, but Wes might have him beat. He just did it quieter . . . with less punching people in the face.

"I know we have to study for exams, but how about one last old movie night tomorrow after my self-defense session with my uncle?"

"Definitely. We haven't had one in a while. We can watch the old DiCaprio version of Romeo and Juliet and call it studying at the same time."

"Ooh, good idea. I love Benvolio in that version. I have no idea why." She glanced at his face and found him trying not to laugh at her. She gave him a playful hip check. "It's a date."

"Ah, Cara?" Wes's face twisted into a curious look. "Is that a knife in your pocket, or are you just happy to see me?"

Her cheeks flushed. She'd forgotten the knife was there, and gave a quick glance to make sure Harrison was out of hearing range, but he was chatting with her uncle several steps behind. "Don't say anything, okay? I feel better having it on me, even if I don't know how to use it yet. I don't want to be helpless again."

"You were never helpless. Rhys told me how badass you were with Lydia, and I was there when we fought her off the first time. But I get it. I've started keeping my bow in my room instead of leaving it with the rest of the team's stuff. It feels better having something nearby."

"Not that it helps us. We don't know what to do with them. I know the Pyx can't tell us how to kill them, but I wish I knew. What if something happens? How are we supposed to protect ourselves?"

Wes reached his other hand across to cover hers where it still rested on his arm. He didn't need to say anything. It was enough to know he was there with her.

The Pyx didn't have to say anything either. She felt their anxiety every time she brought up the topic. She sighed and said goodnight to her uncle before heading to the dorms for a wild Friday night of studying for exams.

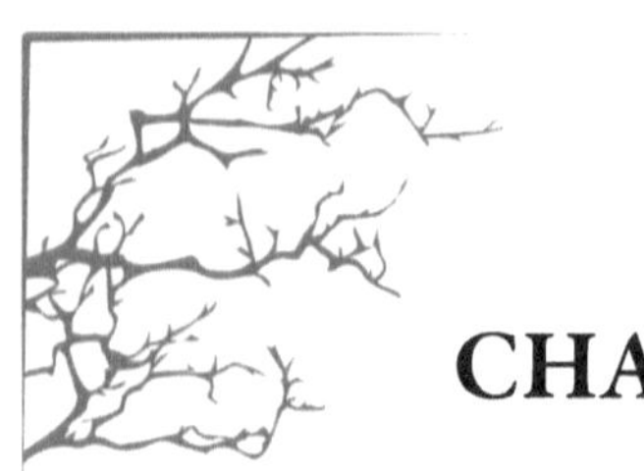

CHAPTER 27

"READY?"

Cara nodded, and Josh's arms closed around her from behind. Fighting off the flash of panic and a shiver at the memory of Messoryx's attack in February, she ran through the steps in her head.

Back up into it. Hips to the side. Twist down and spin. Elbow up.

"Good." Josh blocked her elbow at the side of his head as she spun out of the hold for the dozenth time.

She turned her back to him to start again.

"Ready?"

She nodded, and he squeezed.

"Now this time—" He squeezed her tighter, and her feet left the ground.

Her vision tunneled. Goosebumps rippled down her limbs, and she shrieked. His arms loosened immediately, but not before she flashed back to the dark space between two buildings when Lydia's arms had crushed her ribs and driven the air from her lungs with the super strength of Messoryx's control. Tears made the room swim as she remembered the panic in Rhys's eyes looking back at her and her desperate struggle to breathe.

She dropped to the floor, and bitter hatred flooded her. Messoryx had nearly taken her life the way he'd taken so many others.

"I'm so sorry, Care Bear. I should have warned you first."

Her uncle reached for her as she turned and stumbled a step away from him with the lingering fear and anger surging through her. Jenner leaped up with a growl. He snapped at Josh's outstretched arm and almost caught him before Josh could jerk his hand back in alarm.

"Whoa." She held out a hand to Jenner. All three of them took a sharp breath and froze. When she glanced at her uncle, she found him peering suspiciously at Jenner. She gave her dog the same look. "Jenyx, what the crap was that? Jenner's never snapped at anyone before. What's going on?"

Jenner had relaxed and was now sitting calmly on the carpet with a worried arch above his eyes. He looked like he had destroyed a pair of shoes or torn up a couch cushion.

"My deepest apologies, Joshua. I do not know what happened. When you screamed, Cara, I felt your fear. It was similar to the day the Pyx attacked at the archery range and I knew you needed me though I was a short distance away at the time. But I do not know where the anger came from, and I certainly should not have let it drive my control over Jenner. I am terribly sorry."

"You felt her fear?" Josh asked. "And this happened before?"

"Indeed. I have been giving it a lot of thought since then, and I believe there have been other times. More subtle than the intensity of fear, but at times, it has seemed as though her emotions affected mine in addition to the other way around. I know Cara and I are closely connected after years together, but

I have never known that sort of inherent knowledge of someone in danger. Not before now."

"And the anger?"

"That might have been my fault too," Cara said. "I hate the memory of that attack and knowing everything that happened after it. I hate Messoryx for all the awful things I see in his memories and for leaving me with all this baggage. But mostly, I don't want him to get away with whatever he's planning. It makes me furious he's out there."

"And you picked up on that, Jenyx?"

"It would appear so."

"Did you know he was sensing your emotions, too? Do others?" Josh turned to her.

She shrugged. "Not really. I guess I might have noticed a few times where I can't tell who's feeling what, but I figured that's because my feelings were aligning to match theirs because I can't separate them. I've only noticed it with Jenyx." A memory sprang to her mind of running out of the Dougie after kissing Rhys and Grawllyx offering to take revenge for her anger and confusion. "Maybe once with Grawllyx too. He felt pretty angry one time when I was sort of having . . . a thing. I was a little too wrapped up in my own stuff to notice at the time."

Josh rubbed a hand across his day-old stubble. Cara pursed her lips. Being an empath meant she picked up on the emotions of the Pyx, not the other way around. This was going to be another one of those things no one could understand because she wasn't like other Pyxsees. Why did this keep happening? She wouldn't trade being a Pyxsee. Not anymore. But couldn't she be the normal version of this already not-normal thing? Why did she always have to be an exception?

"Are we done for today? I have a date with Wes."

Josh dropped his hand, and his eyebrows rose.

"Not that kind of date. Like, a me and Wes date. Never mind. It's not a date, but I am supposed to meet him."

"Sure. Of course." He sounded distracted, and she grew more eager to leave. He probably wanted to start calling his Pyxsee friends and contacts to ask awkward questions about how weird she was . . . again.

Outside the castle-like stone building, she looked up to see the red fox sniffing her way through the meadow. Her red and tan fur matched the colors of the grass, unusually dry for the start of June.

"Where's Wes?" Cara asked.

"Right behind you."

She jumped at his voice and whirled around to find him stifling a laugh.

"Didn't mean to scare you. I was leaning against the wall in the shade. That's all."

She swatted his shoulder. "Don't do that. You have no idea." Her head shook with the confusion of the last few minutes, and she looked to Jenner. Did Jenyx really sense her emotions too? Was she going to start having to worry about her angry outbursts triggering her dog to growl and snap now?

Wes fell into step beside her as they started toward the dorms. He walked in silence and waited for her to elaborate if she wanted.

"It's nothing important. Not yet, anyway. Suffice it to say I'm really looking forward to a nice, normal movie night. Can we stop by the Cedars first? I could use a clean shirt."

Wes waited in her lounge while she ran to her room to change, and then they headed over to the Lodge.

"Where's Tomyx?" she asked when they entered the room and she couldn't find Thomas's furry orange shape anywhere.

"Following Jory around."

"Where's Jory?"

"I think he was taking Liv on a hot date to the library." Wes grabbed his laptop. "Studying. Then to the Treehouse, if I remember right."

"Perfect." She stole Jory's pillow and crawled onto Wes's tidy bed, tucking the pillow behind her against his headboard. She nestled into a comfortable spot where they'd watched countless movies together over the past year.

Wes joined her, opening his laptop. "Hang on, I have to find it. Mak distracted me while I was looking earlier."

"Oh?"

"Yeah. I don't know what's gotten into him. He keeps coming over to talk. It started about three weeks ago. Seriously, everyone was acting weird that week."

"Oh." She bit her lip. She was running out of ways to avoid the subject. If Mak had come over right after she'd yelled at him in Rhys's room, then she probably had some explaining to do to Wes.

"Yeah. Rhys was acting strange. Liv noticed too. Something was definitely up with you. You still seem off. And yeah, Mak. He came over that Sunday and asked Jory to leave. Which was my first clue, because he's always happier to talk to Jory than to me. It freaked me out. I thought something happened to Kaiah or our parents. But everything's fine. He just wanted to talk."

"What did you talk about?"

Wes abandoned the search for the movie and held the laptop idly in one hand with a thoughtful expression on his face. "Nothing in particular. He asked how things were with school, and about people. He asked about you. Bonehead still couldn't figure out we're friends and not dating. I think he finally gets it. Oh, and he has a girlfriend now."

Cara grimaced at the part about her before she could hide it under the surprise of hearing Mak was dating someone.

Wes turned his head and narrowed his eyes. "Why do I feel like you know something about this?"

"Yeah. I might be able to explain all those things. Well, not Mak having a girlfriend . . . but good for him."

"So this involves Rhys somehow?"

Her nose wrinkled into a guilty look. The knots in her stomach rolled and tossed around, but she pushed the laptop out of his grasp and slipped her hand into his for courage. "You could say that." She leaned against her friend and spilled.

"I sort of kissed him. Rhys." Her eyes squeezed shut, but she felt his little jolt of surprise against her side. She had to continue before she lost her nerve. "It was after the meeting with the outlaw, after the guardian was killed. When I went over there . . . I don't know. It just sort of happened. Then your brother walked in."

He leaned away from her to look down at her face. "Wait, what?"

"Yeah, um, he kind of caught us. But he was mad because of you. It was sort of sweet in a sad way. He was angry on your behalf because he thought we were a thing. I, ah, might have yelled at him."

His shoulder shook as he chuckled. "Damn, I wish I'd seen that."

"I may have insinuated that he should know you better. I hope I didn't cross a line. Are you mad?"

"No. It's been fine. Nice, even. We're not magically going to be close, but it's good to think we'll do a better job of being brothers since he's graduating at the end of the week. When he goes to college this fall, it would be nice if we still talked sometimes. I can't believe you kissed Rhys and didn't tell me."

Her throat constricted. Wes sounded happy for her. He didn't understand the mess.

"Hey. What . . .? Isn't that a good thing?"

She couldn't speak and turned her head to his chest instead. He brought his arm up and wrapped it around her, pulling her closer. The dam broke.

With the comfort of her best friend and his warm strength enveloping her in a safe cocoon, she let the tears flow. Full ugly-cry style. The worries about being found out, the guilt over Emma, and the ache that consumed her all snowballed together and burst through her walls. The flood of emotion joined forces with the stress of the past few months and her impotence in the face of everything she'd seen from Messoryx, until she was wracked with sobs. Wes had to pass her tissues between gasps for air. Her tears stained his shirt, but he didn't let go. He held her quietly until her tears ran out and her breaths steadied with exhaustion.

"I'm sorry. Do you want to tell me why it's not all paradise and rainbows now? I figured once you two sorted yourselves out, everything would be smooth sailing."

She sniffed again, sitting up and wiping her face with another tissue.

"I don't know why you thought that. It shouldn't have happened. I was asking him about learning how to kill a Pyx, and he was emotional because of the memories that time brings up for him. That's all. It was just a weird vibe and it went too far. It didn't mean what I wanted it to mean. Not to him. He came over to clear the air the next morning at breakfast, and we agreed it had been a mistake. That's when Liv said he was acting weird."

"What? None of that sounds right." He paused, thinking. "I mean, I don't know what led to the kiss, but I know that's not when Liv said he was acting strange. She was over here with Jory before Mak came by and said Rhys was acting weird that same night. Her exact words were "he was practically buzzing." Are you sure he said it was a mistake?"

The knots inside broke apart into a million wriggling worms at the mere thought that Rhys could have been happy about the kiss. But the conversation the next morning, after she'd seen him smiling with Emma . . . she hadn't made that part up. Maybe he had been happy for a little while—her insides flipped over with the idea—but then he'd seen Emma again and things must have changed.

What exactly had he said that morning? Think, Cara. What did you say?

Had she let him say anything at all? She'd been heartbroken and more than a little angry. She hadn't wanted to hear him say the words.

"I guess he didn't say that exactly. But he agreed. We haven't talked about it since, and he's back to normal now. Or getting there." She couldn't bring herself to say Emma's name out loud.

The crush of guilt was too much even though the two of them still looked like they were together.

"No he's not." Wes's low voice beside her ear made her turn.

Wiping her face with her sleeve, she looked at him.

He sighed. "I have no idea what you've been thinking, but he likes you. A lot. Haven't you noticed how he tracks your movements, and the little smile he gets whenever you say something funny? He's drawn to you."

Cara blinked. The words coming out of Wes's mouth made no sense. "He never smiles around me. That's why I thought I made him think of all the bad stuff with Liv. Why he'd never be able to see me for me."

"What? Oh, Cara, no. Okay . . . remember Jory before he and Liv made things official? Remember how his expression changed around her?"

"Yeah. It wasn't his usual grin. He has a different smile for her. Sweeter."

"And . . ."

It took her a minute to see what he was hinting at, but then her head shook back and forth. "It's not the same."

"Why not?"

Yeah, Cara, why not?

She clung to Wes like the world had started spinning in the opposite direction. "I don't know. It just . . . can't be. What are you saying?"

"I'm saying now it makes sense why he's been acting so off the last few weeks. You both have. You said he's back to normal, but I promise you he's not. Actually, I've barely talked to him because he's been so distant."

Her heart threatened to pound through her ribcage. It hammered in her throat hard enough to make breathing difficult. It wanted to fly free with a string of butterflies chasing after it. Only one problem.

"But he has a girlfriend," she whispered.

"What?" Wes pushed her away so he could give her an incredulous look at arm's length. "He doesn't have a girlfriend."

The cage burst open, and her heart sailed. All she could do was stare until her heart returned to its home in her chest. She wasn't sure how it could function properly when it kept flipping over and twisting inside out and back again.

"He doesn't?" she breathed.

"No." Wes pulled her close again. "Honestly. For someone so smart, you are a complete disaster. You know that?"

She gave a shaky laugh, and a few more tears leaked out. She didn't want to ask Wes how long Rhys had been single. Not yet. This way, there was a chance it had been before he'd kissed her. This way, it was possible it hadn't been a mistake at all. She nestled back into Wes's hug and felt the grin spread across her face until her cheeks hurt.

"Okay, screw movie night," Wes said. "You need to go talk to him. You two need to figure out what this is."

Her smile faltered. She had no idea how to do that. "He's probably in town for the weekend, anyway."

"Fine, then text him. You have his number, right? Don't say no, because I'll just give it to you. Or call him . . . Or I'll text him."

"Stop, stop." She was laughing again. "Promise me you won't do anything."

"Why? Why not?"

"Wes. Promise."

She needed to sort out her thoughts after being mad at Rhys for the past few weeks for something he might not have done. Before she could talk to him, she had to shift how she'd been thinking about this and figure out what to say. It had been so long thinking of him as unavailable. How did she readjust? She'd also probably have to work up the nerve to find out when he and Emma had broken up so she knew what the situation really was. If it was after the Valentine's dance, then that changed everything. She'd been so mean about their kiss since that day; she couldn't imagine what he must be thinking at this point. He could have changed his mind by now. There was a lot to think about.

"Fine. I'll promise on two conditions," Wes replied.

"I'm scared to ask."

"The first one is there's a time limit. Two weeks. I'll talk to him myself if you haven't done it in two weeks."

"A month. Come on. This week is exams, and then we'll be settling in at home for the summer. I need time to think and figure out how to talk to him. Jory took four months to tell Liv how he felt."

"And I've been watching you trip over yourself around Rhys for a year now." He gave her a hard look. "Fine. Three weeks. I can't be surrounded by idiots any longer than that." He was smiling, but then his face turned serious. "The second one is you can't pull the stunt you tried at the mansion again."

The bubbly mood deflated. He'd forgiven her easily, but apparently he hadn't forgotten.

"You can call me out for playing the hero, or whatever. I know I can be quick to decide on something that makes sense to me, and I act too fast sometimes. But you can't go off on your own and you can't try to sacrifice yourself for us. Especially me .. . and Rhys too. Not because of any of this other stuff, but because this is our fight as much as it is yours. We're Pyxsees too. And there's no way Jory's letting us take this on without him, either. You don't get to stand alone, and none of us are okay with you martyring yourself to get to Messoryx. Promise you won't try to take off again."

"I'm sorry, Wes. I really am." She'd hurt him more than she'd realized. Starting with not confiding in him after Messoryx had invaded her mind and left her with the memories and visions, and then more when she'd left him out of her decision to leave. "I won't. I promise. And after next week, when we go home for the summer, we'll be together every day. We can train and everything. We'll come up with an actual plan to deal with Messoryx. A Wes-certified plan. Deal?"

"Deal. Still want to watch Romeo and Juliet?"

"Does a rose by any other name smell as sweet?"

He rolled his eyes at her. "Let's ace this English final and get to planning this summer."

She snaked her hand back into his and leaned into the comfort of his shoulder. With friends like this, she could take on any enemy.

CHAPTER 28

STUDENTS AT THIS SCHOOL sure knew how to celebrate the last day of exams. Following their history final, Cara spilled out of the social studies building with her classmates to the sound of joyful shouts and people reveling everywhere. The tops of the trees in the surrounding forest swayed in a rippling wind, but down in the shelter of the clearing, it was a soft summer breeze. Early June heat had made the classrooms uncomfortably warm for writing exams, but outside, the fresh air licked at the beads of sweat on their brows, and Cara swept her hair into a ponytail to feel its refreshing breath on the back of her neck.

A group of juniors had started a raucous game of ultimate frisbee on the lawn between the dining hall and the Dougie. She paused to watch, and Wes stopped beside her. They'd spent the week together, studying and going back and forth from the staff apartments at the castle when she had training sessions with her uncle. Wes had sat in on a few with her. With exams, she'd had to cut back, but they'd managed another session at the archery range, where Harrison had tagged along again.

"Last day blues?" Wes asked.

She had sighed without meaning to. "I guess so. As much as I wanted to leave, and in spite of all the bad stuff that happened this year, I love this place."

"I know the feeling."

"It's okay, though. My uncle left this morning to set up his place in the city. We've got Jory's house as headquarters for hanging out and planning. Liv's already offered up a whole summer of pool parties at her place. It'll be great." She tried to sound convinced, but all the happiness from the students around her refused to sink in.

To his credit, Wes said nothing about her promise to talk to Rhys within the next few weeks, but she could practically hear the gears spinning in his head as he mentally planned out their summer. Was he worrying about being a fifth wheel if things went well? And what if they didn't? She hadn't figured out what to say to Rhys yet, and had still been avoiding him, although she'd managed to give him a small smile when he'd joined them at breakfast one day. She tried not to dwell on the confused look he'd worn, and told herself she'd figure it out once they all made it home and she had time alone to think.

A bit of cool separation kept her from enjoying the moment as much as she'd have liked. She didn't think it was lingering exam stress. Those had gone pretty well, aside from one math question she already knew she'd gotten wrong thanks to Harrison's annoying habit of talking about exams after they were done. She tried not to curse Mr. Meyers for the tricky question.

If it wasn't exams, then this feeling must be related to her reluctance to leave for the summer. She'd have to shake it off and try to enjoy the last day of her sophomore year.

"Want to come pick up Jenner with me? Liv might be down at the stables riding Charlie one more time before we leave tomorrow. Jory's probably there too."

"Yeah, let's go."

"Go where? Hey, Shorty. Hey, Wolfie." Mak loped up from behind them and draped an arm across each of their shoulders.

"Hi, Mak." It was the first time she'd spoken to Wes's brother since yelling at him, and a little flash of the anger from that day wormed through her. She bit it back, embarrassed. "How were your finals?"

"No problem. Solid passes, for sure." He grinned at her, and she hoped that meant all was forgiven. "Things are good all around. Someone gave me a little kick I might have needed."

Wes shook his head. Cara would have been happy with being forgiven, but apparently Mak was actually grateful.

"Guess we all need a good kick sometimes. What's this I hear about a girlfriend?"

Mak dropped his arms from them and turned to his brother. "And I guess some people can't keep a secret."

"Why is it a secret? Are you embarrassed?" Cara asked.

"About dating the greatest girl here? Definitely not. She's just a private person and didn't want to stoke the gossip fires for the last few months of school. But tomorrow . . . tomorrow we graduate and show our epic love to the world." He held his arms above his head with a broad smile, making Cara laugh. Even Wes smiled for his brother's over-the-top happiness.

Cara tapped Mak in the stomach, and he made a big show of dropping his arms as if she'd punched him in the gut, doubling over with a dramatic groan. He was clearly enjoying the fun mood of the school. She tried for a bit of it. "I can keep a secret for one day, then. Who is it?"

He glanced around theatrically, then leaned in and stage-whispered to her. "Emma. You know . . . Rhys's friend. Oh, actually, you know her from cross country and track, don't you?"

She was the one punched in the gut now. Emma . . . and Mak? "Emma?"

Mak was giving her a quizzical look like he didn't understand the confusion and shock on her face. Obviously. It wouldn't make sense to anyone else.

"Yep. Worked up the nerve to ask her at the Valentine's dance. Been together ever since. Best four months of my life. It's not even weird anymore that she hangs out with Rhys all the time. Actually, figuring out the relationship between the two of you"—he waved a hand between her and Wes—"is helping me move past the bit of jealousy I was dealing with. So thanks, kids." He loped away down the nearby path to the grotto to find some other seniors to party with.

When Cara turned back, Wes was staring her down. "What?"

She blinked at him. Mak and Emma had started dating right after Valentine's Day? If Rhys and Emma had broken up that day, then Emma had sure moved on quickly. Was it possible they'd broken up even before then? If so, then they had managed to stay good friends afterward. Maybe that meant it had been a mutual decision and nothing to do with her, or the photo from the gala, or him disappearing from the dance, or any of it. She shook her head. One thing it definitely meant was Rhys hadn't been dating Emma when he'd kissed her. Part of her soared straight up to the bright sun above.

The other part stayed firmly on the ground where a trickle of unease ran down her spine. She wanted to run off to find Rhys and apologize for being so cold. She wanted to explain. But there was something else nagging at her and holding her to this spot.

She was missing something.

She hated missing things.

So what was it now? Her brain ticked through a checklist of the last few busy weeks, but nothing stood out.

As much as she hated them, she reviewed the visions she'd had from Messoryx over the last while. They were more of the same death and anger, but nothing new. This feeling, though, she knew it. It was cold. Calculated.

The pieces clicked in her mind half a second before the men stepped out from the trees.

She froze. Wes followed her gaze and stiffened beside her.

Three men walked out of the forest close to the grotto where Mak had headed and began to cross the lawn toward them. From a distance, the contempt and steely resolve of the Pyx controlling them coiled in Cara's mind. Without drawing any attention, they passed students running joyfully between friends. With three of them, they could cast a strong influence on the minds of the people around them. No one would notice them. Until something happened.

All it would take was one slip of their control or one wrong move . . . There were too many people around. True, everyone was already distracted by the games, shouts, and parties all around them, but if anything happened . . . Add a little fear to this mix and people would see. Once one person did, there was no chance the fear wouldn't spread.

The men coming toward her looked terrifying.

Glowing green eyes stared out from the impassive faces of the controlled hosts. But for non-Pyxsees who wouldn't see that, there was still plenty to be afraid of. Starting with the weapons in their hands.

THE MAN AT THE FRONT wore filthy coveralls stretching across his broad shoulders. He held a huge, savage knife with an easy grip in his right hand. The blade had to be nearly a foot long, with one long sharp edge and a scooped point, making it look like it would be just as deadly pulling back as slashing forward.

To his left, a slimmer man held knives in each hand, with more strapped to a belt around his waist. She recognized their style. They were made for throwing, but had longer edges than the ones she'd been learning with. They would do damage no matter how they struck and could easily be deadly from a distance if thrown properly. She also recognized the man. He'd been at her race and gave her the same cold glare now.

On the other side, a man with messy hair walked in a bizarre outfit. He wore gym shorts, slip on shoes, and a bright-yellow Hawaiian shirt. In another circumstance, it would have been absurd. But when her eye slipped past the hospital ID band on his wrist to the gun in his hand, her gut twisted. She didn't have to wonder what he might have been admitted for, knowing the outlaws had been targeting mental health facilities. This man must have been recently admitted, and from the looks of him, the Pyx had made him escape after grabbing whatever clothes he could find.

The disgust from the outlaws settled in one part of her mind, but the disgust she felt in return was separate. She felt sorry for the men in front of her who had been ripped from their lives and their own struggles to be thrust into this. They stopped directly in front of her and Wes. He shifted closer to her.

She could feel a forced calm overtop of the suppressed hatred radiating from the Pyx. Whether it was because they were trying to mask their feelings from her empathy, or because she'd finally managed to separate their emotions from hers, those feelings slotted easily to one side of the imaginary wall in her mind.

Theirs. Not yours.

Her own fear tasted coppery and real on her tongue. It fell on the other side of the wall.

Yours. Now find a way to use it.

"Don't try your mind tricks on us." The voice grated her senses while it rang through her head and set her nerves on edge. The Pyx wouldn't use the voices of the men they controlled and risk people noticing them—not yet, anyway. It was impossible to tell which one was speaking, but none of them felt familiar. She was certain none of them were Messoryx.

"What tricks?" she asked.

"You can't fool us or use us. We've been warned."

She couldn't figure out what they meant. When she glanced at Wes for help, he stepped away from her side. His throat moved as he swallowed hard and took a step forward. The men tensed. Their hands gripped the knives more firmly. He kept his eyes on them until he turned slowly.

Locking eyes with Cara, he turned his back on the controlled men. He had left himself completely vulnerable to them.

"Wes," she hissed. The blood drained from her face, and every fiber in her body itched to lunge forward and pull him away. The feelings on the "theirs" side of her mind made it clear that would be a bad idea.

"Talk to them, Cara. It'll look like you're talking to me this way so no one else freaks out. They're worried you can change their minds. So do it."

Her heart lodged in her throat. Her head shook with quick tiny motions, and her wild eyes pleaded with him to get away from them. That huge knife was right behind his back. All the man had to do was raise his arm. She couldn't bear it. She was going to get Wes killed.

He mouthed the word "ask" to her.

Ask what? She didn't even know what the outlaws were talking about. She gulped and looked past Wes to the green eyes of the controlled.

"I don't know what Messoryx told you, but he's the only one using you. He's turned you into loyal soldiers for his own agenda."

"His agenda belongs to all of us. It's our agenda too. We chose this. We believe in him."

"What is he planning?"

Anger flared in her mind.

Them. Not you.

The anger filed to one side. Wes gave a tiny headshake. She'd asked the wrong question.

"If you think we'd tell you that, you're sadly mistaken. Maybe you're less of a threat than we were led to believe."

Think, Cara. What are they saying?

With the feelings inside her sorted into two sides, she focused.

Hatred, disgust, fervent loyalty, cold purpose—theirs—on one side. Fear and desperation, a little frustration—hers—on the other side. What did that leave? Why would she be a threat?

Pushing the feelings to each side in her mind, she found a path down the middle. Her thoughts cleared. She found the right question. It was the one she'd been asking all along.

"Why me?"

"Why you?" The grating voice sent a shiver up her arms with its mocking tone. "Messoryx wants you out of the way. You're not the first golden Pyxsee he's come across. Now that you've recognized what you can do, he can't have you around."

Her mind raced. She couldn't let them know she had no idea what he meant. She had to keep them talking until she could figure out a way to get them away from here without anyone getting hurt.

You're not the first.

That was what they'd said. Messoryx had said something similar to her in the garage at Whalton manor.

"My father." The words came out in a sharp breath.

"Obviously." The voice paused with a rush of contempt she shoved to the side. "You know what? I think she's too stupid to have the kind of influence Messoryx thinks she does," he said to his fellow Pyx.

Sparks ignited in the back of her mind, but before she could respond, Wes's eyes widened. Gold flecks in the deep brown sparkled in the bright afternoon sun as he shook his head at someone beyond her shoulder. Her head whipped around. Another pair of green eyes met hers, but they lacked the glow of the controlled. Harrison sauntered down the hill, beaming at them.

He reached Cara's side. "Hullo, love. What's the plan for this . . . beautiful . . . What's going on?" He stuttered as he picked up the vibe from her and Wes. Emerald irises flicked between them.

"Go away," Wes growled.

Harrison didn't move, but he turned his head to Cara. "Tell me."

Wes shot her a warning look. She hesitated, but there wasn't much she could do.

"Remember what I told you about seeing them? Look for three men standing right behind Wes. The one in the middle is a little taller than him." She waited. Curiosity and anticipation rose on either side of the wall she'd established.

Harrison tensed when the scene became clear to him. She'd half expected a flowery British exclamation of surprise, but he was silent. His mouth thinned to a narrow line as his jaw muscles flexed. He appraised each one, including Wes in the center, and didn't move when Hawaiian Shirt raised the gun until it pointed right at him.

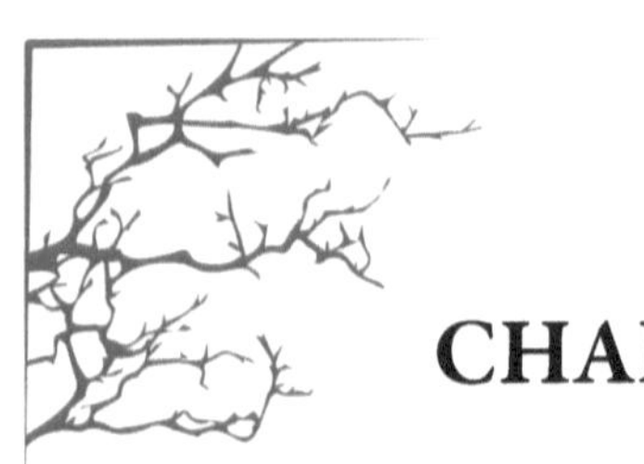

CHAPTER 29

"WELL, WELL. BAD ENOUGH we have a bunch of interfering Pyxsees on our hands. Now you're dragging miserable ordinary humans into things. Perfect. You'll come with us, or he can be the first to die."

"He's not involved in this." Cara's voice rose, and a few passing students glanced over and turned to whisper to their friends. She didn't care if it looked like she was fighting with Wes over another guy. They could think whatever they wanted. As long as they didn't see what was really going on and she could keep them safe and get Wes and Harrison out of this alive.

"Lead people away from here as soon as you can," she whispered to Harrison. Then she took a few steps away.

Wes had to turn to keep her in front of him. The controlled men behind him followed her movements. When she took a few more cautious steps, they moved as well. Hawaiian Shirt kept the gun trained on Harrison and let the other two move past him. For a second, a flicker of uncertainty flashed through her, but it was separate from all her own fears.

Theirs. One of theirs.

"If you try anything, he dies." The voice was a little different this time. This wasn't the same Pyx, and she thought she felt hesitation in spite of the words coming from Hawaiian Shirt.

She took two more steps, moving to the side closest to the forest. "I'm only doing what you asked."

Wes's brow furrowed to a deep crease. "Cara, no."

"Oh, yes." The first voice was back in their heads, and Wes flinched when the man in coveralls raised the huge knife until the point rested against his back. "And it's not just these two. In case you have any second thoughts, I suggest you have a look around."

Cara's head swiveled.

A woman in jean shorts and a plaid shirt leaned against a tree beside the path to the grotto, tapping a pistol against her leg. An older man stood between two trees farther along the edge of the clearing, close to the back of the Cedars. Another woman stared with glowing green eyes from the corner of the Juniper dorm. She scratched her head with a wicked-looking dagger as a group of junior girls walked past her, oblivious to the danger. Altogether, Cara counted half a dozen strangers hidden in plain sight around the school.

She also spotted an unmistakable tall silhouette frozen outside the dining hall in the distance. Like a magnet, like always, her gaze was drawn to him. Her heart cracked and crumbled inside her chest knowing Rhys had seen what was going on. If Wes was right about his feelings, or if all the other times he'd protected her were any indication, he would rush down here. He'd probably come, anyway, no matter how he truly felt, because that was who he was.

She had to act quickly.

She wrenched her eyes away from Rhys's distant form. Wes was glaring at her with his jaw set.

The pain of broken promises crashed down on her, drowning everything else. After everything she'd said to Wes at their movie night, and had meant with all her heart at the time, she couldn't keep the promise. It wasn't just him, although that would have been enough. It wasn't just Pyxsees. It was Harrison and all the other regular students playing games and enjoying themselves behind him.

Her eyes pleaded with Wes to understand. She'd do it, anyway, but she was desperate for him to accept what she had to do. He shook his head.

"No. Cara, you promised."

"I know. I'm sorry."

His face pinched, turning scarlet. She glanced past him to see Rhys sprinting across the lawn through the middle of the ultimate frisbee game still in full swing. She tore her eyes away before they teared up. This wasn't the end. She wasn't giving up. But she had to go with the outlaws to draw them away from the school.

Wes's darkened eyes burned through hers. "Cara, don't do this."

"I don't have a choice. Wes . . ." Her voice cracked.

Before she could turn, a shout drew her attention. A junior in a blue shirt ran toward them, closer than Rhys. For a moment, she was confused, but then she spotted the frisbee sailing through the air. The boy launched himself to catch it with another jubilant shout, and crashed into the back of the man with all the throwing knives. The kid tumbled to the ground and sat up, shaken. His eyes widened to saucers when he saw what he'd run into. Fear kicked in, and he scanned across to the others, taking in the knives and the gun trained on Harrison.

He turned pale. She tried to shush him but was too late. "What the—?"

Rhys reached him before he could yell, and grabbed his shoulders. The guy looked so shocked that he closed his mouth and stared at Rhys, who turned to find Cara.

His nostrils flared at the scene around him. He started to drop his hands from his classmate's shoulders, but Cara stopped him. "No, Rhys, get him out of here. Get everyone out of here. Make something up, but don't let them see. If they see, they'll panic."

"What are you doing?" He choked out the words.

"You know what she's doing," Wes growled.

"No. Not happening," Rhys replied.

Cara turned to the three men. "If I go with you, you'll leave them all alone? You'll let them go?"

"We're not here for a bunch of kids. But we also don't care about hurting them if we have to."

"You don't have to. I'm going."

The faces around her broke her heart in too many ways. Rhys's eyes flashed their anger and desperation with a lightning bolt to the middle of her chest, but Wes's disappointment drove it home and split her heart in two.

She stared back at Rhys and lost herself for a moment. Not that she'd needed any more reason to feel sure of her decision, but gazing into those eyes, she found all the certainty she could have hoped for.

"Get them to safety. For me . . . Please. You said once that you trust me. If you care about me, then trust me now that I know what I have to do."

His shoulders caved as her words hit him. It took him a few seconds to move, but eventually, he swallowed and leaned down to the guy still looking stunned beside him. "Come on, Ben. Looks like you might have hit your head."

Cara couldn't look at Wes again, so she turned to the forest without another word. Footsteps followed behind her, but no one touched her until she passed between the trees into the cool shade, and the sounds of the school faded behind her.

A HAND SHOVED HER ROUGHLY between the shoulder blades, and she stumbled onto the path. Cara glanced across her shoulder before she was pushed forward again. It was the man with all the throwing knives, clearly the same one who had attacked them before. The other two must have stayed to keep her friends in line until they knew she was gone. They had better let them go now that she had surrendered. She tried to catch a glimpse between the trees, but there were too many people in the clearing to figure out what was going on.

The bitterness she'd felt from this Pyx at her race flowed through her without affecting her. It settled easily on the far side of the barrier in her mind, while the other side calmed. She'd be able to hear if panic broke out at the school. For now, the quiet woods wrapped her in hope.

The man grunted behind her when a branch she pushed past snapped back to hit him. Interesting that the Pyx wasn't controlling his pain response as completely as Messoryx had controlled Lydia. Maybe it took practice to fully control a human. From his memories, she knew Messoryx had been doing it for a long time. Most of these others had to be more recent.

"How long have you been his errand boy?" she taunted.

"Don't be ridiculous. Messoryx is a great leader. We have battles, not errands."

"No, I meant the one in coveralls back there. You don't even answer to the top dog, er, top Pyx, do you?"

"Wrong again. You're bad at this. This is my team. I may have missed killing you at the range that day, but we still delivered our messenger who took care of the traitor. Messoryx trusts me to lead this mission."

She hadn't been sure who the leader was here. Now she had to keep him talking until she was sure the other Pyx had left their positions and followed them into the woods.

"A little further, Pyxsee. Unless you want everyone at your precious school to die, you don't want them to hear you scream when I kill you."

"Is that what this is? All you have to do is kill me?" Then why was she still alive? What was his hesitation?

"Finally got something right."

Her thoughts raced back to her friends and everyone at the school. She'd done the only thing she could think of, and she hoped it would be enough. But surrendering to the outlaws didn't mean she'd given up. Now if only she could figure out how to break away from him while ensuring the others left their posts. If she could escape, would they leave the school to chase her down? If she was really this important, they would. Hope flared in her chest.

Again, a strange sense of hesitation came from the Pyx behind her. It wormed in among the bitterness and cold hatred on the "them" side of the wall. With a deep breath, she spun around to face him.

"You don't want to do this."

"Of course I do."

Influence. That was the word the Pyx had used up at the school. Messoryx thought she had influence. Josh thought the same thing, although he might have been thinking about a different kind. Jenner had snapped at her uncle when she was mad. Grawllyx had offered to threaten Rhys when she was upset with him. All those animal pyxides had shown up at the archery range amazingly quickly after the attack there, and again at the race. It was as if her fear had been a deafening cry for help through the area. Was it possible her empathy reached both ways?

Time to find out.

"No, you don't. I feel your hesitation. You don't want to kill me." The bit of fear seeping in probably wouldn't hurt anything, but she tried to push out a sense of calm acceptance. Sending out calm also meant she couldn't expect help from friendly nearby Pyx either. It would be worth it if it worked.

For a second, the calm flickered back to her. Then the man snarled and the Pyx used his host's human voice over the one she heard in her mind. "Nice try."

He lunged forward with one of the knives in his outstretched hand. She jumped to the side. A flash of red streaked out of the brush and darted past her feet. The fox sank her teeth into the man's ankle, and he stumbled with a shout. Cara cried out as the knife slashed across the arm she'd thrown up as a block. Burning pain grew as her body recognized the sharp cut, and her other hand clamped across it. Blood dripped between her fingers.

The man stepped forward, and she moved inside his reach before he could slash again. She stomped on the top of his foot and brought her elbow crashing into his nose. He fell to his knees, and the fox tore at the back of his ankle. He screamed. When she let go, the fox looked to Cara and then in the direction of the school.

"Not me. Him. Go help Wes," she urged.

The fox streaked through the forest the way Cara had come. Blindingly quickly, the man reached for a knife from his belt and threw it after her. Cara knew a moment of panic before the lilting "missed me" sounded in her mind. Then Josh's voice echoed the message he'd tried to drill into her.

Run if you can. Fight if you can't. Don't stop doing either.

She kicked at the man's arm as he raised another knife and sent it spinning harmlessly into the foliage. Then she turned and sprinted. With her arms pumping, she couldn't hold her wound closed anymore, and drops of blood flew in front of her as the arm swung forward with each step. She ran blindly up the path, expecting the bite of a knife in her back or legs with every stride, but she'd made the green team as a sophomore for a reason.

The knife didn't come. She willed her legs to carry her faster. Much faster than any race she'd ever run. Still, the knife didn't come. She chanced a look over her shoulder. The man hobbled after her, but he was falling farther behind. Seeing he couldn't catch her, he reached for the knives.

The Pyx should be able to overcome any pain in the body he controlled and make the man run in spite of an injury, but he couldn't fix something broken. The fox must have severed a tendon to make it so he physically couldn't chase after her. She was far enough ahead by now to see the blade spinning through the air, and ducked.

She threw herself down a side path to put some trees between them. A shout reached her ears. To her horror, she realized the twisting path was leading her back toward the school. More precisely, it was leading her to the grotto where students were celebrating, completely unaware of the lethal chase going on around them. She crashed through the undergrowth to change direction, and came out on the broader trail, slamming straight into another man.

Her heart threw itself into her ribs. Then he turned around, and normal brown eyes instead of glowing green ones looked back at her.

"Mr. Meyers!"

"Cara? I heard a scream. Was that you?"

She grasped the teacher's arms. "No, but you have to help. You know what's been going on. They're here now. They're at the school. You have to get the kids from the grotto and take everyone up to the buildings. Help get everyone inside. Wes and Rhys should be doing that now, but go clear out the grotto."

He blinked at her, and his mouth fell open. He made no effort to move.

"Owen." He startled when she used his name. "You know what they are. You can help. Go."

"But they're invisible. They're hidden."

"Nothing is hidden. You just have to know how to see. These ones are people. They don't belong here. They stand out in the forest. You'll see them if you try. Pay attention to details. Watch for inconsistencies."

He nodded and raced down the path to the right. Laughter from the students enjoying themselves drifted through the trees. A crashing sound in the bushes brought her back to herself. Her mouth went dry, and she turned to run again.

"Cara. What are you doing? Get to the school. Get to safety." Grawlls had found her. The fear coursing through her must have reached out to the Pyx in the area after all.

"I can't. I can't lead them there."

"Of course you can. We're supposed to keep you safe. It's not your job." The bear hobbled forward.

"You're hurt."

His front paw was matted in blood. "Fortunately the human wasn't a skilled hunter, but her knife was still sharp. Don't worry, she's alive and Pyx-free now, though the outlaw did escape."

Cara checked all around her. There was no sign of the man with the throwing knives. She peeled off the thin shirt she wore over her tank top. "Here. Let me see." Finding the top of the blood trail down Grawlls's leg, she felt for the wound. "Don't let him bite me, okay?" Grawlls flinched when her fingers found the gash, but Grawllyx held him under control. Warm, thick blood poured over her hand, mingling with hers. She wrapped her shirt above it and pulled it as tight as she could before tying it in a knot. She had to grit her teeth from the pain when her muscles tensed and the cut across her forearm opened. "There. Now go find help. Find a guardian to look after that for you. I assume they can do that."

"Not until you're safe. You're hurt too."

The thin shirt hadn't offered any protection, but she felt oddly more vulnerable now in only her close-fitting tank top. Running back to school to hide was tempting, but she couldn't.

All of this, including the blood trickling down her arm, would be for nothing. People would probably die.

"You can't run. I can. Now go." She spun on her heel and took off. From the sounds, Grawlls tried to follow her, but his frustrated roar was all she needed to hear to know he'd been forced to give up.

Rays of sun filtered through the leaves above, casting green light across the trail and brightening the gold bands around the trees ahead.

With sudden clarity, she knew where she could go.

She knew the path well.

She surged ahead down the trail between the two gold-banded trees that marked the school boundaries. She made it a hundred feet down the path to the mansion before an ear-splitting crack shattered the air and her face kissed the dirt.

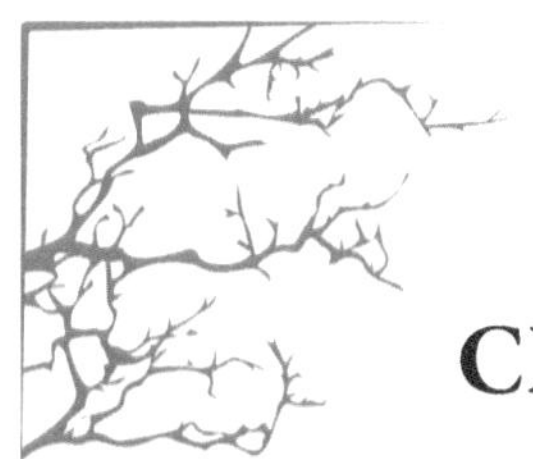

CHAPTER 30

CARA STRUGGLED TO PULL air back into her lungs after having it knocked out by hitting the ground. Her thoughts were a jumbled mess. When a couple shallow breaths made it through, she rolled over to look behind her. A pinch and weird pressure across the top of her shoulder made her look there first. Her brain fought to make sense of it.

Blood streamed down her front, staining her tank top with dark moisture. A hot, wet sensation ran down her back. The heat grew to a steady burn.

On the trail behind her stood the woman in jean shorts who'd been beside the path to the grotto earlier. Realization dawned as the woman raised the gun.

She'd been shot.

She was about to be shot again.

This time, she wouldn't be a moving target.

With the realization, the pain set in. A burning hot poker seared through the top of her shoulder across the base of her neck. Bright spots exploded across her vision.

Her scream stuck in her throat as the gun leveled at her. She was almost grateful. At least the pain would end. The squeak that made it past her lips was lost in a deafening roar when Grawlls threw himself at the woman.

He hadn't given up after all. He'd come for her.

The woman swiveled toward the sound and brought the gun around with her. Grawlls's huge furry mass collided with her, and they both fell to the ground with a muffled bang.

"No!"

"Run," Grawllyx pleaded with her.

Sorrow rang in his voice and through her mind when the bear didn't try to rise. The sharp horror of it belonged on both sides of the wall, and her heart ached. But there was no time to cry. The man with the knives could still be coming, and she needed to draw the others this way too. Anything to take them and their weapons away from the people back at school. What if the woman had already shot someone at the grotto? What if her friends were still being held hostage, or worse?

"Over here," she yelled to the trees, and then let out her pain and anguish in a true scream. She forced her limbs to move past the pain. Adrenaline added to the heat from her shoulder, and she half ran, half stumbled down the path with her body on fire.

She fell several times. Each time, it grew harder to force herself back to her feet, but she did. She fell again when she stumbled from the path into the meadow surrounding Whalton manor. The sight of the graceful stone walls warmed her soul, and she rose to her feet yet again.

She made it to the side door to the garage before a taunting voice grated in her mind.

"Ah, ah, ah."

They'd finally caught up. Without much hope, she tried the knob.

Locked.

The workshop at the end of the garage had only been plan A, but she had no hope for plan B now that they were here. Plan

B had been to break into the mansion and find somewhere to hide. The alarm would go off, and help would come eventually. Now, she'd never have enough time to hide where they couldn't find her. In the state she was in, and with their control over their human hosts, she wouldn't make it across the driveway before they caught her.

Slowly, she turned to face them.

There was only one, and it wasn't who she'd expected. She'd been sure that mocking voice was the man with the throwing knives who'd called himself the leader, but this man wore different clothes.

Familiar clothes.

Her brain had turned a little foggy as she made her way here.

A little voice in the back of her mind told her it was blood loss. She couldn't last much longer. She peered at the man. Hope brightened for a second when she placed him.

"Mr. Meyers?"

No, his eyes hadn't glowed green before. Something was wrong.

"Not anymore. You really shouldn't send pathetic humans to deal with creatures they can't see coming." Her math teacher's face leered at her with an expression she'd never seen on him. "All it took was a little misplaced pity for a hurt, confused stranger in the middle of all those kids. Tragically easy to fool. Your tall friend played right into my hands."

Her first thought was of Rhys. Then she remembered Mak's long legs loping away toward the grotto. Her mouth went dry.

He reached a hand to his waist, to the belt he now wore with all the knives. The Pyx must have traded for a body that wasn't broken after the fox bit his previous host. There was blood on his hand already. Far past anger now, all she felt was fear and horror for her teacher, and terror for what might have happened in the grotto.

"Mr. Meyers, it's me. You know me. I know you can hear me. You have to fight." She kept her eye on him and inched across the driveway.

The green in his eyes flickered, and another wiggle of doubt crept through the "them" side in her mind.

"Yes. Fight. This isn't you. Come on, Owen."

His brown eyes shone through, and she bolted for the side of the mansion. She made it up the steps to the patio before a whistle tore by her ear and a knife buried itself in the oak door as she ran by. If she'd stopped to try the door, she'd be dead. Or maybe this new host wasn't as skilled at knife-throwing as the last one had been. Either way, she rounded the corner with a glance over her shoulder to find the glowing green eyes firmly back in place, visible even from a distance. He seemed to be struggling to lurch after her.

"Don't think a little fight will stop me. Not anymore. This isn't my first hostile takeover." He was out of sight now, but the voice taunted her. "Sure, it's a little harder at first, but Messoryx taught me well."

Down the side of the house, she stopped to pick up an empty flowerpot. Her right arm hung uselessly by her side, so she heaved it with her left as hard as she could. The pot smashed to pieces against the window—the same one she'd snuck through once with Wes and Jory. A giant crack snaked across the glass, but it held. She shook her foggy head and searched around her.

The day was falling into darkness faster than usual. Or was that her?

Rocks. She spotted a line of them in front of a low bush. She took a step toward them without thinking and fell off the edge of the patio. It wasn't high, but it was enough that she fell to her hands and knees in the grass on the other side of the narrow flowerbed, only to have searing pain from her shoulder jolt her upright again. Scrambling into the shelter of one of the larger bushes, she picked up a rock from the row lining the bed.

With a peek over the bush to see if he'd reached the side of the house yet, she lobbed the rock. Left-handed throwing wasn't something she'd practiced, and the rock hit the top corner of the window. The crack groaned and widened, but the glass stayed in place.

One more.

She threw again and hit the middle of the crack. Glass burst into the library with a crash. She dragged herself forward onto the low patio and reached inside to open the lock and yank the window open. A pinch where the glass cut her, and a little more blood trickling down her arm—the left one this time—was a small price to pay for the sweet music of the blaring alarm sounding inside.

"Come now, little Pyxsee. You aren't still trying to hide, are you?"

She scooted back into the bushes with her lungs burning. She sucked in shallow breaths while the world tilted around her. Her heart thundered in her ears. It didn't seem like a good idea for it to beat so hard when it was pushing more blood out of the bullet wound across her shoulder. Putting her head to her knees to quell the nausea, she begged the earth to stop spinning.

Footsteps echoed across the flagstones behind the bushes. They paused at the window.

She did her best to focus and felt for his emotions.

Uncertainty. Fear? Probably scared Messoryx would kill him if he failed to kill her again. Cold determination settled, and she cringed. Could she change that? He'd figured her out last time, but if he didn't know she was doing it this time, maybe she'd have better luck. What did she need?

Her eyes darted across the grass.

The forest was closer on this side of the house. She needed time. Enough to make it to the trees.

She focused on a prickly feeling of curiosity. That feeling of needing to know something. She wasn't sure how to do this, but she pictured the inside of the library with its matching white sofas on either side of the fireplace. The huge desk spanning the space in front of the window. The rows of books lining the wooden walls, and the rolling ladder against the shelves.

Follow me into the library. You know you want to see where I went.

She pushed the feeling out and tried to picture it going from the "her" side to the "them" side in her mind. At the tinkle of glass, she peeked around the bush. He hadn't made it inside yet, but his back was turned. Fighting another wave of nausea, she jumped up and ran.

Any other time, she would have seen the branch across the path and easily stepped over it. But with the dark edges to her vision and the dizziness causing her to stumble, it snapped loudly under her foot. A flash of anger surged through her and helped her stay on her feet even though she knew it came from him as he recognized her trick. The path on this side of the mansion sloped steeply downhill, and she slipped and slid as she tried to run.

Again, she waited for the knife in her back. She could feel him seething behind her, closing the distance between them. When the slope changed and the path leveled off across the hillside, she threw herself down the side instead. She tumbled down the hill. Most of her body had gone numb, but her shoulder still burned and throbbed with each jolt.

She came to rest at the bottom in a small glen. Thick ferns covered the forest floor, and the smell of wet earth against her face grounded her, clearing her mind.

"Not fast enough." Mr. Meyers appeared at the top of the hill and ran effortlessly down the steep incline with perfect control.

He had a knife out from the belt. The blade stroked across his other palm as he gazed down at her. This was it. There was nowhere else to run. His form blurred in front of her, but she managed to struggle to her feet.

She backed away.

He closed the gap.

As she took another step back, her heel struck a rock hidden beneath the ferns. She gasped as something sharp poked her in the shoulder blade directly below the bullet wound. Her vision tunneled, and she fought to stay upright. With her left hand, she reached behind her. Rough bark met her palm. It was a branch poking her shoulder. She tried to inch sideways, but it caught in her shirt, and the pain so close to the fire in her shoulder was too much. She couldn't drop beneath it without getting hung up and dragging the branch across the open wound. That would make her pass out, she was sure. She was already close enough.

Josh's voice came to her again.

Don't stop.

"Owen, please fight." The words sounded far away. She might have been slurring. "Please. Your friend, Josh . . . you know him . . . my uncle. Don't let him do this." She wasn't making sense anymore. It hadn't come out right. She'd meant to tell him not to let the Pyx use him like this. Too late now.

He squared up to her, his eyes glowing, and raised the knife. She recognized it. Her right hand dragged up her leg to her hip where the top of the matching knife stuck out of its sheath. Her thumb fumbled against it. He lunged.

Instinctively, she curled inward and threw herself toward him, away from the tree and under the knife. Hitting the ground, she rolled, landing on her face. She spat out a mouthful of loamy dirt and scrambled forward, desperately trying to regain her footing. Any moment now, she'd feel the searing pain of the knife. Or maybe she'd feel nothing at all. That would be nice.

Don't stop. Get up, Cara. Go.

Time had frozen, and her legs refused to obey the commands her brain was sending. Hollow emptiness drained the rest of her will to fight, and she slumped to the ground. Still, the knife didn't come. Rolling over to meet her fate face to face, she paled at the sight in front of her.

His momentum had carried him. He must have run into the same rock she'd backed up against. The extra strength the Pyx had used to drive forward with the knife had driven him right onto the sharp branch. His body hung limp, with the thick branch protruding from his eye socket and his mouth still stretched in a revolting leer.

Nausea rolled over her again, and she vomited into the ferns. When she looked up again, light had surged from his head. She fell back in shock. It gathered in a flattened circle, looking like a miniature nuclear blast, though the teacher's head was still intact. Slowly, the light rose, hovering. It illuminated him absurdly like a halo and then dissipated into the still air.

Cara tried to remember how to breathe.

She couldn't move.

Footsteps broke the silence, and her head whipped over to the hillside. A bright-yellow blur sailed down the slope and stopped in front of her.

It wasn't over.

Hawaiian Shirt had found her. His gun dangled from his hand, but he made no move to lift it. His eyes were fixed on the body and the last traces of light vanishing into the air.

Don't stop fighting.

But she wanted to. If she could only rest for a while . . . She was so cold. Her hands clenched, and something hard bit into her palm.

Her knife.

She'd managed to free it from the sheath after all.

Hawaiian Shirt started to turn. She would only have one chance. It would have to be with her right hand in spite of the fiery pain from her shoulder. She didn't stand a chance of aiming with her left and he'd be able to raise the gun and fire before she could even transfer the knife to her other hand.

Their eyes met.

The knife fell into place in the groove beside her thumb, ready to throw.

After everything, she couldn't do it. Tears welled in her eyes for the dedicated teacher and understanding dorm parent Mr. Meyers had been. Her uncle's friend had just died right in front of her. She had no way of knowing what else had happened at the school. She thought of Grawlls, and the tears spilled over. With an aching heart, the sudden hollow feeling made sense.

The Pyx was gone.

No matter what he'd done at the end, she wept for him too. He'd lived for millions of years, seen entire ages pass as the world changed, and he'd died for this. For her. For some mysterious influence she didn't even know how to use.

Jenyx was right. All life was precious. The hope that Grawllyx had made it to a new host offered a small consolation. It shouldn't have killed him. She knew how they died now. She had just seen it happen. And now she couldn't do it again, not to another Pyx or to the innocent man she'd have to kill along with him.

With a last tear for the people she would leave behind, she fell back and waited for the remaining Pyx to finish the job his companion had started.

His glowing green eyes didn't leave hers even as her eyelids fluttered. The last thing she saw of the bleary scene in front of her was the green blinking out and the man in the crazy outfit falling to the ground.

In the distance, a voice called her name.

The forest faded to black . . .

. . .

"*Don't leave me.*" A whisper in the dark . . .

Pain jolted her back to her body. Branches bounced overhead, blurring together. Strong arms held her as gently as they could. The face above her was etched with a deep worry, and a tender pull in her chest joined the pain wracking her body. Beyond the silhouette of his hair, the trees above opened to a dimming sky streaked with wispy clouds. Unable to hold her eyes open, she leaned her head into the warmth that smelled of cedar wood and oranges, and thought she smiled.

THANK YOU FOR READING. I hope you enjoyed this book as much as I enjoyed writing it. The story continues in **Daybreak in Green & Gold**, book 4, where a new threat forces the gang to adjust, and relationships change in surprising ways.

If you could spare a moment to leave an honest review on Amazon and/or Goodreads, it would mean so much. Your review helps new readers decide whether to pick up the book, and even a line or two makes a huge difference to independent authors like me, so thank you so much for your help!

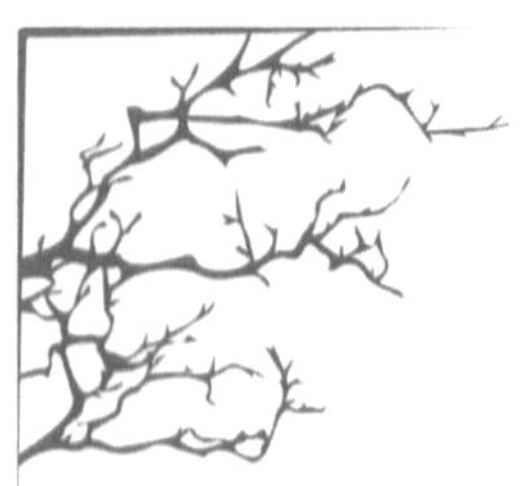

More

REMEMBER THE STORY Jenyx tells Cara and Wes in chapter 2? It's a story about a terrible incident that took place in the town of Vamis in ancient Greece. The events that unfolded when a group of Pyx took over some humans resulted in the unspoken rule against using human pyxides becoming an official part of Pyx law. It also changed the course of a young girl's life forever.

Well, that story was personal. Jenyx was there and you can read the whole tale of that fateful night for free.

Sign up for my VIP reader list at **johollowaybooks.com** and you'll receive a copy of **On Wings And Ash** – a novel full of Pyx, myths, and romance, featuring a pet goose, a tough farm girl, and a couple dashing heroes – as well as other bonus content and, of course, updates on new book releases.

Acknowledgements & Author's Note

THANK YOU TO ALL THE readers who stand by authors you love, and the readers who love to take chances on new authors. Please keep making our world shine brighter with diversity. If you took the time to leave a review, know that I truly appreciate it. Every single review makes a difference in finding new readers. They fuel my soul and boost my motivation in ways I never expected.

To my advance review team—You are amazing people who fill my spirit with the generosity of your time and comments. Huge thanks go to the test readers who helped turn this into a much better book—Lauren, Mandi, Jenni and Angelina—I am eternally grateful for your input. A special thanks to my friend Erika, for saying those first written words aren't so terrible (they are), and for providing a beautiful example of strength when I needed it, and to my wonderful husband who shows that strength daily.

The credit for polishing this book to the state you see now goes to my great editor, Courtney Umphress, and the amazing cover designers at MoorBooks Design. Thank you for doing the things I cannot and making this book into the best version of itself.

THIS BOOK IS BEING released at a strange time in our world in the midst of a global pandemic. While that's not the pending apocalypse imagined by some characters in this book, it's been an interesting lens through which to view the final revisions. Hopefully within a few months we'll be looking back on this time as a small, albeit tragic, chapter in our history. But if we can keep some of the examples of people coming together and sacrificing small comforts for the good of the general population in our minds as we move forward, then maybe some good will have come from it. This isn't why I write, but it's great to see the power we have to effect change when we all decide to act, even in small ways. In the meantime, I'm writing to entertain, so maybe this book has provided a small distraction. I hope so.

I always love to hear from readers. Connect with me on Facebook @johollowaybooks to share your thoughts on any of it, or contact me through my website johollowaybooks.com.

ABOUT THE AUTHOR

JO HOLLOWAY IS THE Canadian author of the Green & Gold series. She lives in Alberta in the shadow of the Rockies with her wonderful quirky dog, Leda. Although always an avid reader, she never really planned to write a book. But some stories demand to be written.

She refuses to choose between cheese and chocolate, but does hold a firm anti-soup stance for reasons no one understands. She loves animals, but traded in riding horses for riding a motorcycle because they don't think for themselves!